ALL I WANT FOR
Christmas

D0096791

REBEKAH PACE

WITH ALEXIS J. PRIDE

This book is printed on acid-free paper.

Published by:
Level 4 Press, Inc.
13518 Jamul Drive
Jamul, CA 91935
www.level4press.com

Library of Congress Control Number: 2019943921

ISBN: 978-1-64630-028-0

eBook ISBN: 978-1-64630-029-7

Printed in USA

Other books by Rebekah Pace

OPERATION SANTA

WALKING WITH THE PROPHETS

THE SANTA WARS

THE RED THREAD

MIRACLE

THE CANNONBALL RUN

UNBOUND

To my dear sister, Sheila—my friend, my inspiration, my gift, and proof that I am favored by God.

1

The early morning sun eased over the horizon of shingled suburban rooftops. Rows of proud chimney stacks were lightly dusted with winter snow that only flirted but wouldn't stay for more than a few cold hours at a time. Without the snow, the tall trees and expansive front lawns that blinked and winked with Christmas lights still seemed naked. It was as if the hush of the morning, yawning awake with color, was a breath held in expectation of something.

An older neighbor navigated the secluded subdivision streets. His leashed dog bobbed happily along and seemed to be walking his master, who muttered white puffs of air into the Chicago wind as he shrunk like a tortoise into his puffy coat. He was approaching a brick home with an impossible number of gables and a circular driveway that boasted His and Hers Lexus SUVs. Last year had been a good sales year, James Harrison told his wife, Fran. But, in reality, it was an expensive apology for all his absences. She wanted a cobalt blue one. He reasoned to himself a silver SUV was more suitable for a man of his position. The real disappointment came when he realized the gift didn't settle her noise.

The dog looked as if he might pause at the Harrison's home. He seemed to be eyeing the fountain. But then, everyone eyed the fountain, in passing. Its stone presence loomed large on the front lawn. In the summer it called attention to itself with an explosion of floral color that encircled its base. No one else in the subdivision owned one. From the fountain, the Harrison's front lawn seemed to stretch for miles before you reached the tall ornate front door, adorned with a gold knocker and flanked by bulbous topiary trees and lilac bushes.

The inside of the Harrison's home revealed everything that the large fountain out front promised: the soaring entryway ceiling commanded heads to look up and admire the majesty of windows with light streaming in from the gables. The white marble floor was surprisingly pristine, given that it had to withstand the constant comings and goings of the clan-of-six Harrison family.

Beyond the entryway, the living room told more of the real story. The stone fireplace was cluttered with family pictures that captured their vacations. The photo of their trip to Disney World, featuring four-year-old Reba, with a squinty-eyed grin and missing front teeth, holding Mickey's hand, stood between an image of Fran and the kids waving from their bikes on a trail in Paris and a photo of James back in the day, goofy smile and open-collar work shirt, holding up a large red-and-yellow plastic choo-choo train. That was taken years ago, when his chestnut hair was still thick and hadn't yet produced a fleck of gray, and, oh, how Fran liked the way the curls wrapped around her fingers. James liked the picture only because it reminded him of how far he'd come since those days of selling toys on commission for a chain store—the days when he and Fran shared the one Chevy, and she made him a bag lunch to save money, and the two kids, Stacy and Jay (Reba and her older brother Elliott were yet to be born), slept in bunk beds because the apartment had only two bedrooms, divided by a flimsy wall. But that was years ago.

James was quite proud of all that he'd accomplished since the long-ago time of tuna melts and apples, and those warm kisses from his pregnant and adoring wife that sent him smiling into his workday. The years had clipped by with him sharpening his skills and chasing buys so that he could finally afford to buy a pair of SUVs on a whim, and a boat that he rarely enjoyed because he traveled so often for work, and the one-of-a-kind this or that that Fran just had to have—things that eventually landed in the minefield in the five-stall garage (a must-have for James's merchandise).

And then there was the grand piano they bought for their oldest, Stacy. It was a stunning piece that punctuated the space between the living room's floor-to-ceiling windows and the stone fireplace, but it sat, lonely, when the girl traded in her musical interest for ballet, and then soccer, and then roaming in packs with her giggling teenage friends to shop at the mall, flicking her blond ponytail out the door as Fran called, "Don't be late for—" as the door slammed shut.

The piano became a good dumping spot for family members in transit: Jay's hockey sticks leaned carelessly against it while he flopped onto the bench in his gear to take off his cleats. (No matter how much Fran complained, he never seemed to use the mudroom for this ritual.) Too often, his things remained just as he'd dumped them.

It seemed the only moments of stillness and quiet were the waking hours of dawn, like now, the morning sun announcing itself by creeping into James and Fran's bedroom. She had the bedside nearest the window. She always awakened before the first ring of her alarm. Now, she squinted toward the sunlight and blinked her vision clear. Brushing blond hair from her face, she turned to the empty side of her bed. She knew it hadn't been slept in.

Saturday morning. The kitchen pulsed with activity. Fran was trying to finish brushing Reba's hair into a ponytail. "Hold still!" she told her daughter, while blowing fallen strands of her own hair out of her face. Reba's ballet instructor had changed the time of the rehearsal for the Christmas recital. A small thing for some, but for Fran it meant moving the chess pieces of her day since the older kids had their own plans and couldn't help out. She would have Reba in tow while shopping, going to her salon appointment, and, finally, delivering Christmas baskets from their church to the nursing home. Fran had missed several of the church's charity event meetings. Guilt had led her to volunteer to hand-deliver the gifts.

"Dad, I need money!" It was Jay, trotting into the kitchen with his hand out, a crooked smile on his face. He was almost as tall as James, but not lanky like his father. The muscles gained from wrestling and football were evident in the thickness of his young neck. Still, though, James had given his son the same dark hair, which Jay wore just long and floppy enough to gain his dad's disapproval. James was slipping one arm into his suit coat while taking a hit of black coffee with his free hand. He gave a look to Fran from across the kitchen island.

"Your son thinks I'm made of money," he said, half joking, but with a tinge of something else in his voice.

She didn't look away from her dexterous fingers working Reba's hair. "What do you expect? He's fifteen."

"Mom, I can't find my soccer gloves!"

Fran threw her voice toward the stairway off the foyer. "Elliott, check your coat pockets!"

"I did!"

"Check again!"

"I can't find 'em. Come and help me!"

Fran was happy to find an indoor winter soccer league for Elliott. Something he could get excited about, show some real interest in besides those video games. It seemed nearly impossible to pull him away from those things lately.

Just then, Stacy skipped down the stairs with a wave, peacoat on, heading for the front door.

"Hey!" Fran called out, stopping her daughter mid-step. "Where you running off to?" She noted the overstuffed backpack Stacy was dragging on the floor.

Her daughter rolled her eyes. "I told you, Mom. Me and some friends are driving up to the Whitaker's weekend place. They've got *everything* there!" A horn honked from the driveway.

"We never talked about this," Fran said, still eyeing the swollen backpack.

"It's just overnight, Mom. And Dad said it was okay."

Fran turned to James, who was knocking back the last of his coffee. "James?" Before Fran could manage the next word, Stacy chirped a goodbye and was out the door.

"Mom, I *still* can't find 'em!"

Sighing, she yelled, "Elliott, look harder! I'm trying to finish your sister's hair!"

"*Ow!*"

"I'm sorry, honey!"

Reba turned just enough to make her point. "Mom, you have to be careful!"

"I know, I know, dear." Fran sighed at the jellied crumbs on her daughter's cheek. "Try to eat your breakfast a little neater, okay, honey? We don't have time to change your sweater."

"Pop-Tarts are just messy. It's not me."

"Hey, Dad." Jay skipped behind his father, who was heading toward the foyer. "How 'bout twenty bucks? Me and some of the guys are going for pizza after the game today."

James slid another look to Fran as he pulled out his wallet.

Fran's cell buzzed to life on the kitchen counter. "It's Mom," she sighed.

"At this hour?" James pulled his winter coat from the closet. "Everything okay?"

Fran remembered her mother had phoned at least twice yesterday, but she'd forgotten to return her calls. Well, at least that's the story she'd tell her. She wanted to ignore her now but thought better of it and answered. James was paused with his jacket sleeve pulled onto one arm, watching, waiting.

"Hi, Mom . . ."

Reba piped up. "Let me talk to Oma!" The excitement was clear in her voice. "Are we going to visit her soon?"

"I know, I'm sorry," Fran went on, ignoring Reba. "It's just been crazy here. You know how it is . . . oh, you mean this Sunday? Tomorrow?" For a second she locked eyes with James, who had already resumed fastening his coat. Shaking his head, he mouthed the word "no." Then he spoke loud enough to be overheard by his mother-in-law. "Love to you, Mom, but we can't make it to church tomorrow. I'm working on something really important."

Reba was reaching for the phone, all happy jitters.

"Mom, Reba wants to say hi, okay?" Fran handed the phone to the little girl, relieved for the interruption.

"Hi, Oma! I miss you! Well, maybe you can come spend the night with us. Are you coming to my ballet recital? I'm a Christmas glitter fairy!"

Fran took the moment to catch James at the door. "How long are you going to be working today?"

"Not sure," he said. "You know it's pretty busy right now. And I've got that new deal I'm trying to pull together."

"I see. Any chance you can break away and meet me at Elliott's game?"

"I'd love to, honey, but—"

"Yeah. Work." She took a step closer, dropping her voice an octave. "Did you come to bed last night?"

"No. I couldn't sleep."

She glanced around to make certain their kids weren't listening. "Again? What's happening with you? I've seen you work hard, but this feels different."

"Listen, I need to get going."

She stiffened. It made him hesitate for a second when he leaned in to kiss her cheek. "I'll be back as soon as I can," he said in a near whisper. She didn't respond this time.

James climbed into his Lexus. He eyed the brown boxes that had taken over the back seat as he cruised down the circular drive, away from the tall ornate door with the lilac bushes on each side. He did love their fragrance in the spring.

He noticed a few of his neighbors on their doorsteps collecting their morning papers. He gave a wave accompanied by a broad smile that was meant to be seen from a distance. Typically, he liked the drive into the city. The view of the calm gray water of Lake Michigan settled him. But it didn't seem to have the same effect today. He felt the tension knotted like a fist along his neck and shoulders. He kept thinking of last night, sitting in his dark living room, staring out onto the empty streets.

Fran had found him in there, the bluish Christmas lights from outside flashing intermittently on his face.

She'd said, "James, it's after four. Are you okay?" There had been an urgency in her voice. He didn't answer, nor did he move.

"James, what's wrong?"

"Go back to bed," he'd told her.

The directive had been quiet but sharp—and stung. She'd watched him for a moment longer before retreating.

His mind replayed sales pitches that didn't take, phone calls from creditors, negotiating with them, reworking his pitches in his head, calculating partial payments.

Stopped in traffic, he pulled out his cell phone and scrolled through the numbers. He had worked his list of options down to Happy Town Parties. Even though they hadn't committed to buying anything, the manager had at least agreed to let James stop in. That's all he needed, James thought. Once in the door, he could sell fat to a walrus.

He called Happy Town to confirm the meeting. He opened the box next to him to look at the toys again. Yeah, they really were garbage. The bobbleheads were supposed to have the likeness of famous ball players, but somehow the ink press screwed up and the eyes and lips were colored in above the facial imprints. The threads of the little bead necklaces broke into pieces when he handled them. Several of the Rubik's Cubes were misaligned and didn't twist properly. He'd used a different manufacturer in China, and they were giving him the runaround on processing the order again. The shipment was supposed to go to Enchanted Castle Playland, had the owner's son not seen the mistakes and refused the merchandise. James had tried to pitch the sale to Goodies and Games. When they groused about the defective toys, calling them junk, he'd attempted to pawn the toys off on Toyland for Tots at a substantially reduced price. The store manager remarked that the products were shameful, not to mention age-inappropriate for most of their customers. So James was off to Happy Town Parties, where he'd had some success before.

He rehearsed in his head what he'd say to the store manager. He wondered if he should lead with the discount. No. He didn't want to look desperate.

It was almost Christmas. He had spent money anticipating the sale of this shipment and had counted on better numbers for this quarter than he'd seen. He'd lost two of his most lucrative contracts to a major competitor and was feeling the pain of it. And then some of his smaller customers started scaling back on their orders. The fact was, the downward trend had been ongoing for some time, but James and Fran's spending habits hadn't changed. In fact, James hadn't told Fran anything had changed.

When he'd come home the other day and seen his bedroom chock-full of Von Maur department store bags, he immediately felt a vein throb in his head. The pain must have registered on his face because Fran had asked him, "Are you okay?" with earnest concern. He'd wanted to ask if she had left any merchandise in the store but decided against it.

He was approaching the strip mall. The stores weren't open for business yet, but many of the merchants were there and could be seen moving about beyond their glass doors. James pulled into the parking spot in front of Happy Town Parties. He saw the manager arranging the display of desk-top miniature elves. His palms grew moist. He took off his leather glove to wipe his forehead.

He eyed the shipment boxes on the passenger seat. "It'll all work out," he said just above a breath. "You can make it happen."

But the manager at Happy Town Parties simply told him, "I'll call you."

James drove to his office downtown. It was a spacious, loft-style room in an old, renovated factory building in Printer's Row. From James's second-floor window, he could see the rush of traffic along the Eisenhower Expressway. Sometimes, he'd find himself staring at the cars racing by below, with his thoughts speeding just as fast. It was then he liked being alone in the quiet space large enough to accommodate several workstations, in the event he should choose to hire support. But for now, it remained his solitary space where he could retreat and think. Work was always therapeutic.

An hour later, his longtime college buddy Gus sidled up to his open door. Gus, a fellow salesman and owner of In Touch Technologies, had a large office suite across the hall from James and often popped in when he'd note James's arrival. There was a puppy-like gladness in the way Gus grinned at him now.

"Man, you look like something the dog chewed up. *Heh. Heh.*" He came farther in and slouched on the small loveseat against the wall that faced James's desk. "How about a drink?"

"It's not even eleven o'clock," James sighed. He leaned back in his chair and rubbed his eyes.

"Well, it's five o'clock somewhere. I say we blow this joint and grab us a couple of cold ones. What you need to do is blow off a little steam, my friend." Gus leaned in, elbows on knees, waiting for James to respond.

"You blow off enough steam for the both of us. Anyway, I've got work to do." James moved a few folders around on his desk meaninglessly. He didn't want to meet Gus's gaze right then because he knew his friend could read him. The avoidance didn't matter.

"Hey, everybody hits a bump in the road every now and then," Gus said. "You'll come out on top. Nothing to sweat over."

On impulse, James looked to the reassurance he was being given. "Thanks, man." He released the tense air from his lungs.

"I still say we should hit our spot. I'm just about done. How about it?"

"I just got here," James chuckled.

"Okay, fine. How about I give you an hour, and then we can grab a bite and a drink?" Gus waited, apparently not moving from the loveseat until he got the answer he wanted. He always persisted until he got the answer he wanted. That was Gus's way, even when they were college kids and James insisted that he couldn't hang out because he needed to study. Gus would keep at him until James caved. In their twenty-plus-year friendship, the only thing that had changed about Gus was his thinning hair and the fact that he now dyed it black. The once ponytail-length hair was cut conservatively short for business.

The fact was, being with Gus was sometimes like being swept back into their college years. Gus refused to acknowledge that decades had marshaled changes evident in each of their lives. And in so doing, he often invited James along for the ride. On occasion, it was a nice distraction for James, especially on days like this. He'd find himself watching as Gus greedily enjoyed the beauty of women, just as he had when they were nineteen-year-old frat boy wannabes. And he still partied like it, too, if the occasion presented itself. Worse still, Gus hadn't grown out of his fondness for goading his friend into petty games of competition. Even though Fran could stomach vinegar better than she could Gus's company, the friendship remained.

Born an only child to doting parents, Angus "Gus" Fowler was as spoiled as a barrel of over-ripe peaches. He was also lonely, and that was something that had never changed. He'd found James at freshman orientation. Both of them were scared and confused, and Gus made James into the brother he'd always wanted. They sampled all new things together, including joining a frat (Gus's idea) in their sophomore year because frat boys got all the hot chicks. Gus would have crossed the burning sands, but James couldn't chug all that alcohol the frat brothers were pushing on him. It landed him in the hospital. When the frat boys kicked him off the line, Gus quit in solidarity. He would have been lonely without James.

He sat alongside James's hospital bed for the three days he was laid up. When James asked him in a barely audible voice, "Why?" Gus told him, "We don't need a frat to get hot chicks." Then he muttered, "Losers," as he slurped his soda.

2

After her ballet rehearsal, Reba was so persistent about seeing her Oma that Fran complied. She sat in the wing chair in her mom's one-bedroom senior residence, intentionally busying herself with scrolling through text messages. Reba and Oma were engaged on the couch.

"I've missed you, Oma!" The way Reba said it even made Fran smile. "See, I wore my costume for you!"

The little girl had insisted on wearing her tutu over her snow pants for her grandma. It was a glittering poof of strawberry pink.

Her Oma's blue eyes, still youthful and shimmering, brightened with equal excitement. Reba twirled in front of her, and Oma clapped her hands in approval of her granddaughter's performance. "Absolutely beautiful! You are the most amazing glitter fairy I have ever seen!"

Reba beamed. "Really?!"

"Really." Oma hugged her warmly, securely.

"Guess what?"

"What?"

Reba whispered too loudly, "I made Christmas presents."

"Oh, my!"

"Uh-huh." She leaned close to her grandmother's ear with a cupped hand. "I made a necklace for Mommy. And I made it out of macaroni and painted it pink because that's her favorite color." She stood erect again, wearing a wide grin.

"You are so talented, my Reba!"

"And I made something for Daddy too," she said. "It's a ball on a string that smells good, and you hang it in your closet so your clothes can smell nice."

"Oh, goodness, what a thoughtful gift for your dad!"

"Uh-huh, and I made one for Grandpa too."

The two women's faces were both surprised and unprepared.

"Reba, honey," Fran said, "Grandpa isn't with us anymore. Remember, we talked about that."

"I know. He's in heaven." Reba turned to Oma. "But you still visit him, right? You said you brought him flowers on his birthday, so I can give you his Christmas present for him."

Oma struggled to smile. She had been mourning for two years. There were times when the pain still felt new. She hugged Reba again. "Of course you can, sweetie."

Fran was watching now. She quickly blinked away the wetness brimming her eyes. She looked over at the small, round end table that held a mint green Tiffany lamp and, next to it, a picture of her father. It was an old photo—one with sepia tones that made his auburn hair look slick and black. Even though the image was of a much younger man (before Fran was born), the broad grin had never changed. Fran felt the aching emptiness brought on by her father's absence.

She turned back to Oma, who'd just released Reba from their hug. Fran remembered how good her mom's hugs always felt. They were better than a warm blanket against a chilly night. She smelled of cookie dough back then. A momentary twang of jealousy broke loose as she thought how her daughter enjoyed the hug she herself could really use right then. Oma caught Fran staring, and it was almost as if her mother were hearing her thoughts. Aware of her, Fran returned to fidgeting with her phone.

Reba asked, "Did you make cookies, Oma! You smell like gingerbread."

"Yes, I did. I made them for my favorite dancing fairy. They're in the kitchen. Can you be a big girl and serve yourself? I want to talk to your mom for a little while."

"Uh-huh. Mom lets me do all sorts of stuff in the kitchen." Reba grabbed a book from her bag and trotted into the kitchen.

Fran called out after her, "Only two cookies, honey. You don't want to ruin your appetite for dinner later."

"You doing okay?" Oma asked.

"I'm fine, Mom." She hesitated, thinking she needed to say more, perhaps because she hadn't been responding to her mother's messages as quickly as she should have. "I've just been so busy lately. You know how it is, the kids always have something going on. And when I'm not driving them around—"

"I know," Oma interrupted, "but you should take a little time to breathe."

"Easier said than done. You didn't have four kids to chase after."

"You look tired." Concern edged her words.

"Yeah," Fran sighed. She touched her cheek. She was recalling the image of herself in the mirror earlier that morning. Her eyes looked darker, duller. She thought she saw more fine lines forming around them. The creams were a waste of money.

Oma interrupted her thoughts. "When you were a girl, I could always tell when something was wrong."

"Really?" Fran smiled. "How'd you know?"

"I could tell because of how quiet you were. You were never quiet unless you were sad. You were a talker since age two and wouldn't quit." Oma laughed as if she hadn't told the story before.

Oma moved to the end of the couch, closer to Fran. "What's wrong?"

"I'm fine, Mom, just a little tired."

"That answer may work on some, but not on me, dear. If I don't know anything else, I know when something's not right with my own daughter. Talk to me."

Fran felt a swell of emotion to the point where her eyes grew wet again. Her mother's words, the care in her tone, threatened every shred of defense and pretense Fran had. More to the point, she didn't want to pretend that everything was fine.

She looked at Oma and didn't bother drying her eyes. "Oh, Mom." The words caught in her throat.

"Tell me. Franny?"

Fran sighed. "James. He's not home much, you know. He works a lot. I mean, I understand that he's trying hard to provide well for us."

"Well, if you're not happy, Franny, you should talk to him about it. Holding it inside won't make it go away."

"You make everything sound so simple."

"I don't mean to suggest that your problems aren't real. Just remember you don't have to shoulder them alone."

"We had an argument a while back about his late nights. Things got heated."

"How long has this been going on?"

"It feels like forever. Sometimes I think about how it used to be when the kids were young. When James seemed happy. He didn't work so much then." She said softly, "We would talk."

Oma touched her hand. "Franny, honey, you have to talk to him."

"I try, but it usually ends up in some kind of argument, or just not a good feeling for either of us. And I really miss it, you know. The talking." Fran picked at invisible lint on her candy-pink cashmere sweater. "I wish I had your faith, Mom. I wish I had your strength."

"You have both. Sometimes I think you don't give yourself enough credit, Franny."

"Thanks, but . . . I don't know. I look in the mirror sometimes and I think, where has all my time gone? And don't get me wrong, I love my kids." She looked toward the kitchen where Reba was, hesitating and then lowering her voice. "I do love them. I just . . . I don't know . . . I just don't feel like I matter."

"Oh, Fran. Honey."

The tears streamed down Fran's cheeks before she could stop herself from giving in to her feeling of powerlessness. "It may sound silly, but it's true. The kids are older now—well, except Reba. James is always working. I take care of the house, do laundry, and taxi the kids around." She gave her mother a pitiful look of helplessness that would rival any little girl's greatest despair.

"Why don't you volunteer at the church?"

"Well, I did. You know the Christmas gift basket thing, the ones for the nursing home? I helped."

"You should do more things like that."

Fran exhaled. "I don't know. James always complains if I'm away from the house too much. He says I have a job—taking care of him and the kids. Anyhow, I'm not sure if more church work would do it for me."

"Why?"

"I felt a little like an outsider. When we'd have our meetings, everybody had somebody they'd sit with, talk to. I can't believe I just said that. It sounds so high school." Her laugh was weak.

"Maybe you should go on Sundays more often. You'd feel more connected." It sounded more like chastising than Oma had intended. But it didn't seem to register with Fran. Instead, she said something her mother hadn't quite expected.

"I'm not sure about the whole church thing."

"What do you mean?" Unconsciously, Oma withdrew a little.

"Mom," Fran said, glancing away, "don't look at me like that. I just meant that it's not doing anything for me. I feel like I'm going sometimes just because it's the thing to do." Oma remained silent. "I didn't always feel that way."

Oma said, "Maybe it would help if you and James had a talk with Pastor Phillips."

"Mom, I—we're both so busy, it's hard to fit it all in." The excuse sounded hollow in her own ears.

Oma told her, "God's concern about us is unconditional, even when we don't make time for Him, He's always ready to listen. Everything is going to be okay, honey. Look, why don't you and James and the kids all come to the midnight Christmas service with me?"

"I don't know. James mentioned something about this thing at his golf buddy's house."

"It's not for a few weeks yet. You've got time to think about it. It would mean a lot to me, and I believe it would help you."

"I'll talk to James about it."

"You do that, Franny."

Reba came into the room. "Oma, I'm sleepy. Can I take a nap in your bed?" She sat next to her grandmother and leaned her head against her shoulder.

Fran told her, "I'm sorry, honey, but we have to go. I have more Christmas shopping to do."

Oma said, "Reba can stay with me while you shop."

The little girl piped up. "Oh, great! Can I, Mom?"

Fran asked, "You sure, Mom?"

"Of course I'm sure. Reba and I have some playtime to catch up on."

"All right, I'll try not to be too long." Fran kissed her daughter on the head. "Be good for Grandma."

Oma and Reba settled on making the remainder of the cookies in Oma's fridge. The old woman and little girl sat side by side at the small table rolling out the dough. Reba liked using the cookie cutter to make all the Christmas shapes: the tree, the snowman, but the reindeer was her favorite.

She asked her grandmother, "If you could have anything you wanted for Christmas, Oma, what would you wish for?"

"Oh my, I'm not sure," Oma said. "Well, maybe a nice pretty necklace. I could wear it to church and show all of my friends."

Reba stopped fiddling with the dough to beam at her grandmother.

Her bright, curious eyes were always alert and anxious to learn something new.

"And what would you wish for?" Oma asked. "Let me guess—a new bike, or maybe one of those video toys all the kids love to play with."

"Nah, that's Elliott's wish. That's all he does, besides soccer. He always plays those stupid games."

"So, what do you want for Christmas?"

Reba went silent, looking down at the cookie dough. "I want—I want God to fix my family."

"Reba, dear, what did you say?" Oma stopped to focus on the child.

Reba continued pressing the cookie cutters into the dough and answered softly, "Nobody laughs anymore."

Oma touched her granddaughter's cheek. "Oh sweetheart, I'm so sorry."

She looked up at her Oma and said, "I want to help, but I don't know how."

"Well," Oma said, "God can do things we can't."

Reba quietly considered her grandmother's words. Not quite sure, she asked, "You think He'll help us?"

Oma said, "Absolutely." Reba carefully placed the cookie dough reindeer onto the baking sheet. She had never asked God to grant a *miracle*. She wondered how she would even go about it.

James said yes to the midnight service at Oma's church. It was just blocks from their home, so distance wasn't a convenient excuse and, besides, Reba pleaded too hard for him to deny her.

3

ran noticed how her husband became more distant, distracted, and pensive. Once, when she made the mistake of mentioning that he should consider hiring an assistant, he snapped, "I'm perfectly capable of handling my business. If I need help, I know where to go for it." She was too taken aback to respond.

Ordinarily, she would call him to ask when he would be home for dinner. It was getting late. But tonight, she decided against it. She'd just finished cooking. She was preparing Reba's plate when she saw her older kids go about the business of getting their own china and drinking glasses, their silverware, preoccupied with whatever activity they had left moments before.

Stacy would disappear again into her room with her meal and her cell phone. Jay would hog the TV in the family room to watch the game. Elliott would scarf down bites between playing NBA 2K19 on his PlayStation 4 in his room.

Reba sat quietly at the table waiting for Fran, who was staring at the other kids. She'd read in one of her self-help books about the importance of family time over dinner. At one point—quite a while ago now—real family dinners had come naturally for them, but those days became fractured and splintered by ragged schedules, busyness, and, over time, general disinterest in the ritual.

Just as her kids were filing out of the kitchen, Fran said to them, "Wait."

Startled, they turned to face her, steaming plates in hand.

"Let's eat together," she said. They knew by her tone that it wasn't open for debate, but Stacy wanted to test her anyway.

"Seriously, Mom?"

"What about the game?" Jay asked, arm extended toward the family room and face crumpled like a five-year-old on the edge of fake tears.

Elliott had already plopped down next to Reba.

"Yes, I'm serious," Fran said. "Sit. You can record the game."

With mumbled protests, they took chairs opposite their younger brother and sister. Fran sat at the head of the table.

The only one who seemed to be happy about dinner together was Reba. "Aren't we going to say grace?" she asked. Her siblings had already started eating.

Fran put her fork down and said, "You're absolutely right, Reba." Stacy rolled her eyes.

"Heads bowed," Fran instructed, the way she would do when they were quite young. "Dear Lord, we thank you for all you have given us and ask that you bless this food so that it is nourishing to our bodies. Amen."

Dinner resumed. "So, what's with the Instagram moment here?" It was Stacy, stabbing at her salad.

"I like it!" Reba chimed, pasta sauce on her chin.

Fran smiled at her. "Napkin, honey." She tapped her own neat chin with a single finger. Then she directed her voice to Stacy. "I thought it would be nice. We never eat dinner together. It gives us a chance to talk."

"What? You lonely or something, Mom?" Stacy said with laughter pushing out her words.

Jay smirked.

"No," Fran said in a tone to match her daughter's sarcasm. "This is good for us. We can, I don't know—share."

Stacy and Jay exchanged telepathic messages. Elliott remained quiet while sneaking his iPhone from his pocket to play Fortnite.

"No phones at the table," Fran instructed.

Elliott groaned but complied. Reba, on the other hand, was excited by the idea of sharing. "I know!" She raised her hand, smiling.

"You don't have to raise your hand, honey. You can go first, if you want," Fran told her.

"We have Daddy's Day Show-and-Tell coming up," Reba said.

Elliott chimed in. "Aren't those like two different things?"

Reba shook her head. "Mrs. Coalson said we're gonna do them together because she's gonna have a baby and has to leave." She turned to Fran. "How do babies come, Mom?"

Fran shot a look to her other kids, who were smiling at her, waiting to see how she would handle the question. "Maybe when you're a little older, honey, we can talk about it. Anyway, tell us more about your big day coming up at school."

"Oh, yeah," Reba continued, "everybody is gonna have their daddies there to do a show-and-tell with them."

"*Everybody?*" Elliott asked.

Jay and Stacy were smirking again.

"Hey," Fran gently admonished.

It didn't affect Reba. "Yeah, and I told my class that Daddy makes toys and we are gonna show his stuff as my show-and-tell."

"Dad doesn't *make* anything," Jay told her.

"Money," Stacy mumbled.

"Hey, guys," Fran said to them, "watch it over there."

Elliott told Reba, "Dad doesn't make stuff like that anymore. People in China do it for him."

Reba pouted, "Well, he could make toys. He used to. Before I was born. He showed me one time."

"You're absolutely right, dear," Fran encouraged her.

"Anyway," Elliott added, "you ask Dad if he could do it? Your show-and-tell thing?"

Reba was wide-eyed, wanting her mom's help in responding to Elliott.

"I'm sure he'll be happy to," Fran told her.

The two older kids murmured something. Fran gave them a warning look.

Jay piped up. "What? What did we do?" He put a hand to his chest as if wounded by his mother's glare, the glint of laughter still twinkling in his eyes.

Elliott was shaking his head. "You should ask Dad, like, super early. You know he's gone all the time."

"He's *working*," Fran clarified.

"Doesn't matter when she asks him," Stacy interjected. "He won't do it."

"Yes, he will!" Reba told her sister, and then looked to her mother.

"Of course, of course, he'd be happy to," Fran said. "But you should ask really soon, like your brother said, so Daddy can make time for it. Your father's very busy right now with work."

"He's *always* busy," Elliott retorted. "And you always say the same thing."

"Elliott!" Fran reproached.

Stacy shrugged. "True, Mom."

Elliott continued, saying, "I asked Dad a whole month before we had that thing with my soccer team. I was the only one whose dad didn't show up. I just left before we took pictures."

"Oh, honey, I know you were disappointed." Fran reached out to touch his arm. "I'm sure he wanted to be there but—"

"He was working." Jay cut her off. His eyes were lowered to his plate as he forked his meal. This time he wasn't smiling.

"He does his best," Fran said to no one in particular. "He does his best for all of us."

"Well, I'm gonna ask 'im." Reba's tone was just short of sticking out her tongue at her brother and sister across the table.

"Yes, you do that, honey. But . . ." Fran paused, her eyes darting around the table to her children, who looked at her expectantly. There was that smirk again on Stacy's and Jay's faces. "But planning ahead is always good." She couldn't bring herself to speak her thought: *Have a backup in case he disappoints you.* The others knew from their own experiences—the promises made and broken. Promises made and out-right forgotten. Stacy's and Jay's smirks were borne out of a defense to the hurtful consequences of such things and the anger that came with them. Elliot was learning. It would one day come to burn Reba too.

The meal went on with Fran asking questions about school, soccer practice, the need to take them shopping for new boots, and Stacy reminding her that she'd rather take the money and shop with her friends. And then it ended, and chairs scraped wordlessly along the wood floor. They all vanished, except Reba, who remained at the table reading a book while Fran cleaned the kitchen. She knew her little girl was waiting.

She closed the last cabinet door from the night's cleanup, then turned to Reba. "Hey, it's getting a little late, honey. Ready for your bath?"

"Mom, can I have a little more time?"

"Well, a few more minutes, but—" Just then she heard the key at the front door. Reba heard it, too, and dashed toward the sound like a puppy after its treat.

James hadn't cleared the threshold before Reba flung her arms around him. "Daddy!" Coming into the foyer, Fran met the surprise on James's face as he returned his daughter's hug.

"Wow!" he exclaimed. "Now that's a welcome-home greeting. What did I do to deserve this?"

Reba pitched her head back so she could look up at him. "I've been waiting to tell you something!"

"Well, this must be important stuff. Should I sit down, or can you tell me while I hang up my coat?" He was already working his way out of his parka.

Fran reached for it. "Here. Let me help."

Another wave of surprise lit James's face.

"We're gonna have a special show-and-tell at school," Reba said, interrupting the few seconds of eye-talk between her parents.

James looked down at her. "Oh, wow. Now that sounds nice."

"But I haven't told you the best part. We're supposed to do the show-and-tell with our dads. We get to do it together in front of the whole class!"

"Oh."

Fran was still standing there, trying to read the moment and her husband's expression. She was poised to intervene and soften anything that may land like a blow on her little girl.

James only nodded, smiling, but the smile didn't reach his eyes. "And when is this?" he asked Reba.

"In three weeks. So we've got a whole lot of time to come up with something really good. I told everybody you make toys. So that's what they're expecting."

He laughed a little. "Oh, really now?" He nodded again. "Okay. Okay. So we've got three weeks to get ready, huh?"

"Then you'll do it? You'll be my partner? That's what Mrs. Coalson calls it."

James knelt so that he was eye-level with his daughter and lightly tapped the tip of her freckled nose. "Of course I'll be your partner."

She leapt and squeeze-hugged him. "I love you, Daddy." Her voice was muffled in his neck.

Fran exhaled. "Okay." She gave a single clap of her hands. "Time for your bath!"

In the hush of the night, Fran and James crawled into bed. The sound of James's deep sigh was a signal that he was shutting down and didn't want conversation. He had the convenient excuse of an early flight in the morning for a business trip. Fran had fought the urge to say anything earlier, but as she lay staring up at the ceiling, her compulsion got the better of her.

"James." She spoke quietly to his back.

"Yeah?" The sterility of his tone signaled she should make this quick.

"This show-and-tell thing at Reba's school." She paused.

"Yeah, what about it?" He hadn't moved to give her his full attention.

"It's important to her. It's a big deal, James."

"She's seven. Everything is a big deal when you're seven, Fran."

"I know. And that's all the more reason to take what's important to her seriously."

That's when he turned to face her. "Are you saying I don't take Reba seriously? Really?"

"I didn't say that, James."

"Okay, care to explain it, then? Because that's what I just heard you say."

"I'm not looking to fight, James."

"Then don't insult me."

"I was just getting at your pattern."

"Pattern? What pattern?"

She hesitated and then said, "You don't always keep your promises."

He sat up. "Here we go again."

"I'm talking about how it makes our kids feel."

"The kids know I love them, Fran. They know that what I do, I do for them."

"Try to explain that to a seven-year-old when you choose work over a school project she's looking forward to, or something else that's a big deal to her. You heard her. She told her whole class about you. She wants *you* to be her partner, James. She wants to show off her dad to her friends. This isn't like the other times when you missed her recitals. I won't be in that classroom for her if you can't follow through this time. Neither will her sister or brothers or her Oma."

He was silent for a long time. And so was Fran. She watched him, not unlike her kids had watched her at dinner, waiting for answers that sounded hopeful but not putting much belief in what they were being told.

James didn't look at Fran when he finally spoke, but he did give her what she wanted to hear. "I won't let Reba down."

4

Saturday morning again. The kids ate breakfast while their parents moved around the kitchen and chatted about the Hollands' Christmas party that night.

Fran had spent weeks shopping for just the right dress, shoes, purse, jewelry, and hairstyle with her crew of fashionista friends on hand for critique and approval: Madeline, twice-divorced and twice richer than everyone else; Kelly, who co-owned a bistro with her ten-years-running live-in boyfriend; and Angelica, a commercial property real estate agent who once dated Gus. Fran forgave her.

Reba stood in her parents' bathroom doorway, watching her mother in the mirror. "Your dress is pretty," she finally said. "I like how it matches your eyes."

Fran turned from her reflection to her daughter, who was smiling behind her. "Oh, really?" She bent to kiss Reba on the forehead. "I think I like it too."

"What does Daddy think?"

James emerged from his closet into his dressing space in the bedroom. "Your mom looks beautiful in whatever she puts on," he said, fidgeting with his bow tie. "Hey." He gestured to Fran. "Give me a hand with this thing, will ya?"

He walked by Reba with a soft hand to her shoulder. She stood a while longer, watching her parents. At moments like these, they were not the mom and dad with angry voices but just like people from the TV shows, especially when they were all dressed up. She remembered the talk she'd had with her Oma about needing God to fix things. But everything seemed fine now. Maybe she really didn't need God's help, after all. To Reba, her parents appeared perfect. Her dad looked like he belonged on the top of a wedding cake, and her mom was like a beautiful blue star. The light in the bathroom made Fran's dress twinkle as she worked on James's bow tie.

"I hate these things." He jutted his chin forward.

"Hold still, James. You fidget worse than Elliott sometimes."

"I like it, Daddy," Reba said.

"Isn't Daddy handsome?" Fran directed her smile to Reba but was aware of James's startled look of pleasure.

Reba covered her face and giggled. Just then, Stacy called upstairs, "Hey, Reba! Pizza's here!"

She bolted for the door. James was still studying Fran as she aimed her attention toward her little girl's footsteps as they disappeared down the stairs.

"Handsome, huh?" he said in a tone she hadn't heard in months.

The way he looked at her then made her smile.

"I've always liked you in a tux."

"Really now?"

She nodded, still smiling.

"What time is it?" he asked, almost whispering.

"It's late," she said.

"It's not late."

"It's too late for anything that won't get us out the door in two minutes."

"I can get there fast, you know."

"I know, but I always prefer it when you take your time. Let's go, Mr. Harrison."

Stacy sat with her lean legs curled underneath her on the couch as she watched TV. She was only mildly aware of Reba and Elliott nearby, both having flopped down on the large Persian rug. Just then, Stacy's phone pinged with an incoming text. It was her boyfriend.

Chase: Sup?
Stacy: Babysitting.
Chase: Working?
Stacy: Nope. Brothers N sister.
Chase: Cool. Want company?
Stacy: Love some but too many eyes.
Chase: Chill in my ride?
Stacy: Eyes have big mouths.
Chase: When R U dun 2nite?
Stacy: Don't know. Mom N Dad at a party.
Chase: Cmon let me see you.
Stacy: 2morrow.
Chase: Okay ☹
Stacy: No ☹. *2morrow =* ☺
Chase: Can't wait.

Stacy felt the same and more. Her thumbs tapped out the words, *Love you.* She paused only for a flicker before hitting the send button. And then waited. Staring at her phone for a reply. No bubbles for an in-progress message. Her heart sank to her taut abs. She cursed to herself. She shouldn't have said that. Her girlfriends said you should never be the one to say it first. Finally, the little bubbles emerged. She bit her lip, still glaring at her phone. Then his reply popped up: *Sorry. Dog peed. Love you too.*

She threw her head back as her whole face, her whole body, combusted into happy. She needed to tell her bestie, Heather Whitaker. After all, Stacy was sure the time spent with Chase during the weekend trip to the Whitaker's place had ramped up their relationship to "I love you" status. So into action her fingers went.

Stacy ignored Reba, who whimpered about her tummy hurting. The messaging with Heather—and then Porsha as an add-on—was too important. Fran was quick to dismiss Stacy's self-immersive moments as just a teenage thing. No matter how frequent the behavior, her consistent response was, "It's just how they are. She'll grow out of it."

Stacy, with her long sun-gold hair, compliments of her mother's genes, glistened at pool parties, to which she had her choice of invitations. She inherited the swarthy skin tone of her father, and it succeeded in giving her a perpetual, enviable tan that was radiant in bright colors. Consequently, her large closet looked like an exploded fruit salad. She took great pleasure in shopping with her friends—Heather, in particular. Heather was famed for her family's money, her sweet-sixteen cherry-red Corvette, and credit cards that let off plumes of smoke as she blazed her way through only the best stores. Stacy was reading Heather's text about the white swimsuit she'd just bought that was a definite for the Whitaker's Christmas trip to Barbados when Reba whimpered again.

"Mom always gives me the pink stuff when my tummy hurts."

Stacy glanced down at her little sister, who looked back at her with sad eyes and a pouty bottom lip.

Stacy sighed. "Elliott."

Elliott, sitting cross-legged and hunched over his Nintendo Switch, responded with mild exasperation. "Yeah?"

"You know where Mom keeps the Pepto Bismol, right?"

"Yeah."

"Well, get it for me. And bring a spoon."

"Why do I have to get it? Didn't Mom say you were in charge?"

"Yep, and that's why I'm telling you to get it."

Stacy: Kid sister might barf. Sending my lil bro to grab meds.
Heather: Eww Lol
Stacy: Tell me about it.

Elliott got up with a grumble and a huff, walking out of the family room, his eyes still trained on his Switch, his adept fingers maniacal. He was transfixed on the world of revenge-seeking Christopher Belmont, who was leaping through castles in his pursuit of Dracula. Elliott would sometimes imagine himself in pursuit, too, his weapon fixed, his stare deadly, and his triumphs set to the atmospheric soundtrack. Transposed into this fantasy world of wizardry and luminescent firepower, his ordinary-boy limbs sculpted into melon-sized muscles that could rip the castle door of the enemy off by its hinges.

He would not be the boy his big brother playfully called "little dude," which in Elliott's ears meant "little runt." He was small for his age, and his spindly legs were so thin his knees looked like doorknobs—at least, that's what some of the kids at school said. He'd sneak Jay's body-building magazines to read, circling words he didn't understand and Googling definitions. Jay knew what was up. Sometimes, he'd tousle Elliott's halo of bronze curls and tell him, "Don't worry, little dude, you'll get there."

But to Elliott, the reach to become his big brother was unimaginable. Jay was a wrestling star and the running back of his school's football team. Everyone spoke in admiration of his dark features and his manlike physique already taking form at age fifteen. "He's gonna be a heartbreaker, Fran," they'd say.

Elliott couldn't believe any such thing would ever be said about him. The Harrison men's curly brown hair was his, which attracted many playful fingers that twiddled, stroked, and fussed. But that was the only nice thing about him, he thought. He had his granddad's nose, James had told him. That might've been fine for an old guy, but to Elliott, it was much too big for a boy's face. He spent a good deal of time looking at that nose situated between his narrow cheekbones. Worse still, it was accented by a spray of freckles that raced along the projectile bony bridge and spread to either delicate cheek. Those were his father's freckles. Fran would kiss them and call Elliott her handsome little man when he was dressed in his suit for church. That didn't help. He figured all moms said those things.

But there were times when he felt his awesomeness, like on the soccer field where his lithe body moved along with the wind's speed. There was also the magic of his video games where he could transform himself into something wondrous.

Elliott was so focused again on his game that he bumped into Jay.

"Hey, watch it, little dude. Look up from that thing when you're walking."

Elliott readjusted the Pepto Bismol bottle he had secured in his armpit while giving his brother the once-over. "Where you going?"

"Got a party to go to," Jay said as he paused to check himself out in the foyer mirror. He smoothed his hand over hair that was nearly wet-black with gel. It made his hazel-green eyes more intense. He'd decided on a V-neck gray shirt and ripped jeans because he didn't want to look like he'd put too much thought into what he'd chosen to wear.

Exasperated, Stacy stomped in Elliott's direction but stopped when she saw Jay. "Hey, where do you think you're going? And is that cologne I smell?"

"I've got plans," he told her. She was sixteen and a junior in high school, only one year older than him, but Jay couldn't quite work up the nerve to steamroll over her authority. And Stacy knew it. He'd hoped to slip out the door when his ride came.

"Mom left me in charge," Stacy reminded him.

"Oh, brother." Jay sighed. "What she said was 'watch the kids.' That would be Elliott and Reba."

The two younger siblings were taking in the exchange.

Hand on hip, Stacy went on, "Well, I didn't hear you ask Mom and Dad if you could go out. Aren't you supposed to be grounded or something?"

Jay laughed incredulously. "You take this babysitting thing way too seriously."

"Like I said, they left me in charge. That means if you don't have

Mom or Dad's okay to go out, you're stuck here with the rest of us." She turned to Elliott. "Just give me the bottle."

He took the Pepto Bismol from his armpit and handed her the spoon.

"My ride's gonna be here any sec," Jay said as Stacy uncapped the medicine and gave Reba a spoonful. Stacy didn't respond. He stepped closer to get her attention. "It's Friday night."

"Yeah. I know," she said, recapping the bottle.

"Look. Don't take it out on me because you got stuck babysitting."

"We're not babies," Reba interjected. "She's just watching us to make sure everybody's okay. That's what Mom said."

Elliott didn't seem to care. He was intent again on his Switch.

Jay sighed. "I got *plans*, Stacy."

"You should've cleared it with Mom."

"Well, I didn't, okay? I just got Chris's text."

"So, conversation over."

"I got a party to go to."

"Where?"

"What do you care?"

"Because somebody needs to know where you are, numb nut."

He rolled his eyes and sighed again. "It's at the Omega House."

Her eyes widened. "Omega? As in frat party?"

"Yeah."

"How'd you get invited to a frat party? You're a flippin' kid." She laughed.

Jay's jaw tightened. "I'm not a kid. And, yeah, I got invited. Well, Tyler's brother is home this weekend. He's getting us in."

She looked him over. "They are gonna be drinking their ass—" She caught herself when she noticed Reba's unblinking stare. "They drink a lot at those things," she amended.

"So what?" Jay challenged.

"So what if you get into some kind of trouble again? What am I supposed to do? If you screw up and I have to call Mom and Dad, *I'm gonna get grounded because I let you go.*"

"I'm not gonna get into trouble."

"Yeah, that's what every kid says."

"Look, I gotta go. I told everybody at school I was going to a college party tonight."

"So you didn't just get the text. "

"Come on, Stace."

She turned to head back into the family room, Elliott and Reba following like little ducklings.

"This is so not cool!" Jay called out behind her. "I covered for you plenty of times!"

Stacy stopped and turned as if to head off what might come next. Reba and Elliott looked back too. "Just shut up, Jay," Stacy told him, and then said, "Hey, guys, go on and watch TV." She gave Reba and Elliott each a hand to the back to move them along.

Jay crossed his arms, feeling more empowered as he got a whiff of Stacy's nervousness. "A trade," he offered. "We don't talk about your boyfriend and the sleepover at the Whitaker's, and I get to go to the party."

"Fine!" She spun on her heel, leaving behind Jay's satisfied laughter. She flopped on the couch, picking up her phone to start another text exchange, but Reba interrupted her.

"What if Jay gets into trouble?" She was sitting on the floor next to Elliott, who was once again lost in his game.

Stacy looked down at her sister's concerned face. "Hey, it'll be okay, Reba."

"But you said—"

"I know. I just want him to be careful, that's all. Nothing's gonna happen to Jay, okay? It's just a stupid frat party."

"They talked to us about drinking and driving at school," Reba said.

"Really? Aren't you guys a little young for that?"

"Nope," Elliott replied without pausing his Switch. "When I was seven they showed us the films too."

Reba continued, saying, "What if Jay and his friends drink? Who's gonna drive them home so they'll be okay?"

"Don't worry, Reba." But Stacy's words were thin and hollow in her own ears.

While driving, James held Fran's hand. How she wished it could always be like that—the way he looked at her, a night out for just the two of them, even if it would be shared with over eighty other guests.

They drove up to the Hollands's mansion where the stately, long driveway was lined with guests' cars that declared their wealth: several Mercedes, too many BMWs to count, a few Lexuses, and multiple limos. James headed toward the row of valets standing in front of the columned double doors like Nutcracker soldiers in matching Christmas-red coats.

Inside the house, they were greeted by two young women with gleaming teeth and form-fitting cocktail dresses. One took their coats, and the other led them through the foyer, where two Christmas trees loomed. Beyond the foyer, a string quartet could be heard playing carols.

One of the young ladies reappeared with two champagne flutes and her brilliant teeth. She handed a flute to both James and Fran. "Enjoy," she said, nodding toward the huge ballroom before clicking away in her stilettos back toward the entrance.

"Wow," James whispered to Fran, "you could play a round of golf in this place."

"James, Mrs. Harrison, so glad you could make it!" They turned toward the voice and saw a woman smiling their way.

"Mrs. Hollands!" James and Fran both exclaimed.

Brunette till death, Mrs. Hollands was a lady of privilege. She was monied, slim, and had a face that defied the laws of physics. She reached out a ring-embellished hand to touch James's arm and then leaned in to Fran to give an air-kiss.

"Thanks so much for inviting us," Fran told her. "Your home is absolutely beautiful. Stunning."

Mrs. Hollands gave a sleepy-eyed chuckle. "I only use this place for parties, you know. It makes for a good magazine cover."

The woman, and her parties, were quite the talk among society types. Her soirees were exclusive, invitation-only affairs where wealthy people talked about their money and traded information on how to claw in more of it—at least, that was James's take, as he had explained to Fran. Being invited was a big deal. The guests were often mentioned in the society pages of the papers with accompanying photos.

The intention behind the gathering was to collect money for charities through a silent auction of overpriced merchandise that earned winning bidders bragging rights, and their names and businesses promoted in the papers. James had met Mrs. Hollands through a mutual acquaintance at The Children's Hospital. He was intending to take a run at pitching his products to the hospital's gift shop when he ran into his friend and hospital board member, Pastor Martin Phillips. The pastor was there visiting the cancer ward. Mrs. Hollands's niece had been recently diagnosed, and she thought donating a sizable amount might increase her niece's prospects of receiving better care, so she was also present.

The chance meeting landed the three of them in the cafeteria, where they chatted over coffee, the young pastor extolling the virtues of the hospital. When Mrs. Hollands offered to make the medical center the benefactor of that year's charity affair, he was overjoyed. And to demonstrate her good-natured kindness even further, she'd turned to James and said, "You're welcome to join us," even though she'd known him all of fifteen minutes.

It was James's "ticket in," as he had said to Fran. With that in mind, he hoped to make connections that could bring him big business.

"I hope you enjoy the party," Mrs. Hollands told them.

"I'm sure we will," Fran replied. "What's being auctioned this year?"

"Well, I would say the real prize to be had this year is a Jackson Pollock sketch. It doesn't rival his *Composition with Red Strokes*, but it should do pretty well, I think."

Someone else caught her eye, so Mrs. Hollands pitched a wave and a smile, then touched Fran on the arm with delicate but cold fingertips. "Excuse me, please."

The crowd of people shimmered under Christmas lights. Servers in tuxes held trays of champagne. The room was filled with the sound of laughter and the clinking of fine crystal. The chamber ensemble filled the large, festive room with music.

"Come on," James said in a resolute tone. "Let's mingle."

He didn't wait for Fran to respond. He placed his hand on her back and guided her into the thick of the room, where he interjected himself into a conversation three other guests were having, debating the merits of traveling on New Year's Day.

A balding man with several strands of hair combed over his scalp was nodding and smiling, ogling a tall brunette. The woman flipped her hair over her shoulder and declared, "There is no place in Europe more beautiful than Málaga. And flying on New Year's is absolutely fabulous. I went there last year, same time, and I was the only one in first class. Fabulous!" The third member of the trio was another woman, equally as striking, with the height and looks of a runway model. She chimed in, "I never do Europe during the holidays. You miss all the good parties here!" Her wrist of bangled bracelets sang out as she sipped from her champagne glass.

"Long-distance travel is always brutal," James supplied.

The brunette touched his arm and told him, "Xanax. I know a good doctor if you're interested."

The balding man was still staring at her and smiling.

The other woman turned her attention to the newcomers. "You traveling this holiday season?" Her eyes moved between James and Fran.

"Well. No." Fran shifted a glance toward James.

"No," he confirmed, "not during Christmas. The kids would rather stay here and enjoy their friends over school break."

"Kids, huh?" The balding man finally spoke. "How many?"

"Four." Fran had an impulse to pull their pictures out of her tiny purse but didn't.

"What school?" the man asked.

Fran answered, "We have two at Kensington High and two at Dover Mane Elementary."

"*Public* schools?" the man asked.

"Good Lord," the gazelle said. Her and the brunette's laughter was soft but blistering.

Fran was about to go on the defense, but another man walked up and clapped the balding guy on the shoulder. "Steve, you see the Pollock piece? Nice. Agnes has got such a good eye."

"Hey, Tom! I haven't checked it out yet, but the wife wants it, so it's a done deal." He flashed a satisfied grin.

"Don't count your sketches before they hatch, my friend," Tom said. He beamed a smile of perfectly square teeth, their whiteness set off by the darkness of his tanning-bed skin.

The gazelle gave a playful eye roll and told James and Fran, "These two do this every year."

"True," the balding man agreed. "With what we spend at these things, we could get your kids into *real* schools." He laughed into his drink.

Fran stiffened. James touched her on the small of her back again.

The brunette said, "Steve, how many of those things have you had?" referring to his drink.

Showing her his teeth, Tom said, "Steve here is gonna need his alcohol. It'll make losing out on the Pollock a lot easier. Right, Steve?" More chuckles and another clap on Steve's back.

"So competitive." The brunette spoke to no one in particular.

Fran observed the look on her husband's face—he was smiling but also calculating his moves. They hadn't even been there twenty minutes, and she'd lost him already. She already knew what would happen next, and she didn't want to stand alongside him listening to a sales pitch. She needed air.

She spotted a clear space near the kitchen entrance. Once there, she leaned against the wall. Its coolness felt good against her back. The band's music swelled. Laughing couples got louder as they claimed space on the crowded dance floor. Fran watched them, pressed against each other, moving to the music, masculine hands on slim hips. Past them, she tried to get a glimpse of James, but the dancing couples blocked her view. It was like watching him through window blinds that opened and closed. She could tell by the way he stood so rigidly that he wasn't having a good time.

Just then, her loneliness turned into something aching and sad. The smell of the Christmas pine trees was suddenly overwhelming. The reflex to cry clenched her throat. She closed her eyes but was soon interrupted by a man's voice. "Hey, you okay?"

It was Martin Phillips, her former pastor—Oma's pastor—and board member for The Children's Hospital. His wife, Charlotte, and Fran had become friends years ago, when she and James were just starting their family. The friendship had waned a bit in recent years, and the fact that Charlotte was no less warm only sharpened Fran's tinge of guilt for not making more of an effort.

Fran always thought Martin looked more like a theater director than a pastor. It was the longish blond hair and the frameless glasses. Clean-shaven, he appeared younger than his years and could easily pass for a man in his early thirties. She liked his kind face, his round eyes that fastened on people with such concern.

"Oh, Pastor Phillips." Caught off-guard, Fran blinked away the emotion she was determined to hide. "I'm fine," she said, aware that her cheeks were now warm and pink.

"You look like you could use some water," he said.

Fran nodded and handed him her champagne flute. He returned

quickly from the kitchen, moving toward her and carrying the glass with purpose.

She took several sips. "Much better. Thank you."

"These things can be a bit much." He threw a glance around the place.

"You don't like the parties? Lots of important people here."

"Well, important work to be accomplished, for sure. As for the people—eh." He intended the last of what he'd said to be taken as a private joke, to cheer her up. "Mrs. Hollands is one of our biggest donors," he continued. "The fact she chose the hospital as her honored charity this year is a big deal. That's what brings me here, otherwise Charlotte and I would be at the movies. She's a sport about giving up our date night when I have to work, though."

"I was looking forward to it." Fran forced a smile when her voice revealed more disappointment than she had intended.

Charlotte was walking toward them. Her hair, the color of red summer berries, was a mass of breezy natural curls that invited a man to lose a hand in them. Everything about her seemed effortless and radiated confidence. Her nearly translucent skin made her mane appear even more vibrant and caused her eyes to glisten like emeralds. Her comfortable V-neck black dress eased down the length of her body to the knee, fitted but not too tight. She had runner's legs, sinewy calves. For some women, their own insecurities would have cancelled the possibility of a friendship with her, but Fran had never felt that way.

Charlotte had this way of touching her lips when she laughed, as if she were in the middle of a shared secret. Anyone who'd been around her for any length of time came to know that laugh, disarming and warm. Pastor Phillips had told Fran and James, when the two couples were out to dinner one time, hearing that laugh was when he first knew he loved her. It was pouring rain on the night of their high school prom, and they were bolting across the lawn toward the school gymnasium for the big dance. His tuxedo was soaked, and Charlotte's hair was in wet ringlets, her saffron dress hanging on her body like a dishrag. They were feet from the door when Charlotte's foot slipped and down she went, onto the wet grass and mud. Martin stopped, waiting for her to cry or curse or something. Charlotte paused just for the second it took for the shock to pass and burst out laughing.

Charlotte and Martin never made it to prom. He would later tell close friends about how the night ended with his marriage proposal.

Charlotte and two friends who trailed her joined Pastor Phillips and Fran.

"Hey." Pastor Phillips kissed his wife on her forehead. "Get any million-dollar donations?" he chuckled.

Fran caught herself staring.

"Nope, but something just as good," Charlotte said. "Meet Jess and Becca. They're human rights attorneys. They'd like to learn more about serving on the board and doing *pro bono* work for the hospital."

"Oh, that's fantastic!" Pastor Phillips shook the women's hands.

"You're doing great work," Jess told him. "We've heard good things about you." She was a middle-aged woman with dark wavy hair streaked with silver. She didn't wear makeup to hide her freckles. Her eyes, under natural black lashes, squinted into crescents when she smiled.

Becca, her law partner, was younger by some years and shorter by many inches. "We've actually been talking about contacting the hospital to ask for a meeting for a while now." She raked her cinnamon hair behind an ear and shifted her feet in designer heels.

"Well, I'm glad we connected tonight," Pastor Phillips said. "We could certainly use some legal talent on the board."

Charlotte was aware of Fran standing there with fixed politeness. "And this is our friend Fran Harrison."

The lawyers shook Fran's hand.

"Are you a board member too?" Jess asked.

"No, not me." Fran gave a small laugh. She raised the flute of water to her face. "Human rights attorneys," she said, searching for something to say and a reason to remain there. "I'm sure your work is very interesting."

"Interesting," Becca agreed, "but not always in a good way."

Charlotte offered, "I'm sure with everything that's happening now with immigration, you're pretty busy."

"Very," Jess said, "but we don't want to bore you with work stories."

"We've been following what's going on very closely," Pastor Phillips told them. "You wouldn't be boring us."

The lawyers launched into a story about a case they'd taken on in which ICE had separated a man named Hector Gonzalez from his son at the border. The child died in a detention center.

There was a point when Fran mentally disconnected from the conversation. Right then, she missed James more than anything. If they were together at that moment, in the way she had imagined their night, she would've led him onto the dance floor.

A server interrupted the group with a large platter of prosciutto hors d'oeuvres. Jess, Becca, and Pastor Phillips helped themselves. Charlotte stole the moment to lock eyes with Fran. There was something sympathetic in the brief, silent exchange she offered. Fran didn't quite know what to feel.

Jess or Becca said something about how work can get overwhelming, but having kids helps: "They ground us."

Charlotte seemed to want to invite Fran into the conversation. "Fran is mother to *four* kids. That's a job by itself."

"Oh, goodness, yes!" Jess still chewed but managed another pinch-eyed smile.

Fran tried to respond likewise, but the smile faltered.

There was a lull, and the lawyers made mention of exchanging business cards before they moved on.

Pastor Phillips turned to Fran and asked, "Where's James, anyway?"

Fran stretched her neck to see beyond the sea of heads in the room. "There. See the tall woman, the blonde? He's with that group there."

She saw James turn and give a small acknowledging wave. She returned the same.

James was glad to see Fran with Pastor Phillips. He didn't have to feel bad about talking business.

"The real money is in tech," Tom was saying while pointing his drink at James. He gave James a shark's grin. Steve, the balding man, nodded, smiled.

The two women stopped listening and soon peeled off from the conversation.

Tom went on. "Just look around you. You got kids, right? How many iPhones and consoles can you count in your family alone? You ever consider expanding your line?"

James listened with the keen sharpness of an animal who hadn't eaten in days and was now fixed on the sound of something moving within reach in the high weeds. He was already figuring out how he could make this happen. His sleepless nights shrieked at him to make this happen. It would take money, more money than he had available right then, no doubt. He had been putting off creditors, making promises, and blowing due dates in the wake of what he'd told himself was only a dry spell. But maybe this was the signal to try something new. Go big.

"Listen to him, Jim," Steve said. "This man knows the market. The bastard made me a mint last quarter on a tip I would've passed on."

"If you want to talk more about it, maybe we can meet over drinks next week," Tom suggested. "I've got people who can get you into the tech space pretty quickly, with the right capital."

James took a breath as if preparing for a deep dive. Music and party noise filled the lag in the conversation. The two men were watching, waiting.

Finally James exhaled. "How much are we talking?"

5

A loud crash. All eyes swept toward the commotion. An aghast waiter was muttering apologies to a woman. It was Fran. Everyone froze, staring at her. She felt the wetness soaking through the front of her dress. She looked down at the wine spill, her mouth open.

Pastor Phillips and Charlotte rushed over to her. "Oh, no," Charlotte breathed, "your dress!"

Fran met their fixed round eyes. Her own were threatening tears.

"It'll be okay." Charlotte touched her arm. "We'll get something to work on that before it sets."

"They should have something in the kitchen," Pastor Phillips suggested.

"Seltzer should do it." Charlotte followed the server with his tray of broken wine glasses into the kitchen, then returned quickly with a cloth and seltzer in hand. "Come with me, the bathroom's this way."

"Thanks. I'll be all right." Fran took the items from Charlotte and tried to smile before entering the ladies' room on her own.

Inside, it was a tomb of white Carrara marble with subtle gray veining. The cheery Christmas music from the string quartet was piped in.

Fran walked up to gilded faucets, taking in her reflection. Her mascara had smudged a bit, the light smears of dark accentuating the crystal blue of her eyes. Her blond hair had lost most of its curl and now fell in relaxed ringlets, just like little girls in turn-of-the-last-century paintings. The overhead lighting angled her cheekbones, and in that moment, she looked all at once tragic and beautiful. She pushed her hair behind her ears, muttering, "Two hundred bucks for these highlights, and he didn't even notice." She turned on the water and rinsed the sticky wine off her arm.

When she walked back out to the party, she was so distracted by the blotch of wetness on the front of her dress that she collided into a man. As she blurted apologies, he turned and steadied her by the arm. "You okay?" he asked with a half-smile.

"Fine. I'm so sorry!" Flustered, she touched her hair, her dress.

"No need to apologize." Then he added, "Haven't we met before?"

She looked closer at him. He did look familiar.

"Dover Mane," he supplied. "You don't remember me?"

"Remember you?"

"Yes. I was one of the chaperones for the kids' zoo trip last spring."

"Oh, yes! How could I forget?" She smiled. "You were the only guy there." She'd only noticed him peripherally back then.

"My name's Adam."

"Yes. Aren't you the police officer?"

"Yep."

"I've seen you at the school for pickup. Your little girl is in the same grade as my Reba."

"Yeah, her name's Erin."

"Oh. I'm Fran."

"I remember. I'm good with faces."

"It's a police thing, huh?"

"No, a man thing."

She blushed. She felt awkward, which made her quiet. But she didn't walk away. She noticed he looked even younger up close and out of uniform. His hair was the color of nutmeg, cut short and wavy on top, hair that would definitely be curly if he'd let it grow longer. He had fair skin and was clean-shaven. And in the pullover sweater and tie, he could pass for a preppy college kid.

She broke the silence. "Well, I was on a hunt for coffee, so—"

"Coffee sounds good. Mind if I join you?"

A quick look for James. She didn't see him. "Sure."

The server met their requests with two cups of French press quicker than she could reply to Adam's compliment: "Nice dress."

Fran mumbled "Thank you" into the rim of her cup. She gazed at the partiers, some milling around, some laughing, some still dancing in pairs, and a few going for it solo.

"Everybody's having a good time," Adam said.

"Yeah." Fran let the veneer slide away and then tried to fix on a smile.

"You okay?" he asked. "You don't look so good."

"Gee, thanks."

"That came out wrong. Sorry. You look beautiful." Immediately he appeared uncomfortable with his honesty. "I didn't mean—"

"You didn't mean it?" She was enjoying his uneasiness.

"Of course I did." He physically shifted, averting his eyes. "I just didn't mean to be inappropriate."

"You weren't."

He saw the smile in her eyes and relaxed.

"Are you friends with Mrs. Hollands?" Fran asked.

"Who?"

"Mrs. Hollands. The host."

"Oh. No. Not at all."

"Oh." Fran was curious about his connection to the crowd but didn't want to ask and risk offense.

He addressed the unspoken question. "I'm here for The Children's Hospital."

"Really? Then you must know—"

"Pastor Phillips and Charlotte," he interrupted, looking past her.

Fran turned to see the couple walking up to join them.

"Adam, I thought that was you." Pastor Phillips extended his hand for a friendly shake.

"Hey, Adam." Charlotte offered him a hug. "It's good seeing you. I'm glad you came."

"Yeah. Quite the gathering here."

"Small world," Fran remarked.

Charlotte queried, "You know Adam?"

"Getting there," Adam replied in Fran's place.

The twinkle in his eye caused her to hide her own response behind a sip of coffee. "Adam was just telling me he's here for The Children's Hospital."

Pastor Phillips said, "Adam has been one of our volunteers for years now. We go way back."

Fran was remembering the kids' field trip. She asked Adam, "You do a lot of volunteer work?"

"I try to make time for what's important."

"Are you going to be here for a while?" Pastor Phillips asked. "There's an idea I'd like to run by you. It'll only take a minute."

"Sure!"

"Great. Let's connect in a bit, okay?"

"Very cool," Adam said, nodding.

Pastor Phillips and Charlotte returned to the thick of the party, leaving Adam and Fran alone again.

"Your husband here?" Adam asked, glancing at Fran's wedding ring.

"Yes. He's somewhere around here."

The coolness of her tone drew his attention. He took the moment to indulge himself but held the look too long. She turned to him, a bit self-conscious.

"Sorry again," he muttered.

"For what?"

"For staring."

"That's okay. I mean, I don't think you were being rude or anything." Fran became intensely aware of the man standing next to her. She felt exposed. "I should go find my husband." She took a step away but then turned back. "Nice meeting you." The feeling behind the words was real.

He smiled before responding. "I'm glad I came tonight."

On the ride home, Fran thought about what Adam had said—"I try to make time for what's important"—comparing it to James's preoccupations as he drove along, locked in his thoughts. There were moments when she thought of mentioning her disappointment but knew it would end in an argument and just make her feel worse.

The house was dark when they got there. Fran peeked into the bedrooms where the kids were sleeping before she and James went to their own room. Fran started to undress, but James headed for the door.

"James, where are you going?"

"I need to check on something. Go on to sleep."

"Check on what? At this hour?"

"I won't be long."

Fran didn't reply as James closed the door behind him. She knew he was going to his office in the basement. Slowly she eased onto her pillow, intently staring at the door. She would fall asleep waiting as James sat alone in front of his computer, clicking through his business spreadsheets. Focusing on the tanking numbers was growing into a nightly obsession for him.

6

James managed to pull together the money for his inventory expansion—the bank loan he'd secured wasn't quite enough, so he'd tried selling his boat but couldn't get any fast takers. He thought it worth the risk to siphon funds from the family's personal resources to meet the demand. Even though he'd spent far more than he'd ever spent for his merchandise of toys, the payoff would be much greater in the end. No risk, no glory. This wasn't part of the deal he'd told Fran. It was a carefully worded chat with his wife as they prepared for bed. She was sitting at her makeup mirror in their bedroom. James was in the bathroom, the door open, talking to her from the other side of the wall.

He led with the part he thought she would be happiest to hear. "I've been thinking about what you said."

Still watching her reflection while brushing her hair, Fran asked, "What did I say?"

"You know. About hiring some help." This had been an ongoing conversation, sometimes to the point of arguing.

She stopped brushing. A half-smile played along her mouth as she spoke. "You're bringing in help at the office? When? When will they start?"

"Well, not just yet. But soon. I got this great tip that I followed up on."

"Oh?" She didn't look as pleased but was poised and waiting for more as she held the hairbrush in her lap.

"Yeah, you remember those guys at the party I was talking to?"

"You mean the benefit thing?"

"Yeah."

"So, what was the tip?"

He walked into the room and stood behind her chair, talking to her reflection. "Do you know people spent nearly a trillion dollars in tech devices last year? iPhones, iPads, gaming systems. Crazy, huh? Almost a trillion. And that number is going up, without a doubt."

"Okay, so what's the big tip?"

"Expansion. I'm expanding my inventory."

"You mean like selling phones and things?"

"Not just phones. All the gadgets that I just mentioned. It's a crazy-hot market, and it just keeps growing."

"Well." She hesitated and tried to tamp down any concern in her voice, in her expression, as James watched her response to his news. "It sounds interesting, honey." He so rarely shared with her these days that she didn't want to ruin the moment. But clearly, she hadn't given him what he'd wanted.

He sighed and seemed to sag a little. "This could be big. Really big for me. For my company. For us."

She smiled. "That's exciting." She wondered about the investment cost but didn't want to go there. Instead she focused on the part of his news that made her happiest. "So when will your new hires be starting?"

"When the inventory arrival date is set. I should know something by next week, I think. Then I can bring a team on to help me move the stuff. We gotta hit it hard."

The gleam in the grin on her husband's face brought a genuine smile to her own face. "Good time of the year for it," she said. "Lots of Christmas shopping."

He leaned down and kissed the crown of her head, his hand on her shoulder. She touched it and closed her eyes.

"This is gonna be great for us," he told her. "You'll see."

The anticipated shipment of goods from China was late. The sales team James hired struggled to place orders when the delivery date was questionable. James called Tom so often that he stopped answering James's voice messages. The most recent word he'd gotten was from Tom's secretary: he was in China.

When the shipment finally arrived, two-thirds of the merchandise was missing. James spent his Saturday morning on the phone trying to get answers. He fought to keep his throbbing head from exploding. He paced the garage, leaving message after message for Tom, calling the shipping company, and rechecking the contents in the delivered boxes as if he expected the absent merchandise to materialize.

Reba appeared in the doorway. "Can we work on our project for the show-and-tell, Daddy?"

He tried not to let the surprise and confusion register on his face. He'd forgotten.

"The show-and-tell is this week," Reba clarified.

"Right. I remember."

He made a mental note to send an email to the team about the shipment and how they should proceed. Then he began exploring other boxes that were stacked against one of the walls. "I know I have them here somewhere," he said to himself with Reba still watching. "Found it."

Reba followed as James went into the basement with a box of his own abandoned toys. They situated themselves on a big area rug. He placed his phone nearby, and they began pulling out the toys. James had memories of making them, but the soul of his inspiration was long dead. Looking at them only made him feel hollow and sad.

Then something shifted as he watched Reba exploring the carved wooden toys with open wonder. He became enrapt by the way she handled each piece with such care, her small fingers delicately probing the fine details.

Reba felt it, too, even though she was too young to have the tools to express it. Still, she watched and evaluated her father with a kind of knowing beyond her years. She placed one of the wooden toys in his hand and kissed him on a cheek. "This one," she said. "Let's choose this one."

It was a carving of a sailboat, a double-masted cutter. There were miniatures of three boys on the boat: one steering the tiller, another near the mainsail who was pointing outward, and a third rotating the pivoting boom.

Reba and James drew big pictures of the different parts of the sail-boat. James wrote notes on how all the parts fit together. That was what he was doing when Fran came downstairs. With surprise and pleasure in her voice, she told them, "You guys have been at this for hours. You hungry? I can make sandwiches."

"I'm starving." James threw a request over his shoulder, "Ham and cheese, please?" and went back to his note cards.

Reba was on the floor coloring drawings of various parts of the boat. She looked up, sparkling with absolute joy in the moment. "Me too, Mom!"

Reba listened as James rehearsed what they would tell the class about the boat: how he carved it, why he liked making toys, and what it meant to him.

James spent more time with Reba that weekend than any of them could remember. Fran was so happy when they finally emerged from the basement, she nearly hugged the breath out of James.

The day of the show-and-tell, James told Reba, "I have some really important stuff at the office to take care of this morning, but I'll be there in plenty of time for our show."

Her silent stare told him she had doubts.

"I promise." And to make his point, he told her, "Hey, why don't you take the sailboat to school with you, and when I come, I'll bring the posters."

"You trust me with your boat?" She tilted her head, looking at him a little sideways.

"Absolutely. Think of it as my promise to show up today, okay?"

Reba nodded.

Fran had missed the conversation and James had already gone by the time she came downstairs with car keys and purse in hand to drive Reba to school. When she saw Reba sitting quiet and alone at the breakfast counter with the sailboat, she paused with a look of concern. Reba repeated to her everything her father had told her, including that he trusted her with his sailboat, and how that was a sign of a promise.

Later that morning in school, Reba rehearsed her father's words in her head as time ticked by. Her attention rested on the sailboat on her desk. She thought she caught her teacher Mrs. Coalson offering her a sympathetic look, but the woman redirected her attention to the father and son in front of the class who were explaining how to build a bike. Mr. Gordon owned three bike shops. The class let out whispered interest as they leaned forward to see Mr. Gordon and Junior demonstrating the proper way to attach a front tire.

Reba and James were supposed to be next. The students were presenting in alphabetical order. She looked toward the door. She was gripping the sailboat at both ends. The class applauded. Reba's attention snapped back to Mrs. Coalson, who was walking up to Reba's desk. She leaned over as much as her pregnant belly allowed and whispered as if it were a secret between them, "Your dad's not here yet?"

Reba shook her head no, unable to say the words as she held onto the sailboat.

"Do you want Ian and his father to go next? That'll give you a little more time."

Reba nodded. That's how it went for the next four presentations. Reba kept being pushed back in the line of presenters to give James more time to show up. And finally he did. Winded, he nearly stumbled into the room, carrying the mounted posters he and Reba had made. She almost leapt out of her seat when she saw him, grinning and waving frantically like he couldn't see her five feet away, and he smiled back. Mrs. Coalson was smiling, too, but put a single finger to her lips to quiet them, as the boy at the front of the room and his father went on about their shared hobby of building model trains.

Mrs. Coalson went over to James, who was still standing by the door. She whispered, "I'm so glad you could make it, Mr. Harrison. If you and Reba need a moment, the two of you can sit at the crafting table at the back of the room, okay? I'll call you up next."

He thanked her, and he and Reba made their way to the rear of the class. The second after he set the posters on the table, Reba clamped her arms around him and murmured, "I knew you'd come!"

He bent to return the hug. "I didn't want to disappoint you." That's when his phone vibrated in his pocket. The motion buzzed against Reba's arm. She let go of him and looked up. He paused just long enough to register an expression of unspoken apology before checking the incoming call. He knelt a little to whisper to her at eye-level. "Honey, I need to take this, okay?"

"But—"

"I'll just be a minute," he interrupted. "This is really, really important. I promise I'll be back in a sec." Before she could respond he was headed for the classroom's rear entrance.

She stood, stunned, mouth parted as she watched her father through the glass window of the door, pacing in the hall.

Mrs. Coalson had seen the last few seconds of their exchange. She came to the back of the classroom, where Reba remained immobile, still fixed on her father.

"You okay, Reba?" Mrs. Coalson put her hand on Reba's shoulder to get her attention.

Reba nodded but wouldn't turn to her.

"Do you want me to talk to your dad, honey? Daniel is just about finished. There aren't any other presenters to call on."

Reba nodded. She watched Mrs. Coalson slip out the back to join James and followed the brief mimed conversation between the two, her father pulling the phone away from his ear and holding up the "give me just one minute" sign to Mrs. Coalson.

She returned to Reba, her expression sympathetic, telling her, "We can wait for a little while. But I'm sorry, if your dad's not available, dear, I'm afraid we'll have to move on with our day."

Reba looked to the door, beyond which her father could still be seen pacing and talking on the phone. "Okay, Mrs. Coalson. I want to wait for my dad." Mrs. Coalson gave her a little smile and then went back to the front to keep the activities going.

Soon, the class applauded when Daniel and his dad finished. Mrs. Coalson allowed for picture-taking of the presenters with their displays. Reba took the moment to run to the rear door because she could no longer see James through the little window. She opened it and quickly looked right and then left down the hall. No James. Her heart sank to the soles of her shoes.

"Reba!" Mrs. Coalson called out. "You know the rules. No opening the doors without permission."

"Sorry, Mrs. Coalson. I was just looking for my partner."

Mrs. Coalson paused, and then said, "Okay, class, we have one more presentation, but before that, why don't we talk about what we've learned so far. Who wants to start?"

As the excited responses ping-ponged around the room, Reba sat at the crafts table staring at the back door, the posters she and her father had made spread out in front of her.

"Reba?" It was Mrs. Coalson. She only called her name, but it was clear she wanted to know what Reba was going to do. Some of her classmates had turned and were looking at her too.

Reba hesitated one last time, looking at the back door, seeing the empty hallway in her mind's eye. She felt Mrs. Coalson staring. She wanted to cry, but she refused to do it in front of everybody. Daniel would laugh at her and get the others to join in too. And he would certainly tease her later when Mrs. Coalson wasn't around. He'd been wanting to get back at her ever since she'd chased him for picking on

Kathy. She thought about what Stacy had said at the dinner table: "He won't do it." And what Elliott had said. And how she didn't want to believe any of it, even if her dad had missed her Christmas recital. This was different. This was really special, and they were partners. And they had spent all that time together on Saturday. The tears fell before she could stop them. Her whole face trembled as she fought to choke back any sound.

She didn't even see when Mrs. Coalson walked from the front of the class, but she was standing in front of Reba now.

"I'm so sorry, Reba," she said.

Reba thought she heard snickering. Turning to gather up the posters, she stole the moment to wipe her face. "I'll do the show-and-tell by myself."

"Reba, are you sure? You don't—"

"I want to. I have all the stuff here."

She would show everybody that she could do things just fine without anybody's help.

"Okay then." Mrs. Coalson gave a single clap of her hands to regain order among the kids, who had grown antsy in that matter of seconds. She grabbed one poster that seemed to be slipping from Reba's small hands as she made her way to the front of the room. Once there, Mrs. Coalson helped her place the posters along the ledge of the blackboard. Reba went to her desk to retrieve the sailboat and then returned to the front of the class.

Some kid said loud enough for several to hear, "She's doing it by herself? She can't do that."

Standing by her desk, Mrs. Coalson held a hush-finger to her lips. She asked Reba, "Are you ready?"

Reba nodded, gave one final look in the direction of the back door, and then turned to the expectant faces of the other kids and some of the dads who'd stayed for the little girl who was last.

"My dad makes toys," she said softly. Her heart was thumping too hard for her to push the words out any louder.

"I can't hear her," a boy whined.

"No interrupting, Ethan, and raise your hand when you want to speak." Mrs. Coalson scowled at him.

Ethan raised his hand and repeated, "She needs to talk louder."

Reba took a breath and belted out, "My dad makes toys." A few laughed. Surprisingly, it made her feel more at ease. She laughed a little too. "He made this boat," she continued in the speech-making voice she had practiced with James. "I have pictures here that we drew to show the parts of it and how they fit together. See?" She stepped aside so they could view the posters. "I asked my dad why he liked making toys, why he made this boat. He told me toys make people happy. And it made him happy when people liked his toys. And he made this boat because he used to think about how one time, when he was a kid, he got together with his friends and made a boat out of this kit they bought. It wasn't like this boat because it fell apart super easy. But my dad said this one reminds him of his friends and how they talked about owning a boat one day when they were all grown up. See, if you look inside the boat, there are little guys in there." She extended the toy in her hand for the students to look from a distance. Some rose from their seats for a glimpse.

"Can we hold it?" one boy asked.

"I see the little people," another boy said. "Your dad made that all by himself? Cooool."

Reba looked to Mrs. Coalson, who was smiling at her. Reba told the kids, "I'll let you touch it, but you can't hold it. You might break it, and it's very valuable." She walked around a bit to let the kids examine the sailboat up close before she returned to her stance in front of the class.

"My dad owns a real boat now," she told them. "He named his boat *Life's Luck*. I thought it was a funny name, but he said that I would understand it when I was all grown up. I asked him to 'splain it to me anyway. He said that steering a boat is like going through life. Sometimes it's really nice on the water, and sometimes it isn't, 'specially if it's too windy. But my dad says if you're lucky, you've got people who love you, and they go through the bad stuff with you, and they help guide the boat sometimes so you don't have to do it all by yourself." She looked past the students to the back door again.

There was a pause with the class still watching her. "I'm done," she told them.

Mrs. Coalson began the applause, and the others joined in. She gave Reba a side hug as she leaned in to say, "Good job, Reba. Very good job."

7

That night, James showed up with a shiny new bicycle for Reba. He wheeled it into the kitchen where Fran was sitting at the table, flipping through another self-help book she'd picked up. She saw the bike and immediately demanded, "What did you do?"

James answered with a question. "Is Reba in bed yet? It took me a while to find a store open tonight that had this thing in stock. This is the one she wanted, right?"

"Yes, that's the one."

He looked toward the staircase.

"James, Christmas is in two days."

"It's not a Christmas gift. Well, sort of, but I'm not waiting until then. I want to give it to her now." His eyes were still trained toward the staircase.

"What happened?" Fran stood up and moved toward James.

"What did Reba tell you?" he asked.

"Nothing. She wouldn't tell me anything. I knew something was wrong, but I couldn't get her to talk about it. She wanted to go to her room to read. James, tell me what happened."

"I'll talk to you in a minute, Fran. I need to see Reba first."

He hoisted the bike and took the stairs, leaving Fran watching after him.

Reba's door was partly cracked. Her light was on. He knocked, and the door swung open wider. She was lying in bed reading.

"Can I come in?" James led with the bike.

Reba glanced at it but focused her attention on James.

"You like it?" he asked. "I went to four different stores to find this bike, you know."

"It's nice."

"Nice!" He made a silly, exaggerated surprise face. "This bike is *awesome*! You even said so yourself." He sat on the side of the bed, still supporting the bike for Reba's viewing.

"Why?" she asked. The tone was even, tinted with hurt and genuine curiosity.

He concentrated on fiddling with the bike before meeting her eyes again. "I'm so, so sorry, Reba. I'd planned to come back. Really, I did. The phone call. The connection kept dropping. I went outside so I could . . . I'm sorry."

"I did the show-and-tell by myself. I thought maybe you'd at least come back to see me do the last part."

"I wanted to, honey, but the call took so long I figured I'd missed it, and then I had to get back for a meeting. I'm proud of you for doing a great job without me."

"Stacy said I should get used to it."

"Get used to what? Doing a great job?"

"No. The doing without you part."

"That's not true. This is just a really busy time for your dad, that's all. It'll be better soon."

"Will you be better?" she asked.

He didn't know what to say because he wasn't sure how she meant it. He had refused to believe that his kids were doing anything less than great. And because he was afraid to hear differently, he didn't want his seven-year-old to explain her comment. But he did venture to ask, "Why didn't you tell your mom about today?" It was apparent Reba had made a choice; she'd decided to confide in her big sister instead.

"I didn't want to get you in trouble," she responded.

He was amazed, and perplexed.

"I didn't want you and Mom to fight. I didn't want you to be sad. I did good. Mrs. Coalson said so."

He sat quietly next to his youngest for a moment longer, contemplating what she had said. It was remarkably one of the most selfless things he'd ever been told.

Without anything more to give, he said, "I love you, Reba."

"I love you too, Daddy." But she felt a mix of other things too: a little sad, uncertain, and somewhat afraid, though she didn't know why. Feelings that churned a need for . . . something—or someone. She thought of her Oma and what she'd said: "God can do things we can't."

When James went downstairs and didn't see Fran in the kitchen, he took the opportunity to skirt the conversation he knew she was waiting to have. He went to his basement office. He would never say the protracted avoidance was planned, but when he emerged and went upstairs, Fran was asleep. He left earlier than usual the next morning, claiming that because it was Christmas Eve, he needed to make up for what would be a shorter day with his team.

James met with them at his office for a talk. The four young men stood silently as he trudged his way through his message: "I know you all are aware of the shipment that went missing. To be totally honest with you, I'm not sure if we'll ever see that merchandise so, well, I'm looking at resources so we can still make good on our commitments, but I'm not in the position to make promises."

One young man among the quiet group spoke up. James listened with a sense of dread of what was coming next. "I'm sorry, Mr. Harrison, but when we had our meeting before, you told us to continue with business as usual. You had us telling clients their merchandise would be arriving . . . *today*. You said, 'Tell them there's been a delay in shipment.' Are we to understand that's not true? We have our reputations to consider, Mr. Harrison. What am I supposed to tell Tech World Global and Electro Plane now?"

"I know," James said, "and I'm sorry." What he'd told them was with the hope that the rest of the shipment from China would be delivered by some miracle. But there was still no definitive word on the whereabouts of the missing merchandise. "Things have taken an unexpected turn," he continued. "It doesn't look like we, *I*, can resolve this anytime soon. We can talk more about this after the holidays."

"Are we supposed to just keep stringing the customers along?"

"That's not what I'm suggesting. Let them know that I'll be contacting them personally. I don't want to lose what you guys have worked so hard to accomplish."

They glanced at each other.

Another young man spoke. "Mr. Harrison, uh, we were supposed to be getting paid today?"

"Yes, yes, of course."

Another man queried, "Does that include sales bonuses? You told us if we met your quota, we'd be given a bonus. We met the quota."

James felt the heat of their collective stares. "Yes, yes, you did," he began slowly, "but we're missing most of the product, and no revenue to collect for it. So—"

"But we met your quota," the first young man interjected.

James paused to suffocate the spark of his own rising anger. "Look," he told them, "I know you worked hard. You guys are some of the most talented, energetic salesmen I know. And I know you're disappointed with how things turned out. Believe me, I am too. But this is business. And if sales don't produce revenue, bonuses can't be paid. Obviously, this isn't your fault. Still, the end result is what it is. I appreciate your work. I'm hoping that we can all come back after the holidays and work like hell to right this ship."

No one responded.

James added, "You'll have your pay on schedule."

They left his office without another word. James thought about the remaining amount in his business account. His professional life was evaporating like steam in front of him. He could see it in the eyes of those young salesmen. They were contemptuous of him. Even in his worst imaginings, James had never considered this day.

The delay in talking with Fran only gave unspoken things time to simmer. When James came home late that evening, she was curled up in a chair by the fireplace reading.

He walked stiffly into the room. "New book?" he asked.

She held it up to show him the cover. "*Seven Steps to Serenity.*"

He saw that she had a notepad and pen on the end table next to her chair. "It's quiet," he remarked.

"Elliott is playing one of those games in his room, probably. Stacy and Jay are out. Stacy babysits the Thomas kids down the street on Fridays now. I told you, James. She took the babysitting job to impress you. I think she figured maybe that might earn her some of your attention."

He was silent but didn't move from where he was standing. "Weren't we supposed to go to that Christmas service at Oma's church tonight?"

"I'm surprised you remembered."

"Reba reminded me. You remind the other kids?"

"Yeah, they should be home shortly." She was examining his face. "Reba like her bike? She's been pretty quiet about it."

"I think so."

"Any reason you couldn't wait till Christmas to give it to her?"

James sighed, bracing himself as he flopped in the chair angled away from her. He rested his face in his hands. "I screwed up," he said, but the words were muffled.

"What?" Fran asked.

He lowered his hands. "I said I screwed up."

"How so?"

"I'd been dogging this buyer in New York for over a week, trying to get in touch with him. He said he was interested in the new line we're selling. But then he went MIA."

"So what was the screwup?"

"He finally called me back, right when we were supposed to do the show-and-tell."

"Oh, James," she breathed. Fran closed her book.

"I had to take the call. I *had* to. I just didn't think it would take that long. I couldn't hear him all that well. I stepped outside for a better connection. Don't look at me like that, Fran. We *need* that sell."

"So you sacrificed Reba to save your deal."

"Look, I said I screwed up, okay?"

"Don't snap at me. I'm not the one who messed up. And by the way, a new bike doesn't cut it, James. You can't just go out and buy a Band-Aid."

"Yeah, I got that," he said, pointing his head up toward Reba's room.

Stacy and Jay came in. Stacy saw her parents' faces and asked, "What's going on?"

"Nothing, sweetheart," Fran said. "Why don't you and Jay go upstairs. You don't have long before we need to leave for the service at Oma's church."

Stacy and Jay exchanged a look and went quietly up to their rooms.

Fran waited until she heard bedroom doors closing upstairs before turning to James. "It's one thing to disappoint me, James, but your seven-year-old daughter?"

"Stop, Fran."

"No, you don't get to shut this down because you don't want to hear it!"

"Look, Reba's fine! I apologized."

"She's *not* fine, James."

"How would you know? I talked to her."

"What did she say?"

"She said . . . she said she loves me. Apparently, she thought if she told you what happened, you'd be mad. Or in her words, she didn't want to get me in trouble."

"That's just sad, James."

"Why would you say that?"

"Because she's trying to take care of you. Heartbroken little girls shouldn't have to protect their fathers when they fail! Do you know how long she'd been talking about doing that show-and-tell with you? For weeks, James. *Weeks*. And she told everybody about it, including Oma and her ballet instructor. That time with you meant everything to her. Just because you don't want to own up to devastating your kid doesn't lessen what you've done."

"Oh, now you're just taking this whole thing to the extreme! Reba wasn't devastated. Yeah, she may have been a little disappointed, but she did great. Her teacher said so."

"Do you take responsibility for any of the hurt you cause?"

"So now we're not talking about Reba, huh? This is about *you*. Figures. Somehow all roads lead back to Fran!"

Their vexed voices drew the kids out of their rooms. They could be seen observing from the upstairs railing. "What's going on?" Jay asked.

"Go back to your rooms!" James ordered, but they didn't move.

"I am exhausted!" Fran shouted. "I have spent every shred of my energy trying to be supportive and getting almost nothing for it but disappointment! You do this all the time to the kids, James. You do it to me. Make promises and then break them. I won't allow you to keep putting us through this!"

"What are you saying? Just put it out there!"

Fran looked up at her children's stricken faces. Reba was crying.

"Stacy," she said, "call Oma and tell her we won't be able to make it to the service tonight."

"What excuse do I give?" Stacy asked. "She's gonna ask me why we're not coming."

"Tell her we're not feeling well." And then Fran said to Reba, "Don't cry, honey. I'll be upstairs in a minute."

The kids went back to their rooms and Fran turned to James. "I mean it. I'm tired, James. I don't have any more to give you, to give *this*."

"Are you saying you want a divorce, Fran?" His voice barely filled the space between them.

"Maybe that's something we should talk about."

"What is it? Or should I ask, *who* is it?"

Fran looked at him, shaking her head. "I need to check on Reba." She headed upstairs.

8

Reba sat on the side of her bed, staring at the closed door. She'd been listening to her parents' loud arguing. And then their voices went quiet. That scared her even more.

When Fran walked in, Reba stood up. She was searching her mother's face as she came closer.

"Reba, honey, I'm sorry we upset you," Fran said.

"Mom," Reba said, "please don't be mad at Daddy."

"Oh baby," Fran sighed, gently touching Reba's cheek. She tried to force a comforting smile, but her expression didn't match her words. "It's complicated grown-up stuff. Try not to worry, all right? Everything will be okay."

"I didn't want you to be mad." Reba started crying again. "Liza Cooper said her mom was always mad at her dad, and they got a divorce."

Fran knelt and hugged Reba. "Don't cry, baby, everything is going to be fine."

Reba asked, "Then you and Daddy won't get a divorce?"

Fran wiped away Reba's tears. "You know we love you, right?" Reba nodded. "That's what I want you to think about, okay? Why don't we get you into bed?"

As Fran helped her daughter settle down for the night, Reba kept thinking about her mom's words, and how she didn't promise not to divorce her dad. Reba lay in bed feeling the weight of blame. She should've made her dad promise not to tell that he'd left her to do the show-and-tell by herself. Why did she even have to be in the stupid show-and-tell in the first place?

She needed to do *something*. It all felt so big, so scary. She needed help. Oma. Oma would know what to do. She was at the church, and Reba knew the way. She sat up in bed, looking at her closed bedroom door. She couldn't leave the house that way. They would see her. The tree outside her window. She always climbed on it in summer. She knew she could climb onto it from her window and make her way down to the front yard. From there she could run to the church lickety-split and find Oma.

Reba got out of bed and put on her hoodie and sweatpants, and out the window she went.

She made it to the church, cold and winded and her hands a little scratched up from the tree. Everyone was standing, singing a Christmas hymn. It only took a second for Reba to spot her Oma near the front. Reba went to her immediately.

Oma was so shocked to see her granddaughter she could scarcely collect her words. "Reba, what in the world?" She looked back to see if the others were with her.

"I came by myself," Reba said.

"Why, honey? You shouldn't be out at night. You shouldn't be by yourself."

"I needed to see you, Oma. Don't make me go back home."

They waited until after the service was over to talk more.

People started to file out, and church members hugged one another and wished each other a merry Christmas as they slowly exited. Oma and Reba sat alone in the pew.

Reba's voice trembled with tears. "I want you to help Mom and Dad, Oma. Make them stop fighting."

"You know how I love them both, honey, but I can't fix their problems."

Reba choked out the words, "Tell me what to do. It's my fault."

"No, dear, no it isn't." Oma hugged her close.

"But they were really mad tonight." Reba pulled away to look up at her grandmother. "Tell me how to fix it, Oma."

"I'm afraid you can't fix their problems either, sweetheart."

Oma was aware of Pastor Phillips now standing within listening distance. She continued, "There's only one person that can fix this, and that's God. The Bible tells us that when two or more ask for help in His name, it will not be denied."

Through her distress, Reba brightened a little. "Oma, can we pray now and ask Him?"

"Of course," Oma said.

Pastor Phillips came closer and looked down on Reba's face, wet with tears. He asked softly, "May I join you in prayer?"

Reba nodded.

Pastor Phillips and Oma sat in the pew and each took hold of one of Reba's hands as she stood in front of them. She started slowly, her earnest little voice heavy with sadness.

"Dear God, please fix my mom and dad. They fight all the time and yell, and I'm scared they won't stay married with each other anymore. We never see my dad, and he missed my show-and-tell because he had to work. He didn't want to miss it, but he did. And my mom is never happy anymore too. If you put my family back together—me and my brothers and sister and my mom and dad—we will all be real happy, and we will be all together and happy all the time. Amen."

Reba paused as though waiting for something. "Oma, did He hear me?"

Pastor Phillips looked at Reba's serious face. "He always hears us, Reba. Now, how about I drive you back home?"

Reba looked at Oma and then back at Pastor Phillips and solemnly nodded. As they left the sanctuary, the two adults talked quietly and then continued down the steps outside. Reba lagged behind, stopping at the top of the stairs. The air was sharp and the sky was clear, no stars. The moon glowed like an orb against the ink-blue of the night. It commanded Reba's attention and made her hesitate.

"I'm parked right over here," Pastor Phillips said, motioning to the lot just beyond the chapel.

I wish I knew for sure, Reba thought. A sudden gust of wind hit so strong it took Reba's breath for a moment. Her eyelids fluttered as a church flyer flew through the air and was thrust against her hoodie and stuck there.

"Reba, honey, come on now. It's time to go."

Reba peeled the paper off her coat and read it. She fixed on the bold headline: "We Have His Promise." And below, "Fear not, little flock, for it is your Father's good pleasure to give you the kingdom" Luke 12:32. Reba thought, *He is answering me! He is!*

"Reba, dear, it's very late. We have to get you home," Oma said.

She stuffed the paper into the pocket of her hoodie. "Coming!" she said, feeling just a bit lighter as she hurried down the stairs to join them.

When Reba and Pastor Phillips arrived at the Harrison's home, there was a police car out front. Reba rushed through the door to the sound of her parents shouting at each other.

"How could you let her sneak out the window, Fran?! You said you put her to bed!"

"Don't you dare blame me, James! This mess started because of your screwup!"

Her sister and brothers stood in a unified knot, watching as the police officers tried to calm James and Fran. Stacy called out, "Reba!" and everyone turned to see her and the pastor standing in the foyer. Fran hurried to hug her. James quickly followed.

Fran said, "You scared us nearly to death, Reba! Don't ever do that again."

James grabbed the pastor's hand. "Thank you so much for bringing her home."

"Glad to help," Pastor Phillips said, eyeing the distressed faces of the other kids and the policemen who were watching. "Anything I can do, James?"

"No," James said, "You've done plenty already, Martin. I can't thank you enough."

Pastor Phillips nodded and said goodnight.

One officer spoke, "Well, it looks like everything is fine now. Glad your little girl is safe. We're going to let you get settled here." He motioned to the door, signaling their exit. James shook their hands and thanked them before closing the door.

Reba and her parents walked farther into the living room where the other kids were.

"Why'd you sneak off?" Jay asked.

"I went to church to see Oma," Reba said.

James bent low enough to speak to Reba face-to-face. "That was a dangerous thing, young lady. I know you were disappointed about not seeing your grandma tonight, but that's no excuse!"

Reba started crying again. "I did it for you!"

"What?" James said.

"I did it for *you*!" she repeated. "I went to church to find Oma so she could help fix you!"

James pointed toward the stairs. "Go to your room, Reba." He turned to the rest of his children. "You too."

Reba was confused. Things were supposed to be different now.

The kids didn't move. Fran looked at James. "Is that all you can say?"

"Don't start with me again, Fran."

"Your daughter runs away for help to *fix* you, and the only thing you can say is 'go to your room'? What happened to you, James? Where's the man I married?"

"You know, Fran, I could ask the same question. The woman I married wasn't self-righteous and quick to criticize everything I do! You think it's easy living with your complaints? Well it's *not*! I work hard to provide for this family, to give you a great house, a nice car. Have I ever complained about the credit card bills you rack up? No, I don't. Well guess what, living like this doesn't come cheap! It takes money. Lots of it. And that means long hours of sweat and hustle and headaches and stress! So I'm not about to listen to you talk about how disappointed you are!"

He stormed off to the entryway closet to grab his coat.

"Dad?" Jay said weakly.

Reba stood watching her father. Stacy and Elliott were stock-still. "James," Fran said, her eyes following her husband, who made for the front door. "Where are you going?"

He walked out and slammed the door so hard the corner Christmas tree shook from the force. No one moved. When Fran spoke again, her voice was dry as if from disuse. "Let's go upstairs, kids. It's been a long night."

Reba studied her mother's face as she tucked her into bed. Fran looked to be fighting back tears. She kissed Reba's forehead, cut off the light, and left the room quickly. Her soft sobs could be heard just as Reba's bedroom door clicked shut.

In the darkness, Reba could hear the stillness of the house. "But I prayed," she whispered, perplexed and angry. "Why isn't everything better now?" She got out of bed and retrieved the crumpled flyer from the pocket of her hoodie. She smoothed it and read again, "We Have His Promise. Fear not, little flock, for it is your Father's good pleasure to give you the kingdom."

She looked out her window at the cold wintry moon shining so brightly.

"Mr. Moon, I asked God to fix my family, and my Oma says God always hears us, and then I got this." She held up the flyer so the moon could see. "So, I know everything will be okay, right?" It came out with all the desperation and pleading her little soul could muster. She watched and waited, her heart tapping a little faster. "I know you can hear me because I see your face up there and you are a special Christmas Eve moon."

And then Reba saw the moon smile at her. She was sure of it and smiled back, feeling relieved. And she got back into bed knowing all was just fine and fell fast asleep, but not before saying, "Goodnight, Mr. Moon."

Well into the night, the house was quiet. Downstairs, the ticking of the grandfather clock in the living room was the only sound to break the silence . . . until the Christmas tree lights' electrical cord cracked and flashed. The force of James slamming the door had jostled the cord enough to ignite a short. There was a split second before the spark lit the dry branches of the pine tree. The flames breathed and lapped at its backside and along the boughs that reached out to the ceiling-high curtains. Quickly, the flames leapt upward, licking the fabric, and spreading downward to devour the piles of paper-wrapped gifts. The fire was alive and hungry and roamed from the living room into the kitchen. It yawned and stretched as it climbed the stairs.

James saw the clouds of billowing smoke long before he drove into his subdivision. He watched them rolling against the night sky as he turned down the street to his house. He was now close enough to see his neighbors in the street, standing in clusters of two and three, coats slung over their pajamas, pointing at the firefighters still rushing around his front lawn. That's when it hit him. It was his house. They were pointing at *his* house. He stopped the car and ran through the crowd, pushing people aside. Smoke and smoldering things made him cough. He could feel the heat from the inferno on his face. He called out, "Fran! Kids!" choking as he got closer to the house that was now a charred shell.

A firefighter rushed to stop him. "Sir, I'm going to need you to step back."

Then James heard Fran shouting his name.

He turned and saw her and the kids amidst neighbors, who'd covered them with blankets. A woman in hair rollers had her arm around Fran. Stacy was crying into the shoulder of an elderly man. Reba was hugging her mother, her face buried in her stomach. Jay and Elliot stood motionless, looking devastated. Fran broke into a loud sob, extending one arm to James as he rushed to her. He held her close and she cried out in pain.

"What is it?" he gasped, pulling away.

"My arm. I fell. I think it's broken. I hurt my back too."

"We need to get you and the kids to the hospital." Then he stretched his arms wide and desperately tried to gather all of his children in, along with his wife, afraid they'd evaporate like the black smoke around them. The wetness of his tears stung eyes that were already irritated by the smoke.

"What happened?" he finally asked.

"The Christmas tree caught fire." Fran's words broke with another sob.

Someone nearby said, "Your family is lucky. They got out just in time."

James examined each of their faces, touching their cheeks, their shoulders. "Are you okay? Are you all right? Jay, your arm." The fire had eaten away at Jay's shirt and exposed red skin.

"It hurts, but I'm okay. I'm okay," Jay assured him.

James was aware that his insides were trembling. He breathed white puffs of air into the cold night, his tongue soured with the taste of the liquor he'd been drinking at a downtown bar.

Another firefighter came over to the family. "The ambulance is on the way. You need to go to the hospital and get checked out. You're a lucky bunch." He nodded his head toward the blackened shell of the house. "That was a bad one."

James looked at what had been their home, the broken windows still spitting smoke. Then he turned to the charred garage door. All of his inventory had been stored in there: the toys that had been his staples, the new tech gadgets from China, even the boxes of playthings he'd handmade. They were all gone now. He closed his eyes slowly and turned to Fran again. "How'd you get out?"

Fran and Jay both responded. "The upstairs windows."

Stacy said, "Everything we have is gone, Dad." She started crying again.

James pulled her into his arms. "It'll be okay."

Jay told him, "Mom's car was in the garage."

Reba turned her tear-streaked face upward to Fran. Her voice quivered as she said, "Mom, I made you and Oma a necklace for Christmas. I put it under the tree. And now I don't have anything for you."

Fran held her closer with her strong arm and kissed her head. "You're all the present I need, honey."

Another firefighter came over. "It's a little burned, but it's still in pretty good shape." He handed them the one thing they had been able to salvage from the fire: a family photo album.

Fran took it with her free hand and thanked the man. She slowly wiped away the soot and dirt, then asked James, "What are we going to do?" Her eyes stretched open with fear.

Without an answer to give, he looked at her, then at his kids, who were all waiting for his response.

A neighbor said, "You all are welcome to stay with us for the night. We have an extra room, some cots."

Just then the ambulance drove up. The EMTs rushed over. James was glad for the interruption. "We'll be fine," he told the neighbor.

9

The X-rays showed that Fran had indeed broken her right arm. An oblique fracture, the doctors told her, as they showed her and James the film of the slanted separation in her bone below her elbow. She'd also suffered muscle strain in her back.

"Use cold compresses," the doctor advised, "and keep the compression brace on for the first few weeks, especially when you go out. Here's a prescription for pain medications. After you're done with them, Tylenol should suffice. I suggest staying off your feet for extended periods of time, even if you think you feel okay. Back strains are sneaky monsters. Pain comes back when you least expect it. I have to warn you, some patients suffer off and on for years."

James was listening attentively, mostly with concern for his wife, but also with some worry over the hospital bills for which he had no money. He no longer had health insurance for his family.

"Hopefully, you'll be one of the lucky ones," the doctor continued. "Six to eight weeks, you'll be good as new, about the same time we'll be taking off your arm cast."

He determined it was best to keep Jay overnight because there was some concern about smoke inhalation (though he kept repeating that it was just a precaution). Jay was the only one who'd suffered burns, which were on his forearm. "You'll have to keep the wounds dressed for the first few weeks," the doctor told him. "The ointment will help with the pain and scarring. In six months the burn marks will barely be noticeable."

"Will I be able to wrestle?" Jay asked. "I'm on the team. We've got a big match."

"Sure, you can," the doctor said. "Maybe in two months, or so. I'd advise against playing contact sports any sooner."

James and Fran spent the night in the emergency room, waiting until the rest of the family had been examined. Stacy, Elliot, and Reba were all fine.

They showed up at Oma's before dawn, covered in soot and smelling like smoke.

There was more hugging and crying when they got there, with Fran convincing her mother that despite the cast and the back brace, she was fine. Oma apologized that there wasn't enough sleeping space for everybody. The small living room seemed to shrink with the six of them simply standing there. She had already made pallets of blankets on the floor for Stacy and Elliott. Reba would sleep on the let-out sofa bed with Fran and James.

"Oh, Mom," Fran breathed. "Thank you for all this."

James echoed, "Yes, thank you, Oma. We're sorry to inconvenience you."

"Oh, nonsense." She waved their gratitude away. "I'm happy to do what little I can. I just wish I could do more. I'm afraid the rules of this place say we're only allowed so many overnight guests a year. I think this puts me at my limit." She was referring to the regulations of her senior citizens' complex, which tracked the number of guests and their comings and goings.

"Mom, you're an angel. And we understand. We're all exhausted and just need a place to sleep." Fran leaned in and kissed Oma on her cheek. "I love you, Mom."

"I love you more, my Franny."

She retired to her bedroom. Stacy and Elliott settled onto the quilt pads on the floor and pulled the comforters over their tired bodies.

Elliott said to no one in particular, "What's gonna happen to us now?"

"We're going to rest up and start a new day tomorrow, son," James responded. "Get some sleep. We're going to be fine."

He helped situate Fran onto the bed, manipulating the covers and trying to steady her at the same time. And then he tucked Reba in next to her. When he didn't join them, Fran asked, "James, you okay?"

"Yeah." He spoke over the sounds of sleep coming from his two children on the floor. "I just need a little quiet time to think."

He went into Oma's kitchen and sat at the table, holding his head in his hands. He felt numb. He feared what would happen when the feeling passed. He feared the prickling sensations, the beginnings of his breaking apart. He thought about the money he had left. The majority was payroll for the sales team he'd hired.

He heard a noise. It was Oma. "James," she said, "you should get some sleep."

He shook his head. "I can't. I mean, I'm not sleepy."

Oma sat across from him. "You need to try to relax. Get some rest."

"I keep thinking about the fire, you know. I keep wondering what would've happened if I'd been home. Maybe things would've turned out differently."

"Stop punishing yourself for not being there," Oma said. "You don't know if your being there would've made a difference. Just thank God things turned out the way they did."

"Yeah," he responded. "Yeah. I keep thinking it could have been worse. But then I think about tomorrow morning, when everybody gets up, and they realize that all we have right now is the clothes on our backs. And they'll look at me for answers, and right now, I don't have any."

"James, you've been through a nightmare tonight. And I know thinking about what happens next has got to be scary. It would be for anybody in your shoes right now. But try not to put so much pressure on yourself. God spared your family tonight. He's going to work things out. Trust Him."

James's laugh was short and dismissive. "Oma, I know you mean well. But here's the thing, everything I worked for is ashes and dirt. Everything I gave my family is gone. Just like that. Years of hard work. Gone. And in a few hours, I have to come up with a plan that keeps my family feeling safe. You hear me? I have to figure out a way for us to survive this. So it's a little hard to take your advice."

"James, try prayer if you're looking for answers."

"I can't wait that long."

"It doesn't take God long to do anything. Sometimes, we may not get what we want immediately, but He knows what's best. He knows when we're ready." Oma paused and then added, "He also has a way of getting our attention."

"Really, Oma? You know, I spent the better part of my life in church. And I was faithful. Even after I got married and we had kids, I never missed a Sunday. And when my business took off, I still gave my tithes when I couldn't make it to the service. That should count for something, right? Well, I think it should. But you're telling me just because I've been a little busy, God's *upset*? And this—all this tonight—is His way of jerking my chain?"

"James—"

"No," he interrupted. "I'm sorry, but I'm not hearing that tonight. I'm not. Because I deserve better. I work hard, and I deserve better. And I'll make sure I get it. I always do. And I always come out on top. And I don't need anybody to make that happen. Thanks for the talk."

His outburst surprised her, but she held her tongue and considered him before getting up from the table. "Tonight, I thanked God for sparing my baby's life and my grandkids. And you. And I'll continue to pray for you, James, and trust God to give you just what you need."

After she left, he sat alone in her kitchen with thoughts that burned and hummed. Eventually, he crept quietly into the let-out bed next to Fran. She appeared to be sleeping soundlessly with her good arm around Reba.

She turned to him with tired, wet eyes.

"I'm sorry I woke you," he whispered.

"Can't sleep," she mouthed with little sound.

He wrapped her gently in his arms, aware of her cast. She smelled like charred wood. He buried his face in her hair. The thought of how near he'd come to losing everyone swallowed him whole again. He felt his very core tremble. He fought to control it. He needed to be strong.

Reba made a sleepy whimper. Fran eased out of James's arms and rolled to stroke her hair. In hushed tones she soothed her little girl back to sleep.

James lay on his back, the rhythmic sound of Fran's low humming only white noise to him as his brain thrummed. *What now?* he asked himself.

"This Christmas totally blows," Elliott grumbled in the morning.

"Listen, kids," James began. "I . . . I know this is rough, but I can pick up some things tomorrow. Everything's closed right now, but—"

"I don't understand," Reba interjected.

"Understand what, baby?" Fran asked, trying to get nearer to Reba. She moved like her legs were made of cement, the pain in her back alive and angry.

"Me and Oma prayed for a miracle. But I shouldn't've asked, and then everybody would have their things," Reba said. The other kids were quiet. Oma emerged from the kitchen. Reba sobbed, "All I wanted is for everything to be good. But it's like God is mad. He let our house burn down! Why is God so mean?"

"Sometimes," Oma began, but Reba ran into her grandmother's bedroom.

"I'll talk to her." Fran started to follow her youngest.

"We both should." James took Fran's hand so she could lean into it.

"Sometimes," Oma repeated, talking to herself now, "God works in mysterious ways."

They were calmer as the day drew on. Fran was in less pain and insisted on helping with dinner, chopping mushrooms from her seat at the kitchen table. The smell of roasted garlic, spicy tomato sauce, and homemade bread soon wafted through the small apartment. On the radio, Bing Crosby crooned as Oma moved around the stove, humming along. "They don't make Christmas songs like that anymore," she said.

"That song," Fran replied, "it makes me think of Dad."

"Me too. 'White Christmas' was his favorite."

"I still miss him so much."

Oma turned to her daughter. "I know. I know, dear. Me too."

"It doesn't feel like he's been gone for two years. Sometimes, it feels like it all happened yesterday."

"We never get over the loss, we just learn to live with it."

"I know it's been lonely for you, Mom."

"Oh, I've been okay, Franny." She gave her a sideways look. "You know, Pastor Phillips asked about you."

"That's nice. He and Charlotte are good people."

"He wants to help."

"I know. But we'll be okay." Fran thought it was best to change the subject. "I'm glad you're going with your friends to Florida this year."

"I feel bad about leaving you."

"Nonsense. Florida is just what you need. How long did you say you and Irma will be down there?"

"Irma says she usually comes back in May or June."

"That's really great, Mom."

Oma looked directly at Fran again. "Are you sure you all will be okay?"

"Mom, don't worry about us. Do something nice for yourself for a change and get out of this cold weather. We'll manage just fine."

"All right, Franny."

They chose a hotel where they were greeted by a doorman. Their two-bedroom suite overlooked a man-made lake with beautiful grounds and was equipped with a kitchen and a bathroom with heated floors and a TV mounted above the Jacuzzi. While there, James would lie in the hotel's bed of silk sheets and dove-soft feather comforter and worry about paying for it all.

Ordinarily, the kids would have been excited at the possibility of the indoor pool and room service. But the drain of the last twenty-four hours had left them quiet and somber. Under Fran's direction, they claimed their sleeping spaces.

Fran called their schools and told them about the fire. It had made the local news. There was an outpouring of sympathy over the phone.

"When I get to the office today, I'll call the insurance company," James told her. He phoned Gus and asked him to get his sales team going because he needed to take care of some things before getting to work. His chest felt tight. When he was done with Gus, he turned to Fran. "If you're up for it, maybe you can have Stacy drive you guys around today. You can drop me off at the Metra and go to the mall. Maybe get some stuff?"

"Yeah. That sounds good," Fran concurred.

"Don't overdo the walking, though. Remember what the doctor said."

"I miss my Nintendo Switch," Elliott groused. "If we're going shopping, can we buy another one?"

Neither of his parents answered him. The three older kids all whined about needing new cell phones.

As Stacy scanned the lot, which was busy with day-after-Christmas shoppers, for a parking space, Fran took note of a tall young man with dark curly hair, his peacoat open and scarf flapping in the wind as he trotted alongside his laughing girlfriend. He was laughing, too, and linked arms with her to speed them up, in sync. Fran realized she was smiling. The boy reminded her of a young James. It was the curly hair. This boy was much thinner than what James had been at his age. Still, the spirit of those two, how they laughed, how connected they seemed right then, it made her think back to the very early times with James.

Stacy cut into her daydreaming by announcing she wanted to go her own way and hit her "fave" stores with the credit card her parents had given her. Jay just wanted some space. Fran told them, "That's fine. But we don't have phones, so how about we meet in the food court in an hour and a half, okay?"

She kept Elliott and Reba with her. Even though she did need to sit to ease the onset of back pain from time to time, she managed to comb the clothing racks to find things for herself and for her kids. They were riding the escalator down when Fran spotted a new boutique across from the food court.

With Reba and Elliott distracted and disinterested, they followed Fran as she wandered into the quaint little store with silk scarves the color of rainbow taffy hanging from an old-fashion coatrack. Shoppers, all women, were fingering dresses and frothy-looking sweaters. They opened little pillbox purses and said things like, "I love this! I know I won't see this one coming and going!" Fran's eye roamed the displays, where there were more bags and purses with exotic finishes: leopard prints, ostrich leather, eclectic patchworks of silk and snakeskin. A voice came up behind her. "Would you like to see one of the pieces?"

"Oh." Fran turned to see a striking woman, a little older than she was, early forties maybe, with luminous eyes lined in smoky gray shadow. Her sleek black hair snaked along the front of her shoulder in a braid as thick as a child's wrist. She wore all black: a form-fitting top that bragged the benefits of yoga, snug pants, and thigh-high flat boots. Still, though, she was tall enough to look Fran in the eye with a perfect smile. "I like the ostrich purse," Fran told her. "The two-tone one."

The woman went to the long extension hook in the corner to retrieve the bag. "You have a good eye."

Reba whined, "Are we gonna be here a long time, Mom?"

Elliott was picking at a hangnail.

"Not long, honey," Fran said.

The woman handed the purse to Fran. "This is one of my favorite pieces." It was in her tone, the pride of ownership, that signaled to Fran the woman was more than an employee there.

Fran ran her hand along the fine stitching that joined the colors of dusty blue and camel. She saw the handwritten tag looped on the handle inside of the silk lining. It read *Originals by Miya* in gold cursive. "You're Miya?" Fran asked.

"Yes." The woman nodded, smiling.

"You designed this?"

"Yes."

"I knew it. It's the way you were admiring the purse. Artists always have that *look* when they like what they've done."

"You're an artist?" Miya asked. "What medium?"

"Me? Oh, no. My husband. Well, he used to wood carve. Beautiful pieces. I remember the *look* once he'd finished something. I want the purse, for sure, but I'd like to look around a bit longer."

"Take your time," Miya said. "If you'd like, I can hold the purse for you behind the counter. Let me know if you'd like to see something else."

Another customer called for Miya's attention at the jewelry counter. Fran strolled over to the pieces under the lights of the casing. She liked the necklaces made of hammered metal. There was one bracelet that caught her eye that was crafted from peach morganite stones. *Stacy would like that*, she thought.

Fran selected another purse to purchase, along with the bracelet, two necklaces, and three pairs of earrings.

"You said we wouldn't be here a long time," Reba said.

"Can we get ice cream?" Elliott queried.

"We're almost done, honey, and yes to the ice cream."

That settled the kids a bit.

Fran watched Miya assisting the customers with ease. She smiled while presenting delicate pieces in her hand under the light for closer examination. Fran imagined herself with the customers—complimenting them as she helped coordinate various accessories—and maybe even having a shop of her own like this one day. She brushed aside the momentary fantasy.

Miya rang up Fran's merchandise. "Thank you for your generous support," Miya said and then apologized for her credit card system working so slowly that day.

Fran filled the wait time with chatter. "Are all of the pieces here your own work?"

"Not all of them. I sell other artists' work too. Mostly people I know."

"It seems like your shop does well."

"Yes," she said, "I'm very fortunate. And this is a very busy time of year, as you can imagine."

"I'm surprised you don't have help here. It was pretty crowded."

"I did, but the girl I hired came down with a bad case of mono. I could use some help. I just haven't had time to post a notice. I was actually going to put a sign in the window today."

On a whim, Fran asked, "How many hours a day? What's the work schedule?"

"Are you interested?" She eyed Fran, taking stock of the tall blonde with effortless elegance. The bulk of the arm cast with curly-cue hearts written on it by her kids didn't seem to matter. She then noticed the message on the credit card machine. "Oh, I'm sorry," she told Fran, "but your card has been declined, ma'am." She looked as if she could feel the heat of Fran's embarrassment. "Perhaps you have another card?"

Fran took the credit card Miya extended to her and stuffed it into her wallet. "I'm not sure what the problem could be." She glanced at Reba and Elliott, checking to see if they'd heard. Miya was still waiting. Fran pulled out another card. "Here, try this one."

Miya's smile lasted for the time it took to run the second card. This time there was no small talk.

Just then Stacy came marching into the store with Jay following. She was on the verge of tears. "Mom," Stacy exclaimed, "you said you'd be in the food court!"

Fran saw that she and Jay were empty-handed.

Stacy stepped closer, aware of the woman behind the counter listening. "My credit card didn't work."

To Fran it seemed the entire store was watching and heard them. Her four children were waiting for her to say something to make everything all right. Her throat went instantly dry. "I'm sure it's nothing to be concerned with, honey."

She saw Miya looking on with sympathy, who then told her, "The payment went through."

Fran breathed in. She didn't pick up the bags on the counter. "See," she said to her kids. "Everything's good. We'll just go back and hit the stores for your things."

Miya asked, "Do you still want the merchandise?"

Fran's first thought was to say "Of course," mostly out of pride. But then another thought came to mind: *credit limit.* The concern over it was completely foreign to her, but she felt it now. She tried to feign casualness over the whole exchange, telling Miya, "You know, I've purchased so much for Christmas, I should probably cool it." Her small laugh sounded strained.

Reba said, "But we lost all our Christmas stuff in the fire."

Fran didn't know what to say. Miya's eyes widened. Slowly she pulled the merchandise from the bags. As she cancelled Fran's transaction, she said, "If you're interested in the job, let me know." She slid a business card to her across the glass counter.

Eyes lowered, Fran thanked Miya and shuttled her four kids out of the store as quickly as she could.

10

James arrived at his office feeling anxious. He should have told Fran to watch her spending, but he wasn't prepared to have a conversation about their finances just yet.

He became aware of a mild pain in his head that was slowly growing more intense. He opened his desk drawer in search of some aspirins, but Gus interrupted, popping through the door James had left ajar.

"Mind if I come in?" Gus had already helped himself to the couch before James could respond.

"Sure," James said, "why not."

Gus melted into a slouch with his fingers laced behind his head. "How you feeling, man?"

"Not good," James sighed.

"No kidding. You look like crap." Gus chuckled.

James gave him a death stare.

"Sorry, dude. How's the family?"

"Doing fine, under the circumstances."

"Where you guys staying?"

"At a hotel."

"A nice one?"

"Yeah, but it's just temporary."

"Why not crash at a friend's place? I'd help you out, but my place has only the two bedrooms and, you know," Gus smiled, very self-satisfied, "with Monica staying over a couple times a week now . . ."

James shook his head. "No, I'm not accepting charity from anybody. We'll be fine."

"Well, I'm sure you'll have your homestead back in no time. Your insurance company will have that covered."

"Yeah." James was quiet, thinking about his lapses in payments. "Hey," he said, shifting the subject, "thanks for taking the reins for me here this morning."

"No prob. I should get outta here. I'm sure you've got plenty to do."

When Gus got up to leave, James called after him. "Close the door, will you?"

Then he sat quietly staring at his phone. He didn't want to call the insurance company because he knew how the conversation would go. Nevertheless, he made the call. They were polite, even when the conversation began to plummet for James.

They told him, "I'm sorry, Mr. Harrison, but you're more than ninety days past due on your premium."

He stood up and began to pace. "That can't be."

"Sir, the last payment on record from you was on September nineteenth. A cancellation letter was sent to your home."

"I didn't receive a letter!" James's mind flashed on official-looking mail that had been stuffed away in his office drawer at home. Overwhelmed by so many notices and phone calls, he had stopped reading what he'd received. Still, he blared through the conversation with the insurance agent. "Look, what is the point of having insurance if you don't deliver on what I've paid for?"

"Sir, that is the issue. The terms of your policy require that you be current with your payments in order for you to exercise your benefits."

"Listen, I've been paying you for over a dozen years. You're telling me because I've fallen a little behind we don't have coverage now?"

"Mr. Harrison, the terms of your policy are clear. According to our records, we attempted to contact you by mail on October twenty-seventh and November fifteenth to address your default. You failed to respond."

"I don't believe this. Haven't you heard a word I've said? We are in crisis here. You understand? We lost everything. *Everything!* We need you to help make this right! That's what I paid for!"

"I'm sorry, sir."

"Don't give me that! Look. I'll make a payment today, all right? How much do we owe?"

"Mr. Harrison, your policy has been cancelled. I am very sorry for you and your family, but we can't retroactively reinstate your insurance."

"This is a rip-off! You take our money, and then when we need to cash in on the benefits, you cancel us because of a couple of late payments!"

"Sir, is there something else I can help you with?"

"Yes, get a manager on the phone! I'm not done with this!"

There was a long wait before a manager calmly introduced himself to James. Amidst James's yelling, the man repeated what the customer service rep had already told him and added, "I advise you to contact your mortgage lender to discuss your situation since I'm required to notify them of your loss, and they'll probably want to arrange for payment in full of their loan."

James hung up the phone and threw his empty coffee mug against the wall. He stared at the shattered pieces on the floor, breathing heavily. A single thought kept replaying—*what am I going to tell Fran?*

James went back to the hotel early that evening, carrying bags. Reba popped up from the floor. "Daddy!" She ran to hug him, stepping on Elliott's leg as he sprawled on the floor in front of the TV.

"Ow! Watch it!" he grumbled before mumbling a "Hey, Dad," along with Stacy and Jay who were lounging on the couch, also watching the TV with mild interest.

Reba announced with pride, "We saved you some pizza!"

"Pizza, huh?" James checked out the new clothes everyone was wearing. "You have fun at the mall?"

"Yeah. And guess what? We went to see Oma again today!"

"You did? That sounds like a fun day. How's Grandma doing?"

"She's okay, except she's got achy knees. She prays for you! She told me."

"That's nice, sweetheart."

"We need new phones, Dad," Stacy said while staring blankly at the TV screen.

"Yeah," Jay echoed.

James didn't address their comments. Instead he asked, "Where's your mother?"

Just then, Fran stepped out of the bathroom with a freshly scrubbed face and her hair tied high on her head in a lopsided scrunchy, the best she could do with one hand. "Hey, you're back early. You know, we need to get phones for everybody."

"Told ya," Stacy retorted.

"Well, why don't we see if Santa has come through for you," James said as he put the bags down. That got their attention.

"You bought us Christmas stuff?" Jay asked, reaching for a bag.

"Hold on now." James snaked out of his coat, grabbed a chair, and pulled it to where the kids were seated. Reba was already clapping. Fran smiled and sat on the edge of the let-out couch.

From one of the bags, James pulled unwrapped boxes of cell phones for Fran, Stacy, Jay, and Elliott.

Elliott asked, "Hey, did you get me a new PlayStation 4?"

"Hold on now." James rummaged through another bag.

"Dad," Stacy said, examining her box, "what kind of phone is this?"

"It's a good phone," James replied.

"How am I supposed to check my Instagram on this thing? Is this one of those pay-as-you-go?"

"I can't play Fortnite on this," Elliott said.

"It'll get the job done," James assured him.

"This looks like something Oma would use," Jay mumbled.

"At least we have phones now," Fran chimed in.

James pulled out two more boxes. One he handed to Elliott. "Here ya go, champ." The other he handed to Reba. "And this is for you, sweetie."

The kids ripped open the packages. Elliot pulled out the department store-purchased soccer jersey. *Lionel Messi, Number 10.*

"Thanks, Dad," he said flatly. "Did you get the Messi cleats I asked you for? I showed you the picture."

"Champ, those things are over two hundred bucks."

Elliott only looked at James as if his statement had little relevance to the more important need for Messi cleats.

"I like my bear, Daddy, and my books," Reba said. "I don't have this series."

"You're welcome, honey, but I had help from your mom."

"Thanks, Mom." Reba got up and hugged both her parents.

James said, "And I have something for everybody to share." He pulled out two board games, handing one to Stacy and the other to Jay.

Stacy read, "Monopoly?"

"This one's Clue." Jay looked at the box in his hands.

"Yeah," James said. "Something you can share."

"I think that'll be fun," Fran said. "I haven't played a board game in years."

"I've never played a board game," Elliott groused. "Does this mean I'm not getting my PlayStation back?"

"We'll see," James replied.

"That doesn't sound hopeful," Elliott muttered.

"Hey." James looked at his kids' faces. "Try it out. You might actually have some fun."

"Is that all the presents?" Jay asked.

Fran and James traded glances.

"Yes," James said. "We've got to be a little more conscientious about budgeting."

"Budgeting?" Stacy seemed to not understand the concept.

James thought of his father in that split second, and he quickly rejected the feelings that came with it.

Stacy asked, "When do we get our house back?"

"I . . . I don't know," James told her truthfully. "But things will be back to normal soon."

Fran added, "We all just have to be a little patient, honey."

"I miss our stuff," Jay said. "This blows."

Fran told him, "Your father is doing the best he can, Jay. Watch your tone."

Elliott groaned, "Worst Christmas ever."

James looked ill.

Fran came closer, examining his face. "Hey, you okay?"

James was aware that Reba was staring up at him too. He asked Fran, "Can we talk?"

She gave a quick glimpse to her children. Reba was the only one who seemed to be taking note of what was happening. "Kids. Your dad and I will be right outside, okay? Be back in a sec." She told Reba, "Watch TV, dear. We'll be back inside in a minute."

Her small face looked worried. Fran smoothed her cheek. "Everything's okay. Watch TV."

She slipped on a jacket and followed James to their car.

Once inside, he gripped the wheel with his head lowered.

"Hey," she said, "what's the matter?"

James paused, trying to pull the words up out of his chest but he couldn't bring himself to do it. The most he could manage was, "The insurance."

Fran grabbed his hand. "Please tell me they're going to make arrangements for us soon! And my car. Did you call them about it?"

"So here's the thing," he began. He couldn't meet her piercing stare. "It seems there's a problem."

Fran withdrew her hand. "What kind of problem?"

"Well, that's what I'm trying to find out. There's some sort of mix-up."

"Mix-up? That's crazy. What are those people talking about? We paid for insurance for emergencies like this."

"I know. I know. That's what I said."

"Well, did you take it up with the manager?"

"Of course I did."

"So what did he say?"

"He said . . . he said he'd look into it."

Fran fell back in the seat. "This is insane. After all we've been through, now this. And what about my car?" She had a thought to mention what happened when she and Stacy attempted their charges that day, but she left it alone.

"It's all the same, honey. You know the insurance is bundled. We just have to wait a little while longer until that company gets their crap together."

"This is the last thing I expected, James. I mean, the kids are going stir crazy in this place. And it's really hard to manage with just one car."

"We won't be here much longer, Fran."

11

That night, Fran and James lay side by side in bed, each hoping their silence would pass as sleep to the other. Fran was thinking about what James had told her about the insurance, mixed in with that awful moment with the credit cards. Her daughter's humiliation that doubled her own. She tried to push all of that away. She thought about being with her kids, taking in the atmosphere and the Christmas music piping from the stores, watching couples at the mall. There was one young family who had their baby strapped to the father's back. *That's what promise looks like,* Fran thought. She'd known that feeling, back when she and James were just as young.

It was when he was newly graduated from college. She was at a friend's Halloween costume party. The tiny apartment was filled with so many people, you had to angle sideways to make your way to the bathroom. The music thumped with incomprehensible lyrics, punctuated by the singer's occasional screams. Some were into it, nodding to the beat and sipping from their red plastic cups. Others claimed spaces on the old furniture to talk in clusters of two or three.

Fran stood alone in a corner. The aluminum star she'd fashioned out of kitchen foil and a headband was slipping. She kept readjusting it and cursing her straight blond hair. She watched the fun going on around her, holding her red cup with both hands, her blue eyes unblinking.

It's not that she didn't want to mingle, but rather, she couldn't. Her Halloween costume was a lit Christmas tree. Her lithesome form, clothed in a black turtleneck and leggings, was entwined in Christmas lights, and her extension cord would only permit her to roam a few feet from the outlet. She'd caught James's attention from over the heads of Count Dracula and a flapper who really seemed to be getting on well.

He gently nudged his way through the crowd, never taking his eyes off her. "A Christmas tree," he said, nodding approvingly. "Original."

"Well, it works with the turtleneck. I get cold easily."

He looked to the extension cord trailing her feet. "How far can you get with that thing?"

"Not very." She took a sip from her cup, eyeing the black peel-and-stick dots angled on the front of his cream pullover. "Let me guess. You're a domino."

"You got it. I can't tell you how many times I had to explain it to people."

She gave his jeans and his dot-covered sweater another once-over. "I'm not sure if you're lazy or clever."

"How about a little of both? Or maybe just clever enough to avoid complicated."

"Hey, I thought you liked my costume?" She was debating how she felt about him.

"I do." His eyes widened, a sincere hand going to his chest.

Someone drunkenly stumbled into him from behind, jostling him enough that he lurched toward Fran, splashing his drink down her costume. She yelped, instinctively leaping back and knocking into the small side table and lamp behind her. James deftly caught the teetering light but dropped his cup and the remaining drink onto her gym shoes.

"Jeez!" she admonished.

"I'm so sorry." He situated the lamp and stood closer to her. The music thumped and blared, and some drunk college student howled, and people laughed, and Fran and James ignored everybody but each other.

"You could have electrocuted me," she said. The tone didn't match the words. She was trying to keep her interest from becoming obvious. Closer to him now, she liked his height. She liked young men so tall she had to tilt her head back to look at them, like now. She liked the color of his eyes, hazel with flecks of green. She liked that the spray of freckles on his nose had remained from his childhood, no doubt. It made him seem harmless, trustworthy. Freckled boys don't break your heart.

"I can get you another drink," he offered.

She peeled her wet sweater away from her stomach. "What I need is a change of clothes."

"I have a sweatshirt in my trunk. You can have it. Of course, it won't do much for your Christmas tree thing."

"Well, I'm kinda tired of the view from here, anyway." She unplugged her extension cord and followed him through the maze of partiers.

They wound up staying in his car, just talking.

"So tell me," Fran said, "what's life like after college?"

"It's not nearly as scary out there as I thought, or maybe I'm just one of the lucky ones. I got a job that I like in sales."

"Oh, yeah? What do you sell?"

"Toys."

"Cool. I should have known, given your choice of costume."

"Ah, yes. I might add I'm a master at dominoes."

"Really now?"

"I'll have to prove it to you. That is, if you'd like to get together again."

"Maybe. If it doesn't involve ruining my clothes." Inside, she had already said yes. He gave a half-smile. "So where do you work, someplace like Toys R Us?"

"Yeah, well something like that. The place I work isn't a big chain or anything, but I'm learning a lot. They make a lot of their stuff locally."

"That's cool."

"I actually sold them one of my designs."

They were interrupted by some grinning guy's face popping up on the driver's side. James let the window down. "What's up, Gus? Kinda busy here."

Gus leaned in to eye Fran and grinned even wider. "Oh, cool, cool." He nodded his approval. "Just wanted you to know that I'm about to split."

"Okay," James said.

"Got a ride with Lana. The one with the—" He stopped himself, still grinning and hoping that James would understand the point of his needlessly coming to tell him this.

"Yeah, cool." James shot a quick glance to Fran, and then told Gus, "I'll catch up with you later."

"Don't wait up." Gus winked at Fran, to her surprise, before he backed up from James's car and shot out a loud drunken howl while running back to the party.

Fran resisted the reflexive eye roll. "Friend of yours?"

"Yeah," James said, "and my roommate." He added, "He's cool."

Fran took his comment to mean, *Don't let him scare you off.* She thought about mentioning Gus's wink but figured there would be no point, and she was right. That would not have been news to James, who was used to his friend flirting with girls he liked, and, arguably, flat out stealing one of James's almost-girlfriends. Later, Gus would try his hand at poaching Fran, but she wouldn't have any of it. Right then, she wanted to forget about him, anyway, turning back to the conversation that had been interrupted. "So, you sold one of your designs, huh? Like a game or something?"

"Oh. Yeah. Not a game. I like wood carving. I made this castle with a little drawbridge that flips down. They really dug it so—"

"That *is* cool. I've never met a wood-carver before."

"My dad got me into it when I was a kid. He used to do construction. He taught me a lot of stuff about building. The wood carving was more of a hobby for him, though."

"So why don't you do more of that? Make more of your own stuff to sell?"

"I've thought about it—more like fantasized, actually. Someday, though."

"You should. Sounds like you've got talent."

"What about you? Got plans yet?"

"Not yet. I graduate next year. I'm not exactly sure what comes next."

"What's your major?"

"Business."

"Well, what do you think you'd like to do?"

"You know, I majored in business because it was safe. And I did well in my classes, but I don't know. I wanna do something that makes me feel . . . important."

"If you could do anything, be anything, what would that life look like?"

"Wow. Anything?"

"Yeah."

"Okay, well, I'd be a fashion buyer."

"You mean like buying cool clothes for stores?"

"Yeah, exactly. I love fashion. I have a good eye and good analytical skills, or so my profs tell me."

"Then why don't you go for it?"

"I wouldn't even know where to start. And I hear those jobs are, like, ridiculously hard to get for somebody like me, straight out of college with no experience."

Unlike Fran, James was very clear-eyed about what he wanted and how he'd one day get there. Fran loved that about him. What questions she'd had about her own path were soon consumed by more pressing matters. They had been married less than a year when she became pregnant with Stacy. While James's income was modest, he was insistent Fran quit her job as a salesclerk at a clothing store. He convinced her that all that standing wasn't good for her or their baby.

They settled in Rogers Park. Their apartment was a small place in a gray stone walk-up, just large enough for a family of three. They loved the neighborhood, electric with young energy: backpacks slung over shoulders, university students running for buses and trains, the sound of steel screeching along the "L" tracks. There were hole-in-the-wall bookstores with wobbly wooden tables for endless reading and coffee drinking. And Fran's family church was there too. James and the newly installed young pastor, Martin Phillips, hit it off immediately.

By the time Jay was born, kids' clothing toys and had taken over the tiny four rooms of their flat. James kissed his young wife on the forehead as Stacy slept between them and Jay slept in his crib.

"I'll work harder for you," he whispered. "I'll be the husband you deserve." She smiled and fell asleep in the comfort of James's promise.

Now, Fran felt James roll over on his side next to her. She wasn't sure if he was still awake. Her mind returned to the problematic credit cards. The potential of the job offer. She thought of ways to mention both. No, perhaps only the job. Things had changed so drastically overnight. Maybe James's thinking would change, too, about her working now. She thought of all the other times she'd mentioned getting a job. The kids had grown, and so had she. But James remained resistant. And when she'd asked him why, he'd always managed an answer that left her defensive. Fran resolved she wouldn't let it happen again.

12

James had set up several drop-by meetings with friends and acquaintances. They had all heard the news about the fire, but he was determined to keep the focus of the conversation on his business needs. But the speech and the responses were generally the same as he went from one posh home to the next.

He started first with Mrs. Hollands. Known for her philanthropy that was largely born out of her boredom, Mrs. Hollands seemed like a good pick for a sizeable investment.

James started by saying, "Thank you for agreeing to meet with me."

"Oh, of course. You poor man." She reached a sun-speckled, bejeweled hand out to pat him on his knee. "I heard what happened to your dear family. How is Frieda holding up?"

"Fran is doing all right, about as good as could be expected."

"A strong woman." She put her splayed, beringed fingers to her chest, adding, "I can't imagine living through such a thing. Losing *everything* . . ."

"Yes, I won't say it's not been difficult, but I'm seeking investors for my business. My inventory was destroyed in the fire. I need to replenish my stock. I have solid relationships with buyers and—"

"Your inventory was lost in the fire too?" she interrupted.

"Yes, yes, it was."

"Oh, dear. But shouldn't your insurance company cover all damages?"

James shifted in his uncomfortable seat. "There seems to be a problem with the insurance," he said.

"A problem? Given your tragic situation, how can an insurance company be reticent about paying?"

"My product line of toys has done very well over the years," James said, in an effort to steer the conversation back to his preferred course. "I have sales records to demonstrate just how successful we've been."

Mrs. Hollands appraised him quietly. Somehow that look told James that she knew what he could not admit to himself: this was his doing, his screwup. She broke the silence. "I do wish you all the best with your business, James, but I personally never undertake risky ventures. I leave that to my brokers." She scribbled in her checkbook then ripped off the check, handing it to him. He saw that she'd written in an amount of one hundred dollars and signed the check but left the rest blank. "You can finish this for me, yes? I do hate to end our visit, dear, but I'm afraid I'm all out of time. I'm expecting friends for cocktails, and I really should prepare."

James stood. "I appreciate your time, Mrs. Hollands. I can see myself out."

He could feel her watching him as he took the long walk to the front door.

That afternoon, he made his way down the list of his meetings, the conversations halting around his house fire. James had to repeat that he had not come for charity. They'd offer him money anyway. One man reached into his wallet to see what he hadn't spent in tips throughout the day at the country club and offered the remaining flimsy bills to James.

When he met with Pastor Phillips and his wife, Charlotte, the conversation turned in an unexpected way.

"We've been trying to get in touch with you, James," Pastor Phillips said. "We left messages."

"I've been insanely busy." James recalled deleting messages from them without even listening to what was said.

"Well, we're glad you reached out to us," Charlotte told him.

"Yes," Pastor Phillips concurred.

James nodded, relieved that this was going to be an easier sell. "I'm looking for investors to help restock my inventory," he began. "Like I said on the phone, the fire wiped us out."

"Well," Pastor Phillips suggested. "I have another approach I'd like for you to consider."

"Oh?"

"Yes. Now hear me out. The Children's Hospital needs a new custodial engineer supervisor. I can pretty much guarantee you the job, if you're interested. The pay is steady. It'll be a solid way to get you back on your feet quickly for your family."

"A janitor?" James gulped.

"You wouldn't have to do much of the physical work, James. The pay is good. And I'm guessing from what you're telling me, you need something steady for your family right now."

"I have a business," James said.

The pastor and his wife glanced at one another before he responded. "I'm sure you'll be able to get your old life back, James. The job at the hospital is just triage until you and your family are situated again."

"Look," James said, "I appreciate the offer, but I have a business. A successful one."

"I understand. If you change your mind, let us know."

James refused the check for two hundred dollars they offered, and he left.

He spent several hours at the office. He couldn't go home just yet. He felt the stench of failure on him after the meetings. It was dusk and cold out. He needed to clear his head. Walk a bit. That always helped. He left work and took off toward Dearborn, near the hub of cafés and shops. Some passersby were nearly trotting for cabs, heading for the Van Buren Street Metra train stop. Others would take on the brisk walk, brushing by James as he ambled along. He passed the old Dearborn Station clock tower, made his way to Wabash, and strolled by Buddy Guy's Legends. Musicians were hustling in and out of the cold to set up for their gig. James blew a hot breath into his cupped hands. In his distracted haste, he'd left his office without his hat and gloves.

He decided to look for a place where he could duck in for a warm coffee. He walked into a small café that smelled of freshly roasted beans. Men and women were killing time before heading to the train station, waiting at small tables while drinking their coffee and reading their newspapers, some on their laptops, others on their phones.

As James eyed the place for a vacant table, someone called out to him. He looked and saw Martin Phillips waving him over. James was caught off-guard by the chance meeting but obeyed, a polite smile fixed on his face.

"Have a seat," Pastor Phillips said, his hand outstretched to the vacant chair on the other side of the small table. "Good to see you again. I just finished a meeting and thought I'd relax with a cup of coffee. Let the traffic die down some, you know?"

James sat down, feeling as if he was coming undone.

"Wow, rough day?" Pastor Phillips asked.

James lowered his eyes. "I could use some coffee." Looking in the direction of the door, he added, "Cold out." He wanted to avoid the pastor's intrusive gaze. James wondered if he would mention the janitor's job again. "Be back in a minute," he said and got up to go to the counter to order. He had such a mixed bag of feelings. He wanted to be alone to wrestle with his worries. At the same time, he found stumbling into the company of the pastor somewhat comforting.

He received his cup of steaming black coffee, hold the cream, two sugars, and in three careful strides was back at the table. Martin Phillips was gingerly sipping his own coffee like leisure time was something to savor.

He looked up as James sat down and smiled. "Stressful time, huh?"

James was tugging at his scarf as if the thing were alive and choking him. "Just a lot going on right now."

"Want to talk about it?"

James made an awkward sound, not quite a laugh. No, the pastor wouldn't mention the job again—at least James wouldn't have to deal with that. He averted his eyes. He had a fleeting impulse to talk about the fire, to tell Pastor Phillips how they'd lost everything, and that he felt he was teetering on a razor's edge. Instead he only said, "I wouldn't want to bore you. Anyway, I'm sure you've got more important things to do besides listening to me go on about work." He was glad to have the coffee cup as his focus.

"This is important," Martin said. "This is what I do."

There was such earnestness in his voice that it edged on urgency. James couldn't help but meet his eyes. Pastor Phillips waited.

James shrugged as he tapped his fingers lightly on his coffee cup. A nervous tic. "I've been meaning to get by the church, you know." It sounded tinny. Immediately, he regretted the hypocrisy. But Pastor Phillips's response was surprising. He laughed. James was unable to mask his surprise.

"I'm sorry, James. I'm not laughing at you. And I certainly don't mean to be rude." He leaned in closer. "Look. I'm not Jesus. You don't have to make excuses to me for not showing up at church."

James was clearly disarmed. He wasn't quite sure what to make of the pastor's comment. All that he managed was, "Oh," with a lift of his eyebrows.

"The tough thing about being a pastor is that people who slack off on going to church start avoiding you like a bill collector." He laughed again at his own joke. The humor wasn't shared. The moment sputtered into an awkward pause. "How many years have I known you, James?"

James sighed at the thought. "Wow. Since Fran and I were first married. Seventeen years."

"Yeah, a long time. When I first met you, I was still pretty new in the ministry. And I remember thinking how nice it was to have church members close to my own age. It made me relax a little. God knew what I needed. He sent me friends in the church."

James relaxed enough to offer a crooked half-smile. "I remember when you would invite us over for lasagna. Your wife still makes the best lasagna I've ever tasted, but don't tell Fran I said that." He offered a real smile.

Pastor Phillips held up two "Scout's honor" fingers. "Your secret's safe." Then he told him, "And anytime you guys want to stop in for lasagna, the door is still open."

"Sounds nice, but my crew has grown since those years when Stacy was two."

"I know. You've got four of them. Speaking of, our youth ministry is planning their annual trip for the spring. You should get in touch with Pastor Sharon. She's coordinating things. Maybe it's something your kids would be interested in."

"Oh. Well, I don't know."

"Well, I know Stacy is a little older now. Junior year?"

"Yeah."

Martin smiled. "You never know. We could always use assistant chaperones. And the other kids are still pretty young, right? How old is Jay? Fifteen?"

"Yes, fifteen." James lowered his eyes as he sipped his coffee. He didn't want to highlight that it had been within those two years that his church attendance, and his family's, had grown spotty.

Pastor Phillips went on. "He's still a great age to enjoy a youth trip. And Elliott is about twelve now, right?"

"Eleven."

"That's great. Perfect age. You should look into it. I know Reba may be a little young for it, but your older three . . . well, think about it."

"I will." James considered adding something about running it by Fran, but he couldn't bring himself to flat-out lie to Pastor Phillips.

"Wow, eleven, huh. I remember christening Elliott like it was yesterday. It's amazing how time flies."

"You're right about that. I can still remember being his age. I was all about baseball."

"Football was my thing."

James went on, "I'd spend the whole summer out on the field, from sunup until dark. Didn't matter how hot it was out there. My mom would fuss at me for coming home all dirty, sometimes scratched up and bleeding from sliding into the bases. But, man, there was nothing like it." He had lost himself in the moment, recalling the dirt lot with the high weeds and the makeshift bases. The sun a fireball in the sky baking down on Timmy McGraw and Frankie Getty from off his block, and Ricky Tate, Frankie's cousin—the regulars who would play baseball until the stench of them blended into one magnificent funk as they walked down the street after a good game, comparing bloody scratches. The four would talk about their daydreams of becoming the next Frank Thomas or Cal Ripken or Fred McGriff. They might get a snow cone, but only if each of them could have one, even if they had to combine their money to make that happen, because that's what friendship was.

"So you still have those lasagna dinners, huh?" James returned his attention to Pastor Phillips.

"Yep," he said, "I'm still amazed how Charlotte can fit twenty people at a table meant for four."

"My mom used to say love makes room. Back when my dad was healthy, she was always inviting someone over for dinner, especially folks who didn't have much. Funny thing was, we didn't have a lot either, but she and my dad, they were givers. She said that was God's way."

"That's one way we show His love. Jesus broke bread with his disciples. It's closeness between friends. It demonstrates how important they are to you, how much you regard them."

James nodded at his coffee cup and said softly, "Yes."

"There's always room for you, James."

There, right there. Martin had spoken to the hidden part of James: the fear and loneliness. So deep were these feelings, they had been kept from his wife, and sometimes, even from himself. He could never, would never, give a name to the things that threatened to overwhelm him. Without warning, he felt emotion behind his eyes. He blinked it away.

His words came out quiet and heavy. "There just doesn't seem to be time for everything, you know?" His hand trembled slightly as he raised the cup to his mouth. He could tell Martin had caught his unsteadiness.

"I know it can feel that way. But you don't have to go it alone."

James looked at him, understanding fully what the pastor meant and what would come next.

"Sometimes," Pastor Phillips began reflectively, "sometimes we work so hard to get it all done or to fix what isn't working that we forget we have a Father who's concerned about everything that touches us. He's there to help when we need it. But we have to learn to get out of the way. We have to learn to let go and let God."

James shook his head with a short, incredulous laugh.

Pastor Phillips didn't speak his disappointment in James's dismissive response. This wasn't like the James he remembered.

James sighed. "Don't take this the wrong way, but problems aren't solved with bumper sticker slogans."

"I see."

Immediately James regretted his words, even if he was being honest about how he felt. Still, he didn't want to somehow disappoint the man he had so much respect for. He didn't want to jeopardize how Pastor Phillips perceived him. James tried to fix things by explaining, "You know me. I'm a man who enjoys conquering the mountain."

"And that's admirable, but there are times when we can't. You know, accepting your limitations isn't a bad thing. At some point, we all give out. We try and try until we become spent. And that's usually when we remember to pray. The good news is, prayer works. But here's the thing, we don't have to come to the end of ourselves before we get the help we need. God is always ready and available. We just have to ask."

"I'll try to remember that," James remarked.

His tone was patronizing, but Martin didn't acknowledge it. Instead he simply said, "I hope so."

James gave the faint laugh again. "Fran thinks I should prioritize my time better."

"Well, what do you think?"

"I prioritize. I know that my family comes first. I know that I've worked hard to show them that, worked hard to give them things they need, stuff they want." He took in an uneasy breath, trying to release the sudden tension in his chest. He felt a desperate need to smother what had happened to his family. For reasons he could not explain, he believed that sharing—*admitting*—any part of his current struggles would make it worse.

Pastor Phillips leaned back, his eyes steady on James. "You know, providing for your family is important. But provision is more than just the stuff you buy off store shelves."

James spoke softly with the rim of his coffee cup at his lips. "You sound like Fran."

"Well, that should tell you something."

James shook his head. "It doesn't tell me anything. It just confuses me."

"How so?"

"Because I'm doing my best here. What the hell else am I supposed to do?" He caught himself. "I'm sorry."

"No worries." Pastor Phillips dismissed it with a wave. "You seem like you're under a lot of pressure."

James swallowed the lump rising in his throat as he nodded, because he couldn't speak it.

Martin leaned in to close the space between them. "Tell me something."

"Sure." James's voice was thin, weak. Despite his efforts at composure, he felt like his insides were exposed and brittle, and that Pastor Phillips had the power to break him into crumbled pieces if he wanted to. But James knew he wouldn't. It was the way Martin fastened on him as if he were looking at a wounded man and trying to figure out how to best handle him with caution and care.

"What do you need?"

"What?" James asked.

"What do you need?"

James blinked as if confused. He couldn't recall ever being asked that question. "I . . . I don't know."

"Well, take a moment. Think about it and say it out loud. It doesn't have to be anything earth-shattering. Just something—right now—that would make you feel good. Make you feel happy, at peace again."

"Okay. Okay." In that beat of silence, thoughts flapped like wings, whirling in his head: he wanted his house back, he wanted the axis of time to slip and get stuck so that he could fix things and outrace what loomed behind him. He said none of this, but instead he said, "I want new golf clubs."

"That's a start. Go on."

"Well, I want a membership to that fancy country club. They denied my application twice."

"Why?"

"Why didn't they let me in?" James asked.

"No, why is it important to you that they *let* you in?"

"I don't know." James shrugged.

"Yeah, you do. Be honest with yourself."

"Okay." James sucked his teeth, thoughtful before answering. "Status," he said, almost defiantly. "It'll give me social status. It's great for making connections."

"I see." Pastor Phillips considered. "So have these things you've bought to provide for your family made you happy for more than a day, a month? Given you peace?"

James looked away. He noticed that the café's patrons were almost all gone. It seemed to amplify his aloneness in the world.

"Temporal things don't deliver in the long term," Pastor Phillips elaborated. "But I'm guessing you know that—at least on some level. How many expensive things have you bought for yourself, for your family, only to crave something else?" He continued with James's attention locked on him. "The problem is, no matter what you buy, that hole—the emptiness—won't be satisfied."

"I work. I work *hard,*" James said defensively. He realized he'd clenched a fist. He took a breath. "I keep thinking, maybe if I just work *more*, come up with new ways to—" He stopped and rubbed his eyes, his lips trembling.

Martin placed his hand on James's arm. "Here's more good news." He waited until James settled himself and he'd regained his attention. "The real price for your happiness and peace has already been paid. Remember, Jesus picked up your tab. I pray for you, James. I pray for your family. And I believe God will answer."

13

When James arrived back at the hotel, it was well past dinner. The kids were watching TV. He was greeted by Reba, who hugged him warmly, and Fran, who looked anxious, as if she'd been waiting for this moment. He spoke to the expression on her face. "Can I get my coat off first?"

"How'd it go?" She couldn't help asking.

There was a pause as he shrugged his shoulders out of his coat and turned to the closet. He didn't want to face her. "Fine," he said. The word was flat, intended to discourage any follow-up. He kicked off his boots and unwound the scarf from his neck.

Fran was tone-deaf to his signals. "You eat yet?"

"No."

"You hungry? There's some—"

"No, I'm not hungry, just tired."

"Well, I was hoping we could talk."

"Is it important?" The tone was edgy, more than he had intended. He looked down at Reba, who was still standing there, watching her parents.

Fran told her, "Honey, why don't you go watch the movie, okay?"

Reba went back to join her siblings without protest.

Fran turned again to James. "Yeah, I think it's important."

He didn't reply. Instead, he headed for the bedroom. Fran followed.

James sat limply on the bed as if drained from the weight of the day. His loud sigh was nearly a groan. "You wanted to talk," he said.

Fran sat and angled herself to see him face-on. "I've been thinking. Now just listen, okay? I know how you feel about me staying at home with the kids, but I think the timing is right for me to get a job."

"Fran, we've already been through this." He glanced at her arm cast. "And anyway, do you think you'd even be up for a job right now? You were just complaining about your back last night."

"Yes, yes, I know, but I think I'd be okay." She took a deep breath. "Things are different now."

"Look, I understand how you feel, but it's going to be okay. I've got this under control."

"I want to help."

"You can help by being home for the kids. They need stability, not more change now. They need you home. Reba needs you home."

"She's fine. You said it yourself."

"You know what that doctor said."

"James, it's been over a year. And you only mention that when I bring up working."

"Are you gonna tell me you haven't thought about it, Fran? Who's to say this fire won't cause some sort of setback?"

Ordinarily, she would have folded then. Not this time. She inhaled deeply and came out with it: "I was offered a job."

"What?" James sat up straighter.

"I was offered a job. Well, I'm pretty sure she'd hire me."

"What job? Where?"

"When I took the kids shopping the other day, I met a woman who owns this boutique at the mall. We hit it off. She needs another sales clerk and told me to call her."

"No. The kids need you home."

"Why are you being so stubborn about this? We need the money."

James felt some of the air leave his lungs, like she had poked him in the sternum. "I said I've got this." His voice was weaker than he had expected.

"James." Fran hesitated. "Our credit cards were declined."

"What are you talking about?"

"At the mall. My card, and the one we gave Stacy."

"But you bought stuff."

"I had the other card on me. That one worked."

"Is that what this is about? Some clerk had a problem with our card, and now you want to—"

"Don't twist this into something else. I want to work because I want to help. I want to *do* something with my time."

"Since when is raising our kids a time waster?"

"Don't do this. You *always* do this!"

The way she looked at him threatened to cut him open. James hated these talks. It had gotten harder to press down his feelings—his boyhood memories. The passing years hadn't released him. It made him angry. He'd always take it out on Fran, his guilt bubbling up and mixing with her confusion. He felt frail. Her expression softened, as if trying to make sense of what she saw in rare flashes: pinpricks of James's vulnerability breaking through.

He needed to harden the air between them. Gesturing to the closed door, he said, "Keep your voice down. These walls aren't brick, you know."

"That's not fair."

"Fran, we've talked about this. Maybe when Reba is a little older we can talk about it again and revise the plan."

A small, thin voice called out from the other side of the door. "Mommy? Daddy?"

Relieved, James admonished, "Now you've gotten Reba upset. I told you to keep it down."

Fran stood up and swallowed her exasperation.

"What if you aren't home and we get another emergency phone call, Fran?"

Fran didn't respond. Instead, she reached for the door. "Mommy's coming, baby."

James exhaled when Fran walked out. He had not been aware that he'd been holding his breath. He stood up with the slow movements of a man in pain. He went to the window and looked out onto the hotel parking lot. It was dark, but he could see his big SUV parked under the soft orb of a streetlight.

Standing at the window, he was once again a boy riding his bicycle down Main Street, past a bakery parking lot. He recognized his father's truck parked there. James had been surprised and delighted as he peddled faster into the lot. He'd glimpsed only his father's profile before he stopped. His father's head was bowed. James couldn't see him face-on, but he knew his father was sad. There was something private about his father's pain that made James hesitate, but his father looked over at him, suddenly aware that he'd lost his moment of privacy.

His face trembled as he forced a smile. "Jimmy, what're you doing here?" His voice was less joyful than it usually was when James would run up and hug him when he returned home from work. James's mother would sometimes complain about the washing she'd have to do to rid her husband's clothes of construction dirt, but James didn't care. He would wrap his arms around his father, enjoy the warm, strong embrace, take in the smells of menthol, hardworking-man sweat, wet cement, and other things James could not name but would recall whenever he'd look up at a building being raised.

That moment, when James locked on his father and saw his eyes shimmer with tears, James knew he was witnessing something that would change things.

"Hey, Dad," James said. "You okay?"

His father's smile wavered. He nodded first, like he needed to find his voice before answering. "I'm okay, son. You go on now. You go ride your bike and play with your friends, okay?" But James didn't feel like this was okay. He knew his father was not okay. He saw him lose the fight with one determined tear that rolled down his cheek. His father's face constricted and trembled. "You go now."

James peddled away fast. He didn't want to see anymore, but at the same time felt the burden of guilt for not knowing what else he could have done.

What happened that afternoon hardened into something even more unsettling later that day. Dinner had been served and eaten, and James's mother was clearing spaghetti plates when his father came home and walked into the little kitchen warmed with the smell of fried onions and simmered garlic. James hadn't yet left the table. His father first looked at him. There was a shadow of something in his expression, perhaps wondering if James had spoken about seeing him earlier. But then it was gone, and he pulled on the familiar happy face James was accustomed to seeing.

"How's my Jimmy?" he said. "No hug for your dad?" Arms stretched wide, his skin smudged with dust, his clothes grimy. A dank lock of his coal-black hair fell over his dark eyes.

His mother grunted. "You show up late and that's all you have to say?" She clanged pots with her back to him and James, who had left his seat to hug his father.

Embracing him now felt different. The man latched on to him. When James pulled away, he looked up at his father, who turned to James's mother. "Spaghetti again?"

"Yep, spaghetti. You complaining?"

"No! I love your spaghetti!"

"Well, it's cheap. It's not been easy, you know."

"I know. I know." An apology edged his quiet words.

"You talk to the foreman?"

"No."

"You said you'd talk to him." She turned, her face hardened in confrontation.

"Dorothy," he said, easy, calming, still apologetic. "The boy."

They looked at James. James was watching, seeing the pleading in his father's face to prevent anything that might come next, and the wear of impatience that sagged on his mother. James had not been aware of this before.

She turned her sharpness to James. "Go. Do your homework." He hesitated. "Now, mister."

James lumbered out of the kitchen. His mother didn't wait. She didn't care that James could still clearly hear them as he passed through the small living room, heading for his bedroom upstairs.

"You said you'd talk to the foreman. You need more work."

"I know. I know."

"So when? When are you gonna talk to him, huh? Tell him you feel fine now. The doctors say you can work like before. No more of this two, three days a week. Who can live off two, three days of money, huh?"

"I'll talk to him. It'll be fine."

James had left the kitchen but stopped at the top of the stairs and sat, listening to his mother's words that were like a wire being stretched tight and threatening to snap. And his father, walking along the edge of those words, teetering and cautious.

James recalled the sight of his father in the bakery parking lot as he listened. And he wondered about the talk with the foreman, and the tears he'd seen in his father's eyes.

The hotel bedroom door opened. Startled by the interruption, James quickly turned from the window. It was Fran, still standing just outside the room. He could tell she hadn't quite forgiven him. Fran had become adept at hiding any sign of her irritation with him when the kids were around. "Bandage wraps," she said. "I forgot to pick some up earlier. Would you mind? Jay's just used his last one."

"No, I don't mind at all." James felt relieved, already plotting to make the most out of his time away from Fran, the kids, and his thoughts.

Tomorrow, he would be heading to New York on business. The thought of it released an easy exhalation.

14

The following night, a shrill noise cut through Fran's sleep. Her eyelids fluttered open to view the dark hotel bedroom. The noise persisted. Instinctively, she reached over for James. The bed was empty. That's right, James was in New York, she remembered. Her mind made sense of the noise. It was the hotel phone on the nightstand. She shifted to rest on one elbow, eyeing the clock. *3:12 AM.* She grabbed the phone.

"Hello." Her voice was thick and raspy.

There was a stranger on the other end. "Mrs. Harrison?"

"Yes. Speaking."

"This is Officer Richards. Adam Richards, ma'am."

"What?" Her heart gave one desperate thump.

"I'm calling about your son."

She sat up immediately, fully alert. Her heart was hammering.

"What . . . what's this about?"

"Jay Harrison."

"What's wrong? What happened?"

"He's not hurt, but we need you to come here to pick him up. Apparently, he's been drinking at a frat party."

"But he's okay? My son's okay?" Her hand was on her chest.

"Yes, he's fine."

Fran struggled to get into her jeans, limited by the use of one hand

and the spike of back pain with each awkward twist of her torso. *This was so much easier with James.* She threw on her down jacket to cover up her nightshirt. She scribbled a note for Stacy, just in case: *Had to make a run. Don't worry. Be back soon. Love, Mom.*

When she arrived at the frat house, there were three cop cars out front of the old Victorian. The police lights pinwheeled flashes of red across the lawn, which had a light powdering of snow. Some of the frat boys were standing on the steps, explaining themselves to the officers.

Fran parked hastily and ran to the nearest policeman, who was standing by one of the squad cars. It was Adam.

"Excuse me. Hi. You, you called about my son."

Adam said, "Right here." He pointed to the back seat of the police car.

She bent at the knees to see inside. There was Jay, miserable and pale, as if he'd vomited out all of his coloring. The boy next to him was groaning with his head tilted against the window.

"Jay? What the hell—" She stopped herself. "May I take him home?"

"Yeah. I'll give your son a pass since he's a juvey. Keep an eye on him."

"Yes, yes, of course. Thank you."

Adam opened the back door. Jay got out and nearly spilled onto the curb. Fran propped him up by linking arms and shuttled him to their car. Even in the cold, she could smell the stench of bile and cheap liquor coming off of him. She gagged at the putrid odor. It was pointless lecturing him, but she couldn't help herself. "You're grounded for a month, mister. You can tell your friends too. That means *just* school and back home again. Are you listening to me?"

Jay didn't look like he could hear anything aside from the acids bubbling and churning in his stomach. He crawled into the back seat and fell asleep.

On the drive home, the shock of the whole situation left Fran feeling as if she'd been turned to custard and at any moment might come completely undone. The thought of it made her angry at Jay for his foolishness, at James for not being there. She shouldn't be talking to cops and collecting her son at three in the morning *alone*. And she felt angry at herself for feeling so weak and vulnerable. She covered her mouth because she didn't want Jay to hear her crying.

Once at the hotel, she led Jay into the master bedroom. She didn't want the kids to wake up and see their brother in this condition. She'd sleep with the girls. She didn't even bother taking off her coat before calling James. He didn't answer. Finally, she fell asleep.

Fran woke up earlier than usual. The room was quiet as a morgue. She sat up, wondering what to do, what to say to Jay. More than anything, she felt scared. She got up. Reba was asleep next to Stacy. Elliott was sound asleep on the let-out couch. There was one of her self-help books she'd left on the table: *Uncovering the Power Within*. She thumbed through it and saw nothing relevant.

Stacy, Elliott, and Reba woke up. Jay was still sleeping it off. Fran offered the car to Stacy in exchange for taxiing her brother to soccer practice and her sister to ballet class.

Once alone, Fran knocked on the master bedroom door. Jay didn't answer. She opened the door and saw him sprawled face down on the bed, like he'd simply fallen forward.

"Jay," she said. "Jay." She advanced farther into the room. It smelled like bourbon, stale breath, and a whiff of vomit. He moaned. "Jay?" She called his name, sounding more apologetic than she intended. It was useless. Even if she got him up and out of bed, he was in no shape to listen to her. She left the room.

She stared at the phone, wondering if she should try James again. Had he even gotten her other messages? The phone rang. She snatched up the receiver. "James?!"

The man said, "No, it's Officer Richards. Adam."

"Oh," she breathed.

Officer Richards went on to say that he had her wallet. She must have dropped it by the squad car last night. Fran couldn't come get it. No car right now. He volunteered to bring it to the hotel. He was in the area.

She met him in the lobby with her hair piled high in a messy bun. Flyaway blond strands fell in front of her anxious blue eyes.

"Thank you," she said, accepting the wallet like she wasn't quite sure what to do with it. There were no pockets in James's oversized sweater. "I'm sorry for the trouble."

"No trouble," Adam told her. "I was on my way to get coffee not far from here. Hey, how's your son?"

"Still sleeping. That's normal, right?"

"I take it you've never had a hangover." She shook her head no. "It's not uncommon." He adjusted his policeman's cap. "Well, I don't want to keep you. Good seeing you again." He headed for the hotel's revolving door.

She watched him, arms crossed against the cold that swooped in as someone else entered the lobby. She debated whether she should ask him for advice. He'd already stepped into the space to rotate the door when she called out, "Wait!"

He turned and walked back to her. "What can I help you with?"

"Look, I know you must be very busy, but I was wondering . . ." She dropped her gaze because she suddenly felt embarrassed. She glanced over her shoulder, making certain she wouldn't be overheard. The hotel clerks seemed occupied behind the front desk. "My son, Jay. I should talk to him. I mean, I know I need to talk to him, but I'm not sure what to say." She stared at him openly, wanting his reply.

He was quiet for a moment as if considering his next words carefully. "It's never easy," he said, "talking to kids about drinking, drugs. Just speak from your heart. Tell him why you're concerned."

"I'm afraid," she whispered. "I'm scared I'll say the wrong thing and it'll just push him away." She saw that he was looking at her wedding ring but didn't speak whatever he was thinking.

"I get it. You don't want to come off sounding like a pamphlet."

She bit her lower lip and nodded.

"You won't. I always tell parents, just let your kids know why you're concerned, but more importantly, *listen*. Ask them what's going on in their lives and what they're feeling. Find out what's behind the drinking, or whatever, and then figure out how you can help them. Make a plan together."

"Yeah. That sounds good. You do a lot of this? Advising, counseling?"

"Actually, yeah." He smiled. "You'll do fine."

He was about to turn away again when she said, "Hey, would you like to get coffee here—with me? Just for a few minutes, maybe? I'd really like to talk a little more if that's okay."

Fran and Adam went to the hotel café adjacent to the lobby. She eased into a chair, her face signaling discomfort at the maneuver. He reached for her instinctively, eyeing the arm cast. "You okay? Can I help?"

Sitting down with a breath, Fran said, "I'm good. The Tylenol hasn't quite kicked in yet."

He kept his questions to himself, pulling off his policeman's cap. She could see his face much better. When he met her eyes, she dropped hers to her cup. She hadn't meant to stare.

He talked about reading the signs before there's a problem. "Every parent I've talked to says pretty much the same thing. They're scared. The thing to remember is, the kids are just as scared, even if it's for different reasons. Scared of not being accepted. Scared of not looking cool. They just need to know that you understand what it's like to struggle to figure things out. Let them know that you're not judging them."

"Thank you," she said. "It helps to hear that. I should go back upstairs to check on Jay." She stood. He did the same. Fran looked as if she were trying to figure out the next step.

"Can I just make one other suggestion?" he asked.

"Please do."

"If you've got some orange juice or tomato juice, give him some.

And aspirin. That'll help. Along with a good breakfast. Let him get his head on straight before you talk to him."

"Yeah."

"Like I said, you'll do fine. Just give him a little room to breathe."

They walked out of the café together just as Stacy was walking in with Reba.

"Hey." Stacy eyed the cop and her mother. "Is everything okay?"

"Fine, everything's fine, honey. This is Adam—Officer Richards. This is my daughter, Stacy."

"Hi, Officer Friendly!" Reba remembered him from his talk at her school on Stranger Danger.

Adam smiled at her. "Hey there."

Fran said, "And I guess you know our little Reba."

Reba was grinning. Stacy continued staring, looking curious and perplexed.

"Well, I should head out. Good meeting you," Adam said to the girls.

After he departed, Fran suggested Stacy and Reba have breakfast at the hotel's restaurant. Stacy wondered about Jay, and Fran replied, "Maybe he'll join you later."

She walked away before any questions could follow.

Fran returned to the suite with a glass of orange juice from the café and aspirin. The master bedroom door was open. Jay was sitting on the side of the bed, leaning forward and holding his head with his mouth hanging open.

She knocked on the doorframe to get his attention but didn't cross the threshold into his space. "Hey there."

"Hey, Mom. What time is it?" He squinted one bloodshot eye at her.

"After ten, I think."

"Where's everybody?"

"Elliott had practice. I asked Stacy and Reba to have breakfast downstairs to give us privacy."

"Uh-oh." He lay back on the bed.

"I was told this will help. Juice and aspirin. Mind if I come in?"

"I don't think I have a choice," he groaned.

She stood over him. "Can you sit up? It's hard talking to you like that."

Slowly, he propped himself on one elbow and took the juice and aspirin she offered.

Fran pulled the chair from the desk over and sat, facing him. "How are you feeling?"

"How do I look?"

"Like you need to get cleaned up and eat."

After downing half the glass of juice, he asked, "Am I in trouble?"

"We can talk about that later."

"When Dad gets home?"

"Yeah, that's probably best."

"Does he know? About last night?"

"No."

"You didn't tell 'im?"

"I called. I couldn't reach him."

Jay turned toward the light coming through the window, but Fran caught the glint of disappointment in his eyes. "He'll be back sometime tonight."

Jay didn't reply.

Fran added, "I'm not angry at you. Well, I am. You could've gotten hurt. Something could've happened to you, and I just don't know what I would do if—" She stopped mid-sentence. "I'm here. I'm here, Jay." She put a hand to her heart when he didn't speak. "I love you."

"I know, Mom. I love you too."

"You should get cleaned up," she said as she stood. "I'll order breakfast for you."

Later that evening when James came home, Fran met him at the door and asked to speak with him outside. Tired, he asked, "Can't I get settled in first?"

She only looked at him. He resigned himself to following her back out the door.

In the privacy of their car, Fran said, "I called you. Jay was caught drinking at a frat party last night."

"Oh? How is he?"

"Honestly, I don't know. I mean, he's not acting any differently, but this whole thing—the parties, drinking. I don't know, James."

"It happens."

"Yeah, I know, but what does it mean? And he's been lying to us."

"He's a fifteen-year-old boy, Fran. Lying happens too."

"You're not concerned about his hanging out with older boys and drinking?"

"Of course I am. I'm just not sure it means he's got some sort of problem."

"Adam thought it could lead to one," Fran said.

"*Adam*? Who's Adam?"

"Officer Richards. The policeman who called me last night."

"First-name basis?"

"His daughter goes to Reba's school. He was at that charity party. Anyway, I asked for some advice over coffee. You know, how to handle things with Jay. He's got a lot of experience with troubled kids and—"

"Wait a second," James interrupted, "Jay is *not* a troubled kid."

"That's not what I said," Fran replied. "Anyway, I told Jay we would talk to him when you got here. I thought it was best to wait."

"Well, I'm exhausted," James said. "Talking with Jay can wait."

James went to the lobby café to work. He couldn't concentrate with all the activity going on in the room, and he wasn't up for the drive to his office. He didn't even hear Jay approach his small table. He just looked up from his laptop and there was his son.

"Hey, Dad."

"Hey! How's it going?"

Jay shrugged. "Okay, I guess."

"Where's Mom?" James looked past him, half expecting Fran to appear behind him.

"On the phone with Oma, I think."

"Oh. You want something, champ?"

"Dad, *champ*? I'm not a kid anymore."

"You used to like being called champ."

"Well, I was eight years old."

"Oh, okay. You want something, Jay?"

Jay fidgeted with his hands in his pockets. "I don't know. Mom said you wanted to talk to me."

There was a pause.

"Okay," James said. "Have a seat."

Jay plopped down in the chair across from him and looked at his father expectantly.

"I heard about what happened," James said. "How long has this been going on?"

"What? Me going to parties?"

"Not just the parties." He quickly glanced around. "The drinking. How long?"

Jay shrugged. "Not long."

"Anything else you're doing we don't know about?"

"What? Like drugs? No, I'm not into that."

"Good," James said. "You don't want to get mixed up in anything like that. You can ruin your life. As for the drinking, you know you're underage, so quit it." His eyes flickered to his laptop for just a second.

Jay caught it. "Is that it?"

"Yeah," James said.

"Right. I wouldn't want to keep you from your work."

"Hey. What's with the attitude? I go easy on you and this is what I get for it?"

"Nothing, Dad."

"No, what gives?"

"I said, nothing." Jay got up and started to walk away.

"Hey," James said. Jay turned to him. "You think I don't care?"

"Tell you the truth, Dad, I don't know. I came down here to see, but I guess this wasn't a good time to interrupt you." He headed for the lobby elevator.

"Jay!" James called out. "Jay!"

But his son didn't answer.

James leaned forward and rested his face in his hands. He thought about following his son up to the room and attempting to explain himself. But he realized he didn't know what to say. The very core of him was being pulled to the point of feeling threadbare.

Not long after, he heard the soft padding of feet approaching. He knew it was Fran.

"What happened?" she asked.

"I don't know."

"What do you mean you don't know, James? We were supposed to talk to Jay together."

James gave her a rundown of what had transpired.

"That's it?".

"Yeah."

"Our son might be in trouble and that's the best you came up with?"

"Are you using this as another opportunity to criticize me?"

His question was a throughway for Fran to complain about his not being accessible when she'd called him after picking up Jay.

James seized the moment to advance his own criticism: "You seemed to manage okay. That cop was sure ready to help out."

Fran retorted, "Don't change the subject, James. I told you what happened."

"Yeah, I heard you. I just wonder, is he that helpful to everybody or just women whose husbands happen to be away."

"He just talked with me. You can't imagine how scary it is to get a call about one of our children at three in the morning. Talking to Adam calmed me down."

James paused before he spoke. "You know, I'm trying here. I really am." In the silence that followed, all sorts of words and emotions bubbled up inside him, but he couldn't manage to shape them. And because he didn't offer more, neither did she. Fran walked away.

15

The holidays were over. James went into his office early. He had plans to talk to his team, give them a pep talk. He was prepared to promise they'd be well taken care of if they hung in there with him. He'd make good on the back end, even if he couldn't offer much up front. He imagined soliciting ideas from them for jump-starting the new year. His wheels were already turning about ways to get enough money for more inventory.

When he arrived, however, he saw one of his sales guys down the hall. He was coming out of the office, carrying a box. He glanced at James and then continued walking.

James quickened his pace behind him and called out, "Hey, what's up, Peter?" But the man wouldn't turn around.

Before James reached his own office door, he could see that Peter had gone into Gus's office.

What the . . . All James could do was stand in his doorway and watch his sales team pack their belongings into boxes with Gus directing them. "You'll see the open door, just a few doors down and to your left. Grab any open cubicle."

It was as if James were invisible. "What's going on here, Gus?"

The remaining three salesmen, boxes in their hands, looked at Gus, waiting to see how he was going to play his hand.

He smiled at James in a nonchalant way, the kind of greeting you'd give someone when passing at the watercooler. "Hey. In early today."

"What's happening?" James's heart was beating faster.

"Listen." Gus took a slow step toward him. "I was gonna call you, talk about this, but I didn't want to interrupt your family time during Christmas."

James looked past Gus's stiff smile and aimed his question to the others. "Where are you going?" He knew the answer. And even though nothing would be gained from asking the question, he'd asked anyway, maybe in a desperate hope that some shred of decency would stop them.

"We're going to work for In Touch Technologies," one of the young men said.

"Gus's company?" James asked, as if he needed to make certain of the betrayal.

"Yeah," another said.

"You can't just walk out without giving me notice."

One young man shrugged. "Actually, we can. A two-week notice isn't written in our agreement."

James turned to Gus as the rest of the sales team filed out past them. "So you steal my team behind my back."

"I didn't *steal* your team. I just gave them a better opportunity to make some real money. Look at it this way—you're strapped for cash. You said it yourself. Now this is one less thing you'll have to worry about."

"You son of a—"

"Hey, you would've done the same thing if you were me. And I would've been man enough to understand, because we're friends."

"You're not my *friend*, Gus. Friends don't step on your neck when you're down."

"Now you're just being melodramatic. You're telling me we can't be friends because I did a little poaching? Listen, I get it. You're pissed because you're in a tough spot right now, but you'll bounce back." Gus touched James's arm, but James stepped away from him.

"Get the hell out of my office, Gus."

Gus sighed and strolled by him. "Suit yourself."

James sat at his desk and took three, four deep breaths to calm himself. He picked up his phone only to find that his service had been disconnected.

16

Fran took Jay to his follow-up doctor's appointment. He had little to say during the drive there. She asked him questions that were shut down with little response.

"You feeling okay?"

"Fine."

"You sure? You've been awfully quiet."

"I'm fine, Mom."

"Jay, honey, I know there's a lot going on right now. And it may be pretty unsettling—"

"Mom—"

"I'm just saying, if you want to talk about—"

"Mom, really, it's okay. We don't have to do this."

"Do *what*?"

"Do the whole mother-kid thing. I'm not a kid. I'm fine."

"Oh. All right."

She glanced at her son in the passenger seat, his bulk slouched with his arms crossed insolently. He was staring out the window. Fran's eyelids fluttered at the feeling of dismissal and uselessness. She was almost glad the ride was ending, as she made some pointless comment about how the parking lot was so busy.

After Jay's physical, Fran sneaked a private moment with the doctor. "He's been so quiet," she said. "I'm not sure what to do, what to make of it."

"He's been through a lot. You all have," the doctor told her. "That's a lot for a young guy like Jay to process. Maybe counseling would help. Here. This is the name of a good therapist who works with young people."

"That's a good idea. Thank you, Doctor."

On the ride back to the hotel, Fran waited for what she thought was a good time to bring up therapy to Jay. He shot it down quickly. That was the last word he spoke to her on the subject.

She felt a little wounded. Unapologetically, she told him he'd have to endure the trip to the mechanic for an oil change. She ignored his groaning sigh.

The shop was large enough for them to get some distance from each other. A glass partition separated two spaces, one of which was a waiting area where a big-screen TV was mounted to the wall. Jay left his mother to head to the other side of the floor-to-ceiling window divider.

Fran watched him through the glass as he slouched into a seat near an older man wearing a Cubs cap and occupied with an auto magazine. She wanted to cry. Frustrated, she pulled at her hair tie and raked her fingers through her hair. She pressed her fingers to her eyes, breathing and counting, like she'd read in *Own Your Moment: Taking Control of Life's Challenges.*

She was aware of other customers in the space, the woman on the other side of the room with dye-fried blue-black hair and a strange orange tan, the color of a melon gone bad. She was on her cell phone and kept repeating, "Can you hear me now? I'm getting the Mercedes checked out." A boy sat next to her playing some sort of game on his phone. Fran thought of Elliott. There was a man a few seats away from them. He was on his iPad, face pinched and eyes mesmerized. *Always working, no doubt.* She was still looking at the man and thinking about James when Adam walked up, his cheeks pink from the cold. The crystals of snow dusted his wavy hair. She hadn't even seen him. She felt unprepared, her voice catching on loose thoughts of her husband.

"Hey, there," he said. "This is a surprise. Mind if I sit, or . . ." He trailed off as he gestured with his thumb to the seats across the way.

She expelled a bit of tense air and waved off his alternative. "No, no, you don't have to. Here, take a load off." She immediately regretted the last of her words, thinking they sounded stupid, or worse yet, like she was trying too hard. She looked down, feeling awkward but unsure why.

He settled next to her. She turned her attention back to Jay, who was focused on the TV.

"How are you guys doing?" Adam asked. He was looking at her arm in the scribbled-on cast, and then following her gaze to Jay.

"Oh, we're fine." Fran kept looking at her son, mainly because she didn't want to face Adam.

"I'm glad you're all okay," he told her.

The way he said that made Fran realize he'd heard about the fire. She was silent at first, and then turned to him. "It's been tough."

"I can imagine."

She swallowed down the tremor in her throat. For a moment she allowed herself to absorb the warmth and compassion she saw in his face.

Then he was the one to avert his gaze. He angled his words to the floor when he spoke. "I know you've probably heard this a dozen times by now, but if there's anything I can do . . ."

Fran was looking through the glass divider again. "Jay. I'm not sure what's happening with him. I'm not sure what to do."

"What's going on?"

She let out a thin, tired sigh. "He doesn't say much these days. Especially to me and James. I thought he was mad at us for grounding him, you know, after the whole partying and drinking thing. But I don't know."

"You think there's more going on?"

The first tear sneaked down her cheek, and she quickly wiped it away. "I'm not sure. I'm just scared we might miss something, you know?"

"Well, have you thought about counseling or therapy? You guys could've died. I can't imagine processing that kind of trauma at his age."

"That's what his doctor said. I tried to talk to him today about it, but he just shot it down. He says he's fine."

The man across the room was called up to the service counter. Fran's eyes followed him for no other reason than that it was easier than looking at Adam. She felt both relief and shame by being so honest with him. At least *he* was willing to listen to her.

"You mind if I talk to him?" Adam suggested.

"Well, I guess, I mean . . . thank you. That's—that's really nice of you to offer." She expelled another breath. "I'm just looking for some way to help him."

Adam accidentally touched her hand with his and then quickly withdrew it. He buried the offending appendage in his pocket. There was a flicker of apology in his eyes, but he didn't speak it. Instead, he said, "I'm no therapist, but I'm willing to help out if I can."

The service desk attendant called Fran's name. She gave Adam a fragile smile as she stood up. "Thanks."

Adam observed Fran for a moment as she walked away. Then he got up and headed for the door of the glass partition. He knew Jay had been watching them, even though he stared straight ahead at the TV and pretended he didn't see Adam headed his way.

It had started to snow, and the surrounding view through the windows gave the feeling of stepping into a snow globe.

"Hey," Adam said.

Jay looked up. "Hey."

"Nice view. Mind if I sit?"

Jay shrugged, his attention trained on the TV. "Suit yourself." As Adam settled next to him, he said, "You're the cop, right?"

"Yeah."

"What? You're here to give me a lecture?"

"Do you need one?"

"Nope."

"Didn't think so. Anyway, lectures never did me a ton of good when I was your age."

"Look, I'm not sure what my mom told you, but I don't need some kind of intervention."

"Well, she thinks you need something. She's concerned."

"I'm fine."

"You sure?"

"Yeah. Totally."

"Okay. I'd say that's pretty remarkable. I mean, if I'd survived what you've gone through, I don't know how put-together I'd be."

Jay shifted just slightly in his seat as his eyes moved away from the TV. "We're okay," he said blandly.

"I know. I know. You guys are very, very fortunate. I saw your mom's arm, but nobody was seriously hurt?"

The part of Jay's arm bandage that wrapped around his hand peeked out from his coat sleeve. Adam saw it. Jay moved his arm but couldn't hide the dressing. "Nobody was hurt bad," he said. "The doctors say I'll be okay. It's just a second-degree burn. That's what they said."

"Yeah, flesh wounds can heal pretty quick. Still, that had to be pretty scary."

"I wasn't scared."

"No?"

Jay didn't answer.

"Listen, being scared doesn't make you any less of a man."

There was another beat of quiet. Jay said, "I'm gonna miss my match," disgusted, almost as if he were talking to himself.

"You'll be in shape for it next year."

"You don't get it," Jay told him. "This win would've sealed the deal

for me. *I* was going to state. And now"—he raised his arm slightly—
"now this."

"You a wrestler?" Adam asked.

"Yeah."

"What class?"

"Middleweight."

"Me too, back in high school. I never made it to state, though. You
must be good."

"Yeah."

"Then you'll be just as good next year."

"No offense, but pep talks don't offer guarantees."

"Well, I got news for you, *life* doesn't offer guarantees. The only
thing we can do is our best—right now, in the moment—and be ready
when opportunity comes."

"You get yours?"

"My what?"

Jay ticked his chin toward Adam's cauliflower ear. "Your opportunity. I'm guessing you didn't get that ear on the mat in high school."

"Oh, this." Adam touched his deformity, common to wrestlers.
"Yeah, I suppose. But I wasn't too smart about it."

"Okay, you got me. What happened?"

"Partying. Drinking happened."

"You tried to go at it *drunk*? Not smart, dude."

"More like hungover, but still not smart. I wasn't the type to listen,
though. I started drinking when I was fourteen. At nineteen, I thought
I could hold my liquor enough to drink anywhere and often. Emphasis
on *often*."

"So, what? You got ousted because you were a drunk?"

"Sounds a lot harsher when you put it that—"

"How'd you wind up being a cop? And don't they have laws against
that or something?"

"Laws against what?"

"Alcoholic cops."

"I'm not an alcoholic."

"But you said—"

"I said I partied hard and it cost me. I never said I did time in A.A."

"Don't tell me. You woke up one day and decided to get clean. I saw that film in health class."

"No. Me getting clean was the judge's idea. And I liked that option better than jail."

Jay looked at Adam. "Okay, I know a setup when I hear one. So go ahead. What's the story?"

Adam took in Jay's quiet insolence. "Maybe I'll tell you one day when you're ready to hear it."

Jay screwed up his face. "What's that's supposed to mean?"

"You party a lot?"

Jay looked ahead at the TV. "Not often."

"Those guys you were hanging with that night, they were kinda an old crowd," Adam said. "Friends of yours?"

Jay shrugged again. "Just a party we were invited to."

"I see."

"You know, my friend's license is gonna get suspended. He wasn't even driving drunk or anything."

"He was behind the wheel of his car when we got there."

"But he wasn't *driving*."

"He would have. And he was drunk."

"You'd think cops would have better things to do than just pick on kids for partying."

Adam gave him a silent look before asking, "You ever see a dead body after a drunk driving accident?" Jay didn't answer. Adam went on. "Trust me, it ain't pretty."

"We may be young, but we're not *stupid*."

"I'm sure if you could ask any one of those boys in the morgue if they'd planned to do anything *stupid*, they all would've said the same thing."

"Everybody drinks," Jay retorted.

"Nothing wrong with drinking, but it's about being smart, being responsible. Like I said, I did my share of partying and hell-raisin' when I was a kid. Lotta memories of some real good times too. But you want to live long enough to make some new ones. Some adult memories. That won't happen if you and your buddies are out drinking and driving. Best-case, you don't die but you end up wasting years in a bottle because you started out hitting the juice at fifteen. Worst-case, you never see those years because you thought you were sober enough to get yourself home."

"Everybody does it," Jay said.

"Does that mean you have to?"

"Now you sound like my dad."

"Smart man, no doubt."

"I wouldn't know. He's not around much."

Fran appeared at the glass door. She hesitated as if she were reading the situation before approaching them. "Hey," she said to Jay, "How you holding up?"

"Bored." He slouched in the seat.

Adam passed a glance between the two. "You know, I should probably—"

"Hey, don't leave on my account," Jay interrupted. He stood.

Fran stopped him before he walked away. "It's going to take longer for them to fix the car."

"What? How much longer?"

"I don't know. There's a part on recall. They're trying to locate it."

"Well, can't you come back for it?"

"I'd rather just get this over with, Jay."

"Awwww, man. Mom. How 'bout I just go home then? Can't I just get an Uber or something?"

Adam signaled that he was leaving. His faint smile was brief. Fran pretended not to watch where he'd gone. *Oh, just to the counter.*

"Mom," Jay said, staring her down. "Uber?"

She huffed. "Fine, Jay. I'll call an Uber. You can go back to the hotel. I don't need you driving me nuts on top of everything else."

When Jay was gone, Adam and Fran got vending machine coffee in the TV waiting room and sat at one of the two bistro tables. He had not told her that his car was ready and paid for. Fran looked past him to the row of seats across the room. "It stopped snowing."

"I'm sure he'll make it back okay. It's not bad out."

She stirred her coffee and pulled at her turtleneck—an old habit she'd never shaken. "How'd it go?"

"With Jay? It went. He's angry. Disappointed. Unsure. Maybe even a little scared."

Fran focused on him to absorb every word. "What did he say? Did he tell you any of those things?"

"No."

"Then how do you know? How can you be sure?"

"Well, I could be wrong on some of it. But I don't think I'm too far off base. His injury killed his opportunity to play state. That's pretty major. He's lost just about every material thing that was important to him. And he's got real attitude issues. That includes his dad, it seems."

Fran placed her hand alongside her neck to control the compulsion to pull at her turtleneck. "It's been hard on the kids. James, he works a lot."

"I see."

"I don't mean to give a bad impression or anything. It's just that—"

"Hey, I'm sorry. You don't have to explain." Adam's cell phone rang. He pulled it from his pocket to check the number. "Work," he grumbled. He held up the wait-a-minute finger and took the call. It was a brief exchange. He hung up with a deep sigh. "I gotta go."

"Oh, I understand," she said, despite her disappointment that the visit was ending. What came next only heightened it.

"Look," Adam told her, "I know you're managing a lot right now. It can't be easy. But while you're taking care of everybody else, remember to take care of you. You don't have to feel guilty about that." He stood up. "This was nice."

"Yeah," she said.

He studied her face as if memorizing it. She didn't turn away.

Adam broke the silence. "Good luck to you and your family, Fran. If I can help in some way with Jay, or anything, you can call."

"Thank you," she said. "And yes, this was nice." She watched him walk away as a pang of sadness hit her.

He didn't look back.

17

The hotel manager approached James late one evening while he was waiting for the elevator. "Mr. Harrison. I've been trying to reach you for the past several days."

James gave him a furtive glance and then turned his attention back to the elevator. "I got your messages. I've just been extremely busy."

"Perhaps we can talk in my office, sir. This way."

He began walking without checking to see if James was following. After pausing a few seconds, James realized he had no choice.

In the manager's office, James was offered a seat so that he could face the prim gentleman with the gold-plated name tag.

"The charges for your family's stay have grown quite substantial," the man said. "As I understand the arrangement, you anticipated being here for the month, and would be retiring the debt at that time. Is that correct?"

"Yes, yes, it is."

"Well, sir, per that agreement, we have attempted to charge the credit card you offered upon registering. However, there seems to be a problem. The credit card has been declined. Have you another method of payment?"

"May I see the bill?" James asked.

The manager slid a sheet of paper to him. James picked it up and scanned the room charges. "I don't have another card available, presently," he said, "but I can write a check and—"

"We don't accept checks, sir."

"Fine." James cleared his throat. "Will you accept a partial cash payment?"

"Mr. Harrison, the terms of our agreement require that you settle your accrued debt at the end of thirty days. We have exceeded that date, given that I have had some difficulty reaching you by phone. The hotel has exercised good faith, sir."

James felt the muscles in his face constrict. Somewhere under the folds of the manager's eyelids rested a familiar impudence, though James had not seen it in a long, long time. The look—arrogant, impatient, contemptuous—was aimed at men with calloused hands, who fiddled with their caps as they cobbled together words, asking for more time to pay, more time to get money they knew would never come their way. These men, who wore bunion-split shoes, whose dignity got mangled by need and fear, had sons—like Jay—who sat and watched. James had been too young to fully comprehend the message behind "We've been patient with you" when the bank manager had said it to his father, but he had grown to understand the power of it, with its sharp, impending threat.

We've been patient with you. Those words brought the memories back. James had vowed that would never be in that position, yet there he was.

"I'll pay the amount due, as agreed," he said. "I'll have the cash for you tomorrow."

"Will you be leaving the hotel then, Mr. Harrison, or will you be requiring our accommodations further?"

Rising from his seat, James gathered his work satchel and straightened his coat. "I'll finalize our plans with my wife tomorrow. Thank you."

James did not go directly upstairs. Instead, he went to the hotel's bar, knowing he would sit there nursing a beer until last call. He was one of two patrons. He overheard the bartender ask the other man if he wanted another drink, and would he be paying by cash, card, or should he charge it to his room? James fished in his pockets in search of a few bills, but his hand grabbed something else in the inner pocket of his coat. He pulled out a bobblehead. He thought of the charity party. The plastic toy grinned at him maniacally. That made him laugh a little—or maybe it was the beer.

He sat the bobblehead on the bar top and watched it wobble. When it slowed down, he poked it into action again. He was recalling how much he hated those things. Always had. But they were good money. And cheap. That's what he had explained to Fran when he'd decided to get into that business. He remembered the glint of disappointment in her eyes.

He imagined telling Fran what the hotel manager had said. He took a hard swallow of his beer. She'd have so many questions. He poked the bobblehead and drank some more. How did things go so wrong? He found himself thinking about his father lately. More than he had in a long time, actually. They were boyhood memories. Part of him wished his father were still alive so he could simply say, "I get it now." Maybe even, "I'm sorry."

James remembered the day his father had said "No" to buying him ice cream. James had cried and cried and wouldn't stop, even when his father, wounded by feelings of ineptitude, confessed that he didn't have the money for it. It was the fear of becoming *him*, his old man, that led James to squander so much of what little he had left at this hotel, all for the sake of avoiding a confession he couldn't bear to make to his wife and children.

His mother's voice had been ringing in his memory too. She wore her misery spectacularly: "I'm blessed to have these hands to work. I have to, you know. My husband hasn't been quite right since his stroke. He tries. God bless him." Her self-anointed martyrdom simultaneously emasculated his father while elevating her among her friends at the church.

She even accepted the charity of others as her personal crown of thorns to be worn for the sake of her family. When his father first got sick, James would hear the whispered words and knew they were meant for them: *shame, pitiful.* He hated the broken, hand-me-down gifts he was forced to accept at the church's charity Christmas party for needy families. Worse still, he hated that his father was no longer the proud bricklayer. During the stretch of three painful years, his weakened left side cheated him of real work. He eventually gave up, as he was relegated to useless odds and ends to make pennies. Eventually, he shriveled inward with little to say. Most days, he spent his time whittling wood on their front porch.

In direct response, James grew defiantly ambitious. He had his first job at thirteen and kept at it until he went away to college. He had earned enough to put himself through school. When asked on his application to tell something about himself, he wrote, "I work hard and I don't accept handouts." It would be the manifesto he would teach his children.

When he went upstairs, the hotel suite was completely dark. He didn't turn on the lights for fear of waking his family. He blundered through the doorway of the master bedroom. Fran was up reading a new self-help book: *Ten Essentials to Right Your Wrong Path.* "Jeez, James. Are you drunk?"

He straightened up, closing the door behind him. He walked steadily. "No." He tossed aside his coat and satchel. "I had one beer."

"It's almost eleven o'clock. Where have you been?"

"Downstairs at the bar."

"Why on earth . . . what's wrong? What's happening?" She studied him as he slipped out of his tie and shirt. He sat on the bedside, head lowered in contemplation. "James, say something."

He cautiously looked at her, her face pinched with tension as she clutched her book. "We have to leave, Fran," he said softly.

"Leave? You mean the hotel?"

"Yes."

"Oh. All right. Did you hear back from the insurance company?"

"No."

"I don't understand. Then why are we leaving?"

"Because it's expensive to stay here. We owe them a lot of money."

"Can't we just put it on the card?"

He didn't answer.

She let out a dull sound like she'd discovered something pricking her skin.

James said, "We can pay them. I'll get the cash from the bank tomorrow."

"Then what? Another hotel? James, it's been over a month. You need to call the insurance company and see what the hold up is."

He took a deep breath and exhaled, slow and uneasy. "I have to tell you something."

She waited.

"It's . . . it's about the insurance. I'm sorry, Fran."

"For what?"

"Our policy." He paused again, turning his eyes downward. "It got cancelled."

The self-help book slid toward the floor as she tried to grab it. "Why? Why would they do that?" She looked assaulted, breathing open-mouthed. "James, *why?*"

"Because . . ." He hesitated. "Because I fell behind on the payments."

"Fell behind? How long? How many payments did you miss?"

"Three."

"Oh. James." Fixing on him, she said, "Do you have the money now? Can you make a payment now?"

"I tried that. They said no."

Tears ran down Fran's face. "What are we going to do? We don't have a home. Our kids don't have a home."

"Fran, I promise, I'll make this right for us. I'll fix this." He reached to touch her hand, and she moved it. "I know you're upset," he said.

She wiped her face. "My Lexus. Is what you told me about the insurance on my car a lie too?" He looked away. "I don't believe this! What else have you been keeping from me?"

"Fran, listen, I wanted to tell you what was happening."

"So why didn't you?"

"I don't know. I was afraid to. I didn't know how you'd react."

"Just how bad is it?"

He inhaled and the air shuddered in his throat before he spoke. "I've spent almost everything we have."

"You mean we don't have any savings left? What about paying the hotel? You said—"

"I have some money in the business account. Mostly payroll."

"James—"

"It'll be okay. I'll replace it."

"Oh, James."

"Look, I know it's a gamble, but we need money now. It's just a chance I'll have to take."

"How? How will you replace it?"

"I'll get another loan from the bank."

"What about the boat? Can't you sell the boat?"

"They repossessed it. Please, don't look at me like that."

"Oh, Lord," she whispered as she closed her eyes and more tears fell.

"I know I've hurt you, Fran. I know I've failed you. But I promise, I'm going to make everything okay."

"How? With what? Our money is gone. All of your inventory is gone. We don't have insurance to replace any of it."

He breathed in before he told her, "I don't know. But I'll figure it out. I always do."

After dropping James at the Metra station, Fran remained parked. It was the first time she'd been alone with her thoughts since James had told her about the insurance, about their money problems. All of it made her feel so dense and heavy. She was in shock, scared of what it all meant, angry at James. She felt confused. She needed . . . what?

She called her mother, who was now in Florida. Oma listened while Fran talked. Fran didn't divulge any details about the conversation she'd had with James. Instead, she talked about how she felt.

"It's all just so much, Mom," Fran said. "I know I have to be strong. I have to be there for my kids, my family. But it feels so overwhelming."

"I can't even imagine, Franny, how tough this must be for you. But try to focus on what's ahead. You'll be settled in your home again. You'll be fine."

"What if . . . what if there's too much damage?"

Oma took a moment. "What are you saying, dear?"

Fran hesitated, her mouth moving before she had the courage to speak the words. "I feel . . . betrayed, and I don't know what to do. And, no, I'm not talking about an affair or anything like that."

"Let me ask you something. Take a moment before you answer, if you need to. It's important to be honest."

Fran waited.

"Do you love James?"

"Yes."

"Are you sure he loves you?"

"Yes."

"Well, then," Oma said, "everything else can be managed."

"Mom, it's not that easy." Fran said, holding the phone in front of her.

"I didn't say it would be easy. I said problems can be managed. If you love your husband, and he loves you, it's worth the struggle to protect what you have. Love costs."

"I feel like I've already paid prices."

"And you'll keep paying them, as long as you're married and want to keep that bond strong."

"But what if I can't? What if I don't have it in me to keep it going?" Fran looked out the car's window, waiting for her mother to respond.

Oma contemplated Fran's question. "You know, I think everyone who's been married has probably said that at some point."

"Well, I guess that explains the divorce rate," Fran said wryly.

"I suppose, but here's what I decided way, way back, even before you were born. That question is like a fork in the road. You can choose an answer that can lead you either way. Stay married and work to build something better, if you two are willing to learn from the not-so-good times, or go your separate ways. Neither option holds any guarantees. That's not how life works."

"But how do I figure it out? How did you know what to do?"

"The figuring out part takes time, dear. And it's time worth taking because there are consequences to big decisions. I suppose for me it wasn't as complicated as it is for women in your generation. We didn't have so many options. And that's what made failing at it so devastating. Thank goodness your father and I weathered that storm before you were born, but for a while, we were both miserable."

"Wow. You were like the happiest married people I've ever known."

"Well, we were very happy—eventually, but three miscarriages can take its toll on a relationship. I remember being pregnant the last time, before you came, how we were so sure God had answered our prayers, *finally*, because I'd made it to my third trimester. We'd not gotten that far before. And, goodness, I'd never seen your father so, so happy. He would sing to my belly." Oma laughed. "I don't mean to embarrass you, dear."

"Not at all, Mom. It's just . . . wow. You've never said a lot about that part of your life with Dad."

"I suppose some things I didn't want to relive, once you came."

"Can I ask what happened?"

"She came too soon. Stillborn. I was in such a dark place after that. I was tired all the time. Didn't feel like eating. I was awful to your father, just awful. He was patient, at first. He even tried to convince me to get help, but I wouldn't. I wanted to punish myself."

"Oh, Mom, why?"

"I felt like it was my fault. Your father was good to me. He was so grateful we were finally going to have a family. And it happened again. I just knew I had to be the reason. Something I did that I shouldn't've. I pushed everybody away who tried to comfort me, tried to pray with me. It was really hard on your father. All of it. At some point, he just couldn't take it anymore. I saw the change in him. We wouldn't even speak to each other half the time. I knew if something didn't change, we'd end up living like strangers. So I had a choice to make. I could get help and learn to pray again. Be thankful for the good husband I'd been blessed with. Or I could one day drive my husband away for good. I knew I didn't want that. And I knew he still loved me, too, despite how we were behaving. I got help. *We* got better. We both needed some healing, and we found it together. That loss nearly broke us, Franny. But the thing is, we grew whole again like fitted pieces." Oma paused. "I don't think that would have happened if we hadn't suffered what we did. We wouldn't have become as strong."

Fran wiped away tears. "I would have never known."

"They say everything is about timing. Maybe now is the time for you to know. Maybe some of it will do you some good."

"Thank you, Mom."

18

Fran drove away missing her mother and thinking about their conversation. She thought of her dad too. "Daddy's little girl," that's what he'd say. And it was true. He was not a man of great means, but he was a man who loved his child with every pulsing beat of his heart. He had waited many years for the day he would have a child and hear the word "Daddy". Finally, there was Francis Ursula, named after her deceased grandmothers.

When he first saw his little girl behind the hospital nursery glass, he cried and mouthed the word "beautiful," mesmerized by the baby's wisps of blond hair from his wife's lineage and crystalline blue eyes that peeked at him through tight eyelids. It seemed his sense of awe and wonder never faded, because for the remainder of his years, he treated Fran like a rare gift to be adored and cherished.

He and Oma worshiped the Lord in gratitude for finally answering their prayers. They taught Fran the Christian way, too, not just taking her to church but explaining the Scripture to her, telling her of God's infinite love. Her parents seemed so assured of these things, Fran believed without question and had never been tested in her lifetime until her father fell sick. That was two years ago.

The news had hit her like a solid blow to her gut. Cancer. It ravaged her father with a spiteful vengeance. Oma, Fran, and everyone at church had gathered and prayed. Surely a merciful God would hear their tearful outcry. He would look down upon a good man whose long life had been ordered by God's word, a man whose capacity to love big had spilled into the lives of so many.

Fran was devastated and astonished that God had not heard, or rather, He had said no. Either way, she was angry. She felt the first fissures in what had been her absolute faith. The fault lines widened into canyons when she and James had to deal with Reba's response to their family's devastating loss. Their little girl wouldn't stop crying as she persisted in asking why Grandpa had to die. Fran didn't have answers.

She turned to self-help books, devouring them for herself, for her child. For months Reba had nightmares, and Fran left her own bed to cradle her child to sleep. And then a phone call from the school turned Fran's world on its head.

Mr. McFlurry, the pet hamster kept by the kids in Reba's class, died. When Reba saw the small animal unmoving in its cage, she screamed—piercing screams—her mouth stretched wide, horrified eyes fastened on the dead rodent, her little fists in knots by her stiffened body. Mrs. Langston, her teacher, couldn't quiet her. The woman tried shushing, talking, growing more fretful as the other children watched. The upset was growing contagious in the rainbow-colored room.

Mrs. Langston called for the nurse. The nurse contacted Fran, who rushed to the school. She was able to calm Reba down, but it took some doing. Fran called James. They spoke with the school nurse and the teacher in the rainbow classroom about the death in the Harrison family, a possible explanation for Reba's meltdown.

The nurse had suggested talking to their family doctor. "I won't claim this to be a true medical diagnosis," she said, "but it may be anxiety."

"Anxiety. She's *five*." James sounded agitated. "Reba's just going through a tough time. She loved her grandpa. We all did."

"James." Fran tried to calm him and the situation. She asked the nurse and Mrs. Langston, "What causes something like that in kids? What's the treatment for it?"

"Mrs. Harrison, your doctor should be the one to talk in detail with you about this," the nurse advised. "As for treatments, there is therap—"

"Hold on," James cut in. "My kid doesn't have some kind of *disorder*."

The nurse was taken aback. She glanced at Mrs. Langston, who also seemed surprised by James's tone.

Fran put her hand on his arm.

The nurse continued. "I was about to mention the option of therapy. There are some really great therapists out there who work with kids. I'm sure your doctor can make recommendations. He can suggest a range of therapeutic options once he has a diagnosis."

The conversations between Fran and James continued into the night, with James finally sounding less defensive.

"I think she's just taking the loss really hard." He was still resistant. "You know how she loves your parents. Anyway, let's not tie ourselves into knots with worry before we see Dr. Stevens tomorrow."

"James, should we tell the other kids?"

"Why don't we decide after we talk to the doctor, okay? This might just be some sort of episode that'll pass. And if it is, there's no need to say something that'll upset the other kids."

The doctor told them, "Reba's anxiety shouldn't be cause for great alarm. It's actually not uncommon. I do recommend therapy, someone to help talk her through this difficult period."

James asked, "Will this keep happening?" Worry and concern were etched on his face.

"I can't say it won't, but the possibility lessens with therapy."

"What can we do," Fran asked, "besides taking her to a therapist?"

"Be there for her," the doctor said. "Make sure she feels safe, secure about things. Reba doesn't need change of any kind right now."

Reba's visits to the therapist were quietly tucked into Fran's weekly routine. Whenever Fran brought up the subject of telling the other children, James would always say no. "It's better this way," he said. Once he added, "I wouldn't want anybody judging Reba."

That caught Fran off guard. "Her sister and brothers wouldn't *judge* her," she replied. "What would make you think that?"

James paused for only a moment before replying, "Nothing. My head is elsewhere. Sorry."

Fran found herself studying his face, wondering about his comment. It wasn't *nothing*. She didn't push it, though. James could be such a private man at times. But as much as it bothered Fran when he shut her out, she found herself absorbing his habit of "respecting the family's privacy," as he put it. It was easier than arguing over such things.

They never told the other kids. It wasn't long before Reba began sleeping peacefully through the night again.

19

Long before there was the worry of unpaid bills, long before the fire and desolation, there had been a time when nothing polluted the fullness of what James and Fran felt for each other.

Back then, James loved the smell of freshly carved wood. The glide and feel of the chisel against the soft and yielding pine. The curled shreds of wood falling onto his lap. He savored the thought of owning his own shop one day—a shop of handmade toys. Everybody loved his toys. He'd make them mainly as gifts. They'd tell him how beautifully crafted the pieces were, with such intricate detail. He never painted his carvings because he wanted to honor the beauty of the natural wood. Maybe a little tongue oil to finish off a piece, but that was it. Let the wood age naturally.

One day he made a pirouetting ballerina atop a small music jewelry box for Fran. He spent several months on the piece. It took a long time because he wanted everything just right. The first effort failed because he couldn't shape the angle of the ballerina's tilt just right. He threw away the second because the legs weren't quite proportional.

The third try, perfection: an elegant figurine, lithe, with one arm positioned above her head and the other curved inward with fingers touching the ripples of her tutu. She spun on the wafer-sized rotating platform. He slipped a second special gift he planned to give Fran inside the jewelry box. He carefully wrapped the present himself.

They went to the annual Holiday Magic Fair at the Lincoln Park Zoo. It was night, but lights were ablaze everywhere, reflecting on the dark lakeshore waters. White strings of them looped along the winding tree-lined walkways, where bends in the path provided benches for couples to enjoy hot cocoa and listen to the Christmas carolers. Whole families were there.

Fran walked alongside James with her arm looped in his. His hands were buried in his jeans pockets. In his excitement about the night, he'd forgotten his gloves.

"You want one of my mittens?" Fran asked, wriggling her fingers. They were covered in electric-red yarn. She smiled brightly under the matching red-knit cap pulled low enough to cover her brows.

"Your nose is the color of your hat," he laughed. "Keep them. You're cold."

"How 'bout we share? I keep one and you wear the other." She'd already taken off a mitten and was holding it out to him.

He stopped walking. "I love you," he said. It was definitive. It was resolute. It was as much a declaration to her as it was an affirmation to himself. She was the one. He had chosen well. No. God had chosen well for him.

"I love you too," she said.

Under the flickering, glittering lights and the full moon her eyes shimmered like rainwater. He touched her face as if he needed to know she was real, this moment between the two of them was real. She closed her eyes and moved just enough to kiss his gentle palm held against her cheek. In that moment, James felt as if he had swallowed the glowing moon, and it filled his chest with something so overwhelming, he felt the power of it running in warm streams down his cheeks. Fran reached up and smoothed his tears away with her mittened hand.

He took her hand in his. "Let's sit for a while." He led her to a nearby bench and when they sat, he pulled his gift from his pocket.

She lit up as bright as the Christmas tree behind her. "Oh, wow! I love presents!" She clapped her mittened and bare hands together.

He laughed. "Well, I hope you like this one."

"I have one for you too," she said. "I just thought we were doing the gift thing on Christmas Day."

"I didn't want to wait that long."

She unwrapped the box, and her wide eyes fastened on the little ballerina. She pulled her second mitten off with her teeth and handed it to James. She wanted to touch every delicate part. They seemed to be in motion. "Oh, James," she breathed. "Did you make this?"

"Yes. I've never made one of those before. I wanted it to be perfect for you."

"It's beautiful."

"It's a music box," he said.

She twisted a little key. Tinkling music started along with the slow twirl of the ballerina. And then out popped a small drawer. Buried in the little velvet cushion was a ring. When she looked up at James again, he was on one knee.

"This was my grandmother's wedding ring. My mom gave it to me and said one day I'd meet the right girl, the one I'd want to share my life with."

"Oh, James."

"Fran, marry me, and I'll spend my life trying to make you as happy as I feel every time I look at you."

When Jay was three, James inherited money from his grandfather. It was enough to make his dream of owning a business happen. But rather than merchandise his own creations, he opted for what he thought would bring in the most cash the fastest. He researched and found a manufacturer in China that could produce cheap little novelty toys for pennies on the dollar—the kind used as prizes at amusement parks, or the type that tumbled out of glass arcade machines equipped with flashing lights and a crane that purposely missed the cheap shiny trinkets kids spent quarters trying to attain.

Over time, he broadened his sales network and eventually

abandoned the small pop-up seasonal amusement parks he'd started with because they would sometimes cancel their orders when they were short on cash. James went after the bigger fish: conglomerates that owned themed indoor party spaces for kids, some equipped with carnival-style rides.

Somewhere during sales calls and pitches, calculating his money earned, the children coming one by one, he had all but forgotten what gave him joy—carving wood and creating toys that brought joy to others.

James was vacantly driving to the bank. He said nothing to the noise around him.

"Why can't we just go back to Oma's?" Reba whined from the back seat.

"Because we can't just squat there," Stacy sighed. "It's for old people, and the place has rules against that. Oma told us, don't you remember?"

Fran angled herself to look back at them. "It'll be okay, honey. We'll be someplace comfortable soon. Your dad just has a few more stops to make, okay?"

Reba groaned. "When are we getting our house back? You said not long, Dadd*yyy*. It's been, like, foreve*rrr*."

There was a stiff moment of silence while the kids waited for James to give them a more definitive answer. He drove on stoically. Fran repeated James's refrain whenever questions about their home came up. "We're working things out—"

Elliott cut her off. "Can we at least go to a restaurant or something?"

James glanced in his rearview mirror and saw his son's pleading face. And that's when James felt it, the beginning of the prickling just before true pain. "No." He fastened his eyes on the road again. He couldn't look at his son as he said these things. A sharp memory of his own father came back to him again. It was that afternoon in front of the ice cream shop. *Why can't I have ice cream?* The angry tears from a son too young to understand his father's pain in having to deny something so small.

"But why?" Elliott persisted. "We've been riding forever. Why can't we go someplace nice, just for a break?"

James couldn't answer his son. Fran caught on. "We'll all be able to stretch our legs when we get to where we'll be staying."

"Where's that?" Jay asked. "Hey, can I pick the hotel?"

"That's my and your father's job," Fran said. "Just hang on for a little while longer, okay, guys? I know this is tough on you, but it'll be over soon." She leaned back in her seat as she stole a glance at James.

He was aware of his wife, her inquisitive look. He was relieved to drive into the bank parking lot and announce, "I'll be back soon."

James took out cash from his business account. He pushed down the uneasiness in his gut that signaled the risks he was taking.

He returned to his family waiting in the car. He considered some of the nicer hotels but knew the money he had wouldn't last, and there was too much to do. He made a choice without consulting anyone. They drove to a motel that had a row of doors resembling storage units.

Jay asked, "How long do we have to stay here before the insurance people build us a new house?"

Fran forced a smile. "There's a Days Inn not far from here, I think."

James told his family without looking at them, "We won't be here long, guys."

They checked into a room: two double beds and a plaid let-out couch with dented cushions. There was a microwave, a mini fridge, and a small TV that had only local channels. Jay fiddled around with the TV remote, fixated on the repetitive loop of the same five stations. "Are you kidding me?" He looked to his father, who seemed oblivious.

James told Fran, "Why don't you take me to the train station so you can keep the car." He offered some money. "Here. We'll have to manage with food we can microwave."

"Can we order pizza?" Reba asked.

"We'll see, honey," Fran told her.

"Has this place even been exterminated?" Stacy eyed the small couch suspiciously.

Later, in the stillness of the night, James and Fran lay in bed. When she spoke, her volume was low but decisive, as if she were interjecting a thought into a conversation already in progress. "I'm going to start looking for work." She knew James wasn't asleep, so when he didn't answer, she turned to him, ready for him to once again push back on the idea. "You aren't going to say anything?"

He looked at her, his face partly hidden in shadows but still readable. "We have to do what's necessary."

That surprised her. She didn't have a ready reply.

"Are you up for it?" he asked. "I mean, are you well enough, Franny?"

She began in a faltering voice, "I . . . I'm okay. My back still hurts some, but I can go back to using the brace, if I need to. And the cast is coming off soon."

20

The bank called in James's business loans for nonpayment. The Harrisons were rationing their money to remain in the motel and to pay for James's Lexus, the cell phones, and food. Despite what had been an obvious death to the life they had known, James remained relentless in his conviction that he could turn things around, even when friends and business acquaintances (potential investors, as he called them) stopped responding to his calls. He looked for work but wouldn't consider anything less than executive-level management.

Fran's own efforts to find a job seemed pointless. With no work experience, she had little to market. No desk job wanted her. She thought about the designer boutique at the mall, but now she didn't have the wardrobe to work at an upscale shop. She could feel critical eyes assessing her, looking at her polyblend clothes that didn't seem to fit quite right. She didn't want to work nights at bars. Being a server at a restaurant wasn't an option with her bulky cast, and, if she was being honest with herself, she wasn't sure she could actually do the job, anyway.

Perhaps the clearest sign of the Harrisons' plight came from the children. Hockey and soccer were now costly luxuries that Jay and Elliott were denied. Stacy's money from her babysitting job was now spent on necessities, not luxuries.

One day, she was sitting on the side of the bed, pulling her savings out of a jam jar. Jay wandered by. "Hey," he said. "You knock over a liquor store or something?"

She gave a snorting chuckle. "Not that much cash in the kitty."

He went and collapsed on the bed across from her. Their confined living quarters had managed to loosen the grip of bad attitudes, rancor, and complaints. They eventually realized it was pointless.

"I need to buy myself some more boots. The seams on the ones Mom bought keep breaking open," she told him.

"Yeah, mine didn't hold up too well, either. Now I just wear my gym shoes with extra socks."

"You don't have boots?"

He sat up, shook his head. "Nah, but it's okay."

"*Okay?*" Stacy stopped counting to look at him. "Uh, have you checked outside? You see all that snow, dude?"

"Yeah, but I don't wanna tell Mom about the boot thing."

"I hear ya. She's totally stressing about money and stuff. One time I heard her crying, her back was hurting so bad."

"I heard her too. I didn't think it was her back, though, you know, that was making her cry."

Stacy looked at him.

Jay lowered his voice. "I wouldn't blame Mom for being tired. *I'm* tired of this." They were both quiet. Jay went on. "You think we'll ever get our house back? I mean, how long does it take insurance people to come through for you?"

"I don't know."

"What? You don't think it's gonna happen?"

Stacy shook her head. "I don't know. I don't know what to think anymore. Dad always gives the same ol' answer when we bring it up. Mom just repeats what he says."

"You don't believe 'em?"

Stacy purposefully shifted her attention to counting her money. "There's a boot sale on. Buy one, get one half off. I'm pretty sure I've got enough here for two."

"Must be nice." Jay slouched again on the bed.

"I'm talking about buying the other pair for you, numb nut."

He straightened himself. "Seriously?"

"Yeah, but don't get too excited. The boots on sale aren't like the cute ones I would've bought. But I guess ugly and warm beats pneumonia."

"So you'd really spend your money on me."

"Of course. One sneeze by you in this sardine can and everybody gets sick."

He brushed away her nonchalance with a wide grin.

"Now don't go looking at me like that," she said, but couldn't hold back her own smile.

Unfortunately, Stacy would eventually have to give up babysitting altogether because the drive to their old community was too far from the motel.

Worse still were the living, breathing reminders that came from the kids at school. The school buses had only picked up Jay, Stacy, and Elliott once, but that was enough. They were teased about living in a "rat motel." Jay got into a fistfight and would've been expelled had the principal not taken pity on him and his family. After that, Fran started driving all her kids to school until something could be figured out.

Elliott, small and frail, didn't fare as well as Jay. He was walking toward his locker when he saw three boys coming. A few other kids in the halls saw too. The boys—the Snow Leopards, as they called themselves—started rolling toward Elliott while the other students slammed their lockers and got out of the way. Elliott would have done the same, but when he turned from closing his door, the pack of Snow Leopards was behind him.

They were bigger, especially the leader, who stared down at him. The boy's eyes were the color of pale stones, pressed into a doughy face. With a quick jerk of his head, he whipped back his bleached bangs. Elliott backed up and knocked into the lockers. The boys standing behind the head Leopard laughed.

"You people got a shower in that rat motel?" the boy spat. "You stink."

"I need to get to lunch," Elliott said.

"The rat needs food." The lead boy spoke over his shoulder to his friends, who laughed.

Elliott tried walking away, but the boy pushed him back into the lockers. "You'll leave when I say you can."

Elliott looked past him to a few kids who hurried down the hall, purposely avoiding eye contact. "Hey. I just want to go before the bell rings."

"Got your lunch voucher, Rat? That *is* what the poor kids use for their free lunches, right?"

"I'm not poor." The words were low and shaky, but the boy heard.

"What?" He closed the space between himself and Elliott, who flattened farther against the lockers. "Well, you sure *look* poor, Rat! Where'd you get that shirt, anyway? Your old man dumpster dive for it?"

Elliott opened his mouth, but his heart was drumming in his throat.

"You got something to say?" the boy demanded.

The bell rang, and the hall monitor's booming voice bellowed, "Clear the halls, people! Or get written up for a tardy!"

The boy took a few easy steps back and fell in line with his friends. "See you soon, *Rat!*"

Even after they'd walked away, Elliott could feel the press of fear on his bladder. He rushed to the cafeteria. The lunchroom provided something that Elliott couldn't get routinely now—food that tasted like a home-cooked meal.

The cafeteria buzzed with talk as groups found their way to their respective islands: jocks at one table, the smart kids at another. There was also a table for the outcasts. Elliott stood with his tray in hand, not sure where he should land. He had tried going over to the table where his former teammates snorted and guffawed while exposing half-mauled food as they ate. He'd hung at the edge of the table and said, "Hey," waiting for somebody to scooch over and let him back into the fold. Some said, "Hey," but they never made room for him.

He wasn't one of them anymore. Everybody knew he'd become fresh prey for the Snow Leopards.

Elliott was walking over to the table of misfits when he felt the sharp ping of something hitting the back of his neck. He jerked at its impact and dropped his lunch tray. The Snow Leopards were hurling pennies at him.

"Hey, Rat!" the lead boy shouted. "Here's some change so you and your old man won't have to beg in the street!"

Snickering from other kids broke out around him. Mrs. Fleming, the English teacher, seemed to appear out of nowhere, her kitten heels loudly clacking on the floor. She shut down the Snow Leopards and told them to report to the Disciplinary Office. She walked over to Elliott, who was looking down at splattered mashed potatoes and the offending pennies on the grown. He was unsure what to do next.

"Elliott," she said with her hand on his shoulder, "I'll get some help to clean this up. Why don't you get another tray?"

He couldn't bring himself to look at her. He simply nodded. Later, when his mother asked him how his day was, he just shrugged. He didn't speak of the Snow Leopards, the lunch, or the pennies. As a matter of fact, he didn't say anything at all for the rest of the evening. He waited until the quiet of the night to cry into his pillow.

As the weeks rolled on and the snow began to melt, so did the shock of the fire. Eventually, they realized this was their new normal. The small motel room. Rationing to keep this shelter. Modest meals.

Reba would whine, "When are we gonna get our house back?"

And Fran and James would take turns answering, "Soon, honey," aware that the other kids were listening, waiting.

There was no expectation of a magical insurance check to right things. In time, even Reba stopped asking.

Desperate conversations were whispered in the bed that Fran shared with James.

"The motel management came by while you were gone," she said.

"They want to know when we'll make up for last week's payment. They said we can't keep running behind."

"I'll stop by their office tomorrow," James assured her.

"Do we have the money to pay them?"

"I'll talk to them."

"Maybe we should find another place."

"Fran, honey, we won't find any place cheaper, or at least not the kind of motels we should have our kids around. I'll talk to them."

"But the man seemed . . . angry. It's the third time."

"I said I'll talk to them, all right?"

"James?"

"Yeah?"

"What about getting a job?"

"I've been looking."

"I know you have. But you've been after management jobs, right? Look, I know you've really got your heart set on starting up your business again. I just mean, maybe you should think about something more temporary. Until things—"

"Fran."

"Yeah?"

"I'm trying, okay? I just didn't think finding a job would be hard. I mean, I've run my own company for Christ's sake. I should've taken that job Pastor Phillips offered me."

"What job? When?"

"It was a while back. I met with him and Charlotte when we were staying at the other hotel. They told me about this job at The Children's Hospital."

Fran propped herself up on her elbow, trying to pierce the dark to see his face. "You didn't tell me."

"It was a job with the maintenance department. I just couldn't, Fran—"

"You should call them. See if that job is still available."

"It's not."

"How do you know if you don't call?"

"I *did* call."

"Oh," Fran said softly.

"That was the worst part. Going back and asking for the job I said wasn't good enough for me. And now, here I am disappointed because they told me they'd filled the position."

"Well, maybe they have something else available."

"I asked, Fran. They said they'd let me know if anything came up."

She lay back down in his arms.

"Sometimes," James began slowly, "sometimes I feel like God has got His foot on my neck."

"Why would you say that?"

"Because everything has gone *wrong*, Fran. Everything I've tried has . . . failed."

"That's not true. We're here. We survived. Our kids survived. And things will turn around for you. You'll get your break. *We'll* get our break."

"How can you be so sure?"

"Because it has to get better."

James and Fran held on to each other in the dark, each with their own thoughts.

21

The children held on to each other, too, even though they weren't as aware of it. Fran saw it. She asked Stacy about her friends—Heather Whitaker and others—the ones she used to always talk about, hang out with. "Why don't you go out with them, honey? Have some fun."

Stacy only looked up at her from the tattered motel couch. "You kidding, Mom? Go out with *what?*"

Jay's response to his own query from Fran was a simple, "I'm cool."

Fran understood. Once, when she was coming out of a buy-for-less grocery store, she saw one of her own friends across the street, twice-as-rich Madeline clicking along in her Gucci heels. Coffee dates with her and the others had ended when conversations about the Harrisons' old house became awkward. Fran ducked back into the store, afraid of being noticed. She thought of that moment often.

More and more, the kids turned to each other. Reba wanted to try one of the board games James had bought for Christmas. Jay said it was stupid, but he was the first to get the box and start setting up the board. Stacy read the instructions. Before long, they were fumbling their way through their turns, laughing and getting loud, scheming to land on Park Place and Boardwalk. They even drew their mother into the game.

They didn't consider watching TV the next evening. They played the game again. There was more magic from a thirteen-dollar box than Fran could've hoped for.

Days passed. The kids didn't talk about what went on at school. Instead, they came together in the common distraction of the games. That is, until Elliott came home with a black eye. Horrified, Fran begged him to tell her what happened. He kept repeating, "Nothing. I fell."

That evening after homework, they claimed their usual game pieces. Elliott was the wheelbarrow, Jay the race car, Stacy the top hat, and Reba the cat. They waited until Fran left to pick up James from the train station before mentioning Elliott's black eye again. As they knelt and sat on the floor around the game board, Jay was the first to speak about it. "Dude, what happened? And don't give me some lame excuse like you ran into a door."

Elliott picked up the dice. "Nothing."

"Don't give us that," Stacy said. She snatched the dice from him. "We're not Mom."

Elliott kept his unswollen eye latched on the game board.

Reba said, "Tell us. You don't have to be sad."

Maybe it was the care coming through in his little sister's soft voice. He couldn't hold it in anymore. Silent tears streamed down his face and splattered on the B&O Railroad.

"Tell us," Stacy insisted. "Who did this?"

The words caught in Elliott's throat. "Some jerks at school. They like making fun of me because . . . because we don't have money now. This douchebag pushed me into my locker. I got tired of it, so I pushed him back. That's when this happened." He gestured to his eye.

"Son of a—" Jay cut a look to Reba and stopped himself.

"You should tell your teacher," Reba said.

"Yeah," Stacy agreed. "Report that guy, and as lame as it seems, you should tell Mom and Dad."

Elliott shook his head. "He's got friends. It'll just make it worse."

"Well, you've got friends too," Jay said.

"No," Elliott said. "I used to. But I'm by myself now." He tried to wipe his tears away.

"You're not by yourself," Jay said. "You have us."

"Thanks, but that doesn't do me much good at school."

They fell silent. It was true that Jay and Stacy had it a little easier. They attended the same high school. And lately, they would find each other on campus just to hang out at lunch.

"Then go to somebody you can talk to at school," Stacy said. "Grown-ups are supposed to protect you from that crap."

Elliott went to sleep that night thinking about what his siblings had said. Instead of going to lunch the next day, he went to Mrs. Fleming's class. She was busily scribbling notes on papers in the empty room. She looked over her glasses at Elliott as he quietly eased his way through the door.

"Can I talk to you, Mrs. Fleming?"

"Of course, Elliott. But shouldn't you be at lunch?"

"I'd rather talk," he said.

"Come. Sit."

He took a front-row seat.

"What's on your mind, Elliott?"

He touched his eye, partly because she was looking at it and partly because he suddenly felt embarrassed. "I'm being bullied," he said quietly, looking down at the floor and not Mrs. Fleming. "I just don't know what to do about it."

"This is an important step," Mrs. Fleming told him. "Just being willing to talk about it. How long has this been going on?"

"Over a month."

"Is it the same boys each time?"

He nodded, still not looking up at her.

"It's going to be okay, Elliott. The school has a zero-tolerance policy for bullying, but you'll need to make a formal complaint. Give names. You'll probably want to talk to your parents about this."

"I don't want to do that."

"What? Give names?"

"Yeah, and tell my parents."

"Why not?

"Just 'cause."

There was a pause.

"Listen, you don't need to tell your parents in order to make a complaint. But you should tell them. I'm sure they'd want to know. They'd want to support you. But as for giving the names of the boys who are responsible, you don't have a choice if you want to make a complaint. If you'd like, I can be there with you."

"Yeah. Yeah, I'd like that." He finally looked up at her.

"Elliott," Mrs. Fleming said, "everything will be okay, even if things are tough right now. And sometimes, believe it or not, good can come out of things that aren't so great. Come here. I want you to see something."

He went to stand in front of her desk. She pulled his work from her graded pile. It was a poem he'd written. "This is impressive work, Elliott."

He shrugged. "I just wrote what came into my head."

"You wrote what was in your heart. That's what makes this such a moving piece. Here. I want to give you something." She pulled out a leather journal. "I bought this when I was on vacation last month. I think this was probably meant for you." She handed it to him.

He ran his hand over the embossed leather. "Thanks, Mrs. Fleming. But what am I supposed to do with it?"

"Write," she said.

"Write *what*?"

"Whatever your heart tells you to. This isn't homework, Elliott. You don't ever have to share your journal with me or anyone else. It's just for you."

Later, he wrote about the shame that kept him from telling his parents about being bullied. He wrote about feeling gleeful when the Snow Leopards were made to give an open admission and apology for their behavior before being expelled. He wrote a poem about uncertainty and how it felt like sand giving way under your feet.

Greenery sprouted in defiance of the cold, wet air. Winter was ending, and it was now warm enough for the motel manager to feel he could demand the Harrisons pay the money that was still due or leave. To keep his SUV, James had been parceling out smaller payments for the motel room and getting further behind in the rent. But his promises were no longer accepted. The Harrisons had to go.

They were silent as they drove away from the motel. All their possessions were in the trunk, packed in grocery bags. Reba insisted on holding the bear she had been given by her dad on Christmas. She sat beside Stacy in the center row behind their parents. In the third row, Elliott was writing intently in his journal next to Jay, who leaned close to his little brother to see.

"What you writing? School stuff? Jay asked.

Elliott held the journal to his chest. "Nope."

"What then?" Jay persisted.

"It's a journal," Elliott answered in a near whisper.

"A what?"

"A journal," Elliot repeated. "A book you write stuff in. Mrs. Fleming gave it to me."

Jay paused thoughtfully. "What kinda stuff do you write?"

"How I feel, mostly."

"Can I read it?" Jay asked.

"It's kinda private." Elliott lowered his eyes.

After another pause, Jay asked, "Do you write about us? Our family?"

Elliott glimpsed his parents in the front seat. He nodded.

Jay lowered his voice even more. "Do you write about this? Us being homeless?"

Elliott looked at him. Jay had said the unspeakable that Elliott had refused to entertain, even with all the mean jokes at school. And as if

James had heard the last of the whispered conversation in the rear, he said, "I don't want anybody to worry, okay? We'll find another place soon. We'll be settled in no time."

Fran offered him a thin smile.

They found a modest place that looked worn enough that it would be an outright dump in a few years. The flashing sign out front read "Mote" because the "L" was no longer lit.

"We're staying here?" Stacy asked, clearly dubious.

Fran said, "It's just for the night, honey. It's late. We have to sleep somewhere."

The fact was, after some searching, James and Fran were faced with the harsh reality that they couldn't afford better. James parked the car in the motel's lot and went in.

The inside was even shabbier, with old carpet that looked like Technicolor vomit. The low popcorn ceilings offered little light, but James could still see the fine spray of cobwebs in the corners.

He asked the man at the counter, "Do you have rooms available? I'll need the largest you have. There're six of us. My wife and four kids."

The man answered, "Yeah. I've got a room. The best I can do for you is two double beds."

"That's fine." James pulled his wallet from his back pocket and put money on the counter.

"It's extra for the room with the double," the man said.

"How much extra?"

"Twenty-five dollars."

James paused for a second and pulled out his wallet again, letting his thumb graze the dollar bills.

"We don't got cable for kids or nothing like that," the man said.

James didn't reply. He placed the additional money on the counter and was handed a key attached to a piece of cardboard the size of a man's palm. On it was the number six, written in black marker.

The Harrisons pushed open the door to Room Six, and the smell of warm beer with hints of urine and Lysol wafted over them. James flicked on a light that weakly illuminated the space where there was the same orange-speckled carpet he'd seen in the small lobby. The two narrow beds were the size of cots and had thin gray blankets rolled at the foot.

"Eeeew," Stacy said, "those sheets look *gross!*"

With a half-sneer, Jay said, "Really, Dad?"

Fran put her arms around Elliot and Reba, who squeezed herself closer to her mom. "James," Fran said, "we can't."

And so they didn't. James collected his money from the manager, and back into the SUV they went. James focused on the steering wheel.

"Does that mean we can't go to a hotel?" Reba asked from the seat behind him.

"We'll find a place, honey," Fran assured her.

"Please, no place gross," Stacy demanded.

Elliott said, "I'm just tired of riding around."

Jay told them, "I'm with Stacy on this one. I can't do gross."

They drove with no luck in finding an affordable place where they wouldn't need antiseptics. It was a busy Friday evening for motels, it seemed.

Finally, despite the reality of their budget, James gave into the tired whining of his children, who were desperate for a shower and a bed.

They rented a large suite at a real hotel that gobbled a chunk of James's remaining money. He didn't mention it, though. What he did say was, "This is just for one night so we can all get a good night's sleep." Fran kissed him on the cheek at the sight of her happy kids spinning in circles to take in the glorious space and playfully rough-housing on the bed.

The night went by like a dream. And the next day they were piled back in the car. The search for a new temporary home was derailed by a trip to Waffle Craze, a breakfast joint that had an all-you-can-eat buffet on weekend mornings. They piled their plates with shameless towers of pancakes.

If it weren't for a few truck drivers and Friday-night partiers getting a waffles-and-black coffee start to their morning, you'd think the Harrisons were back at their own kitchen table. Except this was different. The kids were giddy and enjoyed their playful nudging and the stealing of sausage links off each other's plates.

"I wish we could live here, Daddy," Reba said, looking around at the plastic red-and-white-checked tablecloths and matching curtains.

The rest laughed affectionately.

"Why?" Stacy asked.

"Because it smells like a real home," she said.

Back in the car, night seemed to rush in on wings. Before anybody knew it, they were driving around in the dark. The car was running out of gas. Everyone was running out of patience. That's when Reba said, "Why can't we just go back to the waffle place?"

Fran said, "But they aren't open, honey."

"But they will be," Reba reasoned.

It seemed like a crazy idea, but only for a moment. The boys had already fallen asleep in the rear of the SUV. Parking in the small lot of the restaurant would be safe. James went back to Waffle Craze and told Fran and the girls, "This is just for the night, okay?"

And he watched his family fall asleep, looking over them until his own tiredness lulled him into dreams.

They were the first inside when the restaurant opened. They stuffed themselves with pancakes and eggs under the scrutinizing eye of the server who opened the joint at seven every morning. She had noticed the car in the lot when she'd arrived.

It was so easy. One night turned into a weekend of squatting in the restaurant's parking lot. After a hearty breakfast on the cheap, they could discreetly use the facilities and be on their way.

It was a beautiful Sunday. The bright sun was met by the sound of early morning birds chirping. The last vestiges of winter's frost melted away. The whole family felt it, it seemed, looking up at the achingly clear blue sky that made their eyes water. There was no place any of them needed to rush off to.

Fran made a statement that sounded more like a surprised declaration. "Let's *do* something."

"Yeah, let's!" Reba joined in.

"You up for it, Franny?" James asked. She had complained about stiffness in her back from sleeping in the car.

"Yup." She smiled. "I'm good. And if I need to, I can always sit for a minute."

"Hmmm," James said, as if trying on the idea of a fun day for size. "What did you have in mind?"

"I don't know," Fran said, "but there's plenty to do that's cheap." She leaned over, whispering the last word to James as if budgeting was a secret. As they drove along, Fran watched the cyclists and joggers, couples and young families, even old people toddling along, all of them out taking in the crisp air and vibrant sun. This was beyond good; it was delicious. For the first time during what felt like an unraveling spool of misfortune, Fran felt the frothy sweetness of joy. She leaned back and let down the window so the spring air could wash over her face and play with loose strands of her hair.

They wandered through the city, enjoying the adventure. They fed the geese at Lincoln Park, James and Fran holding hands. The iridescent blue water along Lake Shore Drive lapped lazily against the boulders just beyond the bike path. There was a puppet show at the Lincoln Park Library. Reba loved it. They walked through the conservatory with beautiful flowers already in bloom. They went to Wrigley Field, and even if they couldn't get in to actually see the White Sox play, they stood for a while and listened to the cheers. They walked through the National Museum of Mexican Art, admiring the elaborate textiles, the shockingly bold canvases of abstract paintings. Stacy, sounding breathless at the pleasure, said, "So flippin' beautiful." They even crashed a yoga session in the park. The boys wanted to go roller skating, but James reminded him that they couldn't afford it right now. Unfazed, Elliott joined a small group to watch street poets throwing down free verse. He was enthralled. When the young men took a break from performing, they handed out flyers for an open mic poetry slam. One guy had observed Elliott's enrapt interest. He handed him a flyer.

"You should have your pops bring you," he said.

Jay leaned in to read the flyer. "You wanna check that out?" he asked.

Elliott looked up at his big brother incredulously.

"No joke," Jay said.

The family was peeling away from the crowd and falling into a lazy stroll. "I mean it," Jay continued.

"You'd take me?"

Jay shrugged. "Why not? You really seemed into it back there. And, I don't know, maybe it'll help with the stuff you like writing about."

Jay was looking straight ahead as they sauntered along, but Elliott was full-on grinning at him.

After a quiet moment, Elliott's smile faded. "Jay, are we homeless?"

"Why'd you say something like that?"

"Well, that's what you said. When we were driving. You called us homeless."

"Oh." He lifted his eyebrows. "I meant, uh, I really didn't mean we were, like, *homeless*."

"Then how did you mean it?"

"Well, homeless people sleep in the streets and stuff. We're just trying to figure it out, you know. We're kinda like campers. Just chillin' until our next move."

"So, homeless people don't sleep in their cars?"

Jay shot a look to Stacy, who was walking behind them, holding Reba's hand. He wished for some help with Elliott's question but didn't know how to ask for it any more than he knew how to satisfy his kid brother's demand for answers.

"Well, uh," Jay floundered, "I guess some homeless people sleep in their cars."

"So what's the difference between us and them?"

Jay stopped walking, tilting his head slightly before looking at him. "The difference is we're a family. And that's what home is. Belonging to each other. It's not about where you sleep."

Elliott nodded. "I get it." He sighed with relief.

22

That night, as the sounds of their sleeping children rose and fell from the seats behind them, Fran and James sat awake, looking up at the night sky through the open sunroof. The stars were out. The breeze was chilly enough for them to share a light blanket.

"Good sleeping weather," James whispered to Fran.

"I can't sleep, but it is a beautiful night."

He turned to her. "Why can't you sleep?" He glanced at the family photo album in her lap, the one that had been saved from the fire.

She met his eyes. "Because I don't want the day to end. It was perfect."

He smiled. "Yeah, it was."

Fran sighed. "It felt like . . . it felt like things were normal again."

James fumbled beneath the blanket to find her hand.

"I'd forgotten what that was like," she continued, a tinge of sadness and amazement in her voice. She opened the photo album. "Remember this trip, James?" She ran her finger along the edges of a picture. James was sitting with the kids, who were young enough to have missing teeth and pigtails, laughing around an evening campfire with golden embers, their toasted marshmallows suspended over the flames.

"Yeah," he said. "I remember. We used to go camping a lot back then. We couldn't afford real vacations."

She said to him, "Those camping trips were the most fun."

"We'll get there again," he told her.

"I hope so." She was quiet and reflective. "I wonder how our kids are doing."

"They're weathering it."

"They shouldn't have to."

"I know, but right now we don't have much of a choice."

"You know, I want to talk to them. Have an honest, open talk about how they're feeling, but . . . I'm afraid to. There are so many moments that feel like a live wire, or like I'm about to explode." She removed the picture from the photo album. "But today was rare. A gift. We all got to exhale, just be *us*, you know? Be a family." She folded the picture and slipped it into her wallet to always have it with her.

"Fran?"

"Yeah?"

"Can I ask you something?"

She met his eyes.

"What are you afraid of?"

Fran glanced into the rearview mirror to see their kids snuggled underneath shared blankets. She remembered asking Stacy and Jay about their friends, how embarrassed the two felt about things. She remembered when the kids' questions about the house stopped one day, and she wondered then what they were thinking. She never asked them because she had no answers for them.

She didn't answer James.

The weekend ended with questions about Monday morning. James vowed to find a place for them to stay that day, and as it turned out, he would have to. When he was paying for breakfast, the server, a middle-aged woman with tired eyes, took his money and said quietly, "Listen, I don't want you to get in no trouble, but you can't live in the parking lot." Her eyes shifted as if she'd stolen something from him.

James took in a small, sharp breath. The words were equally as-saulting and alarming. He fumbled for a response. "We aren't—"

"Look. I saw you, your wife, your kids sleeping in that big car you got. I'm just trying to help. If the manager finds out, he'll call the cops for sure."

James nodded and stepped back as the woman fiddled with something behind the counter to avoid looking at him any longer.

Fran walked up behind him. "The kids are ready. You pay the check?" She saw the look on his face. "Hey, you okay?"

"Yeah, fine," he said. "Let's go."

He drove in silence, feeling like he'd swallowed a chunk of ice that had gotten stuck in his chest. And the ice refused to melt. He didn't speak until they had made the final trip to drop the kids off at school. Once they waved goodbye to Reba and Elliott, Fran turned to James. "What? What happened?"

"Nothing," he said, driving away from the school.

"*Something* happened, James, or you wouldn't be acting like this."

"No need to worry, honey. I'm just thinking things through." Just the idea of being caught by the police with his kids sleeping in their vehicle frightened him to his core. But he knew they couldn't afford living in a motel—*any* motel—on the money they had left. Worse still was the cost of his car. He had now fallen irrevocably behind in his payments.

He refused to talk to Fran and the kids about how desperate their money situation was. He didn't want to scare them. Instead, he told them that evening at a pizza restaurant, "We have to be smart about how we spend our money. In the meantime, we'll just hang out and then decide what's our best option. But listen, guys, you can't tell anyone about this. Not your best friends. Not your favorite teachers. I mean *nobody*, okay?"

Stacy and Jay nodded quietly. Elliott only stared, wide-eyed. It was Reba who piped up. "Why not?"

Startled, and with no good response to offer, Fran said, "Well, honey, it's just best, okay?"

"Why? Why is it best?" Reba was looking to her father.

"You're gonna have to trust Daddy, okay? If somebody found out, they could—"

"Take us," Jay interrupted.

Reba's gasp was audible. "What do you mean, take—"

"Nobody's going to take you, baby," Fran interjected, reaching to touch Reba's little cheek.

"Jay," Stacy sighed through her teeth.

Reba was on the brink of tears. James hugged her and kissed the top of her head. "Don't cry, honey."

"This is gonna be hard, Dad," Stacy said. "Like, for how long? How long are we supposed to keep this secret?"

"Your mom and I have talked this through. I'll keep looking for work. I'm sure I'll be able to find something soon, and then we can get settled again."

Fran wore a tense smile even though she felt like she'd heard the ground crack under them. She couldn't turn from the round, unblinking eyes of her kids. Even if James ignored it, she felt her own footing slip. But there was no readjusting to halt the downward slide. The only thing she could do was hold on to the nearest thing to steady herself. She reached over and grasped James's hand.

Fran's conversations with Oma in Florida thinned out. The rare, short phone calls only intensified Oma's vigilant prayers.

That night they started to sleep in a Walmart parking lot. They made a game of looking at the people who shopped late at night. This lasted until spring rain showers were in full swing. They probably would've kept it going, but a few cars had been broken into, and management decided to hire a security patrol to ease the nervousness of their customers. James couldn't risk being caught with his family sleeping in their car. It was time to find another spot.

"I know!" Reba said. "We can sleep at the zoo! I love the zoo!"

"Eeew! Stinky!" Stacy crinkled her nose.

"It has to be some place safe, James," Fran said.

"What about the park?" Elliott suggested.

"Nah," Jay responded, "the cops roll through there on the regular. Hey, what about a truck stop? That's what truckers do. Go there to get some sleep, eat. I bet they even have a place for them to shower."

Jay was right. James found a truck stop that didn't charge. There was a little lounge area with a TV. James told the kids to be careful, though, and not use the lounge too often, just in case someone noticed their regularity. There was a restaurant there and even a small laundry room to clean their clothes. It even allowed James to relax a bit about his SUV being spotted by some repo service.

Despite school marking the days of the week, time became a slippery thing. Stacy couldn't fix it in her mind. Memories of their old house, shopping, and parties slipped and slid into these days of wash-and-wear clothes that were often wrinkled and smelled of dollar-store lotion and cheap buffet meals.

Stacy walked across the campus lawn headed to the library building for the mandatory study time her parents imposed on her and Jay after Stacy had to fess up to the D grade she'd received on an economics test. While econ was never her strongest subject, Stacy had never gotten a D in anything.

"I can't study here," she'd told her parents apologetically because she understood how they'd take the comment. She was right.

James and Fran looked bruised. In response, Fran said, "We'll have to make some adjustments. We need to have library time in the schedule."

James agreed it was a good idea and underscored Fran's suggestion by saying, "We want the best for you guys."

Stacy and Jay thought it was easiest to just stay after school for their study time. James okayed it, not mentioning his thoughts about any extra gas costs with additional travel.

So, Stacy was headed for the library. The spring air was punctuated by the peals of laughter in the distance. Pom-pom girls in mustard-and-grape sports jerseys were running along in packs of two and three.

Then another sound caught Stacy's attention. More laughter from a voice she recognized. She looked around for the source. Heather Whitaker and Porsha, Vivian, and Jazelle—Stacy's besties—were rounding the corner from the library building. Heather was pointing toward the street and screaming with game show hysteria, "OMG, Chase! That is totally *awesome!*" The other girls bounced like happy beans.

Stacy followed their attention and saw her boyfriend Chase drive up in his moped, the one he'd said he wanted for Christmas a long time ago, or at least it seemed so long ago. She watched the girls rush him when he swerved to park curbside. They were giggly with excitement, their shrill voices tangling like thin, hot wires.

"You totally have to give me a ride!" Heather demanded happily.

"First time out with it. My dad said I couldn't drive it 'til spring."

"How fast can this thing go?" Porsha asked.

"Soooo cool." Jazelle ran her fingers along the paint job.

"I wonder if I can convince my folks to buy one for me," Heather pondered

"They just bought you a *car*, Heather!"

"Well, yeah, but it's not a *moped*. Maybe I can pitch it as a graduation gift or something."

"Graduation isn't 'til next year!" Vivian reminded her.

"Maybe an *early* graduation present then! Come on, Chase! Let's go!" Heather climbed onto the seat behind him before he could respond.

Chase turned and saw Stacy watching them. He lifted his hand as he called out, "Stace!"

She trotted toward the library and she didn't stop moving until she'd taken the stairs to the second floor. She found a table by the large windows overlooking the street. She could still see Heather and the group—the way Heather flipped her windswept hair, how she and her friends talked with teeth showing, touching the moped, touching Chase, it was as if Stacy could still hear their voices and laughter.

Since the fire, conversations with Heather had become rarer and rarer. The truth was it was Stacy's fault. Heather had made one last effort, in the new year, coming up to Stacy just as she'd slammed her school locker closed.

Heather offered a tentative, "Hey."

"Hey." Stacy felt a little sheepish because she had been avoiding her friend.

"Listen," Heather said, "me and Porsha and Viv are going to hang out at the mall on Saturday, maybe do some shopping. Okay, *definitely* do some shopping." She laughed. Stacy returned a frail smile. Awkward silence tried choking the moment. Heather said abruptly, "So I was thinking maybe you'd want to come too."

Stacy *did* want to go, except she no longer had the credit card her parents had given her. She'd heard the fight they'd had about her mom getting a job. She couldn't ask her parents for money, that much she was sure of. She thought of her savings from babysitting, and then considered the price tags of the stores Heather haunted. The cost of one pair of jeans would wipe out all Stacy had.

She paused just long enough to notice Heather checking out her outfit, not in a mean-girl way, but with something akin to disbelief and confusion. Shrinking inwardly, Stacy pulled on the hem of her rayon-blend sweater that had been washed only once and had already lost some of its shape.

"I'll think about it," she had said, already moving away from Heather. She never followed up with her, and Heather didn't ask again.

Stacy thought it best to keep her distance.

She pulled books from her bag, occasionally stealing glances out the library window. Heather was snuggled up tight against Chase's back, arms wrapped around him as he pitched himself forward to thrust his moped into gear. The other girls jittered with excitement and seemed to be cheering them on.

Stacy thought of the few times he'd driven her back to the high-rise hotel with the top hat doorman. The words of the textbook pages became a watery blur. A tear dripped onto the words. She quickly smoothed it away. After her family had had to leave the nice hotel, she couldn't stand the thought of Chase seeing the new place, so run-down in contrast. She began pulling away from him too. There had been times when she'd almost dialed his number. But then they couldn't even afford the motel, and she didn't want Chase to find out her family's secret.

She looked out the window. The moped was back, but no Chase. When she heard his voice, for a moment she wondered if she'd imagined it, but then there he was.

"Hey." He flopped down on the seat across from her. "You see me out there?"

They both knew she had. She understood his question to mean, "Why'd you run off?"

Instead of answering, she said, "Nice moped."

"Oh, yeah." He emphasized the word *yeah*, nodding and grinning. He ran his fingers through his shoulder-length blond hair. The late afternoon sunlight coming in through the window caused him to squint. He seemed almost blended with the brightness of the day. The blue skies, his shirt, and eyes were all the same color. The glaring sun washed out the contours of his once-broken nose. Stacy liked his crooked nose. She realized she was smiling.

"What?" Chase asked, grinning back.

"Nothing. Your nose."

He ran his finger along the slant of his bridge. "You're still the only one who's ever called it cute."

She shrugged, still smiling.

He leaned in, his elbows on the table between them. "Hey."

"What?"

"Let's go for a ride on my moped."

"Didn't flex enough with Heather?" Stacy tried to deliver the question as a joke, but a tinge of something else came through.

Chase leaned back with a smirk.

"And what's that look for?" She sounded more defensive than planned.

"You're still into me."

She rolled her eyes and shook her head, giving him a smirk in return.

"Then why the chill, Stace?" He looked at her dead-on, no smiles now. "You know, I totally got the whole thing with your house. I mean, I'd be totally freaked out too. So I gave you some space. But that was months ago."

"Chase, it's . . ."

He hunched forward again. "We were a thing. You couldn't talk to me about it?"

"You wouldn't get it."

"How would you know if you never gave me a shot?" He glanced around the library. There was only one other girl, on the other side of the room, absorbed in her book. He focused on Stacy again. "You know, I've never said that to anybody before."

She knew what he meant: "I love you."

"Me neither," she said.

"Then why the chill? You know, they say I should just step off, move on."

"Who? Your friends?"

"Yeah."

"So, why haven't you?"

"Because I don't know what's up. And I don't think it's me. Heather says you've been the same with her. Like, all distant and everything. And I see you walking around here by yourself. That's not you. So talk to me."

A fist-sized lump formed in her throat. The tears came before she realized she was crying. He wasn't prepared for it. He looked surprised and uncomfortable, glancing around the room again.

She repeated, "You wouldn't get it." It broke through and bubbled to the surface: anger at Chase right then, anger for what had happened to her family, anger at her parents for the albatross of their secret hanging around her neck. More tears ran fast. She wiped them away.

She could see Chase's regret. His nostrils flared with his own frustration. "Not fair, Stace. You can't keep pushing people away."

She wanted to tell him how much had changed, even if she did think about him almost every day. Couldn't he see? But it wasn't just that she'd stopped wearing makeup because it was money she couldn't afford to spend. It wasn't just her hair that she braided because of embarrassing split ends, or her clothes that threatened to disintegrate after too many washings. It was *her*, the girl inside. Desperate survival meant being selfish. She couldn't spare any of herself for Chase.

Her phone rattled next to her econ book, signaling a text coming through. She looked at the message. "It's my brother," she said. "He's on his way here." She noticed Chase staring at her phone.

He raised his eyes and said, "I'm gonna check out, then." He stood with an awkward move of the chair. "A bunch of us are hanging out at Heather's on Friday night." Stacy didn't reply. He added, "I guess . . . I guess we're not doing my prom, huh?"

Her expression opened up with naked sadness. He waited a moment for a response. When she didn't give it, he shook his head and walked away.

More than anything she wanted a real cry. She wanted to expel the pain Chase had exposed. It had been smothered by too much preoccupation with where her family was sleeping and where they were going to get food and keeping to the fringes so they wouldn't get caught. Talking to him was an aching reminder of what she'd lost. Watching him and Heather and the others, seeing the worry-free moped, she felt like a ghost of her former self that would've been right there with them.

She sat feeling heavy, gazing out the window, seeing Chase at ground level as he walked to his moped, got on, and zoomed off. She was still watching long after he had disappeared from sight.

Jay walked up. She didn't even notice. "Hey," he said.

She started and blinked at him.

"What happened?" he asked, his face growing tight.

"Nothing." She looked out the window again.

Jay dropped his backpack on the floor and took what had been

Chase's seat. "Don't give me that." He looked around at the empty tables and the towering bookshelves. The lone girl across the room had gone.

"Chase is going to take somebody else to prom." Her voice broke on the word *prom*, like she might cry, but she choked it back, her eyelids fluttering to clear her teary image of Jay.

He looked a bit surprised, partly because Stacy didn't tell him things like that. "He didn't ask you?" That's all he could think of to say.

"Of course he did."

"Why'd you say no?"

"I didn't at first. I mean, I changed my mind."

"Why?"

"Are you kidding me? Go to prom dressed in *what*? And what about him picking me up?"

"Oh."

"I'm so tired," she sighed.

"I just try not to think about it."

"Well, that's pretty hard to do, you know?"

"Yeah, I know."

She leaned forward and in a delicate voice said, "I feel like I'm moving around, but I'm also trapped inside something where nobody can hear me."

"They'd hear you. You just can't say anything."

"It's so hard sometimes," she said, thinking of Chase. "I've given up all my friends because of this."

"Not saying stuff about home and everything, it's a lot tougher than I thought."

"I'm, like, avoiding people just so I won't slip up." Stacy flung her head back and moaned, "I'll be so glad when this is all over."

"I hear Mom and Dad talking sometimes, late at night when they think we're asleep."

"Me too," she said.

"They're worried about us."

"I know."

"It's gotta suck for them too," Jay said.

"Yeah."

"I heard Dad tell Elliott he's proud of us," Jay said.

"Proud of us for what?"

"He says we're really being strong."

"I don't feel strong."

"You believe him? He could've just been saying stuff, I guess. Elliott is just a kid."

"Elliott is probably doing better than all of us. Him and that diary of his."

"He says it's not a diary, it's a *journal*," Jay said, teasing.

"Yeah, he told me that too."

"So, you believe he meant it?"

"Who? Dad?"

"Maybe he meant it. Or maybe he just doesn't want us to fall apart. My coach used to say stuff like that. You know, how proud he was when he needed to charge us up, even though we were getting our butts whipped."

"Did it help? Your coach saying those things?"

"Yeah. It did. It made us try harder."

"Yeah," Stacy said. "It's pretty cool to hear."

"Stace?"

"Yeah?"

"What do you think is gonna happen? I mean, to us? How did this happen?"

Stacy paused before answering. "I don't know. I never thought anything like this *could* happen—not to people like us."

23

t was a good arrangement. When it ended, each of them would wonder how it all came undone. Did a teacher notice that they'd been wearing the same clothes too many times? Was it the tardy arrivals to school because the truck stop was so far away? Had James been too friendly with one of the truck drivers, and they noticed the family who frequented the stop much too often?

While all these things were true, it was something different that triggered the singular event. The older woman who opened the restaurant called EATS at the truck stop noticed the same blonde doing loads of laundry on the regular. That's when she mentioned it to her coworker, another waitress.

"I think that family is living here," the older woman said one morning as she prepared a pot of coffee before opening the diner.

The younger one stacked napkins in the dispensers. "You think?"

"Yep. You notice how they're always here? Oh, they disappear in the morning, probably to take those kids to school, but they're back here like clockwork."

"How come you so sure?"

"Because I got eyes."

"Ain't that illegal?" the younger one asked, pausing with a handful of napkins.

"I bet it is. Somebody ought to call," the older woman said out loud to no one in particular.

"Call?" The younger one dropped her voice to a whisper, even though there was no one around to overhear them. "You mean like call the *police*?"

"Yeah. And CPS. You know, the ones who come to get neglected kids."

"But they don't *look* neglected. They seem—I don't know—happy when they come in here."

"Well, it ain't right," the older one said. "Somebody ought to report it. Kids ought not be sleeping in cars."

That planted the seed for the singular incident that finally sounded the alarm. Reba was in the truck stop lounge watching cartoons, holding her bear with her legs crossed campfire-style on a little sofa. She had been momentarily left alone when Stacy went to the ladies' room. It was the sight of a child wearing pajama bottoms and socks, with no adult around, that made the younger server from EATS take a second look. She was remembering her conversation with the older server. *It ain't right*, the older woman had said.

The younger server walked up to Reba. "Hey, sweetie. Where's your mama?"

Reba wasn't prepared for the engagement and quickly looked around for Stacy. "She's doing laundry," she said in a soft voice.

The woman checked out Reba's shoeless feet. "You live around here, sweetie? It's okay, you don't have to be scared."

Reba looked behind her again, in the direction of the ladies' room.

"I'm just askin' because I want to make sure you're okay," the woman said, smiling while bending down to meet Reba's eyes.

Just then, Stacy emerged from the bathroom, eyebrows taut at the sight of the woman's proximity to her little sister. "Reba," she said, "time to go."

"But—" Reba tried to protest.

"Time to go," Stacy repeated. She was aware of the woman

carefully watching as she came closer, stiff arm extended for Reba to take her hand.

The two quickly left. The woman remained in her spot where she could see them through the large plate glass window. The little girl had to nearly trot to keep up with the long, determined strides of her big sister. They disappeared into the SUV the woman and her coworker had seen parked on the lot many times.

The younger woman told the older about her encounter with the child. This time, the manager of the truck stop was present. He took the step that the two women hadn't. He made the phone call.

Had Stacy told her parents what had transpired, perhaps the outcome would have been different, but she didn't want to worry them.

The response to the truck stop manager's phone call was swift. Early the next morning, the Harrisons were awakened by a sharp tap on the driver's side window. James blinked his eyes open to see a woman with a stern face staring back at him. Two uniformed police officers stood behind her. She knocked on the window again. This time Fran stirred. "What's happening?" she asked groggily, then yelped when she saw a man peering at her through the passenger side window.

"Will you please step out of the vehicle, sir." the woman said to James.

He rolled down the window.

"We're with Child Protective Services," the woman said. "We need to speak with you."

The kids were roused by the noise. "Dad?" Stacy queried softly, slowly. The others sat up to listen.

"We received a report that you're living in your car with your children," the woman said, attempting to peek in.

"James." Fran gripped his arm painfully tight.

"We're just passing through," James said.

"Where do you live, sir?" One police officer stepped closer. "May I see your license and registration? You too, ma'am."

James hesitated long enough to harden their suspicions. He pulled out his license and registration. Fran handed hers over too.

"This is a local address," the officer said, looking at James. "I'm going to need you to step out of the vehicle, sir."

"Why?" he asked.

"Because CPS needs to examine the space to determine residence. Out of the vehicle, please."

"Dad, what's going on?" Jay leaned forward from the farthest rear seat.

Reba started to cry. Stacy pulled her close and held her.

Hand on the door handle, James didn't know what to do. He looked at Fran, her eyes wide with fear. He saw the man glaring at him through Fran's window.

"Out of the car, sir." The officer's voice was louder, sharper.

He opened the door slowly. The woman stepped back to give him room to get out. "You too," she said to Fran.

And now Elliott was crying.

Fran did as she was told. She ran to where James was standing and wrapped her arms around him. He held her tightly as the woman thrust her upper body into the vehicle to get a good look at the kids occupying the back two rows, blankets spread over them.

"We're with Child Protective Services," she told them. "There's no need to be afraid. We're here to help."

She turned back to James. "I'm going to need you to open the hatch."

He opened the back door remotely, and the woman and her partner went to the rear of the SUV to find plastic bags of clothes, a hairbrush, toothpaste, a math textbook, and a bottle of fabric softener that toppled out when the CPS workers poked their way through the Harrisons' belongings.

"You can't do that!" Jay shouted. "You can't go through our stuff!"

"Just leave us alone!" Stacy demanded.

The woman and man ignored them. She took the lead as they returned to where the officers were standing next to James and Fran. "Mr. Harrison, I think it's in your children's best interest if they come with us."

"What?" James gaped.

The children were looking out the windows.

"You can't do this!" Fran exclaimed. "You can't take our kids!"

"Your children can't live in your vehicle, ma'am," the woman said.

The other CPS worker told the kids, "It's okay, we're taking you someplace safe."

"We're not going with you!" Stacy yelled.

Then the officer said, "James and Francis Harrison, you're under arrest for reckless endangerment of minors." He pulled out his handcuffs. The other policeman had a grip on Fran's arm.

"Don't do this," James said, "Not in front of our kids. We'll come with you."

Fran stood motionless, in shock. James turned to the officers. "Can we have a minute with our kids?"

"Get them out of the vehicle," the officer said.

"Dad!" Jay called out.

James looked and saw the crippling pain on Jay's face. He saw Elliott and Reba crying, her small hands pressed against the window as she watched him.

The CPS workers were trying to coax them out of the SUV. The woman said, "You can't stay here. It's not safe."

The man told James, "Mr. Harrison, we need your assistance here."

"Kids," James said, "come on. We have to go."

"We don't want to go with them!" Stacy screamed, tears and snot streaking her face.

Fran tried reassuring them. "It's just for now. Just for a little while. Come on, kids."

They filed out slowly. Reba wrapped her arms around her mother's waist, crying with heaving sobs. The arms of the others found one another, and soon the Harrisons were one big knot, latching on, afraid of what would come after letting go.

24

James and Fran looked wrung out when they were released the next day on their own recognizance and met with their court-appointed attorney, Mark Cohan. He talked with his hands and leaned in over the avalanche of papers that covered his workspace. He was young with kind, drooping, hound dog eyes and an aggressively receding hairline. He smiled, emphasizing his underbite. "Thank you for meeting me here," he said, "my schedule is pretty crazy these days."

"What's going to happen to our family now?" James asked.

"Will we be getting our kids back today? Where are they?" Fran asked. "Our youngest, Reba, she doesn't do well with . . . change."

The lawyer held up his palms to signal a pause. "Let's deal with the questions in single file, okay? Right now, your kids are staying at one of the foster care group homes. From what I've been told, they're doing fine."

Fran and James looked at each other.

"There's no reason for you to worry. They're safe. Now let's talk about the process to get your family reunited, shall we?"

Fran nodded.

"What we're preparing for is a preliminary hearing. The judge will decide whether to authorize the petition," Mr. Cohan explained.

"Petition?" James asked.

"When the court has determined that child maltreatment has

occurred, the judge enters what's known as an order. It's a document that notes any findings regarding the maltreatment of the child or children. This includes any problems that have to be resolved before the child can safely return home. You understand?"

James and Fran said, "Yes."

"Just know in simple terms, the beginning steps involve the judge's ruling to determine if there's probable cause, meaning, does the judge believe there are grounds for the petition that CPS has filed. Now, if the court authorizes the petition, the judge will then decide where your children will live while your case proceeds."

"Wait, wait." Fran interrupted, hands up to halt the speech. "This is just so much to take in. What do you mean when you say *while your case proceeds*? How long will this take? How long will they keep our kids?"

"I know this is all pretty overwhelming for you," the attorney told her softly. "I can't answer specifically how long this will take. It could be a month or even longer. We'll have a better sense of that after the hearing. Just know that CPS is not looking to keep you separated from your kids. Trust me, the system is overcrowded. The court will determine whether CPS has made reasonable efforts to avoid placing your children in foster homes."

"I can't believe they'd take our kids and give them to somebody else." James looked weary.

"They can't do that! They can't split them up!" Fran shouted. James touched her arm and she jerked away. "You!" she choked out. "You—" She stopped herself from going further, pushing down everything that had been gurgling inside like acid. It was powerful and frightening. The shock and hurt on James's face told her he understood her unspoken rage.

"Please, Mrs. Harrison," the lawyer said.

"Don't give me that tone!" she told him.

"Remember, I'm on *your* side."

Fran held her face in her hands. "Oh, God," she groaned painfully.

James extended his hand to touch her back but decided against it.

Mr. Cohan said, "Mrs. Harrison, can I get you something? Water? Coffee?"

"Oh, God," she whispered again.

"The goal is to get families back together, whenever possible." Mr. Cohan waited, looking at Fran, not speaking again until she had slowly wiped the tears from her cheeks. Mr. Cohan continued in a measured tone: "If reunification can't happen, foster care is the alternative. I just need to make sure you're fully informed of the probable outcomes and what may be involved. If your children are placed in foster care, the court is there to determine whether their placement is appropriate given the needs of your children, which includes proximity to where you'll be living. You're not completely without voice in this regard. We should talk about placement options if the court doesn't immediately return your children to your custody. This is a reality you should be prepared for, Mr. and Mrs. Harrison. Here." He rifled through an erupted volcano of papers on his desk. After a few moments, he unearthed a pamphlet and handed it to James.

"There is a federal mandate to place children in the 'least-restrictive, most family-like, and most appropriate setting available.' But let's consider options that would certainly be better than foster care. Do you know of someone who can take your kids in?"

Fran and James looked at each other. "No," James said softly. "What are the chances the judge will give us back our kids right away?"

"In some cases, the court allows children to return to the parents' custody, but I have to be honest, I'm not sure that's an outcome we can expect. The agency's argument is that your kids would be put in imminent danger if they lived under the conditions they were in with you."

"But our kids weren't in any danger," James tried to assure him.

Fran added, "We have a loving family. We take good care of our kids."

"Mr. and Mrs. Harrison," the lawyer said, "I'm sure you have every good intention, but sleeping in your car is deemed unsafe, without question or allowance for extenuating circumstances."

"This isn't happening," Fran said incredulously, breathlessly. Bewildered, she looked at James and the attorney.

"What if we went back to living in a motel?" James asked.

"That would be a start. I've asked the agency for all records it has about you two and any school, medical, or other information they've collected by investigating you and your family. As for my own research, I didn't find any public records of misconduct involving the two of you—no landlord-tenant proceedings, divorce, no child custody matters."

"Of course not!" James retorted.

"Look. I'm not trying to be antagonistic. I'm being thorough. Is there anything you can tell me? Have there been any incidents of domestic violence?"

"No." James was adamant.

"Criminal conduct of any kind? Anything a witness can report, even though there may not be a public record?"

"No and no."

"You should know that the agency will sometimes look for information from relatives and friends."

"Oh, no," Fran breathed. She was thinking of Oma finding out. She was relieved she was still in Florida.

"The agency tries to be thorough. That's why it's better for me to ask these questions now and get the truth from you, rather than being blindsided later when the agency presents what they've found to the court."

"We don't have some sort of secret life," James protested, realizing that wasn't completely true now. "We just hit a rough patch," he added quietly.

"We can't be without our kids, Mr. Cohan," Fran said. "They need us."

He nodded. "The agency's knowledge of your family is limited to this one discreet event. It's a snapshot. The more the court looks only at the state's depiction of your children's experience, the stronger the claims for the state will seem.

"Because the state has initiated a dependency case, they've drawn negative inferences from this event in your children's lives. Of course, facts can be taken out of context and misinterpreted. It's my job to introduce accurate information and expand the focus past this truck stop incident."

James relished the opportunity to speak of how he had provided for his family, the wealthy friends he'd had, the wealthy business associations. They talked about character witnesses that could be called on. Fran and James had an aside about Oma.

James said, "She'd come home for us. You think we should tell her?"

"Mom shouldn't be traveling yet. She fell and hurt her hip. We've got other options, right? We know lots of people who'd be good witnesses."

James conceded. They ground through a list of friends, acquaintances, and business associates. Mr. Cohan struggled to push them past their embarrassment and humiliation. James and Fran settled on a few names whose knowledge of their plight would feel less searing.

"There are risks and benefits to having the two of you testify," the attorney said. "On one hand, you could testify to important information that could go far in influencing the court, explain more about your actions, for example. But there's always the risk that the judge can potentially get tough with you and just confirm the state's profile of you."

"That doesn't seem fair and unbiased," Fran said.

The attorney leaned back in his chair with a sigh. "Here's what I'll say to that, just between us and these fake walls. The judge may not believe you, no matter how truthful your testimony may be. You should understand this, regardless of your merits as good parents before the bottom fell out. The state could present some witness who's got biases against you. That'll certainly influence their perception of truthfulness about you, about any situation concerning you, even when the testimony you give is true."

"You mean it could come down to a he-said-she-said?" James asked. "Where's the fairness in that?"

"*Fairness*, Mr. Harrison? I'm banking on preparedness and some luck."

There was a string of cases scheduled to be heard in family court that morning, small clusters of people sprinkling the seats, waiting for their names to be called to go before the judge, a petite woman with bobbed gray hair and heavy owl glasses. Despite her delicate frame, her sour face would give anybody pause. Her mouth was permanently set like the drawstring of a bag pulled too tight.

The Harrisons' name was called, and Mr. Cohan led them to a small table up front. Sitting opposite were the CPS workers who had come to claim their children and the agency's lawyer.

The judge made an opening statement: "This is an adjudication hearing, also known as the fact-finding hearing. The court will decide whether the Child Protective Services agency can prove its allegations against you, Mr. and Mrs. . . ." She looked down at her notes. "Harrison. The CPS attorney will present evidence through the testimony of the agency's witnesses. You are not on trial, though the attorneys have the right to cross-examine any witnesses, including you, should you take the stand and present evidence on your own behalf. I'm assuming your attorney has made it clear that the CPS agency needs to sufficiently support its charge of the alleged maltreatment to the court's satisfaction."

Mr. Cohan responded, "Yes, I have, Your Honor."

She looked directly at the Harrisons and asked, "Are you clear on the proceedings to be set forth?"

James and Fran replied too softly. Their lawyer chimed in, looking at the judge, "My clients understand the court's proceedings."

The judge continued to direct her comments to James and Fran. "If this court determines that the CPS agency has provided sufficient evidence, I will issue a judicial determination that justifies continued involvement of the CPS agency and the court. If, however, it is determined that the CPS agency has not provided enough evidence, the case may be dismissed, and the CPS agency will have no authority to pursue its case against you, Mr. and Mrs. Harrison. Counselors, are you ready to proceed?"

Both lawyers answered, "We are, Your Honor."

The agency's attorney presented the state's case, beginning with the testimony of the lead CPS worker. Dressed in navy blue, she sat stiffly in the witness chair, hands folded.

"How many cases do you handle a year, Ms. Crayton?"

"Too many," she responded dryly.

"And how many involving white-collar families?"

"Surprisingly, it's a growing number."

"Why do you think that is?" the lawyer asked her.

"It's the economy. So many wealthy families just suddenly lost their means of support. It's usually fathers who were the providers but are now suddenly unemployed and without the means to maintain their lifestyles. The downward spiral starts when they can't adjust to having less, spending less. And before they know it, they've exhausted their resources and haven't found another job that permits them to continue their status."

"Would you categorize the Harrisons in this demographic?"

"I would."

"Why?"

"They fit the pattern. Mr. Harrison, in particular."

"On what basis have you made this determination?"

"We've interviewed people who know the Harrisons well."

"Thank you, Ms. Crayton. I have nothing further."

The judge asked Mr. Cohan, "Do you have questions for this witness?"

He stood. "Yes, Your Honor." Without leaving the defendants' table, he asked, "How well do you know James and Fran Harrison, Ms. Crayton?"

"Well, I don't."

"Yet you're confident in your assertions about them—about their lifestyle, values, attitudes. You've made some pretty sweeping remarks about people you admittedly don't know."

"We make it our business to collect information through interviews and other data."

"Really? So how much time did you spend interviewing my clients?"

Ms. Crayton shifted a look at the judge.

"Answer, Ms. Crayton," the judge said.

"We didn't," the CPS worker confessed.

Mr. Cohan demanded, "Will you please speak up, Ms. Crayton?"

"I said we didn't," she repeated louder. She didn't look at James or Fran but kept her attention on the attorney.

James could tell the question had gotten to her. He could tell Fran thought so too. He squeezed her hand.

"I have no further questions," Mr. Cohan said. "Thank you."

Ms. Crayton removed herself from the witness box with a slight smoothing of her blue suit coat.

Mr. Cohan continued, "The respondents would like to call Pastor Martin Phillips to the witness stand."

Eyes turned to see Pastor Phillips rise from his seat toward the middle of the courtroom. He took a second to look at his wife, Charlotte, who had accompanied him. As he walked to the front of the room, he met the eyes of James and Fran and offered an almost imperceptible smile, with warm, sympathetic eyes.

In the witness box he was asked what kind of man he knew James Harrison to be.

"A family man," Pastor Phillips said. "He loves his wife. His kids. He takes a lot of pride in caring for them."

"And how long have you known him?"

"For about seventeen years now."

"In what capacity?"

"Friends, but we're professional acquaintances as well, and I'm the pastor of the church they used to attend."

"You heard the prior testimony, correct?"

"Yes, yes, I did."

"Do you agree with the generalizations used to describe Mr. Harrison?"

"Not entirely."

"How does your assessment of him differ?"

"I don't think status is the reason James has worked to be successful. He wants to be a good provider. He's a man of solid character. Strong, Godly values."

"Besides knowing Mr. Harrison well, on what basis are you qualified to make a personal assessment, sir?"

"I'm a certified counselor through my church. I've served in this capacity for nearly twenty years. I've worked with hundreds of couples and people struggling with issues related to the care of their families."

"No more questions."

The agency's attorney stood. "Permission to cross," he said to the judge.

"Granted."

The attorney flipped through his notes. "You claim that Mr. Harrison is distinguished by his love of family. Is that correct, Pastor?"

"Yes."

"Have any of his actions ever challenged your perception of him?"

"No."

"I see," the attorney said. "Not even when he refused the job you offered him?"

Pastor Phillips didn't respond, clearly surprised the lawyer had found this out.

The judge said, "I'm interested in hearing your reply."

"It was a difficult adjustment for him," Pastor Phillips said.

"It seems like you're making allowances. Does that also mean there's an exception to your general opinion of him?" the attorney asked.

Pastor Phillips hesitated.

"For the benefit of the court," the lawyer urged him, "why don't you explain what transpired around this job offer you made to Mr. Harrison that he, in turn, rejected, despite the financial struggles of his family you claim he loves so much."

Pastor Phillips took a breath. "What do you want to know?"

"Well, for starters, what kind of job was it?"

He looked at James before answering. "It was custodial engineer supervisor for The Children's Hospital."

"Supervisor?"

"Yes."

"I see. Good pay? Benefits?"

"Yes."

"And Mr. Harrison turned you down."

"Yes."

"He didn't pause, ask for some time to think about it?"

"No, he didn't."

"Would you say you were doing most of the work to sell him on accepting the job?"

Pastor Phillips didn't answer.

"Sir, please answer the question."

"Yes," he said.

"Would you happen to have any insights into what Mr. Harrison's financial situation was at that time?"

"I'd say dire."

"Why is that? Had he run into trouble with his business?"

"Yes."

"Big trouble?"

"I assumed so."

"Why the assumption?"

"Because he came to us looking for a loan for his business. He needed an infusion of cash after losing everything they had in the fire."

"And despite being in desperate straits, he turned the job down cold," the attorney said. "Now does that sound like a man who just wants to be a good provider'?" As he recited Pastor Phillips's words, he was looking at James shifting in his seat. The agency's attorney turned again to Pastor Phillips. "You called him a man of solid character, sir. You still feel that way?"

"Yes, I do. No man is without . . . no one is perfect."

"That'll be all." The agency's lawyer resumed his seat.

When Pastor Phillips left the witness box, he didn't look at James as he returned to sit with Charlotte.

The agency's lawyer called the arresting police officer to the stand and asked him procedural questions, questions about his observations of the children.

Attorney Cohan followed with Mrs. Fleming, Elliott's English teacher, who talked about how Mr. and Mrs. Harrison had always shown themselves to be very concerned parents, and what a bright boy Elliott was. But things shifted when she added, "He used to be a happy boy."

The words hung in the room, and it was clear the agency's attorney smelled blood. He stood up and walked to Mrs. Fleming during cross, talking to her as if they were having a conversation over coffee. "Mrs. Fleming, you mentioned Elliott *used* to be happy. What do you think changed?"

She sighed. "You know, I've been teaching for over thirty years. I've seen a lot. Kids can be cruel sometimes when another child is going through a rough time."

"Was it obvious that Elliott was going through a rough time?" He turned to look at James and Fran.

"Yes," Mrs. Fleming said.

"How so?"

"Well, it started with the fire. That poor family, they lost everything.

That would be devasting for anyone, children in particular. Afterward, things just changed for him. Drastically."

"In what ways?"

"Living in a motel, for one. The other kids found out about it and started making fun of him. They said some pretty awful things. They made fun of his clothing. You know, because he wasn't . . ." she paused and looked sheepishly at James and Fran, "dressing as well." Her eyes lowered. "It didn't help that he had to quit the soccer team. He told me."

"He would confide in you?"

"Sometimes. I was concerned. I asked what was going on with him. He told me his parents couldn't afford the expense of him being on the team anymore. There were a lot of things they had to give up, he said."

"Sounds tough."

"It was, I'm sure. But the worst part was the bullying."

Fran gaped at Mrs. Fleming.

"He was being bullied at school?" the lawyer asked.

She nodded. "Yes, and it just got worse over time. I did what I could. I'd intervene when I saw something. You know, send the kids who were causing trouble to the principal's office. I tried to convince Elliott to talk to his parents about it. He said he didn't want to."

"Did he give you a reason?"

"Maybe he was too ashamed. It's like that with some kids."

"Do you know if he ever told his parents?"

"I don't think so."

"And why is that?"

"I was with Elliott when he made his formal complaint, you know, against the students who were bullying him. His parents weren't there."

"Thank you, Mrs. Fleming. No more questions."

James and Fran sat looking shell-shocked. Their attorney stood and addressed the witness. "Mrs. Fleming, is it your testimony that Mr. and Mrs. Harrison had no knowledge of their son Elliott being bullied at school?"

"As far as I know," she replied.

"If you were certain of this, why didn't you contact the Harrisons?"

"Well, I didn't think it was my place."

"Whose place would it have been, Mrs. Fleming? You said you sent the bullies to the principal's office. Should it have been the principal's place?"

She blinked in rapid succession. "I don't know."

"You're confused about what should have happened to address the problem, yet you expect an eleven-year-old boy to have answers. Mr. and Mrs. Harrison can't be expected to respond to a problem they don't know exists. No further questions."

Rattled, Mrs. Fleming descended from the witness box. The agency's lawyer called Gus to the stand. James watched as he strolled to the witness chair, careful not to meet James's eyes.

Gus looked smug as the lawyer asked questions to establish that he knew James "better than anybody." He talked about their college years, being roommates, intimate conversations with James, whom he still referred to as his friend. But the sly grin that came and went as Gus spoke allowed James to really see him, maybe for the first time. It was like watching a moray eel feed off other eels.

"And how long was Mr. Harrison aware that his business was tanking?"

"Oh, I'd say a good six months before it folded. We used to talk about it all the time. All the signs were there. He was running the Island of Misfit Toys. Nobody wanted 'em." He chuckled.

"Did Mr. Harrison ever discuss with you alternative plans to his failing business?"

"Do you mean was he looking to pack it in and get a regular job?"

"Yes."

"Not that he ever mentioned. Like I said, we talked a lot about how things were going for him. He never mentioned wanting to quit and do something else."

"Did he ever express concerns for his family, in light of his failing business?"

"Not that I remember. Nothing changed. They spent money like James owned a printing press for it. He was never big on the rainy-day principle, you know. So I wasn't surprised when he had to dip into the money that was supposed to be for his payroll."

"Excuse me?" The lawyer took a step toward him.

James stared down Gus, who refused to look at him. "He dipped into his payroll because he needed cash. For himself."

"Are you saying he misappropriated funds?"

"Well, I don't know how he squared it with the IRS, I only know that he took it. He told me."

The judge looked at James. He felt his heart thumping louder.

"When did he tell you he was using his business's funds for his personal use?"

"Oh, just before Christmas. That's when things were really going downhill for him, I think. The sales guys he hired were grumbling. Nobody was happy about how James was handling his business."

"Thank you, Mr. Fowler. No more questions."

"Cross, Your Honor," Mr. Cohan said, standing up. The judge nodded to him, and he approached Gus. "You mentioned that James Harrison talked to you about his business affairs, correct?"

"Absolutely. Regularly. We were like brothers."

"Brothers?"

"Absolutely."

"You said you *were* like brothers. That's past tense, Mr. Fowler. What changed between you and Mr. Harrison?"

"I'm not sure."

"Oh, I think you do, sir. Isn't it true that you poached his sales team?"

"I wouldn't call it 'poaching'."

"Mr. Harrison came back to work after Christmas, looking to work with his team to repair his business when he saw you shuttling his salesmen out of *his* office and into your own. He was caught unawares and was devastated."

"Listen, James couldn't pay those guys going forward. *He* knew it. *I* knew it. The way I see it, I did everybody a favor."

"I'm sure Mr. Harrison would argue differently. You took away the support he had that was necessary to improve his circumstance. This was a critical step toward his business's downfall."

"Hey, you're reaching. James was on that mudslide long before I hired those guys. And if the situation had been reversed and he was in my place, James would've left me twisting in the wind. It's called *business*. The only difference between me and James is I wouldn't have gotten my panties in a bunch over it."

"Is that what you tell yourself so you can sleep at night? Look at him, Mr. Fowler." Gus held his eyes steady on the lawyer. "James Harrison lost his home. You helped with the failure of his business. His family is in shambles now. I'd say that's far worse than leaving a man you call a friend twisting in the wind."

The agency's attorney stood and said, "Your Honor, Mr. Fowler is no more responsible for Mr. Harrison's lack of business acumen than I am. As unfortunate as his circumstances might be, it's Mr. Harrison's responsibility to make good decisions for the well-being of his family. He doesn't get to scapegoat his way out of these charges."

"Counselors," the judge interjected, "we have a witness on the stand. Mr. Cohan, do you have any more questions?"

"No more questions, Your Honor."

"Then I suggest we break for lunch. The court will reconvene in one hour." With a slam of her gavel, the judge dismissed everyone present.

25

Huddled in the courtroom's hallway, James and Fran talked with their lawyer.

"I'm not feeling good about this," James said.

"Neither am I," Fran admitted.

"Look, I know this hasn't been easy for you two, but all isn't lost."

"Can you tell us that we're winning this thing?" James asked.

The attorney didn't respond.

"Well, that says everything right there . . . your silence."

"It's not that cut and dried, Mr. Harrison. It never is. You have to understand, CPS and their attorney believe they're operating in the best interests of your children, even if you see things differently."

"You're right. I do see things differently."

"They're making my husband out to be some kind of selfish . . . failure," Fran said. She turned away as if that would hide the anger flushing her face.

"I know this is upsetting, but remember, this is only a preliminary hearing. Fact-finding."

"I get that," James said, "but you told us this could determine the outcome of things, how the judge will decide what should happen next. That's based on what she thinks about *me* and my ability to take care of my family. And listening to what happened in there just now, we've got a right to be upset."

"Just try to calm down," the attorney urged.

"Can't you fix this?" Fran questioned.

"The only thing we can do, Mrs. Harrison, is what we're doing . . . presenting testimony on your husband's behalf."

"Well, it doesn't look like that's good enough," Fran said.

"Then I should testify," James offered.

"I'm still not convinced that's in your best interest."

"I think you should," Fran told James.

"I need to speak on my own behalf," James said. "I need to set the record straight."

"The outcome can go either way."

"Can it be any worse than what we've seen already?" Fran asked.

"Yes. Yes, it could," Mr. Cohan said.

James told the attorney, "It's a chance I'm willing to take."

"All right, we'll run through some questions. The agency's attorney might try to goad you. The judge could even weigh in."

"I'll be ready for it," James said.

When James took the stand, his lawyer asked questions that demonstrated the best of James Harrison. He was an upstanding citizen with no record of activity contrary to the law. Mrs. Harrison had been a stay-at-home mom since the birth of her children. Mr. Harrison was a successful business owner for nearly fifteen years.

When Mr. Cohan concluded and the agency's attorney felt satisfied in dispensing his own bruising, the judge glanced up from the CPS workers' notes she'd been given.

"What happened, Mr. Harrison?" She eyed James over her reading glasses.

"I'm not sure, Your Honor," he said softly.

"Can you speak up, sir?"

"I'm not sure," he repeated. "Things were great, and then I hit a dry

spell, I guess. I borrowed money to turn things around. But I couldn't."
He glanced at Fran.

"How long have you been homeless?" the judge asked.

James bristled at the question. He didn't see himself that way, no matter what the agency had claimed.

"Did you hear me?" the judge asked.

"Three months," he said.

"And during that time, did you seek employment?"

"I reached out to investors for my company. I knew I could make it all work again if I could pull together enough capital."

"I mean, did you try to find traditional employment, Mr. Harrison, a job, anything that would ensure provision for your family?"

"Well, yes. I applied at a few places."

"How few, sir?"

"I don't remember the exact number."

"Twenty? Thirty?"

"No. No, Judge."

"Fewer than twenty?" When he hesitated, she continued, "Mr. Harrison, I'd like an answer, please."

"Yes, Your Honor, fewer than twenty."

The judge went quiet, leaning back in her chair and folding her arms while looking at James.

James fidgeted. His lawyer awkwardly sifted through some papers. Fran picked at a hangnail.

The judge spoke again. "When did your company go bankrupt?"

"February, ma'am."

"When did you start looking for work? I mean a traditional job?"

"Well, I filled out some applications in March."

"But the majority of your time was still spent trying to revive your business."

"Yes, because I knew if I could just get enough cash together, I could make it all work again."

"According to the agency's interview records, you were living at the

. . ." She checked her notes. "Four Clover Inn since January. You had been given several warnings up until March that you could be evicted because of late or missed payments. Yet you waited until March before you filled out your first job application?"

"I had a successful business, Judge."

"*Had*, Mr. Harrison. Past tense. You *have* a family to provide for. The fact that you were willing to gamble their well-being because you couldn't reprioritize is troubling."

"You have to understand, Your Honor. This—what's happening now—it's not my life. It's not the life I gave my family. We had a beautiful home. I gave my wife everything she wanted. My kids had everything. It's hard to just give that up, give up everything I've worked for and settle for some *job* somewhere."

"Mr. Harrison, are you listening to yourself, sir?"

Fran looked at James. How fragile, fearful, and broken he seemed. He had mastered hiding it. But now it was on display for everyone to see. The whole world seemed pressed into that courtroom. Her tears came fast for him. *Oh, James. Oh, my dear James.*

The judge continued, "Everything you've mentioned, sir, has passed. The life you enjoyed, I'm sorry to say, is over. You need to focus on the *now*. I'm talking about putting your own ego and self-interests aside and do what's *necessary*."

"I did."

"Yes, you filled out a few job applications."

"And I wrote proposals and met with investors and—"

Attorney Cohan interjected, "If I may say, Your Honor, my client understands his missteps. He is prepared to do whatever it takes to right his living situation, including finding stable employment."

"Are you, Mr. Harrison?"

James cleared his throat. "Yes, absolutely. I'll do whatever it takes to get my family back." His declaration sounded shredded with defeat.

Fran was quietly crying.

The judge studied James for a moment before she launched into her own declaration. "I'm willing to give you an opportunity to prove that. You'll appear before me in two weeks, at which time you are to provide proof of employment, Mr. Harrison. And in the meantime, you and your wife are to take residence at a shelter. Or choose some other legal residence. No more living in your vehicle. And you must provide proof of your living accommodations, as well. You can rejoin your wife and your attorney, sir."

"Thank you, Your Honor." James left the witness chair and went to Fran.

The judge asked Mr. Cohan, "Have you discussed interim living arrangements with your clients for their children?"

"Yes, Your Honor, but no determination could be made."

"All right then. The Harrison children will remain in the custody of the state agency, which will provide for them appropriate housing. The sooner you can get your lives together, Mr. and Mrs. Harrison, the sooner we can arrange for you to be reunited with your children. Are we clear?"

"Yes, Your Honor," James confirmed.

"Your Honor," Fran said, "when can we see our children?"

"Arrangements will be made by the caseworker assigned to this case. These will be supervised visits."

"*Supervised?*" James and Fran said almost in unison.

The lawyer whispered to Fran, "This is customary."

"Let me also add," the judge said, "if the conditions I've given you are not met upon your appearance in this court in June, Mr. Harrison, longer-term considerations for your children's welfare will be discussed."

The judge lowered her gavel and dismissed the court.

"Don't worry," Mr. Cohan said. "This will all work out."

The CPS workers approached the Harrisons as Mr. Cohan packed up his briefcase. The woman extended a slip of paper to James. "Here are the names of some of the better shelters."

He only glared at her. Fran took the paper from the woman's

outstretched hand and said, "Thank you. What will you do with our children?" The last of her words wobbled.

The woman spoke in a voice that was surprisingly kind. "We'll certainly try to find them a good place to stay while you and your husband are working through this."

"How soon can we see them?" James asked.

"We'll contact your lawyer. He'll go over the details with you. Right, Mark?"

He nodded.

"Good luck to you," the man said, as he and the other CPS worker moved to leave the courtroom.

Mr. Cohan said to James and Fran, "I have a little time. Let's sit and talk about what's ahead."

James and Fran nodded, following him out to the place in the hall where they'd spoken earlier.

He carefully met their eyes. "Here's what's going to happen. There will be a caseworker assigned. They will contact me to talk about visitation. We need to decide what your requests will be, and then I can negotiate where possible. What type of parenting time would you like?"

"I don't even know what that means," Fran said. "They're my kids. I want to see them every day."

"I understand, Mrs. Harrison, but in all likelihood, that's not going to happen. Let's come up with a frequency that's reasonable, under the circumstances."

"At least once a week then," James said.

"Okay, I'll ask, but remember these are requests, which means they can be denied. Assuming the kids are at one of the CPS group homes, would you like the visits to take place there?"

"I don't like the idea of visiting my kids in a place that feels like an institution," Fran said.

"I'm sure, but it's not quite like that. I mean, granted, these group homes are state-owned, but they do try to make them comfortable for the kids. And there are spaces provided for family visits."

"I'd like to go elsewhere," Fran insisted.

"My kids like pizza," James said. "Can we take them to a pizza place?"

"Remember, these will be supervised visits. You can't just take them anywhere you want."

"Oh." James sounded as if he'd been punctured and his breath was leaving him.

"But they can meet us at a nice pizza place, right?" Fran asked.

"I can certainly ask," Mr. Cohan said. "Now, here's something that might make things a little better for you, for the kids. Do you know someone who'd be willing to supervise the visits and can pass the agency's background checks?"

James and Fran looked at each other. "No, we don't. My mom is in Florida. Anyway, she lives in a retirement community. They wouldn't allow four children to stay with her."

"There's no one else?"

Fran and James were silent.

"I see," the attorney said. "The caseworker can make arrangements, if necessary. Okay, this should do it for now. Keep your cell phones on. If that becomes a problem, let me know and I'll help. In the meantime, check out the shelters. I'll find out where your kids have been placed and how to contact their caregiver and anything else I can find out for you. I'll be in contact very soon. Good luck to you, Mr. and Mrs. Harrison." He gave them a nod before taking long, brisk steps down the hall.

26

James and Fran went back to pick up the SUV. It took them three buses. It should have only taken two, but they didn't know what route to take, and then they had to pay six dollars and forty cents for a cab to take them the rest of the way to the truck stop. All the while, Fran said nothing to James.

When they arrived, they glimpsed a few of the workers staring at them through the plate-glass window of EATS. Admittedly, they were both starving, but they'd find food elsewhere. They climbed into the SUV and sat.

"This feels unreal," Fran said. She let her whole body go limp.

James rested his head on the steering wheel. "I keep replaying the last few days in my head."

"I can still smell them," Fran said in a near whisper.

James sat up. "What?"

"It smells like the kids in here." Reba's little girl sweat, Stacy's scent of Ivory soap, Jay's earthen woodsy deodorant, and Elliott's sweet bubblegum aroma filled the air.

James took her hand. "They'll be fine."

"How do you know that?"

"I know because I can't bear to think any different."

"Do you think Mr. Cohan will call us tomorrow? You know, and tell us about the kids—if we can see them?"

"I hope so."

"If he doesn't, we'll call him," she said. "James?"

"Yeah?"

Fran told him with a tremor in her throat, "I don't want to leave here."

He looked at her eyes that shimmered, wet and fearful. "Why not?"

"This is the last place we were all together. What if we don't get that back? What if—" The tears ran fast.

James wiped them away, and with his hand to her cheek, he said, "Don't be scared, Fran. We'll be together again. Leaving here doesn't mean the end of anything. I'll make this right."

Her face hardened. It wasn't an expression he'd seen before. Slowly he pulled his hand away, his eyes still locked on hers.

"You blame me?" The words came out raspy.

She got out of the car and he followed.

"Your selfishness. Your pride. Why couldn't you . . . ?" She stopped and looked at him, her face red. She was trembling and struggled to say the words but they caught in her throat. "Our kids, James! Why couldn't you *do* something?"

"I—" he began, but she screamed at him, "How could you let this happen?!"

He reached for her but she slapped his hand away. "You kept telling us everything would be okay. I trusted you. We all did. 'Everything will be okay. Everything will be okay,'" she mocked.

"Fran, I tried my best."

"Don't give me that! You did what you *always* do—whatever you want."

"That's not fair. Everything I've done, I did for us. Even if things didn't turn out the way I wanted, I tried."

"Really, James? We've been living in our *car*. Our kids, they've lost—they've lost everything—not just the house and clothes, I'm talking about their friends, the security they had with us. And now they've been taken! Taken from us because they say we're unfit parents. Can you really stand there and tell me you tried your best?"

James didn't respond, so Fran barreled on.

"You couldn't even admit we were sinking. All those times when I offered to help, you pushed it away until, until . . . this." She gestured at the car. "Tell me something. Was it worth it, James?"

"It's not like that, Fran."

"It's not like *what*? What am I missing here?"

"I made some mistakes, I'll admit that—"

"You could've made different choices!" She buried her face in her hands. "God, help me."

"Don't you think I think about that too?" He hit his chest. "Don't you think I hurt?"

She looked up at him. "Then why?"

He let his head fall back, stared up at the sky. "I needed to take care of you and the kids. *I* needed to handle it."

"But you should have said something."

"I couldn't."

"Why?"

"I don't know."

"I don't believe that!"

James was quiet again. He looked at Fran, then down at the pavement. "When I was a kid, my dad—you know, I told you—he got sick. A stroke. Everything changed. Especially when my mom had to work." He glanced quickly at Fran, whose eyes were fastened on him. "She took care of him and did what she could to earn money for us. I knew it ate my dad up on the inside. Not being able to do what was necessary to provide for his family. He was such a proud man.

"Our house was tiny. Just a couple of rooms with two small bedrooms upstairs. Anyway, after he got sick, I used to try and keep him company in the living room and watch baseball with him. People from the church would come by to visit. They'd say a little to him, but he wasn't much for conversation then, so they'd spend most of their time with my mom in the kitchen. You could hear everything between those two little rooms. And my mom, she had a voice on her.

"This went on for a long time, even after my dad got better and tried to go back to work. Except he couldn't do a lot. After a while, we all knew that his situation wasn't going to get much better, so my mom's role as breadwinner was pretty much fixed. I remember this one time she and this lady from our church were talking, and she says, 'I'm so sorry for you. It's got to be hard.' And my mom says, 'It's like not having a husband at all.' I swear to you, Fran, I looked up at my dad, and it was like somebody was crushing the air right out of him. He didn't say anything. He just kept staring at the game. And my mom and her friend just kept talking like it was nothing.

"I used to think about that day a lot. I used to wonder if my mom wanted my dad to hear that."

Fran and James just stood there. Finally, Fran spoke. "James, we're partners, right?"

"Yes."

"Sometimes roles change, or situations change . . . You should have talked to me."

"I know."

"So why didn't you?"

"I was just scared, I guess."

"Scared of what?"

"Scared of you looking at me differently. Scared of ending up like my father. I didn't want to be a man who couldn't take care of his family."

"James, you're *not* your dad. And I'm not your mom."

There was silence before James spoke again.

"Fran?"

"Yes?"

"You know I never meant any of this to happen."

She wouldn't look at him. "I'm replaying the last few days in my head and thinking what I should have done differently."

"If," he began slowly, "if you could choose again, what would you have done?"

This time when she turned to him, he couldn't read her. She studied his face and then finally answered. "That's just it. I don't know. I only wish something would've been done so I'd still have my children."

"Fran," James said in shallow breaths because his heart was beating wildly. "Are you going to leave me?"

"Why would you ask me that now?"

"Because I've made so many mistakes." He couldn't look at her just then.

"Is that what you want?"

"Of course not." He turned to her again, hoping to make his declaration even stronger.

"It's not what I want either," she said. "Punishing you, being without you would only make my pain worse. I don't want to feel any more broken. I need you to help me through this."

He reached for her hand. "I love you, Fran. I'll do whatever it takes to get the kids back."

James and Fran tried several shelters. All but one had a waiting list. It was a long cinder block building with a low ceiling and a ramp for wheelchairs. It looked like it may have been a warehouse of some kind, at one point. As they approached the building, they caught the glares of a line of men standing nearby smoking cigarettes. Their skin and clothing looked the same murky gray. The orange tips of their smokes lit up their dirty faces. At their feet were big plastic bags filled with whatever they had collected in the streets. A few had grocery carts crammed with tumbling garbage. Fran clutched James's hand as he curved past them to the entrance.

Inside, the place had the assaulting smell of ammonia, so strong it made James blink away tears. More people hung around in a ragged line. They seemed to be waiting to talk to the three people who were working behind a sheet of bulletproof glass. The word "Intake" was painted on the window.

James and Fran eyed the small crowd. No one approached the window, so they did. "Excuse me, ma'am," James said to a young woman wearing jeans and a stringy ponytail. She had the acne of a teenager but the worry lines around her eyes of a much older woman.

"Yeah?" Her voice was muffled through the thick glass.

"We were wondering if you have a room available?"

The woman's face crinkled. "A *room?*"

"Well, do you have *space* available?"

The woman's eyes drifted from James to Fran, and then back to James. "We have beds. You two together?"

"We're married," Fran said.

The flashing neon lights and siren of an emergency vehicle whipped through the space. The doors burst open with EMTs shoving a gurney and yelling, "Coming through, folks!"

James and Fran leapt out of the rush as the men parted the line of onlookers. James turned back to the woman behind the glass. Her two coworkers came from behind the counter to lead the medical team down a hall and around a corner.

"What happened?" James asked the woman.

"Some drunk guy fell trying to crawl down from a bunk. They say he knocked himself out cold. Cement don't give." She spoke to the question on James's face. "It happens. You wanted a bed? We've got one for you now. How long you plan on staying?"

James looked at Fran, who was painfully gripping his hand. "I, um, I don't know."

"Well, if you're looking to stay the night, we just need you to sign on this sheet. Here." She slipped a form to James. "These are the short-term-stay rules—all the stuff that'll get you kicked out, and the times you can take showers and eat meals. If you don't get in no trouble and you wanna stay longer than just a coupla nights, then I can set you up to talk to Pastor Murphy. He runs this place. He'll want to interview you and tell you the rules for long-term stays. And, oh, yeah, don't leave nothing you like where you sleep. Folks like to steal."

"When would I need to talk to . . ."

"Pastor Murphy. Anything longer than two nights, you need to get the okay from him."

They only peeked into the dining hall. It was a large room, not too different from a big high school cafeteria. There was a sign on thin white office paper taped to the door: "Tonight's Sermon by Pastor Murphy: What to Do When Your Road Runs Out, 8:00 p.m." A long line of people holding food trays shuffled along like an inchworm. There were rows and rows of plastic picnic tables filled shoulder-to-shoulder with men and women. Some seemed too young to be there. They ate with their backs hunched, scooping spoonfuls of food into their mouths. No one talked.

That night, James and Fran huddled together with their arms linked, her face in his chest. They lay fully clothed on a twin bed with questionable sheets.

"We should try the other ones tomorrow," she whispered, aware of an arm dangling off the bunk above her, and the snores encircling them from both sides. In the dark room, there were lumped silhouettes of bodies laid out on narrow slab-like beds, stacked double-deck across the length of the room. It smelled of musty bodies, liquor breath, and sickeningly sweet aerosol.

James whispered against Fran's forehead, "We'll put our names on the list at the place with the porch swing, the one that takes in families."

"They seemed nice," Fran exhaled. "They said they have a long wait, though."

"I know, but maybe we'll get lucky. We got lucky here."

For some reason that struck them both as funny. They tremored with shorts snorts of stifled laughter.

"At least we can tell Mr. Cohan we've complied with what the judge said," Fran sighed.

"Yeah, that's got to mean something."

"Maybe they'll let us see the kids sooner. You know, because we're staying here."

"Yeah, and maybe if we get into that other shelter—the one that takes families—we can get the kids back."

"But only if you get a job, James. They won't do it if you don't get a job."

He paused just briefly and said, "I know."

She tilted her face upward as if to look at him, even though her head was still beneath his chin and it was too dark to see details. "You're going to do it, right? Get a job like the judge said?"

"I want our kids back. I want our family together again, Fran. I'll do what it takes."

She lowered her head and nestled against him again. She could hear his breathing and the steady tap of his heart. The rhythm of it was soothing.

"Fran." Though he'd whispered her name, it still felt jarring to hear it.

"What?" Her voice signaled that she was riding the edge of sleep.

"Why did you tell Mark Cohan, 'No,' when he asked if you wanted to testify?"

"Well, he'd said that he wasn't sure it was a good idea."

"He said it was probably not a good idea for *me* to testify. He didn't say that about you. He asked you, and you said you didn't want to. Why?"

"I don't know."

"Were you scared?"

She contemplated her answer.

"You can say it," he said. "I really want to know."

"That other lawyer," she began, "he made everybody who testified say something awful, twisted their words . . . I didn't want to say anything bad about you."

"I can handle your honesty," he said. And when she remained silent, he added, "I want to know."

She began slowly, "You were so proud to tell them everything you'd accomplished, everything you'd given us. I didn't want them to know what it really cost. I didn't want to tell them how lonely I was, how many times the kids needed you and we had to make do without you. Had I testified, then that lawyer, the judge, they'd know your neglect didn't just start. It's been there a very long time. You just couldn't see it."

They were both quiet. It was pointless for him to apologize when they both knew he had not been sorry for those times, for all of those hurts and disappointments.

"And after all of that," he said, "after everything I've put you through, you still chose me. You're still here with me." He held her tightly, as if he wouldn't survive if he let go. "Oh, Franny." He kissed her hard and long on the crown of her head. "I want to be worthy of you again."

She fell asleep in James's tight embrace, feeling warm and secure, and slipped into a dream.

They sit in waist-high mud. James is beyond reach in front of her. Slimy and hot, the mud stews around them with the smell of animal feces. She feels more bewildered than disgusted and looks to James as if expecting him to answer, even though they don't share words. He appears puzzled as he attempts to stand, reaching for her, and then collapsing on his backside. He tries again and fails. Even when she reaches both arms forward for him to rescue her, he can't quite manage it. Their slimy fingers almost touch, straining, trembling to connect, and James falls back, breathless, and ashamed of his failure. She hears his thoughts: I can fix this. She is sad. She feels her heart crying. Then James speaks a single word: "Oma."

Fran looks, and there is her mother, standing alongside the mud pit. "You don't belong in there, Franny." She pushes her words out with incredulous laughter. "Here, take my hand." She is reaching for Fran. A clean towel appears in her hand. "Come on, Franny. Your time here is over. You need to come home. Get clean."

Fran returns her attention to James, who remains stuck in his spot, still shame-faced as Oma won't acknowledge him. Fran will not allow it. "Not without James, Mom. I won't go without my husband."

Oma only repeats, "It's time to go, Franny. You need to come home."

"Not without James!"

But when she looks to him again, he is gone.

27

Fran didn't tell James about her dream the next morning as they ate their shelter breakfast of burned coffee, dry toast, and runny oatmeal.

"What's wrong?" he asked.

She nibbled cautiously at her toast. "Nothing."

James quietly observed her from across the table. He assumed she was still upset about being at the shelter. He gave a surreptitious glance to the others who flanked her. The woman on her right grunted and snorted her way through her bowl of oatmeal. The man on Fran's left busied himself with his false teeth, which he was pulling from a wadded cloth.

"We'll go there this morning," James said, his volume low. "You know, what we talked about last night."

"Good," Fran said.

He studied her face. No, the shelter wasn't it. There was something else wrong. "Fran," he said, pausing to get her full attention.

"Yeah?"

"Talk to me. What's wrong?"

Only briefly, she thought about sharing the dream. But to say the words in her head sounded silly even to her. Still, her heart remembered the tears. They felt real. She reached for James. She needed to touch him. He took her hand. She clasped his.

"We're in this together, right?" she asked.

His brow furrowed. "Of course." He didn't follow up with the question of what prompted her to say those words. Instead, he just continued to hold her hand tightly in return.

The nicer family shelter with the porch swing told James and Fran that it would be impossible to determine their length of time on the wait-list, but they were free to add their names, if they chose.

Less hopeful, they returned to the shelter where they had stayed the night.

James said, "I think we should talk to the pastor who runs the place. Maybe we'll be able to keep our place there while we look for something better." Fran agreed.

They sat in the office of Pastor Murphy, the shelter's director. His desk held a small plaque that faced the twin seats occupied by James and Fran: "I can do all things through Christ that strengthens me. Philippians 4:13." Most of the wall space was covered by teeming book-cases and posters of an inspirational variety: men passing out coffee to needy people on the street while women handed out blankets, a family warming themselves around a burning barrel with the American Red Cross extending a care package. On the wall just behind the desk was a blow up of a news article with the headline: "Murphy's Law: There Are None Too Low Who Can't Be Reached With a Helping Hand." It featured the pastor in an arm-over-shoulder embrace with one man and a few others grouped around them, smiling. They were standing in front of the shelter.

It wasn't a recent article, apparently. In the photograph, the pastor was noticeably younger, though he was still rocking his Willie Nelson ponytail and beard. His wardrobe of a T-shirt and ripped jeans had also survived over the years. He rested his elbows on his desk like he want-ed to position himself to study James and Fran. "So what's your story?"

"Well," James started, looking to Fran before facing the pastor full-on. "We need a place to stay."

"That much I figured, but why here? How'd you wind up here? You don't seem to fit the usual profile of folks who come our way."

"Oh." James ran his hand over his wrinkled, double-woven silk shirt. The shaggy growth of his curls made him look handsome, rakish. "It was a process. We lost our house in a fire. We didn't have anywhere to go. Social Services took our kids. We have to have a place to stay while we work to get things back on track." Fran nodded, agreeing with his summation.

"I see," Pastor Murphy said. "You got a drug or alcohol problem?" He asked James, who was surprised by the question.

"No," he said.

"What about you?" Pastor Murphy turned to Fran.

"No, nothing like that."

"Okay then. Here's the way it works. You both need to be gone during the day, looking for a job, preferably. The shelter here can help you with that, if need be. If you want, you can apply for one of our in-house programs and find work here, maybe in the kitchen or with cleanup duties. Now, once you start collecting paychecks, we'll manage your money, and you'll contribute some for your keep. Ten percent goes to help this place stay afloat. You get to keep twenty percent for anything personal you might need. Seventy percent goes into the bank for safekeeping until you're ready to move on from here.

"You stay out of trouble, and you can stay here as long as you'd like. You get into any kind of trouble, you're gone. No drugs. No booze. No fights." He handed James a list with the heading "Rules" in bold black print. "Read this. And I'd advise keeping anything of value out of the rooms. We're not responsible for what happens otherwise. Questions?"

"No," James said, and then asked if he could do some work in exchange for parking privileges in the alley garage. Pastor Murphy agreed.

"Thank you," Fran said.

They shuffled out of Pastor Murphy's office to check in with Mark Cohan. They sat in James's car with his cell phone on speaker. "We've found a place to say," James said.

"Great," Mr. Cohan said. "Where are you staying?"

"Green Pastures Mission," Fran told him.

Mr. Cohan paused. "Well. Okay, okay."

"What about our kids," James asked. "Any news? When can we see them?"

"Soon," the lawyer said. "I'm working on it. Stacy, Elliott, and Reba have all been placed together. They're staying with a woman who's registered with the agency. She has other foster kids."

James and Fran locked eyes.

"Other kids?" Fran asked. "How many?"

"I don't know."

"What about Jay?" James asked. "Is he with them too?"

"I'm afraid not. He's still at the CPS group home. But he's fine. And soon you'll be able to see for yourself. Keep your cell phone on. I'll be in touch."

They hung up the phone, still face-to-face.

"I don't like it, James," Fran said. "I don't like that our kids are being warehoused with a bunch of other kids. Who knows what goes on in places like that?"

"Jay can take care of himself, and I'm sure they have people there—watching."

"I'm more concerned about where they put our other kids. How many foster children does this woman have? Is she collecting them?"

"I don't know, Fran. Maybe she's just kind-hearted."

She looked at him with naked skepticism.

"Okay, so we don't know what her deal is. But we'll get a chance to ask the kids. Stacy won't have a problem telling us, and if it doesn't feel right for them, we'll talk to Mr. Cohan. Maybe he can help find someplace better."

Fran nodded.

More conversations about the kids came over the next couple of days when they received a visit from the caseworker. She was a young woman who looked fresh out of college, overwhelmed with gray eyes and ruddy cheeks like a baby's bottom.

They sat at the edge of a dining table near the close of dinner at the shelter. They didn't care about the people moving by them, around them, because no one seemed to notice their conversation.

Fran and James asked, "How are our kids?"

Fran continued, "Our youngest, Reba. I'm worried. The separation isn't good for her. It's not good for any of them."

The caseworker said, "Reba is doing okay. Your oldest is quite good with her." She focused on the mild panic rising in Fran's face. "They're adjusting, Mrs. Harrison. The placement home we found for your daughters and Elliott is one of our regulars. The woman's name is Miss Allison Pringle. It's a good home for your kids during this interim period."

"I hear she has other kids there," Fran said, "foster kids."

"Yes," the woman confirmed.

"How many?" James asked.

"Mr. and Mrs. Harrison, it's a good situation. Most of your kids are together. That's rare. Some kids can't get placed at all because the system is so overcrowded with these cases."

"My kids aren't a *case*," James said.

"That wasn't meant as a derogatory term, Mr. Harrison. I simply mean that there are too many of these circumstances where children need our help, and we have too few resources to accommodate all of them."

"Where does this woman, Miss Pringle, live? Is she near the kids' school district?"

"I'm afraid not," the caseworker said.

"What about school?" James asked.

"Well, we're in the process of getting them transferred to the nearest public schools, which is a bit of a miracle."

"Wait. What schools?" Fran asked.

"Miss Pringle lives in a good school district. She's not far from some of the better public schools in the city, Mrs. Harrison. The classrooms aren't so overcrowded that teachers can't remember the kids' names. They actually have computers. That's a big deal."

"But what about the schools our kids already attend?" James said. "The school year is almost over. Can't you make some kind of arrangement to get them there?"

"I'm afraid not, Mr. Harrison."

"Why not?"

"Because the kids have to attend school in their home district."

Fran and James glared at the young woman.

"Temporary home," she amended.

"This makes no sense to me," Fran said. "They've already been taken from us, and now you're disrupting their lives further by taking them out of their schools—*good* schools—and away from their friends."

"I'm sorry, but there's nothing I can do. And as I said, your kids are some of the lucky ones. We can't always arrange for school transfers so quickly and easily. Sometimes kids' records get held up, and students wind up missing months of school. I've even seen situations where kids have had to repeat a school year because of some hold up in the transfer process. We're doing the best we can."

The house on Plymouth Street where Stacy, Elliott, and Reba were placed had three bedrooms and one bath. In it lived a portly woman, Miss Alison, who ate with her fingers. She had five children. Two of them she'd birthed: a ferret-like little boy who ate boogers and enjoyed sly, stolen moments of torturing his mother's cat, and another child who was a year older and given to fits of biting and violent temper tantrums. The remaining three were foster care children who had been placed in the small home and presumably forgotten. They never had requested visits from their relatives. The oldest of the three was close to Elliot's age. The other two were younger than Reba. They cried themselves to sleep routinely.

Miss Allison was grateful for the call about the Harrison children. They represented a sizable income increase. And more still, the oldest was a teenager of some age. Surely she would be useful. It was always such a handful dealing with the young ones, but Miss Allison preferred them. The county paid more for their care.

Reba refused to leave Stacy's side after the little boy with a fondness for boogers pulled her hair. Stacy told her, "He just likes you."

To which Reba replied, "He's gross!"

Miss Allison smiled often at the Harrison children, but her eyes delivered a different message. She watched them scowling at the canned soup steaming in their bowls for dinner. They weren't eating it savagely like the other foster kids. And when she caught Elliott eyeing the pizza Miss Alison's own children were enjoying, she carped, "You don't seem to like your soup, Edward."

"My name is Elliott," he said evenly.

Her mouth puckered like she'd tasted something bitter. Her Booger Boy gave a cunning smile beyond his years, as pride of ownership curled around his chewing mouth. This was all within the first eight days of the Harrison children's placement in the home. To them, it seemed far longer.

Stacy was "asked" to clean up after dinner. Elliott was told to help. Reba wouldn't separate from her big sister's side, so she volunteered too.

"How long do we have to stay here?" Reba whined.

"Keep your voice down, Reba," Stacy said, giving a cautious glance over her shoulder. The kitchen was empty, except for the three of them, but that didn't mean they couldn't be overheard. But, in the living room, there was some sort of squabble going on between Booger Boy and a few of the other kids. There was lots of screeching and squealing, like cats in a bag, with Miss Allison yelling and threatening.

Stacy turned back to washing dishes, and then handed a plate to Elliott to rinse and dry. "We'll be gone soon," she whispered to Reba, who stood near her hip.

"I miss Mommy and Daddy." Her voice quavered.

Stacy held Reba's chin with a soapy index finger and thumb. "Hey, don't cry, okay? It'll be over soon." The caseworker was right. Stacy had assumed the role she'd observed of their mother. At night, when Reba would lie next to her crying, she'd hold her little sister and hum softly until she fell asleep.

"But why can't it be over now?" she asked. "I liked camping in our big car."

"Because those people said we couldn't," Elliott said curtly.

His anger caught Stacy's attention. She was trying to think of something to say to him when Miss Allison shuffled in with the mincing steps of someone whose thighs fight in transit. She paused for a second to regard the three children who had suddenly stopped talking.

Stacy felt the need to say something. "We're almost done."

"Good," Miss Allison said. "One of the others wet the bed again last night. Always something with that one," she mumbled. "Anyway, those sheets need changing. You wouldn't mind helping, would you?"

Stacy turned to meet the woman's hard eyes that didn't match her fixed smile. "Sure, I'll do it."

They waited until Miss Alison's raspy feet couldn't be heard moving down the hall.

"That one kid is *always* wetting the bed," Elliott said. "I hate sleeping with that little boy."

"Then sleep on the floor," Stacy grumbled.

"I can't," Elliott said. "Not enough covers for that. Hey, do you think she'll let me sleep in the room with you guys?"

"Where?" Stacy asked. "You know we're already two to a bed in there. Bunk beds and that little stinky cot she's shoved in there."

"I'm glad you don't smell bad," Reba said to her big sister. "I like sleeping with you. You smell like soap." She grinned at Stacy, and that made her laugh.

"And he farts too," Elliott groused. "He says the soup gives him gas. I told him, 'Then don't eat it.'"

"Fat chance of that happening," Stacy said. "Eight days and the only thing the woman can serve us is soup."

"She bought pizza," Reba said.

"But that wasn't for us."

"Oh, yeah. You think we'll get pizza when we see Mommy and Daddy?"

"I hope so," Stacy said.

"I miss pizza," Elliott added. "I miss *real* food."

"Tell me about it," Stacy concurred.

"Do you think Jay misses pizza with us?" Reba asked.

"I'm sure he does," Stacy assured her.

"I wish we still had our phones," Elliott said. "We could call Jay if they hadn't taken our phones."

"What difference does it make? We ran out of minutes on those things. Dad didn't pay for more minutes."

"Still, they didn't have to take them," Elliott continued. "What did they think we were gonna do?"

"Prison break," Stacy said, causing all three to burst into soft giggles.

Jay sat near a table used for family visits and stared out the window. He hadn't eaten. His stomach hurt, but he refused to take the meds the evening-duty nurse had offered. She couldn't answer his questions about where his sisters and brother had been taken, where his parents were, and when he'd see them.

Another boy slid into the seat across from him.

"Fresh face," the boy said. He was lean like stretched taffy. He smiled wide, but he made Jay feel uneasy. Jay sat up a little straighter, as if on alert.

"Don't worry," the boy said. "I'm harmless." His crooked teeth looked as if they were intended to maim. "I'm Casper."

"As in the *ghost?*" Jay took in the startling blackness of the boy's skin.

The boy laughed. "That's not my real name. That's what my friends call me."

"Oh," Jay said, "like some kind of joke."

Casper shrugged. "I like it. You got a name?"

"Yeah," Jay said, but nothing else.

"Well?" Casper raised his eyebrows in query. "You want me to guess or something?"

"I don't much care," Jay sighed. That was intended to signal he didn't want the intrusion.

Casper took it as an invitation for game play. "Okay, cool. Ricky. Did I get it right?"

"Ricky? No way do I look like a *Ricky*."

"Okay, okay. How about Ted?"

Jay rolled his eyes. "You have got to be kidding me. Seriously? Ted? What do you think this is?"

"Well, help me out here. I don't know a lot of white kids."

"Well, I don't know a lot of black kids, but I could've done better than *Ted*."

"Would you have come up with Casper?"

"Well . . ." Jay thought for a second. "No."

"See?"

"Fine, my name's Jay."

"Okay. Okay, that suits you," Casper said. "This your first time?"

"First time?"

"In foster care."

"Yeah. You?"

"Nah," Casper answered, sucking food from a molar.

"How long you been here?"

"In here? 'Bout a month, but I been to lots of other places. I been to Bedford, Hope Gardens—now that was a serious dump—Langley, which had the best food, and now here. This place is nicer. You got lucky."

"There's nothing lucky about being stuck in this place."

"You'll get used to it."

"I won't have to."

"Oh. They say you leaving?"

"No, I—"

"Like I said," Casper interrupted, "you'll get used to it." He smirked.

Jay got angry. "I'm going home."

"Yeah, that's what most of us said at first."

"Well, I'm not like *most* of you. I'm going home."

The little smile slipped from Casper's face. "What makes you think you're so special?"

"Because my parents aren't crackheads." The words flew from Jay's mouth without thought, and the second the poison was released, he regretted it.

Casper looked insulted and angry. "You saying mine are?"

"I didn't say that. I don't know your people. Parents."

"Well, you implied it. You shouldn't be going around saying things you don't know. Don't believe the hype, dude. Not every kid is here 'cause they got crackhead mamas or something."

"Hey, I didn't—"

"Yeah, yeah," Casper said, cutting him off again. He got up and mumbled, "Can't be nice to some people."

"Sorry." The word was limp and aimed at the empty chair.

Casper turned back to Jay. "My parents died in a car crash three years ago. I had an auntie who took me in at first. She got sick. I didn't have any more people for CPS to call on."

"I'm sorry," Jay said again.

"Yeah, I got that."

Another boy sauntered over, hoodie pulled up and hands in his pockets. He was large in a beefy way, like the wrestlers Jay knew at his school. He looked a lot older than high school. It was the way his heavy brows creased over his dark eyes. He had a scruff of facial hair that looked in need of a shave.

The boy was sizing up Jay while he said, "What's up, Casper?"

Casper noted the boy's interest. "Just chillin', Rodriguez."

"Who's the newbie?" the boy asked, still looking at Jay.

"You can ask 'im, but he's not much for conversation."

"Well, maybe he just don't like what you have to say." The boy laughed, but he didn't seem to be joking around.

Casper's expression confirmed it.

"You should take off," the boy said. "I can keep the newbie company."

Jay looked at Casper, who paused and then sat back down. "Nah, I don't think so. I'm cool right here."

The boy took a moment to evaluate both of them before saying, "Three's a crowd," and walked away.

They watched him retreat back to the TV area.

"What's his deal?" Jay asked.

"You wouldn't want to know," Casper said. "Or maybe you would. You might be into what Rodriguez got."

"I don't get high, if that's what he's about."

"Yeah. Right. You just like accusing people's mamas of that kinda thing."

"Look, I said—"

"Hey, I heard you."

There was a pause before Jay spoke again. "Thanks."

"For what?"

Jay jutted his chin in the direction of the other boy who'd left them alone.

"Oh."

"So why'd you stay?" Jay asked.

"You mean why'd I stay after you pissed me off?"

"Uh . . ." Jay trailed off.

Casper sucked his teeth. "I don't know."

"I can handle myself," Jay said.

"Oh, yeah?" Casper's laughter mocked him.

Jay's nostrils flared in mild anger.

Casper told him, "This ain't *Sesame Street*, sunshine."

28

When the Harrison family was finally permitted to see each other, they were so excited, they all seemed to be talking at once.

"I've missed you kids so much!"

"Dad! You hug too hard!"

"Stacy, are you okay? You look tired."

"Mom, you smell like bell peppers."

"Reba, I think you've grown some!" Fran checked Reba's arms, her cheeks, as if looking for signs of illness. "How are you feeling? Are you doing okay?"

"Jay, how you holding up, son?"

Jay didn't answer.

"Elliott, you have to eat. You're looking thin."

"The kid they make me sleep with pees in the bed."

They had met at a pizzeria, where the pizza went cold before they slowed their all-at-once chatter to eat. The assigned caseworker was gracious enough to take a seat at the next table over, where she enjoyed coffee and read a magazine. Stacy and Jay talked about access to computers so they could message each other.

"When are we gonna be together again, Dad, like for good?" Stacy asked. She was sandwiched between her brothers. Jay was reaching in front of her for an end piece of pizza but had his eyes on his father, waiting for the answer.

Elliott said, "I hope it'll be soon. I'm so over sleeping with that stinky kid. Did I tell you he pees in the bed?"

"It'll be soon," James said. "Your mom and I are doing everything we can to make that happen."

Reba, sitting between her parents, asked, "Can we camp in our big car again?"

Fran caressed her daughter's hair. "I'm afraid we can't do that anymore."

"Can we visit Oma today?"

"Oh, honey," Fran said. "I'm afraid not. Oma is still in Florida, remember?"

Stacy was watching the exchange. "How soon?" she pressed. "How soon before we're outta this?"

"I can't stand that place," Elliott mumbled.

Jay looked at Elliott and then Stacy. "Where's the house where you're staying?"

"Plymouth Street," Stacy answered.

"It's an ugly old blue house, and I hate it there," Elliott added.

"It'll be over soon," James said. "Come on, guys. Eat, okay? Elliott, I got half pepperoni because of you. Eat up."

James focused on his own plate of food. He was glad for the distraction because he didn't want to see the neediness of his kids right then. He swallowed hard to keep a lump from rising in his throat. He chewed his pizza and drank his water and chewed some more. He feared that if he raised his eyes, the small fissure in him that threatened to break open would burst. He couldn't have that. He couldn't let his children and his wife witness him crumbling into broken bits. His kids were all expecting answers, relief he couldn't deliver. He wondered how long it would be before they blamed him for failing them. He soon got his answer.

"Dad," Stacy said, her voice low, trembling, but commanding.

James looked up at her and met eyes that shimmered with wetness.

"How could you let this happen to us? Why can't you fix this?" She held her gaze on him.

James couldn't break away. The other kids were watching him too.

Fran spoke up. "Stacy, honey, your father is trying. We're both trying."

Stacy closed her eyes as tears began to fall. She tossed her napkin onto the table and walked out of the restaurant.

Fran got up. "I'll talk to her."

"No," James said, "let me." He followed his daughter's path toward the door. He had no idea what he would say to her, but it was clear old promises would not do.

By the time James reached the street, Stacy had already made it up the block at a brisk pace. "Stacy!" he called out, and began trotting after her.

She kept going.

"Stacy! Wait!" James was almost running to catch up. "Please, honey, let me talk to you!"

She stopped suddenly with a sharp turn. "What?" she barked, pitching herself forward to hurl the word at him.

Her anger hit him hard and stopped him in his tracks. Her look of contempt left him dumbly groping for words. He felt small and powerless because he had none. Stacy stared him down, and James could see, even from that distance, the pain writhing beneath her resentment.

"Oh, Stacy," he said, slowly walking closer. He looked at his daughter, who was standing on the sidewalk, watching him and waiting. "I'm so sorry."

With no better options, James and Fran asked Pastor Murphy for work at the shelter. James was assigned to help with cleanup, and Fran was placed on kitchen duty.

James was introduced to an old black man whose dentures were so large they seemed ready to leap out and bite without warning. He walked quite swiftly, surprisingly, looking back impatiently at James because he couldn't seem to keep up. James skip-trotted down the hall toward the linen closet where all the cleaning supplies were kept. The old man gave James a pair of rubber gloves, a mop, a pail, and some advice: "If anybody starts to retchin', save yo'se'f some trouble. Clean up after they pass out."

Later in the evening, as James sloshed the big soapy mop along the cement hall floor, his memories taunted him. He thought about the job Martin Phillips had offered him. He thought of his boat, the one he'd enjoyed bragging about even if he didn't take it onto the water much. Now was the time of year when he'd be preparing his boat and having conversations with Gus about it. Gus. *Gus.* James clenched his jaw to the point of pain in his head. He swung the mop too wildly and slammed it against the wall. The loud thud rang through the hall, and the evening check-in clerk snapped her head around from watching TV to inspect the noise. James threw up an apologetic hand. He thought about his old home, the perfume of the lilac bushes that would be budding purple right about now. There was the memory of sleeping in his king-size bed with his wife, the feel of silk sheets against his skin. The smell of Fran's morning hazelnut coffee. Feigning fatigue at his kids' requests for money, back when he had plenty of it to dole out and an ego to match.

Fran came at her new job with purpose. She scoured pans without hesitation, often fighting through back pain but refusing to give in to it for the sake of her children. She chopped, stewed, and doled out helpings as if her survival depended on it. And it did.

After dinner was served, she was allowed to take a coffee break. She almost fell into the chair, massaging her lower back. She listened to the clinking of silverware against plastic trays in the large hall. She smiled, feeling accomplished.

A woman who also worked cooking detail slid into the chair across from Fran. She wore a headscarf that was situated tight and low on her forehead, just above where her eyebrows should have been. Instead, there were shadows, like caterpillars, where her brows would return. Her faint golden lashes were already sprouting and caught the light in mesmerizing ways.

She smiled with chapped lips and coffee-stained teeth. She drew her water glass to her mouth and said, "Lord, am I tired. My feet would probably run off and quit me if they could." When she realized her joke had gone ignored, she said to Fran, "You look like you'd rather be where your head is."

Fran let out a sigh. "Just thinking." She stretched her back.

"About what?"

"My kids."

The naked caterpillar skin jerked up. "Oh? You saw your kids?"

"Yeah. A few days ago. Gosh, it feels like forever since we were with them." Fran's face crumpled just slightly as she gave in to the tears. Quickly, she fanned them away.

The woman said, "That must be tough."

"You have kids?"

The woman shook her head with a terse smile. "We didn't have kids."

"Oh." An awkward pause followed. Then Fran asked, "You're married? Is your husband here too?"

The woman said, "I was married. He died a few years ago."

"I'm sorry." Fran wondered if he had been close to the woman's age, to *her* age. Too young to die. "How long were you married?" she asked in a tone reserved for respecting the dead.

"Eighteen years," the woman said. "We met in grad school."

"Grad school?" Fran was unable to hide the surprise in her voice.

The woman made a sound akin to laughter. Fran wasn't sure how she had taken the response. She wanted to say something to fix it, partly because she did think it unbelievable that someone well-educated could end up in a place like this, but then Fran considered herself and James.

"You know," Fran said, "I feel silly for asking, but what's your name?" They had seen each other frequently enough during their common shifts in the kitchen for polite introductions to have been done with.

"Oh, don't feel silly," the woman said. "Judith. My name's Judith."

"Lovely name," Fran said.

"You're Fran, right?"

Fran nodded.

"My husband used to call me Jay," Judith went on.

"Really? That's my son's name."

"Cool. I got the nickname because his mom was named Judy. He said our names were too similar, you know, for him to feel, well, comfortable." She gave a little waggle of her missing eyebrows, grinning with her stained teeth.

Fran blushed, laughed. "Yeah," she said. "So, grad school, huh?"

"Yep, we met at a frat party at U of C. I'm not sure if it was the cheap beer or his charm, but we hit it off right away. I fell for him hard, I tell you."

"I met my husband, James, at a party too."

"Seems like a lifetime ago," Judith said as she adjusted her scarf.

Fran quietly sipped from her cup.

"Losing him was hard." Judith's voice faltered on the word *hard*. "The toughest part about getting sick was not having him with me, you know?"

"I'm sure that must have been really rough."

"Yeah, yeah, it was. It was the first time I really felt alone and scared. I tried everything. You name it—meditation, self-help books."

Fran nodded. "I used to read a lot of those too. My husband liked making fun of them."

"Well, none of it did me any good."

Fran didn't respond.

"I was at the end of my rope. I just about gave up."

"What changed?" Fran asked.

"You know what's funny? I was never religious. Two years ago, I would've rolled my eyes if somebody said something about the scriptures and whatnot. But I guess what they say about timing is true. I was leaving the hospital one day and walked by the chapel. I went in and sat. I didn't know what to do, really. I just sat there. This pastor approached me. He was easy to talk to. He told me about Jesus, and how He's there for us. I didn't have to be afraid, worried. He prayed with me, and I tell you, I never felt so much peace. That was a real turning point for me once I just let go."

Fran listened with focused attention, to the point of staring at Judith.

Judith noticed and said, "I don't mean to come off as some crazy person." She let out a nervous laugh with jazz hands to underscore *crazy*.

Fran blinked, appearing a little awkward. "Oh, no, no, not at all. I just . . . I just wasn't expecting that. It's good, finding something, finding God."

"You're a Christian too?"

Fran hesitated just long enough for her response to seem questionable. "Yes . . . well, I haven't been to church regularly in a while."

"They have a chapel here. Actually, it's the dining hall-turned-chapel on Sunday after breakfast, and every Wednesday at eight."

"I've seen," Fran said. She had actually done more. The last two Wednesdays, when she'd worked the dinner hour, afterward, she'd heard them filing in for the service. She had stowed away in the kitchen to listen, though she had never joined them.

"You should come," Judith said. "I know Pastor Murphy doesn't look like your typical preacher, but that's a good thing. You should hear him."

Fran felt an inexplicable pang of guilt. She shifted and fumbled with her coffee cup. She offered a terse smile again. "I should get back to work. I don't want to overdo the break thing. It was nice talking to you, Judith."

Judith seemed a little surprised and disappointed, her eyes following

Fran as she stood. "It was nice talking to you too, Fran. Think about it, okay?"

Fran nodded and walked away. She didn't like that talking with Judith touched something deep inside her. She wanted to finish putting the dishes away in a hurry and find James.

Old man Carl's laughter was almost soundless as he watched James struggle to finish mopping the hallway, his rings of armpit sweat the size of plates. James paused to take a deep breath and wipe his forehead, trying his best to ignore the old man, who was leaning against a wall, his grinning lips straining against his enormous false teeth.

"It's a wonder you ain't give yourself a heart attack," Carl said. "Let the mop do the work for you. Push it and relax a bit, push it and relax. Don't fight the thing." And a moment later, he said, "Here. Gimme." He took the mop from James and began a kind of dance with it, side-stepping and swerving its head, the soapy residue zigzagging in its wake. He thrust the handle forward, extending his arm like he was swinging a partner, and then brought it closer, shifting it to the left, then right. Carl was humming. James was watching intently.

Finally, James asked, "You like doing this?"

Carl inhaled deeply and looked at James like he had grown a third eye. "What? Man, you crazy?" His short laugh came with a wheezing sound. "Ain't nothing fun about working."

"It's just that—" James stopped himself before he said something about the humming.

Carl leaned the mop against the wall and patted his front pockets looking for his smokes. "You got any squares on you?" he asked James.

James looked confused.

"Cigarettes, man."

"I don't smoke." James was almost apologizing.

Carl shrugged. "It's cool. I can get some air without my smokes."

He sank the mop back into the bucket and wheeled it against the wall. After several steps toward the door, he looked over his shoulder at James, silently inviting him to follow. James took his cue.

Outside, the evening air was crisp and damp. The city streetlamps shone on puddles from an earlier rain. The buildings along the block were still and dark. Some of the windows had steel gates, signaling shutdown for the night. An emergency vehicle whined in the far distance. Carl sat on the stoop with a satisfied groan. When James didn't sit, Carl gave him that look of expectation again. James eased onto the stoop next to him. He was aware of the cold wetness that threatened to seep through his jeans, but he didn't say anything.

"I like it like this," Carl sighed.

"Like what?"

"Quiet."

The siren wailed again.

"I like the quiet too," James said. "I used to like sitting in my backyard late at night during the summer. It helped me to think."

"Backyard, huh? Where you from?"

"Oh, just the suburbs. Pretty far from here," James said softly as if speaking to himself.

"The *'buuuurbs.'* " Carl elongated the word in contemplation. "You had a nice house there?"

"It was a beautiful house."

"You had a dog?"

"No dog."

"No dog?" Carl swiveled to give James a disbelieving eye.

James laughed a little. "No dog."

"Huh," Carl said. "I had a dog."

"Yeah?"

"A nice dog. The house, though? Not so much. But it was mine. The house and the dog."

"What kind?"

"What kind of house?"

"No. What kind of dog?"

"Ooooh. Well, I couldn't say. A mutt, I guess. I found him poking around a garbage can back behind this restaurant where I used to do cleanup. I fed him, and you know how the story goes from there, I couldn't get rid of him. The owner told me to stop feeding him. I wouldn't, so the guy, the owner guy, got mad and said if I didn't stop, he'd fire me."

"You kept feeding the dog?"

"Yep. And I got fired too."

"Well, why didn't you just take the dog home so you could keep your job?"

"I liked the dog more than I liked my job. Anyway, that restaurant threw away more food in a day than I had at my place in a month. It was just throwaway stuff I was feeding the dog." Carl shrugged. "Heartless," he went on under his breath.

"What happened to the dog?" James asked.

Carl was staring out at the wet, empty streets. He didn't answer. Finally, he said, "I miss my house too. Wasn't nothing fancy. But I miss it. Funny how things turn out sometimes. I always thought I'd get back there, you know? My place. My spot. Maybe get me another dog."

James paused before saying, "Can I ask you something?"

Carl said, "I'm listening," with his eyes fastened on the dark, wet puddles in the streets.

"How long have you been here?" There was hesitancy in his tone, like he was tiptoeing into a room where he had not been invited.

Carl's split-second glance told James he *was* intruding. Still, though, Carl answered. "Too long. But it beats sleeping under the viaducts." He appraised James again. "I guess you wouldn't know nothing about that. Sleeping under a viaduct."

"No," James said, "can't say I do."

"Yeah. Didn't think so. That's a whole different kind of lonely. A different kind of low. That's when you know."

"Know? Know what?"

Carl inhaled until his chest swelled. "You know you've hit bottom."

James thought of the many faceless homeless people he'd seen over the years and at the same time *not* seen, as he rushed to his meetings, raced to his car to get to his golf games, brushed by them on his way to meet Gus for drinks. The thought of it both frightened and shamed him. He wanted to ask, *How does that happen? How does sleeping under a viaduct happen?*

But somehow he knew the answer. *The bottom* is insidious. It rises up to swallow the solid ground beneath your feet. And before you know it, there you are, looking out with scared desperate eyes, faceless and voiceless.

James had felt the ground crack and buckle beneath his feet that day the police came with the CPS investigators. And now he was sitting next to Carl. James felt sweat collecting in his armpits even though the evening breeze sprinkled his skin with goosebumps.

James couldn't bring himself to voice pointed questions about *the bottom*, but he did ask, "How did you find out about this place?"

"The rev here. He bought me a drink."

"What? You're kidding me?"

Carl laughed a little, showing those aggressive teeth. "Naw, I ain't playing. And that look on your face right now was pretty much the same for me when he offered."

"So what happened? I mean, *how'd* that happen?"

"Well, he didn't just hand me a forty-ounce, if that's what you mean. He was stopped at a light, right at the viaduct where my sleeping stuff was. I walked up to his car asking for money. You know, the usual. And that's when he said, 'how bad do you want that drink?'

"I tried the old line about being hungry and all that business, but the rev ain't hearing it. He asks me again, 'How bad do you want that drink?' I was so outdone I couldn't answer right off, you know what I'm saying? Now, by this time he's got folks honking at him to move 'cause the light turned green. But he don't care. He's waiting for me to answer. And I tell him straight up, 'I want it *bad*.' And that's when he says, 'Bad enough to come sit with me, get something to eat, and let me tell you some good news?' Now, truth was, I didn't care about no *news,* but I sure cared about that drink. So I let him take me to some restaurant round the corner where we sat and talked—well, he did most of the talking, but I drank and listened. Then I found myself doing more listening than drinking."

James nodded. He was remembering many years ago, when he and Fran were young and first married. They worked with their church's youth group in street ministry. "Good news," he said out loud. He felt the play of a smile along his lips when he said those words, though he wasn't sure if it was the memories of passing out Bibles and blankets to the homeless or recalling the refrain "I've got *good news* for you today!" that prompted it.

"Yeah," Carl said. "The good news was about the Lord loving me. Loving *me.*" He patted his chest with the word *me.* "Crazy. That's what I told him. But then he opens his Bible to this verse, John 3:16. And he tells me to see for myself." Carl was shaking his head back and forth slowly, his eyes fastened on the street again. "I couldn't believe it. Not that I didn't wanna believe it, but Jesus dying for somebody like *me?* I couldn't wrap my head around it. I ain't never been much. Hmph. My own mama would have a thing or two to tell you about that."

"So did Pastor Murphy invite you here?"

"Yeah, and he put me to work too. He told me a vet ain't got no business being unemployed."

James said, "I miss that too."

"You a vet?"

"Oh, me? No." James laughed awkwardly. "I was thinking about ministry work. I used to . . . well, that was a long time ago."

"You was a preacher, huh?"

"No, not a preacher. I was part of a youth group ministry. But that was a lifetime ago."

"Were you any good at it?"

James laughed again. "I believed in what I was doing. I enjoyed helping people."

"So why'd you stop?"

James quit laughing, and he stopped smiling. "Life got in the way, I guess you could say. My wife and I started having babies. I worked more and more . . ."

"Your wife, she the pretty blonde in the kitchen?"

James nodded. "Yeah."

"Lucky man," Carl said. After a pause, he asked, "You ever think you'll get back to it?"

"Get back to what?"

"Being a preacher."

"I wasn't a preacher." James sounded more irritated than he actually felt.

It didn't seem to faze Carl, who just shrugged and asked again, "You think you'll ever do it again?"

"I doubt it."

"Why not?"

"Well, I wasn't called. It was just something I enjoyed."

"Were you called to work yourself crazy?"

James faltered, surprised at Carl's question. "No, I guess not, but that's what happens when you have a family to provide for."

"Yeah, I get it. But tell me something, you ever think about work and find yourself smiling?"

"What?"

"Smiling. Like you just did when you was talking about being a preacher back in the day."

He didn't bother correcting Carl this time. "No. No, I can't say that I have."

"Then that ought to tell you plenty. No man ever died wishing they woulda worked more. You're still young yet. Think about it. Figure out what you wanna do when you leave this place."

James didn't know what to say and was relieved when Fran interrupted at the entrance behind them. "There you are," she said. She was smiling as if she'd just satisfied a long search for James.

Carl looked at her, too, and then turned back to James. "Lucky man," he said again. "I'm going in."

James made a motion to get up, but Carl waved at him to be still. "I can finish up," he said. "Nice night to sit and talk to a pretty girl." He winked at James and gave a nod to Fran as he passed her. She smiled in his direction.

"I like him already," she said, giggling like the girl she used to be as she situated herself next to James.

29

CPS had its own small bus that would drop the kids off and pick them back up from neighborhood schools. The high school campus didn't have much lawn space in front of the towering building. The patchy grass was covered by all the people gathered outside. The place was like its own city of kids. Some rushed by Jay because he was moving too slowly. Some walked in packs with their caps turned backward and pants riding low on their behinds. Some had music going and took turns dancing to entertain growing crowds, the dancers popping their limbs and spinning on their backs. There were clumps of smokers, laughing their hot, acidic laughs.

Casper walked up alongside Jay and told him, "It's best not to stare." More instructions followed: "The stoners hang out over by the fire escape. Don't cut through there. See that? Those are gang colors, north of that block over there. The Tech Geeks are cool, but showing smarts isn't always a good thing. You don't want to get pressured into doing somebody's homework. Never stop walking if somebody asks you a question on the street, even if they ask nice. You never know if it's a setup. Those guys over there, we call them The Prison Pipeline because that's where they'll end up, no doubt. They're cool with The Stoners but are into more than just enjoying some herb. Watch out for them. They like to recruit."

Rodriguez was bumming smokes. Yards of school grounds separated them, but Jay could feel Rodriguez glaring at him.

When lunchtime came, Jay was prepared to find some isolation and eat as quickly as he could. The cafeteria vibrated with high-pitched, fevered talk and punches of laughter. He took an end seat at a table of people who had little interest in each other.

Jay was examining his fish sticks when Casper appeared. "Hey, what's up?"

"These things look like amputated fingers." Jay held up a withered fish stick.

"It's better if you don't look. Just chew and swallow."

Jay crammed the fish stick into his mouth.

"See. Told you," Casper said. "Me and my friends got a seat, unless you like eating solo."

"I'm good," Jay said, mauling his next mouthful.

"Cool."

Jay waited until he walked away before looking up to see which table he was headed to. Casper's friends were a mixed bag of kids several spots away, some with beaded braids, a few with hip horn-rimmed glasses, and at least one white guy with crinkly shoulder-length hair. When Casper made it there, Jay could tell there was conversation about him because one girl looked his way and pointed while talking to Casper.

Later, Jay would learn more about Casper's friends. "We call ourselves The Anti, 'cause we ain't into anything but ourselves! We got street smarts, but we got book smarts, too, which makes us *twice* as smart." Casper's savvy group read a lot, shared oranges, and argued about things that mattered. Jay would have an opportunity to sit and watch intense debates over their views of the world and whether Burrito King was actually better than Los Loco Tacos.

"We got enough swagger to use the school library without anybody giving us crap about it," Casper would tell him. "We're going places—and I ain't talking about the county jail, like Rodriguez and the rest of The Prison Pipeline."

Casper and his friends aspired for a world beyond the cinder blocks of the high school and were equipped to stare down anything that got in their way. They were the survivalists who would one day give inspirational talks about overcoming desperate circumstances to generations to come.

Presently, Jay went back to his dry fish sticks.

He was relieved when the bus from the CPS group home showed to pick them up. Kids filed on, laughing and hollering, ignoring the driver who told them to pipe down. Jay lagged behind. When he got on, he saw a few seats available, including the one next to Casper. Looking out the window, Casper pretended not to notice Jay as he came his way. Jay slid into the seat next to him. The bus lurched into motion with a fusion of yelping teenagers, shout-outs to the bus driver, who ignored them, and the occasional bodily function that caused barks of laughter.

Jay asked Casper, "How come nobody hassles you guys about this bus? They gotta know what this is about."

"Yeah, everybody knows what's up, but most got their own issues, or their people got issues. So some things are just off-limits, you know?"

The electricity of noise ate the silence between them.

Casper said, "Tell me something."

"Shoot."

"What was up today?"

"What?"

"How come you diss me and my friends at lunch?"

"I didn't—"

"Hey, you know what, it's cool. I was just trying to be nice." Casper looked out the window as a gas station and small park rolled by.

"Your girlfriend was staring at me," Jay said.

"Who?"

"The one with the long braids. I saw her staring at me. She pointed at me when she was talking to you."

"Yeah. And?"

"Well, what'd she say?"

"I don't remember."

"You don't remember, or you won't tell me?"

"Take your pick."

"You sulk like a girl."

Casper whipped a look at Jay. Then the two burst out laughing.

More composed, Casper told him, "You'd better be glad I feel sorry for you."

In the few moments that passed, Jay worked up the courage to say, "Can I ask *you* something?"

"Go for it."

Jay still hesitated before saying, "You've stayed in a lot of these places, right?"

"Yeah."

"How come you didn't get placed with a family?" The question hung there. When Casper didn't answer right away, Jay felt uneasy and embarrassed for bringing it up. "I was just curious," he mumbled.

"It's cool, it's cool. They couldn't find a home for me. People don't much care for taking in black teenage boys, I hear. They think we're trouble. I guess they all believe the hype too."

"Oh." Jay was expecting to leave the question alone after seemingly exposing the underbelly of something raw.

But Casper surprised him when he continued. "After my auntie died and CPS showed up, they'd talk to me about families who took kids in. They'd make it sound all nice. They'd tell us about families like yours, you know. Sometimes, they'd have us dress up to meet some people who were looking for kids. And the people, they were all excited—until they saw me. I could tell. Even though they fake-faced the interview with me, I knew. So after doing the show pony thing another six or seven times and getting rejected, my caseworker stopped trying, I guess."

"That sucks."

"Yeah. It does. I won't lie. I made myself okay with it, though. I just don't think about it much. I read a lot. That helps. All sorts of books. And I'm cool, most of the time, except when it's something big like Thanksgiving or Christmas, and I think . . . well, that's when it's hard. Real hard."

"What do you do?" Jay asked. "I mean, like at Christmas, what do you do?"

"Well, last year this church invited us kids to their banquet hall for dinner. They had it all fancy with tablecloths and stuff. And they had a Christmas tree with presents for us. That was cool. And there was a Santa Claus there for the little kids. After all that, the preacher gets up and tells us that God loves us like we're His kids, and He wants to give us what we need, just like real dads do. Then the preacher says, the only thing we have to do is pray and ask. So we bowed our heads, and he taught us how to ask."

"What did you ask for?"

"I can't tell you."

"Why not?"

"'Cause that's between me and Him." Casper gave an uptick of his head, signaling skyward. "And anyway, I'm still waiting for His answer."

The bus rocked and jostled everyone with a hard swerve that pitched the noise higher. The bus driver announced an upcoming stop on Plymouth Street.

"Plymouth Street," Jay said. "The house where my sisters and brother are staying is on Plymouth."

"Yeah?" Casper was more occupied with the books and notepads that had toppled out of his bookbag.

"Yeah, an ugly blue house," Jay mused. A thought came: what if his parents never came to get him from the CPS group home?

Casper said, "Question."

"Yeah?" Jay was still partly distracted.

"How come you ended up here?"

"My parents—there was a fire. We lost everything." He couldn't bring himself to tell about living out of his parents' car.

"Wow. But don't they got insurance for stuff like that?"

Jay didn't answer. Instead, he diverted the conversation. "Another question."

"Shoot." Casper shrugged.

"Suppose you never got to live with a family?"

"We talking about me or *you*?"

"I'm just talking. So, what'll happen?"

"What do you mean?"

"Well, do you stay in this place forever?"

"Not *forever*. Just until you hit eighteen. After that, you're on your own."

"Just like that? They kick you out?"

"More like you age out. At eighteen, you're grown, says the law, so the county won't be responsible for us anymore." Casper seemed nonchalant about it.

Jay struggled to remind himself what his parents had said: "This will be over soon." But he wasn't feeling it. And worse still was the prospect of being out on his own once he was too old to stay at the group home. In the new school, his aloneness became more real. He ached painfully for his dad, his mom, Stacy, Elliott, and Reba. Messaging through social media helped, but he missed their voices.

"You look like somebody stole your lunch money," Casper said.

Jay didn't respond to the joke. "What are you gonna do?"

"About what?" Casper asked.

"When you leave here. Where are you gonna go? Join the Army or something?"

"See, there you go again. I got a 3.7 GPA, dude. I'm going to college. I like to read. Not much else to do around here. What about you?"

"I don't know. I hadn't thought real hard about it. College, I guess. My dad always talks about how important that is."

"School's not really your thing, huh?"

"Sports is my thing. Football. Wrestling. Hockey. I liked playing on my school's teams. I miss it."

"A school with a hockey team? Sounds like money to me."

"Yeah."

"Now that face I just don't get. What do rich dudes have to be depressed about?"

"Past tense, remember? Or I wouldn't be sitting on this bus."

"Okay, point taken, but still, must be nice to even have some memories of that kinda cash."

"Yeah, I guess so."

"You *guess* so?"

"It's not all it's cracked up to be, dude."

"Yeah. Right."

"Seriously. I mean, I won't say having stuff isn't nice, but—"

"But *nothing,* man."

"Hard to believe, I know, but it's true. I won't lie, it was tough at first, like right after the fire, it sucked. I mean, no iPhone, no cash to hang out with my friends. I used to take all that stuff for granted because we always had it. And then we didn't. We just had . . . us."

"So you're telling me you don't miss all that?"

Jay considered Casper's question before answering. "You know, when I saw my sisters and brother the other day, and my mom and dad, I didn't think about any of that other stuff. I was just happy. And it was over so quick."

"Dude, your old man had you living like a *baller.* I wish!"

"Yeah, but my dad was always working. I mean, like, *always.* I used to really be mad at him for never having time for us. We all were mad, including my mom. She used to try to hide it from us. Back then, everybody was into their own space. But that whole thing with the fire, it changed *everything.* We started hanging out together—my dad, me and my sisters and brother, my mom. We were together all the time. And it felt really cool. Way cooler than anything my dad could've bought us. And then somebody sicced the cops on us, and CPS split us up."

"That's tough. Your family sounds real cool. You're lucky."

"Casper?" Jay asked as the bus pulled in front of the group home. The kids began collecting their backpacks and falling in line to disembark.

"Yeah, Jay?"

"How would I get to Plymouth Street from here?"

30

It was almost twilight when Jay found his way to the ugly, old, blue house—Miss Alison's house. He stood on the porch, his tall frame and tousled dark brown hair, just like his dad's, illuminated by the soft glow of the lights coming from inside the house. Miss Allison stood squinting at him through the screen. She breathed out vodka when she asked, "Who are you?" She wasn't expecting anyone. She resented that her evening of drinking her "special tea" to calm her nerves had been interrupted.

"I'm here to see my sisters and brother," Jay said.

"Who?" The woman appeared to sway a bit and then steadied herself.

"My sister Stacy, she lives here with you, right? And my baby sister, Reba, and my brother, Elliott. They told me this is the foster care home they got sent to."

The woman was assessing Jay's words as if she wasn't sure if she should respond. But then Stacy came running into the living room at the familiar sound of her brother's voice. "Jay!" she shouted, pausing to blink as if she wasn't sure what she was seeing. "How'd you get here?"

"The bus." The words pushed out with excitement and laughter.

Stacy rushed past Miss Allison to hug Jay, who was still standing under the porch lamp. They ignored the woman, who looked both concerned and irritated. Soon, a few of the other kids came from other parts of the little house to see what the noise was about. Reba shrieked

Jay's name, and Elliott came running, too, exclaiming with amazement. They laughed and talked over each other on the porch. Miss Alison, standing and watching, ignored her own kids, who whined about being hungry. She would have told Stacy she should be fixing food for the kids, but the brother was there. This one was older. He might say something to one of those CPS workers. She kept her mouth shut about making dinner, but she did say, "It's a school night. Keep the visit short." She turned away and did not invite Jay in.

The kids sat on the steps, huddled together to ward off the chill of the evening air. By the time the streetlights flickered on, they'd shared stories about their new schools and wistful memories about living at the motel.

"I liked it when we played the board games," Reba said. "I wish we still had them."

"I miss sleeping in my own bed," Elliott whispered.

Stacy leaned in closer to Jay and spoke quietly. "Mom and Dad are working at the shelter. They're saving up so we can all be together again. We'll be out of this place."

"I can't wait," Elliott said. "I want to go back to my old school."

"I thought you hated it there," Jay reminded him.

"I hated the bullies," Elliott said.

"What's worse than bullies?" Reba asked.

"Bullies who might really hurt you," Elliott told her.

Stacy looked surprised. "Elliott, did somebody hit you? Threaten you? Why didn't you say something?"

"Who hurt you?" Jay asked.

"Nobody," Elliott said. "Well, not yet, anyway."

"Why didn't you tell me?" Stacy repeated.

"Because you're a girl," Elliott blurted. "What's my big sister supposed to do?"

Stacy looked at Jay, bewildered and not knowing how to respond.

"Hey," Jay said. "Nobody's gonna hurt you."

Elliott countered with, "How do you know?"

"Hey," Jay repeated, hunching a bit to meet his little brother at eye level. "I said nobody's gonna hurt you, and I mean it."

"That sounds real good, but what happens when they catch me someplace, huh?"

"If somebody's been threatening you, you need to tell somebody, Elliott," Stacy said. "Talk to one of the teachers, somebody you trust."

"Tell the principal," Reba piped up.

"Stacy, that won't do any good," Elliott said. "These kids aren't like the ones from our old school. They're not just mean. They get even. If I get them in trouble, who knows what they'll do."

"You can't walk around scared like that," Jay told him.

"Easy for you to say. I'm not some wrestler like you. I don't hang out with jocks."

Jay sighed. "We'll fix this."

Elliott shook his head. "I don't see how. I'm stuck in that crappy school, alone."

"You have me," Reba said.

"I'll just be glad when Mom and Dad can come and get us." Elliott kept his eyes glued to the ground.

"Hey," Jay said, commanding Elliott's attention. "It's gonna be okay."

Rosa Maria Gonzalez had plump cheeks that her *abuelas* loved to pinch and kiss. She squealed when she laughed, and her brown eyes squinted into little crescents. She loved sharing her *polvorones de canela* because she said no one made them better than her *abuela*. She gave one to Reba because she looked sad.

Reba sat across from Rosa at the school cafeteria table, both of them munching on the cinnamon cookies. "My Oma makes cookies too," she told Rosa. Reba was remembering the last time she helped her grandma bake cookies. That was before Christmas. Before the fire. Before she had asked her Oma to pray for God to fix her family. The cinnamon cookie lumped in her throat. She leaned closer so her soft voice would carry across the table. "I miss my Oma."

"Why don't you visit her then?" Rosa asked. The words came out padded with cookie crumbs.

"I want to. It's almost summer. My mom said Oma would be back by now."

"Then you should ask your *mamá* to take you there."

Reba looked down at the bitten cookie in her hand. "I have."

"So what did she say?"

"She said I have to wait."

"Why?"

"I don't know. I wish I knew how to get to my Oma's house."

"Do you know the address?" Rosa asked.

"Uh-huh." Reba recited what her Oma had taught her.

"You could take a cab there," Rosa suggested. "Or a bus, or you could hitchhike like they do in the movies."

Reba whispered, "Isn't that dangerous?"

"Not in the movies," Rosa said. "And *mis tíos* do it all the time in Mexico."

"Really?"

"Yup."

"I have some money still. I saved it. I could pay for a ride."

"You should do it," Rosa said.

In the dark quiet of night, Stacy and Reba lay side by side in the bed they shared. Neither slept. The air was filled with the soft rise and fall of sleeping sounds from the other children nearby, being carried away in their dreams.

Reba was holding on to the bear she'd gotten for Christmas. Her small voice cut through the velvet padding of noise. "Do you think he'll be okay?"

"Who?" Stacy rolled onto her side so she could face her sister.

"Elliott," Reba said. "He said those boys were mean to him. They might do something bad to him if he told anybody."

"Elliott will be fine. Nobody's going to hurt him."

"But how do you know?" When Stacy hesitated, Reba spoke what they both felt deeply. "I wish Mommy and Daddy were here. Or Oma. Oma would know what to do. She knows what to do about everything."

"Yeah," Stacy sighed. "I wish we were with them too. But everything is going to be okay."

"I don't believe you." Reba's voice trembled.

"Why not?"

"Because you don't sound like you believe it."

Surprised and quieted for a moment, Stacy collected herself, thinking of something to say that would sound more convincing. "I know what Oma would say if she were here."

"What?" Reba asked.

"She would tell us not to worry because God will protect Elliott."

"You think so?" Reba sounded hopeful.

"I do."

"How can we be sure?"

"Because God doesn't like bullies. Remember David and Goliath?"

"David threw the rock and hit him with it."

"That's right. God anointed the stone, and that was the end of Goliath. No more picking on people smaller than he was." Stacy sighed, satisfied, and told Reba, "Now get some sleep."

The next day on the bus to their new school, Reba sat with Elliott and reminded him about the story of David and Goliath. But the outcome was quite different for Elliott.

When he returned to the bus at the end of the school day, he had a black eye.

Miss Allison and her Booger Boy laughed at the purple bruise and swelling setting in. Elliott went to the room where he slept that was not his. Reba ran to hers and pulled her long-saved birthday money from a hidden sock. She would go to Oma's today. She would wait for

Stacy's bus to bring her home, and she would tell her what happened to Elliott, and she would ask her to come to Oma's too. Oma would know what to do.

Reba waited on the couch, watching the door. When Stacy came in, she asked her, "What's wrong? What happened?"

"Elliott," was all Reba said.

"Elliott!" Stacy called out, taking anxious steps toward the boys' room.

Reba heard Miss Allison laughing, a kind of wet laugh from her throat. She always laughed like that when she drank her special tea.

Stacy stormed back into the living room and went for Booger Boy's laptop on the table near the TV. She plopped down next to Reba and flipped it open.

"What are you doing?" Reba asked.

"I'm messaging Jay. I'm telling him about what happened to Elliott."

A minute later, Booger Boy came into the living room looking for his laptop. He was ready to play his games. That's when he saw Stacy. "Gimme my computer!" he shrieked. "Maaaaa!"

Miss Allison rushed in like she expected to see her son bleeding. "What?"

Booger Boy ran over and snatched the laptop from Stacy, but his grip slipped and it went crashing onto the Spanish tile floor. The screen went black. "You broke it!" he screamed, scrambling down on all fours to pick it up, fumbling to reboot it.

"I didn't break it, you dropped it!" Stacy said.

"That computer cost me good money!" Miss Allison shouted. "You're gonna pay for that!"

"It wasn't her fault!" Reba said.

"You stay out of this. Entitled little brats."

"Ma, my computer won't turn on!" Booger Boy sobbed. "You broke it!" he yelled again at Stacy.

Miss Allison told her, "You're gonna pay to fix that thing!"

"It wasn't my fault!" Stacy argued.

"I saw," Reba said. "He dropped it."

The commotion drew the other kids into the room, all except Elliott.

"It doesn't matter," Miss Allison said. "You had no business touching it! You'll work it off. You'll start by stripping off the boy's wet sheets."

"I just washed them yesterday."

"Well, they need washing again."

"I hate this place!" Stacy said between gritted teeth.

"You think you can do better?" Miss Allison retorted. "You think anybody else will take you in?" Stacy didn't reply. "Just like I thought. Get in there and get that laundry started. I'm gonna need help with dinner."

Stacy walked away toward the bedrooms. Miss Allison put her arm around whimpering Booger Boy as they went into the kitchen. The other children retreated to the crannies they had come from.

Alone in the living room, Reba contemplated whether she should go after Stacy or just simply go. She slipped out the door unnoticed and was down the street, lickety-split.

Reba turned several corners, not quite sure where to go and not sure at all where she was. Still, she was determined to make good on her mission. She would see her Oma. She had walked far enough that she had found the busy streets. Cars were rushing and honking. There were buses that pulled up along the sidewalk—collections of people climbed on.

She slipped her small hand into her pocket and squeezed her dollar bills. She came close to the curb to watch the cars zooming by. None of them looked like cabs. She thought of what her friend Rosa had said about hitchhiking. She also thought of Stranger Danger and how Officer Friendly had visited their school and taught them about being careful. She needed to find someone nice, someone she could ask to drive her to Oma's house. She could give them money for helping her. She saw a strip mall up the street and knew she would find people there.

When she reached the small parking lot, she saw a couple with gray hair putting a small grocery bag in the back seat of an old car.

They looked nice. Their gray hair reminded her of her Oma. She ran up to them.

"Excuse me!" Reba called.

They turned to face her.

"Will you take me to my Oma's house? I'll give you money for it." And just to make sure they believed her, she pulled out the fistful of dollar bills and held it up to them. "See, I have money."

The two old people looked at one another. The man asked, "Where does your Oma live?" assuming the child was looking to return home and didn't know the way.

Reba gave them an address, but she didn't know that Elmwood *Street* and Elmwood *Place* were two different things. The address Reba gave raised their eyebrows. "Oh," the woman said, "that's far from here."

Reba held steady eyes on the man. "I have money," she whispered.

She could see his eyes soften. He spoke to his wife but kept watching Reba. "It's not that far, Lou Ann. We could take the outer drive."

"Rush hour," the woman said.

"She needs to get home," he persisted.

"Maybe we should find a policeman or something."

Reba lowered her eyes. "Thank you anyway," she said, turning away. She saw a man up ahead lighting a cigarette outside his car. As she walked toward him, he gave her a squinty-eyed half-smile and exhaled smoke.

"Wait, dear!" the woman called out.

Reba turned back to the elderly couple.

"Come back," the man beckoned. "Come on. We'll take you."

They drove along Lake Shore Drive and Reba watched the water shimmering like blue diamonds beneath the sunlight. Soon she would see her Oma. Reba thought of all the things she would tell her: how the family camped in the car, the big place where kids live with no parents, Elliott and the mean kids who hurt him, and she would definitely tell Oma how much she missed her. But just as important, Reba had questions.

When they came to the neighborhood streets, the big houses looked like what Reba remembered, but not the same. Finally, the old couple pulled up in front of a white two-story place with aluminum siding.

"Is this it, dear?" the old woman called to the back seat where Reba sat.

She looked out at the house. "No, this isn't where my Oma lives."

The man eyed her in the rearview mirror. "But this is the address you gave us."

Reba shook her head. "My Oma lives in a building with lots of other people, not a house."

The old woman said to her husband, "Stanley, we need to take her to the police. She's lost."

They drove to the nearest station and explained the details of their journey. A nice lady officer sat Reba at a desk, asked her all sorts of questions, and gave her cookies she had left over from her lunch that day. She told Reba she was going to make some calls, but not to worry, she would be returned safely home.

Soon, the female officer walked away and left Reba alone to watch the foot traffic of policemen and women. And then she recognized one who had stopped for a drink at the watercooler. She hopped down from her chair and walked over. "Hi, Officer Friendly!"

Officer Adam Richards turned to the child, his expression quizzical but warm.

"I'm Reba," she said. "You came to my school to tell us about Stranger Danger. And you drank coffee with my mom."

"Ooooohhh," he said. "You're Mrs. Harrison's kid. Yes, I remember you. But, Reba, what are you doing here?"

"I came to see my Oma, but maybe she moved or something. It's been a long time."

"Let me take you home. You live on Briar Street, right?"

She shook her head. "Not anymore. We had a fire."

"Oh, right, right. I'm sorry. Where do you live now? I'll drive you there. We don't want your parents to get worried."

"I don't live with my parents."

He hesitated before asking, "Are they okay?"

"They're okay. They just live in a different place from us. They said the court made them. But Mom says we'll all be back together soon."

"I see," Adam said softly. "Well, do you know the address of the place you're staying, or maybe a phone number?"

"Yes, but I need to see my Oma first."

"I'll take you, but we should call the home where you're staying. They'll be worried."

Reba nodded.

"Do you know where your Oma lives?"

Knowing the area well, Adam figured out what the elderly couple could not: the senior citizens complex where Oma lived was located on Elmwood Place, one block over from Elmwood Street.

Oma burst into happy tears when she opened the door and Reba yelled her name. But then she relaxed her embrace when she noticed the officer standing behind the child.

He extended his hand. "Adam Richards, ma'am."

"That's Officer Friendly," Reba filled in. "He gave me a ride."

"Reba, where are your parents?"

Adam responded to her concerned expression. "Everything is fine, ma'am."

"I came a long way to see you. I missed you." Reba hugged her grandmother like she never wanted to let go.

"I missed you, too, my Reba. Come in. Come in."

"I can give you two some privacy, ma'am," Adam said. He told Reba, "How about I come back in thirty minutes, and then I can take you home, okay?"

Reba's face clouded. She didn't like the idea, but she nodded.

In Oma's kitchen, Reba enjoyed one of her favorites—warm milk with a touch of cinnamon. Before her cup was half gone, she had told her Oma everything.

Oma tried to hold back her tears but couldn't.

"Don't cry, Oma," Reba said. She got up from her seat to hug her grandmother tightly around the neck.

"I had no idea," Oma said, talking mostly to herself. "I only knew to pray."

"No, Oma. We prayed, and everything went wrong. Our house burned up. We lost everything. I asked God to protect Elliott, and those mean boys gave him a black eye. Why won't God listen? Doesn't He care?"

"Of course, God cares, honey. And He does listen."

"But it doesn't feel like it."

"It never does when we're going through a troublesome time. You were just saying how you and your sister and brothers would play those board games you'd gotten for Christmas, and how much you liked it. Did it feel like you'd lost everything then?"

"No."

"And when you went to the zoo, all of you together, and then got pizza after. What about then?"

"No. But we aren't together right now."

"That may be true for now, but you haven't lost that. You still have your mom and dad, you have Stacy, Jay, and Elliott, and you have them now in ways that you didn't before the fire. Do you remember what we prayed for?"

"Yes. We asked God to fix my broken family."

"Did they feel broken while you were together, even though you didn't have the house and all of the things you used to?"

"No. I liked it. Everybody was happy."

"See, God *does* listen. He heard your prayer, Reba. *Our* prayers."

"But what about Elliott? And why aren't we together now like we used to be?"

"Don't you worry, dear. God isn't done yet."

Miss Allison opened her door. Her eyes went to Officer Adam Richards first, and then to Reba, who stood in front of him. She grabbed the child and squeezed her to her bosom. "Oh, honey! You gave me the worst scare! How dare you run off like that? Thank you so much, officer, for bringing her home."

"My pleasure, ma'am."

Reba tried to move herself away from the woman as Stacy emerged and stood in the small archway leading to the living room. "Reba!" she called, surprised and relieved. Reba bolted out of Miss Alison's arms and ran to her. The other kids came slinking around like old cats—everyone except Elliott.

When Stacy recognized the officer, Miss Allison saw the connection between them and fought to hide her displeasure.

"How are things?" Adam asked.

Stacy flashed a glance to Miss Alison. "Things are okay." She didn't attempt a smile to sell her answer as truth.

Adam studied Miss Alison, who was keenly fixed on Stacy. "Ma'am," he said, "would you mind if I had a word alone with the young lady?"

Miss Alison's head snapped back in Adam's direction. "Why?" she blurted.

"Is that a problem?"

"No. No, of course not." She gave a tight-lipped smile and stepped aside to invite him in.

"I'll come out on the porch." Stacy gently touched Reba on the head and then passed Miss Allison and closed the door behind her. Miss Allison hadn't moved.

"I'm sorry about everything that's happened to your family," Adam said.

"Thank you." Stacy quickly blinked away sudden emotion.

"Are you all together? Your brothers and sister, I mean."

"No. They've got Jay at a group home. They couldn't find anybody who'd take him in. He was the lucky one."

"You're not treated well here?"

"She's got me here because she needs a maid and help with too many kids."

"Does she hurt any of you?"

"If you mean does she hit us, no."

"If she does, you call me, you hear?" He gave her his card.

"They took our phones." Her voice faltered, and without warning tears streamed down her face. "It's so hard." She stared down at the card. "I try to be strong for Reba, for Elliott, but it's hard. And now this thing with Elliott. I don't know what to do."

"What's wrong?"

"Bullies. It's gotten worse. Somebody hit him. He won't talk to me. He won't say anything. I wish Jay were here. Maybe he could help." Stacy swiped at her tears with the back of her hand.

"What school does he go to?" Adam asked.

"Xavier."

"Don't worry," he assured her.

31

Cutting class was easy. Jay just slipped out during lunch and trotted to the bus stop. Xavier was two bus rides away. He could see Elliott and then be back in time for his own bus that would take him back to the group home. Nobody except Casper would know. He had told Casper about the message he'd received from Stacy, about the bullying, the black eye, and how Elliott wouldn't talk. Casper warned Jay not to do anything stupid: "Stupid has consequences."

That didn't matter to Jay. His only thoughts were of his little brother. They had consumed him since he'd read Stacy's message. "Wish you were here" was how she'd ended it. "Please, help us" is how he'd read it. This felt more desperate than the time before, when Elliott first told them he was being bullied. They were fractured. Jay understood why Elliott felt alone. He understood his fear.

Jay arrived at the old mossy building and went through the front door. He was immediately stopped by a security guard, who came up to him from behind a large metal detection device shaped like a goalpost. "Son," the security guard said, "may I help you?"

"I'm here to see my little brother." Jay looked past the man to the empty hallways and classroom doors.

"We don't allow visitors, son."

"Seriously? What if I had a kid in this place? What if there was some kind of emergency?"

"You don't, and this isn't." The guard rocked on his heels. "And you should be in school yourself."

"Hey," Jay said, "I'm not looking for trouble. I just need to talk to my kid brother. Can't I wait in the office or something? Can't you call him in there?"

"No," the man said. "Now please leave."

"I just need a few minutes with him. He needs to know I'm here."

"I don't want to have to ask you again," the guard said.

"Come on. I'm not trying to start anything, okay? His name's Elliott. Elliott Harrison."

The guard put his finger to Jay's chest. "I won't ask you again."

Jay raised his hands in surrender. "Please, I don't have a lot of time. Just five minutes, okay? My brother, he's being bullied. Somebody punched him. He's scared. I know he is. And he's alone, or he thinks he is. But I'm here. *I'm* here."

Another security guard strolled up. "Everything okay?" He gave Jay the once-over.

"Everything's fine," the first guard said, his eyes steady on Jay.

The other man hesitated, then nodded and walked on.

The first guard turned back to Jay. "How old is your kid brother?"

"Eleven."

"Tough age."

"Yeah."

There was a pause, the two of them just looking at each other.

"Policies are strict here," the guard said. "We don't allow loitering, but I've already done my required check on the outside of the school grounds." He dropped his voice. "They've got teacher meetings today. School lets out in a few minutes."

Jay gave a grateful nod and headed back out. He took a few steps and then sat down on the cold cement step closest to the sidewalk. It was a quiet little one-way street with light traffic. The cop car rolling toward him easily caught his attention. At first he thought the guards had ratted him out. But then, when the officer lowered his window, Jay recognized him.

"You should be in school, Jay," Adam said.

Jay took in a breath and rubbed his now-moist palms along his jeans. "I . . . I had a half day."

"Don't you know it's never a good practice to lie to a cop?"

"Fine. I came here to see my brother. You're gonna bust my chops about that?"

"No, but I might bust your chops for doing something stupid."

"I don't do *stupid*."

"Really? You've cut school. You're sitting on the steps of an elementary school about to do God knows what because some kid punched out your brother."

"Who told—"

"Stacy. Your sister. We had a talk."

"When did that happen?"

"I can tell you about it in the car if you want. Let me take you back to school or back to that place you're staying if it's too late for school. I'll handle this. I told Stacy I'd check in on Elliott today."

"Wait, you drove all the way out here just for this?"

"Yeah, I did."

"Wow." Jay paused. "Okay. Okay, I'll go back to school with you, but after I see my brother. I didn't come all this way for nothing."

"Fair enough."

Jay went to the squad car, and as soon as he reached for the door, the dismissal bell rang. He turned to see a flood of kids erupting from the double doors. Adam got out of the car.

"You see him?" he asked Jay.

"Not yet."

The CPS bus pulled up behind the squad car. There were shouts of names, peals of laughter, hoots and hollers. Groups of giggling girls peeled away from the outpouring of kids leaving the school building. Knots of boys swaggered off down the street. And then Elliott's spindly limbs lurched from the crowd, flailing and stumbling. A boy had pushed him. Three were laughing and pointing. One was much bigger than the rest, like he'd been held back a grade or two.

Adam was already at Jay's side as he went toward the boys.

"Hey, Elliott!" Jay called.

"Jay!" Elliott screeched, struck by disbelief.

The bigger bully stood a little taller, the two smaller easing behind him. The remaining crowd of kids stepped back and waited to see what was going to happen as the cop and the older boy came closer. They squared off with the bullies, Elliott in the middle. His eye, the one that wasn't blue-black and swollen shut, looked relieved but anxious.

The CPS bus driver had the door open and yelled out, "Hey, is that other kid coming or what?"

"I'll get him home!" Adam called back. The driver pulled away. Adam turned again to the bullies. "What's going on here?"

"Nothing. Nothing officer," the older boy said.

"We were just playing around," one of the other ones said from behind him.

"Playing around?" Adam looked at Elliott's black eye and said to the older boy, "You did this?"

The boy's eyes shifted.

"I'm talking to you," Adam said. "Did you hit Elliott?"

Fear skipped over each of their faces when Adam referred to Elliott by name. They looked at the policeman and then at Jay, who seemed tall and broad enough to blot out the afternoon sun. Elliott was smiling.

"We were just messing around," the older boy said. He backed up just enough to stumble into one of the boys behind him.

"Yeah, we didn't mean nothing," the second kid said.

"Well, I don't call punching my kid brother *nothing*," Jay snarled.

Adam placed a hand on Jay's shoulder, then asked the three boys, "You think you'd like doing time in juvey?" They didn't answer. "I suggest you keep your hands off of Elliott—you and anybody else you know who likes *messing around*. And don't think I won't find out."

The boys stiffened. "Okay," two of them said and then ran off down the street. The older boy remained, silent. His eyes moved from the cop to Jay and then to Elliott, who was standing next to his brother, looking satisfied.

"I won't do it again," the bully said, his eyes still moving between the three before settling on the cop. "Sir."

"All right then," Adam said. "You can go, but just remember, I can come back if necessary."

The boy ran off in the direction his friends had gone.

Elliott looked up at Jay. "I can't believe you came."

Jay took him by the chin to angle his face for a better look at the black eye. "Jeez. He did get you good."

Elliott lowered his eyes, embarrassed.

"Don't worry," Adam said. "I had plenty of 'em when I was a kid. They heal, and you get better at ducking and swinging."

Elliott said, "Easy for you to say," taking in Adam's height.

"You'll hit your growth spurt." Jay put his arm around his brother and pulled him forward as they headed for the squad car.

"I gotta say, this is cool," Elliott said.

"What?" Jay asked.

"Having my big brother and the cops roll up."

"Glad to help," Adam told him.

"Cool." Elliott smiled again.

They rode along in quiet thought for a few minutes before Elliott spoke again. "Jay, can I ask you something?"

"Sure, dude."

"Were you serious? About what you said?"

"About what?"

"Me, getting a growth spurt or whatever."

"Of course. You think you're gonna be like this forever?" Jay chuckled and tousled his brother's hair.

Elliott sighed irritably, pulling his head away from Jay.

Jay said, "Look, before you know it, you'll be shoulder to shoulder with *me*."

Elliott's expression softened as he turned his healthy eye on his brother. "But—" He stopped himself.

"But what?"

"What if . . . what if they still make fun of me because I like to write?"

"Then that's their idiot problem, not *yours*. Just ignore them."

"I tried that," Elliott said, eyes downward. "They wouldn't let me. They took my journal. I tried to get it back. That big guy you saw today, he ripped out some of the pages. I tackled him to get it. That's how I got this eye." Still focused on his lap, Elliott added, "I know it was stupid."

"No," Jay said in a voice that pulled Elliott's attention. "That took guts. You know, you don't have to be some big dude to have courage. And as for them not thinking writing is cool, so what? So. What. I got this buddy, his name is Casper. Smart dude. He hangs with other smart dudes who are into all sorts of stuff that some people might not think is cool, but guess what? They don't care. Seriously. They are totally cool with being who they are. That can be you, dude. Be totally down with who you are. And when people pick up that vibe, they'll step off and leave you alone. But until then, I got your back."

Elliott gave a relaxed sigh and leaned his head back. He looked peaceful.

Jay caught Adam's eyes in the rearview mirror. Even though he couldn't see the rest of his face from the back seat, Jay knew Adam was smiling.

32

Seeing that cop again set Miss Alison's teeth on edge. When Adam dropped off Elliott, she tried to be polite, but she couldn't hold it together any longer than she could hold her water after drinking a fifth of vodka. She nearly slammed the door in his face as soon as he said goodbye to Elliott.

She had gotten a call earlier that day from the CPS worker, something about needing to speak with her in person. It wasn't time for their routine meeting and evaluation. More disturbing still was the fact that the woman had called Miss Allison at work but refused to give any more details other than confirming a time and day for their face-to-face.

Miss Allison had come home from her shift at the nursing home, taken off her scrubs, and made her special tea. This daily ritual of hers occurred earlier than usual on this particular afternoon. She needed to take the edge off. But despite being two teacups in, she remained all prickly and jagged. She stared, blurry-eyed, at each of the children from her perch at the kitchen table. Those who had been around her long enough recognized the mood, including her own birth children. They knew to tread lightly to avoid setting her off. They talked in soft tones and shied away from the kitchen altogether, if possible. Everyone knew this rule of the house, except the Harrison children.

It was Reba's fault. That's what Miss Allison would later say in her defense to the CPS worker and the investigating officer. Reba went into the kitchen to look on the china cabinet shelf for the crayons she thought she'd left there. She was happy Elliott was more like his old self again and wanted to draw her brother a picture. She found the crayons right next to Miss Alison's open purse on the cabinet, where she regularly dumped things when she came home from work.

Miss Allison stewed as she drank at the kitchen table, watching Reba flitter around like a butterfly, annoyingly happy. The little girl was even humming. She sat at the table opposite Miss Allison and began to color her picture for Elliott.

"Can't you do that someplace else?" Miss Allison demanded.

"There is no place else," Reba told her. "I can't draw without a table."

"Well, you shouldn't be drawing at all. I'm sure you've got homework to do."

"I don't have any. I did my homework during library time."

"You'd better not be lying."

Reba's eyes widened. "I wouldn't. I mean, I really did do my homework already."

"Well, I'll find out if you're lying," Miss Allison mumbled. She stood and teetered, then regained her composure. She was getting a headache and went to her purse for her aspirin.

Reba went back to coloring and humming. Then she asked, "Can me and my sister and brother have pizza, too, for dinner?"

"What?"

"Can we have pizza too?" Reba repeated. "I'll give you some of my money for it."

Immediately, Miss Allison yanked at the opening of her purse, unzipping the inside compartment where she kept her money. The twenty dollars she could have sworn was there, was not. She had no recollection of spending it. She spun on her heel to face Reba, nearly toppling in the process but gripping the china cabinet ledge in time. "You say you've got money?"

"Uh-huh." Reba was still concentrating on her crayon creation.

"Where'd you get it?"

"My Oma. I spent some, but I have some left." She stopped coloring and looked at Miss Alison. "Elliott is better. I'd like to celebrate, and we like pizza," she grinned.

"You stole my money, didn't you?"

"No." Reba shook her head. "My Oma always gives me five dollars for my birthday."

"You lying little . . ." Miss Allison picked up the bag, shaking it at Reba, yelling, "I had twenty dollars right here in my purse!"

Stacy rushed in. "What's going on?"

"Your sister is a thief and a liar!"

"No, I'm not!" Reba cried. She told Stacy, "I didn't take her money."

Stacy went to her. "Don't cry. I know you didn't."

"Of course, you'd cover for her!"

"You don't know what you're talking about," Stacy said. "My little sister is no thief! Check with one of your own kids."

"Don't you dare try to blame my kids for this. I had that money right here!" She shook her purse so hard this time coins popped out and rolled across the floor.

Drawn by the commotion, the other kids came and clogged the kitchen entrance. "Hey, what's happening?" Elliott asked.

"Your kid sister is a thief, and this one here is trying to cover for her."

"I am not!" Reba cried.

"You, all of you, walking around here like you're so much better than the rest of us. Like you're, you're—something!" Miss Allison went to grab her cup from the table but stumbled and knocked her drink onto Reba's crayon drawing.

Reba gasped. Miss Allison cursed, snatched up the soggy picture, and flung it on the floor. "And keep your crap out of my kitchen!" she screamed.

Stacy and Elliott looked at each other, not knowing what to do. The other kids ran off.

Sobbing, Reba picked up her drawing from where it lay crumpled at Miss Allison's feet, stood, and screamed back, "You're just mean, and you don't like us!"

The slap across Reba's face came so suddenly, the moment didn't register until Miss Allison saw the little girl fall to the floor, heard her cry out, heard her sister yelling, and saw her own hand trembling and suspended from the strike.

The caseworker asked to meet with James and Fran. They both assumed it was about their appearance before the judge, as the date was rapidly approaching. They learned differently.

"She did what!" Fran yelled at the woman across the cafeteria table. James and the caseworker looked around, the noise having drawn the attention of the few who remained after the lunch rush.

"Calm down." James put his hand on her shoulder.

She shirked it away. "Did you hear what she just said, James? That woman hit our Reba! She hit Reba!"

"I know. I know. I'm upset, too, but they've taken our kids out of that place. Right?" He looked to the young woman to reaffirm what she had just told them moments ago.

"Yes, yes, that's right, Mr. Harrison."

"James, we have to get out of here. We have to get our kids back," Fran said.

"We will. We will."

Fran told the caseworker, "We want to see our kids. "When can we see them? I want to know they're okay."

"As soon as I can arrange it," the caseworker said.

"When? Tomorrow?" Fran demanded.

"Not that soon. I have other commitments, Mrs. Harrison. Let me check my schedule. I'm so sorry. I know this is terrible to hear. I've never had a situation like this before."

"Or maybe it's just never been reported."

"We do try," the caseworker said mildly.

"You said a police officer called you?" James asked.

"Yes, yes, that's right."

"What happened?" Fran questioned. "Did Stacy call the police?"

"Well, yes. She told me the officer—last name Richards, I think—is a friend of your family's. She said he told her to call him if there was ever a problem. And she did. He was the one who came to get them, and arrested Miss Allison on abuse charges. And then he called us."

"Richards? Adam Richards?" Fran asked.

"I think so," the caseworker said.

Fran told James, "He's the policeman who was trying to help out with Jay. You remember that thing with the frat party."

"Yeah, I remember," James said, and then to the caseworker, "He came for our kids?"

"Yes. According to the report, it took him less than twenty minutes to show. That's pretty amazing since he was coming from across town."

"Are you going to try to place our kids somewhere else?" James wondered. "Or can they stay with Jay at the group home?"

"We'd prefer to place them with a family, if possible. Space is limited at the group home."

"But you see how things turned out when you put them with that woman," Fran pointed out. "Why can't our kids just stay at the group home until after our court date?"

"Are you sure you'll be moved by then?"

"We've been saving up. And we've been looking for a place," Fran told her.

"I'm sorry, but I can't make promises based on good intentions. Our job is to find temporary homes for these kids so we can make room for anyone else who needs it."

"Look, it's *your* good intentions that put our kids in the hands of that whack job," James said.

"I know this must be frustrating for you, Mr. Harrison. I can just imagine what you must be feeling."

"No," Fran said, choking on her words. "I'm afraid you don't know what this feels like. Our children have been *taken* from us!"

"If you know of anybody who would take them for now," the caseworker said, "that would solve everything."

James didn't acknowledge the caseworker's comment. He simply tried to hold on to Fran, who again shirked his embrace.

Later that evening after dinner, Fran was still in the kitchen when she heard a few people coming into the big dining hall. She looked out and saw them moving tables and chairs to organize them into rows. She remembered then, *Wednesday night service.* She could've left quietly and discreetly, but she didn't. Instead, she watched from the kitchen doorway as the men and women worked purposefully to get everything set up before Pastor Murphy entered. When a glance was thrown in Fran's direction, she retreated just enough to remain undetected.

Pastor Murphy came through the door with such energy, it was like he was preparing to deliver prayers at some prominent cathedral and not the spot where they had enjoyed lentil soup just an hour before.

They had pulled out a small lectern from the pantry. Pastor Murphy stood behind it with his back to Fran. She remained partially hidden in the kitchen doorway, watching him address the small gathering of men and women.

"God created the angels and gave them many jobs," he said. "They have charge over all sorts of things, like guiding us when we can't see our way, shielding us when we need a protector, speaking faith and encouragement into our hearts to give us strength, even when we feel hopeless. No, *especially* when we feel hopeless."

While listening, Fran moved out a little farther from the door. She felt the pull of Pastor Murphy's words and wanted to see him as he spoke. Judith, seated in the front row, met Fran's eyes and smiled at her. Fran returned the acknowledgment.

"The Scripture tells us," Pastor Murphy continued, "'For He will command his angels concerning you to guard you in all your ways. On their hands they will bear you up, lest you strike your foot against the stone.' That's just how attentive our Father is to our needs, brothers and sisters. You have His promise that He will carry you through, *always*. Stand, and let's thank our God for the provision of His protection. Let's thank Him for all of His blessings and pray that His angels will continue to do His predestined will for us."

After the service, Pastor Murphy invited anyone with a special need to come up to pray about the matter with him. A few walked up to thank him. Judith went up and hugged Pastor Murphy. She gave a shy wave to Fran before leaving.

Pastor Murphy turned and walked to Fran, who was still standing in the kitchen doorway. "Next time, I hope you'll join us and take a seat," he said.

She stepped out a little farther still. "Next time, maybe I will."

He tipped his head back, eyes narrowed, while examining her from behind his glasses. "Agnostic or Lost Lamb?"

"I'd like to think I'm neither," she said, but then she amended, "truth be told, I'd probably fit more into the second camp."

"I see." He nodded.

"Why not ask if I'm an atheist?"

"I saw you standing there when I came in. And you didn't move the entire time. An atheist? No. I'm a good messenger, but I'm not *that* good." He chuckled.

"Don't sell yourself short, Pastor Murphy. You had the crowd. You had me too."

"Well, that's good to hear. Maybe that's why He gave me this message. Maybe it was for you. Fran, isn't it?"

"Yes."

"You know, sometimes it sounds like a cliché when we've heard it so often. But everything will be okay." He smiled and was turning away when she called out.

"Pastor Murphy."

He faced her again. "Yeah, Fran?"

"I haven't been to church in quite a while. I think about how long it's been sometimes. I think about what God must think of me—being absent for so long. Tell me something. What you said about angels protecting us, does that still go if we haven't been to church for a long time? Will angels still look after our kids?"

He came close to her and took both of her hands in his and squeezed. "Fran," he said, looking into her eyes, "there is no expiration on God's love for you, or His promises to you, and that includes loving and protecting your children, even when you can't give them your best. You have to trust Him. You have to let go of the worry about your own limitations and let God do what He is more than able to do."

"Thank you." She waited for the room to clear. The kitchen was always the quietest at this time of the evening. Fran found a chair to sit and contemplate what Pastor Murphy had said.

She thought of the self-help books she'd read and all that she had tried and failed. She thought of her children at the mercy of someone else. She felt a surge of helplessness. She buried her face in her hands and wept. She now understood what it meant to be at the end of one's rope. Words from Pastor Murphy's sermon came back to her, along with old remembrances of what she'd been taught about God's love and faith. She had been so angry with God, she had not spoken to Him. But like any loving father, she knew that He would forgive, and He would answer if she called on Him in her desperate time of need. And so, for the first time in a long time, she prayed.

33

The apartments James and Fran had considered previously had all been cancelled out for one reason or another: location, size, cost, risky parking that wouldn't permit James to hide their car each night. But their meeting with the caseworker and the looming court date solidified their urgency: they had to secure an apartment now.

They found one with three bedrooms north of the shelter. The landlord had a thick accent and James couldn't understand him too well, but two words were repeated emphatically: bring cash. So they got their savings from Pastor Murphy and put it in an envelope that Fran held on to tightly in her purse.

When they reached the neighborhood, James didn't like that there were so few side streets for parking. He had to be careful where they drove the car. He told Fran, "We've been lucky so far. I don't want to push it."

"But it has three bedrooms, James. We're not going to do better. And we need a place *now*. We have to be able to tell the judge we've got a home for the kids to come to."

"You know we have four kids, right?"

"We're not going to do any better than this."

Sighing with reluctance, he stopped talking as they drove through the veins of heavily trafficked streets, with strip malls chock-full of taco-take-out restaurants, laundromats, liquor stores, and small convenience stores with Big Win lottery signs plastered outside. Dogs roamed the streets with no owners nearby. Women strolled with shoeless babies straddling their hips. Old folks pushed carts carrying heaps of things found from the street.

The apartment building was a brick walk-up. It faced a busy street, where there was a bus stop with a smattering of bored-looking people.

They circled the block trying to find a parking spot. "I don't like the idea of living in front of a bus stop, Fran. We've got young kids."

"I know," she said, "but the building has a walkway that's rather long. It's not like the front door is right at the sidewalk."

"You really want to make this happen, huh?"

"We can't face that judge without a place to stay, James. We just can't."

James gave another resigned sigh as he rounded a corner. He was doing a lot of that lately.

"Oh, look," Fran said, pointing ahead, "somebody's pulling out of that spot. Right there, see?"

James parked, and they walked the short distance to the apartment building, aware of the stares that the neighborhood kids shot their way. One man seared Fran with a look so intense, she grabbed James's arm. He didn't seem to notice. He was looking at the bars on the first-floor windows. "We're getting out of this dump as soon as we can," he said.

"I won't argue," she concurred, stepping through the vestibule door that James held open for her.

A teenage boy bounded down the stairs as they reached the second floor. He was in such a hurry he bumped into Fran and nearly knocked her off-balance.

"Hey, watch it!" James shouted, steadying his wife.

"Sorry! Sorry!" the boy called back, still bounding down the stairs by twos toward the main entrance.

The landlord was waiting at the third-floor landing when they arrived, winded and holding on to the banister. "Good exercise, no?" he laughed. His belly shook in his ill-fitting jogging suit.

Fran nodded.

"Come see." He opened the apartment door. He threw the words over his shoulder, "You'll like."

James and Fran passed by him, taking in the empty apartment.

"Wow," Fran breathed. The pictures online didn't show the panoramic view of the city. And from the third floor, the distant skyline seemed to be poking the clouds. "I like it," she said to James, her eyes bright.

He put a hard toe to the scratches and scuffs on the hardwoods. "These floors have seen better days." There were obvious pet pee stains that had left marbled shapes of darker brown in the mahogany wood.

"It's quaint." She turned to the landlord, who was still hanging back by the door. "Can you do something about the smell?"

"Si, si, si." He grinned and nodded vigorously. "Before you moof een, spick-an'-span!"

Fran grabbed James by the hand. "Let's check out the bedrooms."

The rooms were small boxes with tiny spaces where items could be hung. They were more like recesses in the walls than actual closets.

"Your walk-in in our old house was the size of this bedroom," James said.

"Well, I don't need that kind of space anymore." She looked around the room as if her eyes were a tape measure.

"How are we supposed to fit four kids in these little rooms?" James asked.

"Bunk beds. Have you forgotten?" She was smiling now.

"Ah." He took a step closer. "That was a *looong* time ago. The kids were tiny back then."

"We were tiny then." She gave James's middle a backhand tap. She laughed when he grabbed her hand and pulled her close. "James," she said in mock embarrassment, "we're not alone!" She motioned toward the smiling landlord near the doorway.

James turned just enough to see their solo audience. He smiled in return, and then let Fran loose.

"I know it sounds crazy," she said, looking around the bedroom, "but I like that it's small, mostly because it *does* remind me of when we were just starting out. Back then, moving into that two-bedroom apartment was a big deal, remember? We had a bedroom of our own again." She gave James such a warm expression. "We were so happy."

"Things were simpler then."

"It's like we're starting fresh."

"You mean we're starting with nothing."

"You make it sound like the worst thing in the world."

"I'm just not romanticizing the situation we're in." His face hardened.

"You take apartment? You like?" the landlord asked, walking up to them.

They broke their concentration on one another.

"Yes, it's fine," James told him. "We'll take it."

The landlord nodded, all smiles. James gave Fran a look that cued her to hand over the money she was carrying. She opened the zipped compartment in her purse. Nothing. She thought she'd put it there after removing it from the outside pocket with the snap and flap. It was empty. Her hands fumbled, and her brain scrambled to make what wasn't there materialize because she desperately could not accept the obvious.

"What?" James's voice was tinny, the way it always was when he was nervous or anxious.

She looked up at him with wide, horrified eyes. Her mouth opened soundlessly.

James grabbed his head with both hands. "You don't have it? You don't have the money?"

She shook her head. "I know I had it." Her tears glistened in the early afternoon sun shining into the room.

"Did you check every pocket there?"

"I checked, James."

"Well, dump your things out."

She dropped to her knees, upending her purse and raking out the contents. James joined her on the floor, helping her rifle through everything: tissues, a comb, chewing gum, her wallet, a picture of the kids, eight dollars, a pocket calendar. No envelope.

"I know I had it." Her tears came fast.

"Wait," James said, still fumbling with the inconsequential things from her purse, "did you leave it in the car?"

"No. No, I put it in this part of my purse. I know I—" She stopped and locked eyes with James. They were thinking the same thing.

"That kid. That son of a . . ." James spoke through clenched teeth, biting down to hold back the last of his words. His face was red, menacing.

The look frightened Fran. She'd never seen him so angry.

"You no take apartment?" the landlord asked. "You no take, then I have more peoples to show." He sounded impatient now.

James stood. He reached down to help Fran to her feet. "We should let the man get on with his business."

Fran turned to the landlord. "Can you hold the place for us?" Her voice was feeble and childlike, as if she knew the question was pointless.

"You have cash. You have apartment. No hold," the landlord said with an umpire's exaggerated cross-sweep of his hands.

"Come on, honey." James guided Fran to the door with his hand on the small of her back. He told the landlord, "Thank you for your time," his eyes focused on the ground.

They said nothing as they walked down the street toward their car, until James suddenly stopped, looking up and down the block like he had lost something.

"What are you . . ." Fran trailed off as she was struck with the same realization her husband had obviously just had. They both stood on the sidewalk, mouths slackened with disbelief, staring at the spot where they knew they had parked, only now they were staring at an old Chevy with rusted spots arching over bald tires. The Lexus was gone.

"We have to report this to the police," Fran demanded. "I can't believe this. My . . . the photo album was in the car, James!"

"We can report it," he said, his voice husky, as if he might cry.

They walked up the street to the Taco Loco restaurant for bus directions to the nearest police station. They rode along in awkward silence as the bus sputtered and belched gas fumes. People jostled against them in the narrow plastic seats. The air throbbed with the noise of crying babies who needed changing and the smell of armpits.

James and Fran spilled out of the crowded bus onto another busy street right in front of the police station. They rushed in, talking at once about their stolen car. The officer pointed them to a desk where another policeman sat working behind a sheet of bulletproof glass. They hurried there and once again began their story. The policeman didn't look too concerned or interested. He gave them a form to fill out and told them to return it to him when they were done.

Officers passed them with brisk, self-important steps. They were invisible. James felt less than invisible. "I didn't want to push our luck," he repeated in self-reprimand.

"You couldn't have known, James," Fran said softly.

"No, but I could've avoided the risk."

"Are you blaming me?"

He walked away to exit the station, his words trailing him, "I didn't say that."

Fran followed, widening her stride to fall in step with his agitated pace. "That tone. It sure sounds like it."

When they reached the steps outside, he spun around to face her. "You were so insistent."

"You *do* blame me! I don't believe this!"

"If we hadn't gone to see that dump, we'd still have my Lexus!"

"We went there because we need a place to live. Or have you already forgotten the whole point of trying to make this happen?"

"Of course I haven't."

"Well, stop acting like the whole world is coming to an end because you lost that stupid car. You can get another car. We can't get our pictures back. That's all we had left."

"My car was the last thing we had, Fran!"

"You mean the last thing *you* had. Let it go, James. What we had—
that life—it's over and done with."

"That's easy enough for you to say."

"Excuse me? What's that supposed to mean?"

"It means that everything I worked for is lost. What *I* worked for!"

"You arrogant . . . I don't believe you. For the last two and a half
years, I've been practically begging you to let me work, let me do *something* with my life besides taking care of you and the kids. But you had
to have it your way. And now you want to stand there and talk to me
like I've been riding on some gravy train?"

"That's not—"

"Don't interrupt me. I'm not done. Let me make one thing clear,
James. I have always done my part. I have always been willing to do
whatever is necessary for our family, including working like a dog in a
slop kitchen for slave wages to help save money. And you know what?
I'll go back there to that crap hole and do it again and again if it'll get
us that much closer to getting our kids back. Because that's all that
matters to me. Not that stupid car. Not anything else." Fran wiped
away angry tears, her chin trembling.

James turned his face upward. "God." It was a single word, a prayer
of anguish and pleading.

He took her in his arms, and they held tightly to each other. It
didn't matter about the comings and goings of people around them.
For that moment, they hid themselves away in the safety of each other.

34

It was near the end of Fran's shift. She was putting away the last of the breakfast dishes. James came into the kitchen with a strange expression on his face. He was carrying his mop but had no pail, and she was going to say something when she saw Oma appear behind him. Then she understood the look on his face—a mix of astonishment and embarrassment.

"I have a few more things to finish," James said. "I'll let you two talk and catch up."

Fran nodded, still not quite able to find her voice. When she did finally speak, she told her mother, "Please don't look at me like that."

"Like what?"

"Like I'm pitiful." She wished she didn't look so tired and sweaty right then, her blond ponytail dirty and stringy. She brushed strands of loose hair away from her eyes.

"You're not *pitiful*. You're far from pitiful. But Franny, how—"

"It just . . . it just happened, Mom." She turned away to shelve the last of the pots. Before facing her mother again, she took off her apron and smoothed the wrinkles in her shirt.

"Are you done working?" Oma asked. "Can we sit and talk?"

"Sure."

Fran led her mother to an empty table.

"I was worried when I hadn't heard from you after getting back."

"How'd you find us?"

"Reba came to see me."

"What?"

"Yes. She came to see me."

"How'd she get all the way to your place?"

"A policeman brought her. Reba said he's a family friend."

"Adam? Adam Richards?"

"Yes, yes, I believe so. Anyhow, she told me everything."

There was a pause. Then Fran answered her mother's unspoken question. "I wanted to tell you, I really did."

"Then why didn't you? Why did I have to hear about it from Reba? Don't you know you can talk to me about anything?"

"I know, I just . . ." Fran didn't finish the thought.

"What?"

"I didn't want you to worry—" Fran began but stopped herself. "I didn't want you to judge me."

"I wouldn't. I'd never judge you, and I certainly wouldn't try to persuade you to do something you don't want to do. You're strong, smart, and determined. The only thing I've ever wanted to do is support you."

"I know."

"Then you should have trusted me enough to tell me."

"I know. I know. I guess, more than anything, I was ashamed."

"You needn't be. Hard times can fall on anybody."

"I know, but still, I didn't want anybody finding out or, I should say, I didn't want any more of our friends finding out."

"Who'd you talk to about this?"

"Charlotte and her husband, Pastor Phillips. We didn't actually talk to them about it. Our lawyer had Pastor Phillips come in as a character witness for us in family court."

"What happens now?"

"We have another court date next week. We're supposed to be settled someplace, be ready to take our kids to a home of our own."

"I see." She didn't ask the obvious question, but she didn't need to.

"We're not ready, Mom."

"Maybe they'll give you more time."

"If we don't have a home for our kids, they told us they'll put them in long-term foster care. *Foster care*, Mom. Our kids aren't *foster* kids. We love them. We want them back."

"Well, have you thought about asking someone to take them in while you and James work on getting settled?"

"Funny, had you asked me that a month ago, I would've been too proud to consider it. Now when I think about it, I realize James and I just don't have anybody we could go to for that kind of favor. We have four kids. That's a big number."

"You have lots of wealthy friends. Couldn't they help just a little while?"

"We knew people who invited us to their expensive parties, and I served on committees . . . I learned that doesn't qualify as friendship."

"Fran," Oma began slowly, "I was talking with Pastor Yaeger the other day. You remember him, he's the one who oversees missions for our church. Anyway, he's taking a group to join up with some other missionaries in Honduras. He says he usually travels with his secretary, but she's just had a baby, she's on maternity leave. He's looking to hire someone for the trip. All expenses paid."

"Why are you telling me this, Mom?"

"Well, it sounds like a good opportunity for you to make some real money."

"Honduras? I don't want to leave James, the children."

James heard only Fran's comment as he walked into the dining room. "Leave?" he asked.

Fran and Oma turned to see him.

"Mom was telling me about a job. Some short-term thing, but I'm not interested."

"Oh?" James pulled up a seat to join them.

"I was saying that one of the pastors at the church needs a secretary to travel with him to Honduras," Oma said. "He's taking a group to help flood victims."

"For how long?" James asked.

"Oh." Oma's face lit up with surprise. "Six months, maybe seven. But he says it depends on how smoothly things go. It could be longer. He's the chief engineer for a lot of the rebuilding they'll be doing. I was telling Fran it's an opportunity for her to make some good money. The trip is covered by the church."

"Thanks, Mom, but I said I'm not interested. Anyway, he's probably got more than enough qualified people who are."

"Maybe, but he says if you want the job, it's yours."

"Excuse me?" Fran said.

James shifted in his seat.

"I said Pastor Yaeger is offering you the job—if you want it."

"Wait, why would he do that?"

"Don't talk to me in that tone, Franny. You'd think I'd done something wrong."

"You discussed my personal business with someone I barely know."

"He's not *someone*, he's Pastor Yaeger."

"I don't believe this."

"I think you should take it," James interjected.

The two women just looked at him in astonishment, so he repeated himself. "I think you should take it."

Oma was pleased but Fran was even more upset. She rounded on James. "Why would you say something like that?"

"Because, Fran, it makes sense. We need money to get back on our feet. This is an opportunity."

"But I don't want to leave. I don't want to leave the kids for six months, maybe longer."

"Wouldn't you rather have them with us for good instead of just having visitation rights? Of course you would. Well, this is your shot, and I'll look for mine."

"Six months, James? And you heard her. What if something goes wrong? I could be there for who knows how long. And what if something else happens, like that crazy woman Miss Alison?"

"Let's think positively."

"That's a little hard to do after what's already happened. I will look for work here."

James asked Oma, "When does Pastor Yaeger need an answer?"

"Soon. They're leaving in a few weeks."

"Fran, do you really think you can find a job in a few weeks? You know we've tried. This is being handed to you. To us."

"I don't like being pressured."

"We didn't mean to pressure you, honey," Oma said. "We just want you to consider the opportunity you're being given."

"Well, it feels like pressure." Fran got up from the table and walked toward the exit. James trotted after her, throwing words over his shoulder: "Excuse us, Oma." Once they'd reached the hall, he pulled at Fran's arm to stop her from going any farther.

"Hey, what's the problem?" he asked.

"Six months away and you don't see a problem with that?"

"I know it's a long time, but eyes on the goal, right?"

"James, I could never forgive myself if something happened to one of our kids and I wasn't here. To be so far away . . ."

"I know. I know. But we've got to break out of this rut we're in, Franny. We need more money than we're making, and we need it now."

"I know."

"And maybe, if we can tell that judge you've got something lined up to make some real money, even if it's short-term, she'll cut us some slack."

"Maybe. I don't know."

"Your mom will need an answer soon."

"I'll tell her I'll give her an answer in a week if I can't find something local."

"Fair enough. Just keep an open mind, okay? Big picture."

She wasn't so sure but said, "Big picture."

Along with the photo of her family, Fran kept a small pocket calendar in her purse. She carried it with her everywhere. She'd "X" off the days as they drew closer to their court day. There were only a few left, during which she and James put in job applications anywhere they could. She also knew that her time was running out to give an answer to Pastor Yaeger's offer. James was still firm on the idea that she should call Oma and take the job. Fran remained resistant. "Anything could happen," she told him. And it did.

There was a new girl who came to the shelter: young, heroin-thin with sleeves of multi-colored tattoos that obscured her habit. She was introduced to Fran as the new kitchen help. The girl had a buzz cut on both sides of her head, and what remained of her hair was short, spiked into a mohawk, and dyed the color of brilliant blue peacock feathers. She liked running her slender fingers over the top of her hair. She moved around the kitchen wiping down this, putting away that, but all the while Fran sensed the girl watching her.

Fran emptied the garbage into a large barrel for James or Carl or one of the other guys to pick up. She'd only had her back turned for a minute before her thoughts fell on her purse. It was put away in one of the lower cabinets, right where the new girl was storing the cleaned pots.

Turning quickly, Fran crossed the space in broad steps, heading for the cabinet. The girl had eased to the other side of the small space, wiping down a counter that had already been cleaned. Fran yanked open the cabinet drawer. She exhaled when she saw her purse, but thought to check it. Rifling through it, she saw immediately that her wallet was missing, and her small calendar.

Still holding her purse, Fran turned to the girl. "My wallet is missing," she breathed.

The girl kept wiping idly.

"I said, my wallet is missing," Fran repeated, louder, with panic and anger flushing her face.

The girl paused just long enough to glance at her. "Not my problem."

"It is if you took it. And my calendar. That calendar is important. Give me back my things."

The girl kept at her mindless job, slowly moving the rag in circles.

Fran took a step closer. "I want my wallet back. Give me back my calendar!"

"Look, I don't know what you're talking about."

"You stole my things! Don't try to play dumb. No one else has been in here."

"It's not smart to go around accusing people."

"I'm reporting this. I'm reporting *you*."

The girl came at her fiercely, causing Fran to take a reflexive step back. "I said I didn't take your wallet, lady. Got it?"

"It was in my purse." Fran's voice shook with anger. "I know I had it in there before you showed up. My kids' picture was in there, and my calendar. I need that!"

The girl walked away, and on impulse, Fran grabbed her arm. Just as swiftly, the girl spun and slapped Fran. "Keep your hands off me, lady! Who do you think you are?"

Fran gasped, holding her face. With all the hurt, fear, and anguish boiling up and bursting its way out of her, she hit the girl back.

They flew into each other, shrieking and pulling and screaming, knocking over dishes and pots. The calamity of noise brought three other workers rushing into the kitchen. One man reached in to tear the women apart as he yelled to the others, "Get help! Get Pastor Murphy!"

Fran and James sat in two small chairs in front of Pastor Murphy's desk. Fran's eyes were lowered as tears ran steadily down her bruised cheek. James held her hand. They each had a garbage bag full of their personal belongings.

"I'm sorry," Pastor Murphy said. "I'm very sorry, but we have a hard rule here about violence."

"But that girl *stole* my wife's wallet and things," James repeated.

"Violence is never the answer, James. That's what we try to teach here. You see why I have to ask you to leave? If you stay, it negates everything I've said. And then the rules don't matter. I can't give one person a pass, or else I'm gonna be faced with ten or twenty possible situations just like this, and maybe the outcome will be worse." Pastor Murphy shook his head. "I'm guessing you wouldn't reconsider staying, James, and we could try to find another shelter for Fran."

"Thanks, Pastor Murphy, but absolutely not."

"It'll be much harder to find a place that'll take you both. Most shelters don't take couples and families. Not enough room."

They were silent for a moment. Pastor Murphy went on. "I really am sorry. I like you. I like you both, but you've put me in an impossible situation here."

"I see." James looked over at Fran. She remained still, staring at the floor, her jaw tensed. James squeezed her shoulder and whispered, "It'll be okay."

"Do you have any idea where you might go?" Pastor Murphy asked. James said, "No."

"Well, try Hope House. They used to take couples. Maybe they still do. And listen, if your situation hasn't improved soon, give me a call." He handed James his card, and then he gave one to Fran.

"It's the address of the church where I pastor. It's just a couple of blocks from here. We're there most evenings. My number is on the card too. I always answer."

James stood and extended his hand to Pastor Murphy. "Thank you. We appreciate everything you've done."

When Fran stood, Pastor Murphy came from behind his desk and hugged her. He lifted her chin to look her squarely in the face. "It will be all right, Fran. Remember, your angels are with you wherever you go."

35

ope House no longer took in couples, only women, but Fran wouldn't stay there without James. Hope House recommended Our Lady of Peace Shelter, but they were overcrowded. Good News Shelter was for men only. Garden Missions suggested they come back at the end of the week. Lots of turnover during the weekends.

The moon hung like a white plate against the dark sky when James and Fran finally stopped their search and stood at a bus stop, their feet clotted with pain, arms aching from carrying all their worldly possessions with them. The traffic was steady on Michigan Avenue. Fran held her garbage bag of items limply at her side. "What now?" she asked James.

He looked frayed, his curly brown hair hanging in his face and clinging to his damp forehead. "I don't know, but we need to find someplace to sleep."

"How much money do we have left?"

"Maybe enough for a night or two at a motel, but that would leave us with nothing."

"We need money to get around. We need money to find jobs."

James nodded. "I agree." He looked across the street to Buckingham Fountain. The water spouting up was lit in shimmering jewel tones—a Chicago summer tradition. "Hey, what about Grant Park over there?"

"The park?"

"Yeah."

"Isn't that kind of dangerous?"

"We're downtown. This neighborhood isn't bad. It's a busy street. And the park's got lots of trees. We won't be seen."

"I don't know, James."

"Well, you just said you didn't want to spend our money on a motel."

"Are you sure? I mean, about the park?"

"Yeah, yeah, we'll be okay. We can take turns sleeping. I'll keep look out first. And tomorrow, we can try more shelters."

They dragged their garbage bags stuffed with everything they owned to the center of the street, where they stopped for passing traffic. They crossed the rest of the way to the shady park. Neither said a word.

They found a tree that was situated close enough to the streets that James could observe foot traffic. He sat under the broad branches of an elm tree, which cloaked them in shadows, and helped Fran nestle next to him, her head on his lap. He covered her with a sweatshirt drawn from his own garbage bag of clothing.

"James," Fran said quietly.

"Yeah?"

"We have to call Mark Cohan."

"I know."

"All of my notes were in my calendar."

"What notes?"

"Everything I'd planned to tell the judge."

"We'll do fine, Franny. Get some sleep, okay?"

A breeze rustled through the trees and skipped along the fallen leaves around them. She hadn't heard James. She was already dreaming.

The attorney's receptionist, sitting just outside his office door, seemed to hesitate for a moment when James and Fran walked up and said they had an appointment. Then she remembered her manners. "Yes, yes, of course. He's expecting you. Go right in."

They walked into a room that wasn't much bigger than the law-
yer's desk, which was covered in haphazard stacks of manila folders.
Mr. Cohan beckoned at them to come in while talking on the phone.
The room had no windows, only file cabinets and a single bookshelf
where the attorney reached for a book. He said something about the
"PROTECT Act of 2003" and then hung up.

He looked at James and Fran. "Wow, what happened to you two?"

They dragged their garbage bags behind them, cups of coffee in
their hands, bought from a fast-food restaurant whose facilities they
had used to clean up. Still, the wear of the night before was evident.
James needed a shave, and Fran's stringy hair, twisted into a sagging
knot, needed shampooing. Both were red-eyed and looked exhausted.

"We didn't get much sleep," James said.

Mr. Cohan extended a hand to the seats in front of his desk.
"Please. Sit."

Fran melted onto the chair. Every part of her body ached.

Cohan took in their bags. "What's this?"

"We got kicked out of the shelter. These are our things," Fran said.

"What?"

"Yeah," James echoed. "We got kicked out."

"Why?" the attorney asked, his eyes moving between the two of them.

"I, uh, I got into a fight," Fran told him.

Mr. Cohan could only lift his brows. "So you're . . . ?"

James and Fran looked at each other. "Well, um, we've no place to
stay." James spoke for both of them.

"This isn't good. This is *not* good," their lawyer said. "We're supposed to show *progress*."

"Hey, it's not like we didn't try," James snapped. "We've been working our butts off to save up nickels to get a place."

"So what happened?"

"Our money was stolen."

"We had an apartment picked out and everything," Fran added.

"Wow. I'm sorry to hear that."

"It's been a nightmare," she admitted.

"Well, the judge is expecting an update. Like we talked about, that's the point of this next hearing." He rifled through notes in a folder. "Your kids' caseworker tells me they're back at the group home."

"Yes," Fran said. "I was relieved, frankly. At least they're all together." She sipped her coffee gingerly.

"That woman who took them in is crazy. She hit Reba," James explained.

The attorney interjected, "The police got involved. Have you given any thought to some sort of temporary living arrangement? Anything that we could give the judge to show you're on your way to solid ground again?"

"Honestly," Fran said, "we don't even know where we'll be staying tonight."

"Well, do you have any job prospects? Something?"

Fran was silent. James put in, "Fran has a job offer."

"Oh?"

"It's just a part-time thing," Fran said.

"But it's an offer, right?" the lawyer pressed. "What is it? Tell me about it." He picked up a pen to take notes.

"It's a secretarial job. Traveling, actually, with a Christian mission group from my mom's church."

"That sounds great. But you don't look too interested."

"I'd rather find something here," she said.

"Well, how much traveling are we talking about?"

"Six or seven months, maybe more," she said.

"James?" Mr. Cohan waited for his take on things.

"I'm fine with it. It's a great opportunity to make some real money. We need it." He was looking at Fran, who kept her eyes on her coffee cup.

"It sounds like that's something for you two to work out. But I'd suggest deciding fast. The fact is, the judge isn't going to be too gracious if you have nothing to show for the past couple of months. Look,

I know you've been trying hard. And I hate to say it, but the only thing that matters is results."

"What will happen to our kids if we don't show results?" Fran asked.

"The judge won't change her position from what she told us the first time. The next step in the process will be to find a long-term home solution for your kids. If you're not prepared to take them, the state will." He paused before adding, "Look, Mr. and Mrs. Harrison, you're good people, and I know you love your kids. I'm telling you, from what I've seen, you don't want your kids to become wards of the state. Their facilities are overcrowded. The likelihood of your kids staying together is almost nil. The CPS workers, they try hard to oversee the process of placing kids in decent homes, but the fact is, it's a crapshoot. *Decent* becomes a relative term. And kids often fall through the cracks when it comes to proper oversight, once they're placed. You got lucky. It could have been very different if you didn't have that cop friend looking after yours." He aimed his next statement directly at Fran, "Do whatever you need to do to get your kids back."

After they left the attorney's office, they went to a small sandwich shop around the corner. They sat in a back booth where they could inconspicuously tuck their garbage bags out of view.

"We have three days, Franny," James said softly.

She knew what he meant. "I know. I know." She poked at her salad. "I'm not very hungry. We shouldn't have wasted money on this."

"You need to eat," he said and bit into his tuna melt.

"You know how much I love our kids, don't you?" she asked.

"Of course I do, and they do too."

"I just don't want you to think that I'm not thinking of them, or that I don't get what's going to happen in the next few days. It's just that . . . I'm not even sure how to explain it." She breathed out as she leaned back in the booth, gazing down at her uneaten salad. "I feel like we're all like little broken pieces barely held together, and I'm just afraid of us breaking apart completely if I'm gone that long. We're a family, James. Family means being *together*. You and me and the kids."

He took her hand. "Fran, I love your devotion to us. I know how you feel, but I think we're stronger than that. Look at all we've survived. We'll make it okay if you take that job. We will."

"But for the kids—it's not over yet. And what about you, if I go? What will you do?"

"Keep at it. My luck has been so bad, I figure something's gotta change at some point." He gave her a quick smile. He found himself observing Fran. She looked so tired. She'd lost weight, the fine lines around her eyes more noticeable under the harsh lighting of the sandwich shop. Her lips had lost their natural pinkish color, and she'd developed a nervous habit of biting her lower lip, like now. He blamed himself for putting her through so much stress.

His piercing gaze called her attention. "What?" Her dry mouth forced a smile.

He picked up his sandwich, needing to distract himself.

"What were you thinking?"

"Nothing."

"Don't give me that. Staring at me like that. What?"

"Okay." He put the sandwich down, briefly glancing out the window at the passing traffic. "I was thinking how much I love you. How I don't deserve you."

"James."

"It's true. All those years, I thought I was the one making sacrifices, being *generous*." He laughed lightly at himself, shook his head, and laughed again. "I'd forgotten what I'd been given. You. Our kids. How fortunate I was."

"Oh, James."

"It's true. All true. And the thing is, you tried to tell me, tried to show me, but I just didn't get it. I don't know, I guess I didn't want to get it. Maybe it would've burst some sort of bubble for me. It just seems foolish now."

"We have both been different people over the years. That's just how life is. We go through things, have a bunch of experiences—some good, some not so good—and they change us. Hopefully for the better."

"Yeah."

"Hey. Don't sound like that. You gave us a good home. You made us feel secure. I believe your heart was in the right place, we just needed more of *you*."

"Well, in the end, what did it amount to anyway? I lost it all, Franny."

"That's not true, you still have me, you still have our family."

"A family I couldn't hold together. You just said it yourself. We're broken pieces."

"And you reminded me that we're stronger than that, as long as we can hold on to each other."

"You just deserve so much more, Fran."

She sat up. "I have what I want. And when we get our kids back, I'll have *everything*."

36

James and Fran were late for their court appearance. They arrived breathless, having run from the bus to the county building. When they got off the elevator, Mark Cohan was standing outside the door of the courtroom, checking his watch and looking for them.

"You're late," he snapped. "You get lost from the motel? I've been calling you repeatedly."

"I'm sorry." James croaked, out of breath from running. He was trying to control his panting. "Our phone is out of minutes. And no, we didn't get lost."

"We missed our first bus." Fran, too, gulped air.

Mark Cohan had given them money to stay at a motel for the night so they could be rested and get cleaned up. James had splurged on a ten-dollar haircut and a shave. Fran opted to twist her hair into a French knot that would disguise her split ends.

James kept adjusting his sport coat that was now a little too broad in the shoulders. His weight loss was evident, and the jacket looked borrowed for the occasion. When their attorney looked to be appraising them, Fran touched the side-tie of her wrap dress and wished she had been able to wear her skirt instead, but it was too loose in the waist now. She thought the wrap looked more dignified than most of her clothing options, but now everything was loose.

"It's too late for a review," the attorney said. "We have to get in there. We're the first case to be heard. The judge will take the bench any minute now."

James nodded, and Fran did, too, with her hand on her heart.

Cohan touched her arm. "You okay?"

"Yes, yes, I'm fine."

"There's one development I wanted to talk with you about, but we can address that later. We're late. Let's go."

They filed into the courtroom just as the Harrisons' case was being called. The judge looked over her glasses and said, "Good of you to join us this morning, counselor," as they rushed to take their seats.

Attorney Cohan said, "My apologies, Your Honor." He rifled through the notes he'd left on his seat before he'd gone out in search of the Harrisons.

The judge asked, "Are counselors ready to proceed?"

"Yes, Your Honor," the CPS lawyer said.

Mr. Cohan said the same.

The judge looked over at the Harrisons. "This is a dispositional hearing. I'm certain your lawyer has explained what will happen today, but for the record, I will determine whether your children should return home, stay in the care of CPS, or in the care of another family, if you are not in the position to resume responsibility for them. The objective is to ultimately work toward finding a safe and permanent home for your children, Mr. and Mrs. Harrison. Is that clear?"

"Yes, Your Honor," James and Fran responded.

The judge looked to the CPS caseworker and the agency's attorney seated across the way from Fran and James. "Do you have your records prepared?"

"Yes, Your Honor," the caseworker said. She handed typed notes to the lawyer, who gave them to the judge.

The judge perused the documents for a moment and then looked to them again, her glasses sitting low on the bridge of her nose. "Ms. Atkins, would you care to report on progress?"

"Yes, Your Honor. Following the adjudicatory hearing, Stacy

Harrison, Elliott Harrison, and Reba Harrison were each placed in the care of Allison Pringle. Jay Harrison remained at the CPS group home. We were not successful in finding placement."

"Were you able to arrange for consistent visits for the parents with their children?"

"Yes, we were."

"How frequent were these arrangements?"

"Mr. and Mrs. Harrison wanted visits once a week, but that was just more than we could handle. Managing the other caseloads wouldn't permit me to devote that much time to the Harrison family."

"Well, again, to my question: how often were these parents granted visitation with their children?"

"Every other week."

The judge looked to the other side of the room where the Harrisons sat with Mark Cohan, watching and listening to the young caseworker.

"Every other week," the judge repeated. "And so they've seen their children three times since their placement?"

"No, Your Honor," the caseworker said.

"No?" the judge queried. "Explain."

"The third visit was interrupted by the incident that led to the children's removal from Ms. Allison Pringle's home."

The CPS lawyer said, "You have the police report there, Your Honor."

The judge paused to flip through the documents. "I see," she said, still examining the page. "It appears you've removed Ms. Pringle from your viability list."

"We have."

"And the children haven't seen their parents since this incident?"

"No. No, Your Honor." The caseworker shifted in her seat and gave a quick glance toward the Harrisons.

"Why?" the judge asked.

"We tried, Your Honor, but there were scheduling issues."

"Of what nature, Ms. Atkins?"

"Well, actually, there was a mix-up on the visitation date. I found that I was doubled-booked. The issue wasn't resolved before our hearing today."

"That's very, very unfortunate." The judge kept scanning the notes. "And how are the children adjusting?"

"Well, they're doing as well as most, ma'am."

The judge looked up. "What does that mean, Ms. Atkins? Can you be a little more specific?"

"Oh, yes, yes, of course. They're in good health, physically, but there was some anxiety."

"Would you recommend counseling for them?"

"I don't think so. They're back together now at the group home. They seem happier. They miss their parents, of course." She glanced at the Harrisons again. "That's all they talk about when I see them. They asked if kids could testify in your court. I said yes, but not in a hearing like this. The youngest one . . ." She looked down at her notes. "Reba. She even wrote you a letter."

"Oh?" The judge returned to flipping through the notes.

"Excuse me, Your Honor, if you're looking for the letter, it's not there."

"You didn't include it?"

"Well, no." She looked to the CPS lawyer, who dropped his focus to his own notepad.

"Do you have the letter, Ms. Atkins?" the judge asked.

"I think so. I had it in my bag." The caseworker poked through her large purse, pulled out a folded sheet of paper, and held it up. She looked relieved. "Here."

"Well, read it," the judge instructed her.

"You want me to read the letter?"

"Yes, Ms. Atkins, I believe those were my words. The child wrote the letter to the court. We'll hear it."

The caseworker unfolded the paper and began reading.

Dear Judge,

My name is Reba Harrison. I am seven years old. I have one sister. Her name is Stacy. And I have two brothers. They are Jay and Elliott. We all live in this big place our lady caseworker calls the Group Home. And before that, me and my sister Stacy and my brother Elliott got sent to live in a house with smelly sheets.

I miss our real house, but mostly I miss my mommy and daddy. When we lived in our big house with the big pretty fountain in front, everybody seemed sad, especially my mom. So I prayed with my grandma Oma for God to fix our family. And then we lost our big house. I thought it was the worstest thing in the whole wide world. But then it wasn't.

We were together all the time. We played games. We drove to places in our SUV to see things. And my mommy and daddy looked happy again.

But the police came, and the people who take kids away from bad families came too. They took us away from Mommy and Daddy. Except they are not bad parents. They are good parents, but bad things happened, and we had to camp in our SUV. Mommy and Daddy love us big bunches. That's what my mommy says. And they are the only ones who know how to take care of us. Mommy knows how to make my warm milk with cimmonin.

Ms. Atkins stumbled on the word and looked up at the judge, then continued.

My grandma Oma taught me just because bad things happen doesn't make it the worstest thing. It sometimes makes good things start. Your sister will make you warm milk, if the lady with the smelly sheets will let her. Big brothers will teach you how to spit far. Don't tell my mom.

One time my dad told me being in a family is like being in a big boat. If everybody is in the boat, then we are safe if a scary storm comes. That only works if everybody is together. It's scary in the boat without Mommy and Daddy.

The lady caseworker says you can put us all back together. Please do it. We miss our mommy and daddy. I bet they miss us too.

Very yours truly,
Reba Harrison

P.S. If you do it, I can draw you a nice picture of a family in a boat. But don't tell my sister. She says bribery is a felluny.

The judge resisted a smile. She took off her glasses. "Thank you, Ms. Atkins." She focused on the Harrisons. James had his arm around Fran. She needed a tissue but wiping away the tears with her hand would have to do.

"You're fortunate, Mr. and Mrs. Harrison. Your daughter is quite amazing, I'm sure. If she's any indication of the work you've done, you're raising your children well." Then she addressed Mark Cohan: "Counselor, have you prepared an update for the court on Mr. and Mrs. Harrison's employment and living accommodations?"

"Yes, Your Honor, and if it would please the court, I have included statements made by Pastor John Murphy, who operates Green Pastures Mission. Mr. and Mrs. Harrison took residence there and were both employed at the facility. Pastor Murphy speaks very favorably of both the Harrisons."

"Approach," the judge said. Mr. Cohan took the documents to her. She looked the papers over and homed in on the termination date of the Harrisons' stay at Green Pastures Mission. "I see they're no longer residing at the shelter."

"No, they aren't, Your Honor. May I be permitted to speak about the progress my clients have made?"

"Please."

"They have been model residents at Green Pastures Mission, as you see from the letter Pastor Murphy has provided. As stated, my clients were also employed at the shelter, dutifully saving their resources to stabilize their situation."

"And have they, counselor?"

Mark Cohan paused because he hadn't had time to speak to the Harrisons about Fran's decision on her job offer. "Mrs. Harrison can better update you concerning the employment matter, ma'am."

He looked at Fran. James was waiting too.

"I have a job, Your Honor," Fran said. "Well, I have a job *offer*."

"That sounds promising," the judge told her. "Congratulations. Please share the details."

"It's an assignment, actually," Fran began, "with a foreign Christian mission group."

"What's the job, Mrs. Harrison?"

"Secretary to the chief engineer, ma'am."

"For how long?"

"At least six months, possibly longer."

"That's a lengthy assignment. You said *foreign* mission group. Where, may I ask?"

"Honduras."

"And what happens after the six months?"

"I'd try to find something else. And maybe have better success because I'd actually have some experience on my resume, not just my business degree."

"I see. And what about the care of your children? Is Mr. Harrison now in the position to resume responsibility?"

Mark Cohan said, "Mr. Harrison is still seeking full-time employment."

"I see," the judge said again. "This job offer, will it offer sufficient pay to cover the living expenses of your family while your husband pursues employment?"

"I don't know, Your Honor," Fran said. "I haven't had that conversation."

"There's not been an official acceptance of the job?"

Fran glanced at James, who was watching her. "No, ma'am, there hasn't."

"I'm sensing hesitation, Mrs. Harrison."

Fran didn't respond.

"I'll take your silence as a tacit admission." The judge addressed Mr. Cohan. "The court mandated that stable housing be secured before the children are to be released into the care of Mr. and Mrs. Harrison. According to the information you have submitted, they're no longer residing at the shelter. You mentioned that your clients worked at the shelter and accumulated savings for better housing provisions."

"That's correct, Your Honor."

"Well, what's the progress on securing a place to live? Where are they living now?"

"Right now," Mark Cohan began, "they're living in a motel."

"A motel? For how long?"

"I'm not certain, Your Honor," he said, even though he could very well have given an exact date, based on the money he'd given the Harrisons.

"Mr. Harrison," the judge said, "can you provide a more specific answer? How long will you be living at the motel, and when do you think you'll have an apartment secured?"

James inhaled deeply. "I'm sorry, but I don't have a good answer for either of those questions, ma'am."

"Can you at least give an estimate, sir? A week? A month?" The judge waited. "Sir, are you or are you not financially prepared to secure a residence for yourself and your family?"

James hadn't been aware that he was breathing heavily until then. "No," he said.

"Speak up, sir."

"No," he repeated.

"Can you tell me why, sir? Don't you have savings prepared for this very purpose?"

"We . . . we did," James said softly.

"Speak up, Mr. Harrison. I can't hear you."

"We had money, but it was stolen when we went to see a place, Your Honor."

"All of your money was stolen?"

"Most of it. We have a little left."

"Enough to secure an apartment?"

"No."

The judge leaned back in her chair. Whispering could be heard coming from the caseworker and CPS lawyer on the other side of the aisle from the Harrisons.

The judge leaned forward again, adjusting her glasses and looking at the documents in front of her. "If I'm understanding the current situation correctly, the Harrisons have not secured a home for their children, nor are they in the position to do so immediately. Nor have they attained employment that would ensure sufficient provision for their children. Am I correct?"

"Yes, Your Honor," Mark Cohan said, "but some consideration should be given to the traumatic circumstance of having their resources stolen from them. I submit to the court that any shortfall on the part of Mr. and Mrs. Harrison is *not* from lack of trying. They looked for jobs, but like many in the country right now, they couldn't find work. Mr. Harrison was a successful businessman who willingly labored as a janitor at the shelter to earn money for his family. Mrs. Harrison worked double shifts in the kitchen when they permitted her to do so, just so they could scrape together more money more quickly. They did their best, Your Honor."

"I can appreciate their effort, counselor. It's commendable. But I'm afraid the circumstances warrant more than just *trying*." The judge sighed and removed her glasses, aiming her attention at Fran and James. "Mr. and Mrs. Harrison, I'm sorry for what must've been a heartbreaking experience for you. You certainly have been through plenty. That said, your children need a home, and you need proper resources to care for them, including the provision of a home. I'm afraid, based on what's been presented before me, I have no choice but to mandate that the Harrison children remain in the custody of Child Protective Services. Foster care placement of Stacy Harrison, Jay Harrison, Elliott Harrison, and Reba Harrison will begin forthwith for the provision of long-term care in a home or homes deemed suitable."

Fran broke into a sob, sounding like a wounded animal. James wrapped his arms around her as she wept uncontrollably against his chest.

"Excuse me!" A voice came from several rows behind them.

The judge met the attention of the red-haired woman who had

raised her hand. Mark Cohan turned to see, as did the caseworker and CPS lawyer. James still held Fran, whose body contracted with soundless grief.

"Ma'am," the judge said. "I'll ask that you respect this court and its proceedings, or I'll have to ask you to leave."

The woman stood. "I'm sorry. I'm sorry. I mean no disrespect, Your Honor. My name is Charlotte Phillips, and this is my husband, Pastor Martin Phillips." She touched him on the shoulder.

James angled himself enough to see them, just as Martin Phillips stood up next to his wife.

"We were here before," Charlotte said, "for the first hearing. We're friends of the Harrisons."

"We'd like to volunteer to take care of their children for them," Pastor Phillips said. "They've been through so much, Your Honor."

Fran looked up the curve of James's neck, her tear-streaked face looking astonished. James whispered to Mark Cohan, "Did you know about this?"

"I did. I wanted to talk to you about it, but I couldn't get you on the phone."

The judge said, "Well, your timing is impeccable. Can your home accommodate the children?"

"Yes, Your Honor," Pastor Phillips said. "We have sufficient space. And we have the means to take care of them."

The judge addressed James and Fran. "Are you amenable to this offer given by . . ." She paused, looking again at the standing couple.

"Charlotte and Martin Phillips, Your Honor," the pastor supplied.

The judge nodded, continuing, "The offer extended to you by Mr. and Mrs. Phillips?"

"Absolutely," Fran said.

"Of course, of course," James confirmed.

"Very well then," the judge said. "Arrangements can be made and will be facilitated by Ms. Bernadette Atkins, the assigned caseworker. So ordered. We are dismissed."

James and Fran stood up in happy shock. They quickly shook hands with Mark Cohan, and then rushed to greet and hug Charlotte and Martin. The caseworker and the CPS lawyer paused before the small group just long enough to get the Phillips' contact information and tell both couples to expect a call.

"How did you know about today?" James asked.

"Adam," Pastor Phillips said. "You know, the policeman. Apparently, he's been talking to the caseworker since he got your kids taken out of that other home."

Charlotte said, "He's a really great guy. He wanted to know if we had any ideas on how to help."

"Well, this was it," Martin added.

"I'm grateful," James said, "to you guys, to Adam. You saved us. You saved our kids."

Fran hugged Charlotte again. "Thank you. Thank you with everything I have in my heart."

37

When the Harrison children got the news, they literally jumped for joy. Word spread quickly among the residents of the group home. Casper approached Jay when he heard. "So you're leaving this place, huh?" He didn't do well at hiding the glint of sadness in his eyes, even though he tried smiling.

"Yep," Jay responded. Then he asked Casper, "You gonna be cool?"

He shrugged. "Of course. I'll be here schooling the newbies when they come through."

"And watching their backs," Jay added.

"Yeah. Maybe not so much since Rodriguez got transferred."

"No joke?" Jay felt undeniable relief, even if he did know that the place would be history to him soon.

"No joke. I heard he got into something. It had to be major because the guys he was rolling with got arrested."

"Deep."

"Yeah, that's the story of this place. But it's not your story, Jay. You stay up."

James and Fran splurged on pizza and talked about seeing the kids as often as they wanted, and how everything would fall into place now. It just had to. And even though James knew they were nearing the last of the money they had, he still suggested they stay at the motel where Mark Cohan had gifted a night to them. It was by far nothing fancy, but the small lobby smelled of Pine-Sol, and the clerk at the desk insisted that guests help themselves to his little bowl of Starlight Mints. The sheets in the room were old but clean, and the bed was big enough for James and Fran to spoon by choice.

They strolled languidly along the busy street, holding hands, heading toward the bus stop.

"It's such a nice afternoon," Fran said, "let's walk the rest of the way to the motel."

"I'm tired. I feel like a deflated balloon."

"I'm tired too. But I'm happy too." She turned to him and took up both of his hands. "Let's walk."

There was something in the way the summer wind played with her hair, the way she squinted and fought the strands that whipped across her face, so he couldn't deny her. She was smiling at him as if she remembered nothing that had ever been scornful or hurtful or regretful about James Harrison. He captured some of her soft golden hair between his fingers and delicately tucked it behind her ear. He couldn't resist this beautiful woman.

He started strolling with her hand clasped in his, arms swaying in that casual way that says no worries, no rush.

"I can't tell you how relieved I feel," Fran said, like she hadn't spoken these words at least four times before.

James gave the same reply he'd given previously: "I know the feeling. Like an anvil has been lifted off my chest." He moved the conversation in a new direction. "We have to find a place to stay after tonight, and we may not be able to stay together." He gave her a side-eye glance. She didn't respond. "We can't keep sleeping outdoors, Franny. It's not safe."

"We haven't had any problems."

"Because we've been lucky. I don't want to keep pushing our luck, not with you out there with me."

She paused a beat. "What does that mean?"

"I just mean that I don't want to keep putting you in danger, putting *us* in danger, for that matter. And if we can't find a place that'll take us in together, then we'll just have to separate for now." He kept walking, aware that her fingers had grown a bit slack. "It's not like I want to," he added. "I hate the thought of it. And maybe we can find places that aren't that far, you know? I could catch a bus or even walk to where you'd be."

"Sounds like you've got this planned out." She tried to sound casual about it but failed.

"I'm just thinking out loud, Franny, I haven't planned anything. It's just how it is right now, but not for long, right?" He stopped and commanded her attention. Eyebrows raised, he repeated, "Right?" He waited. She struggled to look conciliatory. He leaned in and kissed her forehead, never letting go of her hand.

"Well, we'll have tonight together." She sighed.

"Absolutely. And a hot shower that's private."

"And who knows, maybe we'll get lucky tomorrow when we look at the shelters again. I mean, look what happened today. Charlotte and Pastor Phillips coming through like that. Who would've guessed that, right?"

"Right."

"So anything can happen tomorrow. I'm not giving up hope." She dropped James's hand so she could drape her arm around his waist.

James gave her a side-hug. He was aware of so many little things about her. The way her hair caressed and tickled his arm, the smell of her baby powder sweat mixed with dollar store apple shampoo, the way her hips moved and bumped him as they walked together, the way she chewed her lower lip when she was thinking, like now. He wanted to take it all in. Breathe it all in. Let it fill up his chest 'til it burst.

Fran woke up and squinted toward the single motel room window, where the mellow orange of the setting sun streaked the sky. She looked down at her clothes, remembering now that she'd told James she was going to lie down just for a minute and then get up to shower after him. She was fully dressed and felt rumpled, and the room was eerily quiet.

Her bare feet landed soundlessly on the nappy brown carpet. She looked around and, even though she knew she was alone, she called his name. "James?" She noticed his garbage bag of personal effects was gone. She rushed over to the corner where the miserable black plastic bag had been slumped next to hers. It was gone. She looked over to the small desk and saw he had left money—eighteen dollars and sixty-four cents. Most of it was in singles, neatly placed, along with a short pile of coins. There was no note. She called out his name again, but this time it wasn't a question. "Oh, James."

She made her way to the bed again, sitting on its end. Fran waited. She didn't know what to feel. In her head was a whirl of thoughts. *When did he go? Did he tiptoe out? Did he try to wake me? He didn't say goodbye, so maybe he'll come back.* Her insides churned. And she waited.

There were noises of muffled laughter from the other side of the thin drywall that separated the rooms. There were the sounds of car horns and tires rolling by on pavement outside the motel. There was the gurgling noise from deep within Fran's belly. But then something, or rather someone, interrupted. The knock was persistent. Fran heard her name being called. She recognized the voice.

"Mom?" She was reaching for the doorknob even before she'd gotten to the door. She pulled it open and saw Oma standing in front of her. "What are you doing here?"

"James called me. He asked me to come and get you."

"What?" Fran blinked. "And take me *where?*"

"Home with me. I came in a cab." Oma gestured behind her. Fran looked past her mother to see the idling car. "Can we talk about this in the cab, Franny? We can talk about everything on the way home."

Fran paused. "No."

"What?"

"No."

"Franny, honey, it's time to go. It's time for you to come home."

"I don't want to leave. I'm not leaving."

"Franny, please."

"James might come back here looking for me."

"Fran, he called me to come and get you. He wants you to go. He's . . . he's not coming back."

Fran looked hard and mean when she heard those words. "How do you know? Did he tell you that?"

Oma sighed. "Honey, I can't imagine what you're feeling right now."

"How do you know he's not coming back?"

"Because he told me he waited until you were asleep before he called me. He paid for the room and said he'd told the manager I'd be coming for you. He wanted to be gone before I got here. He asked me to look after you."

"Why?"

"Honey, I don't have answers. I only know what he asked me to do. Please, come with me, okay?"

Fran wiped away tears that wouldn't stop. "I need to get my bag," she said.

It was true. The manager confirmed what Oma had said. And now, riding silently next to Oma, Fran looked out of the back seat window onto the streets, shards of memories breaking inside her: James holding her hand, the feel of it, how often and natural it had become over these last months; the sound of his laughter; sighing next to him after working all day; hopeful, whispered plans they shared at night in their narrow bed. Then it hit her. *Green Pastures Mission. Pastor Murphy.* He'd said his church was just a couple of blocks from the shelter. Fran began raking through her purse, dropping things on the floor of the cab. "It's got to be in here," she murmured.

"What? What are you looking for, Franny?"

"The card. His card."

"Whose card?"

"Pastor Murphy. He gave us his card. It has the address of his church on it. Got it!" She held it up, angled to see the small print. "Grace At the Cross." She told Oma, "Mom, I have to go there."

James had walked miles and miles, carrying his garbage bag of clothes, allowing buses to pass him by. He needed to think. He wondered if he'd done the right thing. He wondered if he should have left a note. But then, the very reason he hadn't left a note was painfully evident to him: he couldn't bring himself to admit his own failings in writing.

He knew that no amount of words, no expression of apology would be big enough to fix the great rupture he'd caused. Fran had been gracious, but the consequences of everything he'd done wrong was clear. Even though he was powerless to right things, he could at least move out of the way so that Fran could do what was necessary. He refused to think of any heartbreak other than his own and the pain he was convinced he'd already caused Fran and the children.

He heard the songs and tambourines even before the church came into view. Then he saw it up ahead, a beacon of white with a steeple. He moved more swiftly toward it, feeling his pulse thumping in his veins.

By the time James reached the church, he was panting and weak. He slipped in through a rear door to the full swell of the congregation singing. He dropped into a pew at the back with his ragged bag at his feet and let the music wash over him. When they finished singing and sat, he saw Pastor Murphy at the altar.

"Of all the parables of the Bible, the prodigal son is among the most commonly rehearsed and most relevant today," he said. "It remains current to our everyday existence because it speaks so clearly to both man's and God's nature. Man, with his tendency to live only to satisfy his flesh, then finds out that worldly goods will never satisfy. And more important, when the goods are gone, what you are left with is brokenness."

A few in the congregation said "Amen;" some wept. James was enrapt, listening and remembering his own worldly treasures, his preoccupations with them. He became painfully aware of the plastic bag next to him. How foolish he felt. He had worked with the strength of every cell and sinew of his mind and body to attain—*what*? To end up with what? All his worldly possessions in a black plastic bag?

"But here is the good news, my friends," Pastor Murphy went on. "The nature of God is that of a loving father. Like the father of the prodigal son, He sees us when we are far away from Him. He sees us, and He is waiting anxiously for our return home. We only need to head in His direction, and He is more than willing to forgive our transgressions and wrap us in His garment of love. He's waiting, my friends. If you'll come to this altar tonight to accept Him, He will heal your brokenness."

Someone began another congregational hymn that the others picked up on while Pastor Murphy intoned, "Won't you come?" his arm extended toward the crowd. "Won't you come?"

James was not aware that amidst the loud singing of those around him, his crying was audible. It was with tears streaming down his face that he began to see everything clearly.

He had been given so much—Fran, Stacy, Jay, Elliott, Reba. He had been entrusted with so much, and he had not treated it as the treasure it was. He remembered back to the time when he *had* known. How he would go to church and kneel and thank God for blessings one could never earn. James remembered and longed to return to that place of peace.

As he observed others walking to the altar, James stood up too. He made his way to where Pastor Murphy was waiting, nodding in affirmation.

When James was within reach, Pastor Murphy held out his hand to him. "Our Father has been waiting for you, James."

James nodded. "And I'm ready to come home."

As the pastor prayed for James, others in the congregation shifted into another song. No one heard the door when it creaked open.

Pastor Murphy hugged James after the prayer, the church still vibrant with music. James turned and saw Fran coming down the aisle. Oma was standing by the door.

"I thought I'd lost you!" Fran shouted, reaching out for James, who moved quickly to meet her. He wrapped her so tightly in his arms that her feet lifted off the floor. He relaxed his grip just enough to see her face.

"I thought you'd be better off without me."

"Never," she said through her tears.

"I'm sorry, I'm so sorry for everything I've put you through these last years. But no more. I see now. I'm just grateful to God that He gives . . . do-overs." He almost laughed through his tears.

Pastor Murphy walked over to them and whispered, "Don't leave. If you two are still looking for a place, I can help. Let's talk after the service ends."

Later, as the parishioners made their way out of the church, James and Fran told Oma what Pastor Murphy had said.

"Oh!" she responded. "I'll wait here. My hip could use a rest. You two go on."

Pastor Murphy led James and Fran up a flight of stairs to a garage apartment alongside the church. "Brother Kennedy was our groundskeeper for the last eight years," he explained. "He'd been sick off and on for a while. His daughter finally convinced him to hang up his tool belt and move in with her family. He says it's gonna be permanent. He was going to remodel the apartment but never got to it. We need a new groundskeeper, so, I'm thinking, if you two need a place to stay, maybe we can help each other out. The apartment needs a lot of work, and it's small, but private. One bedroom, one bath."

James and Fran walked in. It was a spacious, open room with an old kitchenette marked by a breakfast bar. Dark laminate pretending to be wood covered some of the floor, while the rest remained exposed plywood. The redeeming feature was large glass patio doors that led to a sizable deck.

"This is wonderful. We can fix it up. James is a woodworker." Fran spoke with pride, looking at her husband.

James smiled at her as he walked toward the patio doors. "Yeah, it is nice."

Pastor Murphy said, "Well, if you want the job, it's yours. We can only afford one salary, though. The church covers the expenses for this space."

James turned to him. "Wow. This is perfect. Of course we'll accept. We can't thank you enough."

"Pastor Murphy," Fran added, "there are no words." She hugged him tightly, like a child hugging a grandparent.

"I'm glad to help," Pastor Murphy said. "We were all pretty bummed about Brother Kennedy moving away. But there is a reason for everything."

Fran and James returned to where Oma was waiting in the church downstairs. "Mom," Fran said, "we have a place to stay now. Everything's going to be okay."

38

Charlotte and Pastor Phillips's home felt like a warm hug and smelled of oven-baked sugar cookies. It was apparent that the couple wanted to ensure the Harrison kids felt welcomed. The boys were made comfortable in the attic space that served as Pastor Phillips's private den and office, heavy with books and a turn-of-the-century antique desk. They were fine with the let-out couch and futon that allowed for a clear view of the large TV. The girls were given the spare bedroom, decidedly feminine with buttercream walls and paintings of gardenias. They slept deeply in the shared bed made ready with a new lightweight flowered comforter.

Unable to break herself from what had been her role at Allison Pringle's house, Stacy would immediately get up to clean after every meal until Charlotte followed her into the kitchen and told her, "It's really nice that you want to help, Stacy, but you don't have to earn your keep here."

Stacy turned to her from where she was putting plates and glasses into the dishwasher. "I want to help."

"Well, that's very nice. But know you have a place here. You don't need to work for it."

Chin quivering, Stacy let out a loud sob. She attempted to cover it but was unable to stop the eruption of so much she'd been feeling over the past months. Charlotte rushed to embrace her. "It's all right. Everything is all right," Charlotte said, attempting to soothe Stacy's tears.

The sound drew Pastor Phillips's attention. He came to the kitchen entryway. "Everything okay?"

Stacy couldn't stop crying. Charlotte held on so she could let it out. She turned just enough to make eye contact with her husband. "We're fine. Would you mind giving us a moment, honey?"

He nodded. "If you need anything, I'll be in the family room."

Stacy lifted her wet face, her eyes red and puffy. Charlotte looked right into them. "You're here now. That nightmare is over. You will never, *ever* have to live through that again."

Stacy nodded and hugged Charlotte, letting out a deep sigh in her arms.

Adam dropped by to see how the kids were doing and stayed for dinner one evening.

Reba told him, "Thank you, Officer Friendly, for helping us."

Everyone around the table smiled.

"I made something for you," Reba said.

"Oh!" Adam was genuinely surprised.

"Wait here." Reba looked to Charlotte for an okay to be momentarily excused from the table. Charlotte gave a little nod. Reba dashed away and returned with a crayon drawing. "It's a certificate."

"Wow," Adam said as he accepted the drawing. He read the lopsided purple words surrounded by a rainbow of curlicues: *For Ociffer Friendly, the Bravest Police Man I Know.* "Well, this is very impressive," he told Reba. "This has got to be the nicest certificate anybody has ever given me."

She told him, "You can hug me now, if you want." Everyone laughed.

After dinner, Pastor Phillips and Adam hung out in the living room, talking. Jay wandered in. He looked at Adam like there was something he wanted to say. Pastor Phillips read the cues and said, "Let me check with Charlotte to see if there's any of her chocolate cake left."

Jay was still standing when Pastor Phillips walked past him toward the kitchen.

"You doing okay?" Adam asked.

"Yeah. Everything's cool. I mean, we're doing great."

"You wanna sit?"

Jay took a few long strides toward the couch then paused. "They told us what you did."

"Come again?"

"Pastor Phillips and Charlotte. They said you told them about us being stuck in that place. So I wanted to say thanks."

"Don't mention it."

"Charlotte says you help a lot of kids."

"I try to do my part."

"You like it? Helping kids?"

"Yeah."

"Cool."

"It is."

"So did you always wanna be a cop?" Jay asked.

Adam smiled. "The answer is no. Truth is, I didn't know what I wanted to do with my life. I was kinda messed up as a kid."

"Seriously?"

"*Very* seriously. My dad took off. It was just me, my kid brother, and my mom. She had to work, so I had plenty of opportunities to screw around. I told you, I started drinking when I was fourteen."

"So what happened? What changed?"

"A car accident happened. Me and a few buddies of mine were out drinking. I'm sure you know where this is going. We get into a car crash that totals our ride and nearly kills the other guy when we T-bone him."

"Jeez."

"Yeah. I was fifteen. Anyway, one of the cops liked me, or felt sorry for me. He told my ma about this program for troubled kids run by the police department. He became my mentor. That's how I got the idea in my head I wanted to be a cop."

"I met some kids at that group home . . ." Jay shook his head, not finishing the thought.

"Well, sometimes kids can turn out different if they're given a shot."

"They weren't all bad. Some of the kids at that place were cool. There was this one guy, Casper."

"Casper?"

"Yeah, he was cool. He's been in that place, like, for *years*. No family to take him in. But he's, like, crazy smart. Life just screwed him."

"It happens a lot. Smart kids who don't catch a break. That's why mentoring is important. When you're pretty much out there on your own at that age it's kinda easy to end up doing something stupid."

Jay thought of Casper and his Anti group and how determined they all were not to be the stupid ones. Even Rodriguez may have turned out differently if he'd had somebody. And Jay thought of his own situation. What if he didn't have his family? What if he didn't have anybody to put him in check? "So what kind of places you volunteer at?" he asked.

"Well, there's this program called Teen Rescue. We meet at the Y."

"Is it a cop thing?"

"No, it's not all cops. There's lots of other people too. And kids your age."

"Doing what? Like, helping out?"

"Yeah. Sort of a big brother kind of role. The kids who volunteer are great. They're good at getting the other kids to open up. You ever think about doing something like that?"

"You mean like working with kids?"

"Yeah."

"Nah."

"Not interested?"

Jay shrugged. "I wouldn't know what to do."

"The only thing you have to do is be *you* and hang out with them. Maybe play some ball. Talk to them."

Jay was quiet. Pastor Phillips returned with a slice of cake.

"Any more of that left?" Jay asked.

"Yep."

"Cool. I think I'll go for it." Jay got up to head for the kitchen.

"Good plan," Pastor Phillips said. "How about you, Adam?"

"Thanks but no. I've had my fill for the night. Anyway, I should get moving." He stood and called out, "Jay."

Jay turned to him.

"Think about it, okay?"

The kids loved their parents' new place. They squealed and turned around in the big open room, they pulled open the rickety cupboard doors, and they went out to the patio to look at the stretch of sky and the big trees on the church's property.

"What's that structure over there?" Stacy asked.

"That's a stable, or it was," Fran told her. "Pastor Murphy says this place is over a century old. It's a city landmark."

"Wow. Do they still have horses in there?"

"No, they just use that building for storing things."

"Can we move here too?" Reba asked.

"Well, not here, honey," James explained, "but you can stay over! You all can, and soon your mom and I will have a place big enough for all of us."

"I can't wait," Stacy said. "Charlotte and Pastor Phillips are awesome, but I miss *us*."

The boys echoed, "Me too."

The kids helped fix up the apartment. The girls painted. Jay and Elliott worked with James to finish installing the floor and securing the lopsided cabinet doors. The church bought a nice new white fridge for them. Oma gifted a baker's rack, where Fran placed wicker baskets to increase storage space.

When the work was finally done, the family ate pizza. This quickly became their Friday night ritual. Afterward, they would play board games until exhaustion and then the kids would spread out on sleeping bags in the big main room. "Camping!" Reba called it. The kids came Friday evenings and stayed the weekend. They were a family again.

Fran was job searching in order to save up to help rent a home for the whole family. The Honduras job was long gone, but Fran was determined to find work. When Pastor Murphy heard this, he offered more assistance. "I know that Good Shepherd needs a kitchen manager at their place. You did good work for us. I can put in a word for you if you want."

It wasn't what Fran had in mind, but it was a job, a job she needed. She was grateful for Pastor Murphy's offer. "That would be amazing," she told him. "Thank you so much."

Kitchen duty at Good Shepherd was rough. It meant blistered hands (despite the rubber gloves) and burning back pain on some days—a reminder of the fire. There were times she'd limp to bed to fall asleep with James massaging away her aches.

Sometimes, she'd stare at her face in the murky bathroom mirror, studying her lean jaw that seemed hardened around the edges now. Her blue eyes were more intense, more knowing. Her blond hair, no longer salon-kept, hung loose in dull, tousled waves. The elongated sinew of her neck met the sharp blades of her collarbone and severe shoulders. Stacy had told her, "You look fierce, Mom." Fran stood more erect, defying the pain. She examined the small spots of dead, calloused skin on her palms, permanently burnished pink from hard scrubbing.

Once, when she was leaving the shelter, she saw her old friend Madeline again, or rather, they saw each other, even though Madeline pretended not to notice Fran. For a second Fran considered letting the pretense ride, as Madeline seemed to be rushing for her car door. But then in the next moment, Fran called out, "Maddie!" The woman put on a surprised smile and waved.

Fran laughed to herself. Walking closer, she adjusted her backpack of work clothes. "How have you been?"

"Great. Great." Madeline tightened the sash of her ivory silk jacket. Her eyes shifted from Fran's flannel shirt and jeans to the shelter in the near distance. Two men stood out front in janitor's coveralls on a smoke break. "What brings you to this neck of the woods?" Her smile was stiff and frozen.

"Just leaving work," Fran said.

Madeline looked confused.

"Kitchen manager at the shelter." Fran pitched her thumb to the miserable gray building behind her where the janitors were hanging loose. "Oh."

"And you?" They both understood what Fran meant; it was a shock to see Madeline in a city neighborhood with patchy lawns and liquor stores, where people and animals roamed as if they belonged to no one and had nowhere to go.

She flicked a manicured hand to gesture beyond Fran. "I bought a couple of three-flats down the street. My accountant's idea." After a beat she added, "I've been meaning to call you."

"Don't worry about it."

"No." Madeline angled her face away from a city bus that rolled by, burping gaseous fumes. She looked at Fran again. "I should've called."

"I'm fine. Listen, you take care. It was nice bumping into you."

Madeline smiled again—a genuine smile this time. "I'm glad everything's fine, Fran. You take care too."

Once Fran got home, Reba noticed her hands, touching the rough places and saying, "Mommy, your hands are different. Do they hurt?"

"Only sometimes, honey."

"I don't want you to hurt."

Fran said, "Don't be sad. It's okay. Mommy's fine."

"How come they hurt? What did you do?"

"Work."

"Maybe you can get a nicer job someplace where your hands won't hurt."

She pulled Reba onto her lap and smoothed back her flyaway golden hair. In a flash, Fran recalled all sorts of fanciful daydreams. "You know, sweetheart, I used to think about that—working someplace 'nice,' but I learned that any job that's honest and helps you take care of the people you love is a good job."

"Even if it hurts?"

Fran paused thoughtfully. "We have to be strong—not just on the outside, but on the inside. And when we're strong, we can do *anything*."

"*Anything?*"

"Yep."

Reba looked at her mother's hands again and then at her face. She beamed at Fran. "When I grow up, I wanna be just like you, Mommy."

On hot August nights, the family used blow-up mattresses to sleep on the patio under the stars.

They each knew the gift of these moments, especially James.

"I prayed for this," he said, taking in the sight of his happy children bathed in moonlight, Fran beside him.

Fran leaned her head on his shoulder. "I think we all shared that prayer."

"I owe you guys so much." James met the eyes of each of his children. "I wasn't fair to you. I'm sorry."

His kids sat up, paying closer attention to him now. "It's okay, Dad," Jay said. "It's over."

"Yeah, but I still need to make things right with you guys—not just move on and try to forget the last eight months."

Jay and Stacy gave one another a glance.

"What you went through was because of my own arrogance, my own . . . fears."

Fran sat up to look at him. She encouraged him without saying anything.

He continued. "I promise to be a better father to all four of you. A better man, a better husband. I never want any of you to feel you have to keep a secret because of shame. I want all of us to know we can be honest, we can talk to each other."

It was the beginning of real communication and real healing between the Harrisons. Later it would be continued and fostered in the therapy they all needed after their trauma.

On another such night, Fran and Stacy stayed up talking in quiet slumber party tones, marveling at the sparkling jewels in the dark sky.

"When your father and I first got married, we'd sleep out on the balcony of our apartment on hot nights. The apartment was little, with no AC, but it had a great balcony. Those were really good times." Fran seemed lost in the memory.

"I remember the pictures. You guys looked happy."

"We were."

"This is good too," Stacy assured her.

"Very."

In a small voice, Stacy said, "I still dream about it sometimes."

Fran's smile fell away when she realized what her daughter was referring to.

Stacy continued, "Not so much now. Just sometimes. I'm back in that woman's house, but I'll wake up, sometimes really late at night, you know, and I'll be like, *okay, it's just a dream. It's just a dream.* I'll keep telling myself that until I fall back to sleep."

Fran stroked her daughter's hair, leaned and kissed her head. "I'm so very, very sorry you guys had to live through that whole ordeal. I can't tell you how much my heart ached thinking about you at that woman's house."

"I know, Mom, but the whole eight months weren't all bad. I got to hang out with you guys more. I did some fun stuff I didn't know I liked—like visiting that cool Mexican art museum."

"Yes, that was very cool." Fran nodded, taking in the night air and remembering. "Maybe we can go back there again. Make a day of it."

"I was telling my friends about it."

"Oh?" She was happy at Stacy's mention of friends. It had been a long time.

"Yeah. I texted a few of them. Just to say hey, you know."

"So you've made some plans?"

"Yeah, nothing major. Just hanging out. Heather is, like, always wanting to shop, but I was like, we should try something else. So much other stuff out there to do."

Fran grinned at her.

"What?"

"Oh, nothing." Fran was looking at Stacy more deeply, recognizing that her daughter had grown. There was a quiet moment when soft snores could be heard from the other sleeping bags. Fran whispered, "Anybody else going with you guys?"

"Just the usual group." She hesitated. "Okay, and maybe this other guy I know. A boy."

"What's his name?"

"Chase."

Fran could hear the significance of his name in her daughter's voice. "Are we going to meet him?"

"Yeah. Yeah, you will."

Labor Day weekend was marked by the celebration of Elliott's birthday and an outdoor barbeque at the Harrisons' apartment. Some of Elliott's friends from youth church came, and Charlotte and Pastor Phillips.

In addition to the new bike James and Fran gave their son, James wanted to offer Elliott another gift. As the party came to an end, they sat talking near the big picnic table where Fran and Charlotte were packing up leftovers and cups and plates.

James handed Elliott a package wrapped in plain paper with a raffia bow.

"I've got to confess," James said as he watched Elliott open a book of poems, "I had some help from Jay. He says you really like reading poetry."

Elliott smiled, looking at the book's table of contents, slowly flipping through the pages. "Thanks, Dad."

"I don't know much about poetry, but I asked the lady at the bookstore for some suggestions. She said this was a good one. Really popular."

"Yeah," Elliott said, "Terrance Hayes is really cool."

"And your brother said something else too. He told me you've got real talent."

Elliott looked at James. "Did Jay really say that?"

"Yep. He did." He added, "He said you don't think so, though."

Elliott shrugged. "My teachers like my stuff. They try to get me to do the poetry readings at school."

"Why don't you?"

Elliott shrugged again. "I don't know."

"You should do it."

"But what if nobody likes it?"

"Your teachers like it, right?"

"Yeah, but they're supposed to tell you stuff like that."

"Maybe, but I don't think they'd try to get you in front of a crowd if your poems weren't any good."

Elliott gave his father a dubious look.

"Seriously," James went on, "I bet they only ask the kids who are *really* good."

"I've never done something like that before. All those people watching."

"You played soccer plenty of times in front of a crowd."

"But that was different. I wasn't onstage by myself. What if I mess up?"

"Well, sometimes that happens, people mess up, but sharing your work is bigger than that. It's bigger than whether or not you make a mistake." Elliott was listening closely. "Look, sharing your gift is about touching people, speaking to their hearts. And that's what they remember. How you make them *feel*. I'd say that's the reason we're given talents. We're supposed to put them out there to affect the world."

"Dad," Elliot said softly.

"Yeah?"

"Can I . . . Can I write a poem about us being homeless?"

James paused just long enough to hold Elliott's attention and give weight to his response: "Write whatever is in your heart, son."

39

The autumn that year burst forth with radiant colors. The towering elms on the church grounds were aglow with shimmering gold leaves tinged with orange and red. From the apartment patio, the early morning sky could be seen emerging from the darkness. Fran and James would sit together watching the sun rise before their workday started. This was their favorite time of day.

They settled in nicely with the congregants of Grace At the Cross. They were the bus drivers, plumbers, kindergarten teachers, lunchroom ladies, housekeepers, and construction workers who gathered together in glorious worship, calloused hands stretched high in full-throated praise. Fran and James were right there with the wholeness of their hearts. Fran served on two special events committees. And in October, she joined the toy drive for the needy with James.

The church received boxes of toys, some new from department stores, most used. Members of the committee questioned whether some of them shouldn't just be thrown away because of their condition.

James told them, "I can fix these."

"James used to make toys," Fran chimed in. "My husband can fix just about any toy they manufacture. When our kids were little, he would fix their toys all the time."

"It'll be fun," James said. "I kind of miss working with toys."

The committee was happy to hear it. They arranged for James to use the garage below his apartment as a workshop and stocked it with the essentials. Fixing the toys was easy enough. But what really ignited the light inside James was a pile of old wood, left over from one of Brother Kennedy's projects, no doubt. James decided to make a few small toys to donate.

Everyone was impressed. Pastor Murphy said, "James, you've got quite a talent. You ever think about teaching kids?"

"I'd love to," James enthused. "I've just never had the opportunity."

"Well, would you consider giving classes here? I've been thinking about outreach programs we could offer our young kids at the church and in the neighborhood. You know, something to keep them occupied and off the streets."

"I think that's an amazing idea. I'd love to help."

Fran told him, "What a beautiful way to use your gift."

"Can I be your student, too, Daddy?" Reba asked.

"Better," James said. "You can be my assistant."

She squealed with delight. James, Fran, and the kids printed flyers and passed them out at the local grocery stores, dry cleaners, and restaurants.

By February, each of James's four workstations had two or three little would-be woodcarvers whittling away. Fran took pictures. They made more flyers. And then James had another thought. He asked Pastor Murphy, "Do you think the church could reach out to places like CPS? I've been talking a lot with my son Jay about the kids stuck in the system. It would be great if we could include them. I'm sure a lot of kids would love something like this."

Pastor Murphy told him, "That's a great idea. We have a couple of social workers in our congregation. I'm sure they could give us some direction."

By spring, James's woodcarving classes were full, and he was making more toys of his own, as well. Stacy created a simple website to start selling his merchandise, and it was Jay's idea to videotape his father at work and upload it to YouTube.

Pastor Murphy suggested moving the woodcarving lessons to the barn to accommodate all the kids. "You could also do your carving out there and use the space to sell your toys, James," he said. "I think it'll be a win for the church. The walkway passes right by the church's front door. We may get a few who'll wander in."

Several of the church members helped James clean up the barn and turn it into a real workshop. People donated tables for the kids to work at and shelving to display pieces in progress. Someone bought a cash register for James's new business. Several pooled their money to buy him a new computer.

The money earned from selling the toys online helped with James and Fran's savings to move to a bigger place. Summer and fall came and went before they thought they'd saved enough to venture beyond the little apartment. The tough part was finding a space big enough for a family of six. Every home that was large enough was still too expensive for them. But they were ready to be together again.

Frustrated, James told Pastor Murphy about their ordeal. Pastor Murphy took it upon himself to talk with his friend and church member, Brother Clive, who owned a small house he desperately needed to rent.

He told James, "It needs work. I'm thinking, if you're willing to put the muscle into fixing it up, I can pay for the materials you'll need. And I'll rent it to you at a cost that can work with your budget."

The gingerbread-style brick-and-stone bungalow was in a suburb north of the church. It looked quite lovely from the driveway, but Brother Clive hadn't exaggerated about the work needed on the inside.

When James, Fran, and the kids walked through the space, their jaws dropped, and not in a good way. They eyed the sun-faded, peeling floral wallpaper, the abandoned garbage bags toppling over in front of the stone fireplace and under the bay window. Unrecognizable stains were petrified on the wood floor. The ceiling had fallen and lay on the floor in big chunks of wet drywall. Looking up at the naked rafters, Fran drew Reba nearer to her. "Stay close to Mommy, honey. Be careful."

Brother Clive had stayed in his car. He'd offered them a few minutes of private time to walk through the house and talk. They understood why.

Jay's response was, "Not again. *More* renovations?"

Stacy groaned.

"I like the big window," Elliott said.

"Me too," Reba added.

James tamped down his dismay. "Well, it's got potential."

"Honey," Fran said, "how long will this take us?"

"How long will it take us to afford a place this big?"

"Point taken."

Brother Clive walked in. "Well?"

They finished just days before Christmas, with the help of tradesmen and others from the church who volunteered: scraping, patching, nailing, sanding, painting. Their final job was to hang a large, framed drawing by up-and-coming local artist, Reba Harrison. The masterpiece was situated above the mantel of the stone fireplace. It was a picture of her family, along with all of the people who "had been really nice," she said: Pastor Phillips and Charlotte, Officer Friendly, Pastor Murphy, and "the nice judge lady."

With their sweat long dried and the hardwood floors now refinished, James and Fran brought their kids and Oma to visit the house again. The rooms had been transformed with airy shades of cream and angel white. Fran had decorated with donated furniture and new rugs that softly sprouted between naked toes.

The kids ran through their new home, opening doors and jogging up and down the short staircases, laughing and talking excitedly about game nights in front of the stone fireplace.

The girls quickly claimed the two bedrooms on the main floor as their own. The attic had been converted into a cozy master suite with its own reading nook, where Fran now read books on small business and marketing. The basement had been completely renovated. It offered two additional bedrooms for the boys, and a sprawling lounge area that would see Jay's friend, Casper, in a sleeping bag on many weekends. Not only did Casper now have a family to welcome him, but he would turn out to be a great support and tutor for Jay.

The neighborhood was rife with babysitting opportunities for Stacy and a convenient location for Jay to connect with Officer Adam Richards when the two would volunteer at Teen Rescue.

"This couldn't be more perfect," James said in wonderment, standing in the living room, remembering the house before he and many helping hands had transformed it.

Fran turned to Oma, who was absorbing the joy of the moment. "Mom, I love the potbellied stove we picked out. You and I are going to have a great time cooking here."

"Indeed," Oma agreed.

Reba glinted with happiness. She thought of that Christmas Eve at the church, praying with Oma. She'd asked God for a miracle. It seemed so big, so *impossible,* and it had taken so long to happen. Worse still, when everything had gone horribly wrong, she wondered if He'd even heard her. But now she knew: God can do *anything!* The sureness of this bubbled up in Reba's heart. "Oma, you were right," she said, head flung back, spinning around in the living room. "God *does* listen!"

"Yes, He does," Oma declared.

It was gratitude that prompted James to create his most seminal work. That spring, he dedicated all his spare time to it, cloaking it under a sheet in the barn workshop, much to Fran's playful frustration. "Just a quick peek," she'd plead.

James laughed but wouldn't concede. "You'll be the first to see it when it's done. Promise!" He'd punctuate his statement with a quick peck on her cheek.

Eventually, he led Fran by the hand to the barn for the big reveal. The carving stood on his workbench and was as tall as a small child.

He pulled the sheet from it. Fran's hands immediately went to the grooves and details of the wings, the sword, the painstaking expression on Jacob's face as he wrestled with the angel. Inscribed at the base of the statue was "I won't let you go until you bless me. Genesis 32:26."

"Wow," Fran breathed, her eyes moving from the carving to James, her hands again touching the finely chiseled lines. "I had no idea. Jacob and the angel. What made you—"

"Jacob was granted his transformation. Me too."

"To say it's beautiful doesn't . . . it's awe-striking. I've seen your carvings before, but nothing like this."

"Well, I've never done anything like this. I guess I was inspired."

Pastor Murphy came by to see the wooden art piece for himself. "I've heard all sorts of talk about it, James. But I have to say, words don't do this justice. It's absolutely amazing. You've got a real gift, son."

"Thank you," James said humbly.

"What do you plan to do with it?"

"Well, I hadn't thought about it."

"It should be seen, James. This is a testimony."

James paused thoughtfully. "Is there a place for it in the church?"

"I'll make a place for it, if you'd let the church buy it."

"No, I couldn't take money. You and the church have done so much for us, I'd be happy to donate it."

"Well, that's awful generous of you. I'll make sure it's put in a proper place that'll honor your work and your message."

Pastor Murphy arranged for it to be mounted and placed inside near the entrance. And in the same grateful spirit, the Harrison family returned regularly to Green Pastures Mission to volunteer in thanksgiving for everything they had received.

By the following December, the store, All I Want For Christmas—the name was Reba's idea—was officially launched to much fanfare and promise. They had a new website, and thanks to Fran's marketing savvy, newspapers and magazines did features on the husband-and-wife business partners, James and Fran Harrison.

Pastor Murphy's comment proved prophetic: the foot traffic along the winding stone pathway to the quaint little store often led to inquiries about the church, visitors on Sundays, and sometimes, new congregants.

It was the week before Christmas on a cold snowy Friday afternoon. It was getting dark and James decided to knock off early. Just as he was preparing to pack up, he saw a customer coming down the stone walkway, a man holding a little girl's hand. She skipped and trotted along the snowy path to hurry her father along. The closer the pair came into view, the more James believed he recognized the man. When the store's front door chimed open, James was certain, and so was the man staring back at him.

His little girl broke away, exclaiming, "See, Daddy! Look at all these toys! Just like I told you! Just like we saw in the magazine! Isn't this cool?"

The man stepped farther into the store, not taking his eyes from James.

"So how's business at In Touch Technologies?" James asked. Though the chance meeting with someone from his old sales team surprised him, James was even more surprised by the absence of resentment or anger. He felt no bitterness as he recalled this man and the rest of his team abandoning him for the likes of Gus Fowler.

"Well, I'm no longer there," the man said, coming closer. "Gus's business isn't doing too well. I heard the IRS shut the place down."

"Oh." James had nothing else to say.

The man looked over at his daughter, who was admiring the wooden carvings along the wall. Then he said to James, "Hey, I'm sorry about how things ended. It's just that I have a kid, see—"

James held up his hand. "No need to explain. You did what you had to. I should apologize to you."

"Listen, I never thanked you for sending us those bonus payments. Most people would've—"

"Don't mention it."

The man gave a slight nod, acknowledging what he thought was James's wish to leave the past where it belonged.

There was a pause, and then the man said, "My daughter has been asking me to bring her to this store for weeks. All of her friends have an 'original James Harrison'. My wife has two of your pieces in our house."

"That's nice. Thank you."

"Looks like life has been treating you well," the man said, studying James's face.

"Yes." James smiled. "Does your daughter have a particular toy in mind?"

The little girl, with her missing-tooth grin, said, "That one!" She pointed to a shelf over her head.

The father smiled and then said to James, "An early Christmas present."

James went around the counter to retrieve the marionette. "Excellent choice, madam." He gave a princely bow to the little girl, and she giggled.

James eyed the clock on the wall. "Oh, man," he said in a near whisper. He moved back to the counter with more speed.

"Problem?" the man asked.

"Just running a little late."

"Business to get to, huh?"

"No," James said, wrapping the toy. "My son Elliott is in the end-of-semester poetry recital at his school. It's a bit of a drive from here."

"Oh," the man said, genuinely surprised.

James caught the look. It made him smile. He handed the package to the man. "Merry Christmas."

The man nodded and took his daughter's hand. He looked at the package he was holding, and then briefly again at James.

James wasn't paying attention. His mind was already traveling to the auditorium of St. Mary's Middle School where his son would soon be standing onstage reading his poetry. That was what was important to James these days. That and the home-cooked meal they would come home to—meatloaf, Elliott's favorite. Then there would be the family's customary Friday night game of Monopoly. And later still, James would sit with Fran by the fire, the Christmas tree twinkling, enthralled with the absolute knowledge of what riches he possessed.

Rebekah Pace Collection

(Faith, Inspirational, and Christmas)

ISBN: 978-1-64630-030-3

When a 90 year old Holocaust survivor reconnects with his childhood sweetheart in a strange world of shared dreams, he must venture out of the safety of his lonely life and go on a mission to rescue his lost soul mate from impending tragedy.

ISBN: 978-1-646300-36-5

When a postal manager is transferred to rural Appalachia as punishment, she discovers the importance of helping others.

ISBN: 978-1-64630-086-0

When a street gang moves into the neighborhood of an aging, alcoholic actor known for his James Bond - like iconic role he desperately tries to relive his past glory by saving his community.

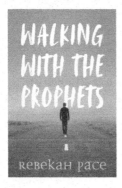

ISBN: 978-1-646300-50-1

A hedge fund manager and quant in NYC receives enlightenment and is commanded to walk across the United States with nothing but a walking stick and begging bowl.

ISBN: 978-1-646300-32-7

When he learns that his wife is thrilled at the prospect of divorce, a man decides to make her fall in love with him again so that he can punish her by leaving.

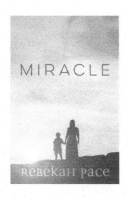

ISBN: 978-1-646300-34-1

When the decision is made to stop life support for their mother, a daughter must justify that decision to her siblings and reconcile her own feelings of guilt.

ISBN: 978-1-64630-087-7

Inspired by the actual illegal cross-country road race. When the computer in their self-driving car comes alive, a boy and his companions must win the race to save his family.